A NOBLE **KILLING**

BARBARA
NADEL

A NOBLE **KILLING**

headline

First published in 2011 by
HEADLINE PUBLISHING GROUP

1

Cataloguing in Publication Data is available from the British Library

ISBN 978 0 7553 7160 0 (Hardback)
ISBN 978 0 7553 7161 7 (Trade paperback)

Typeset in Times New Roman by Palimpsest Book Production Limited,
Falkirk, Stirlingshire

Printed and bound in Great Britain by
Clays Ltd, St Ives, Plc

Headline's policy is to use papers that are natural, renewable and recyclable
products and made from wood grown in sustainable forests. The logging and
manufacturing processes are expected to conform to the environmental
regulations of the country of origin.

To all my wonderful female friends, to Kathy, Pat, Ruth, Jeyda, Elsie, Sarah, Jenny, Vivian, Gilda and to my agent, Juliet.

Cast of Characters

Çetin İkmen – middle-aged İstanbul police inspector

Mehmet Süleyman – İstanbul police inspector, İkmen's protégé

Commissioner Ardıç – İkmen and Süleyman's boss

Sergeant Ayşe Farsakoğlu – İkmen's deputy

Sergeant İzzet Melik – Süleyman's deputy

Metin İskender – younger İstanbul police inspector

Dr Arto Sarkissian – police pathologist, an ethnic Armenian

Constable Hikmet Yıldız – İstanbul police constable

İsmail Yıldız – Hikmet's brother

Hatice – police psychologist

Flower – one of Süleyman's informants

Gonca – Süleyman's gypsy mistress

Şukru – Gonca's brother

Hamid İdiz – piano teacher based in fashionable Şişli district

Ali Reza Zafir – teenage pupil of Hamid İdiz

Murad Emin – teenage pupil of Hamid İdiz

Izabella Madrid – piano teacher based in Balat district

Cahit Seyhan – father of victim Gözde Seyhan

Saadet Seyhan – Cahit's wife

Lokman Seyhan – Cahit and Saadet's older son

Kenan Seyhan – Cahit and Saadet's younger son, Lokman's brother

Gözde Seyhan – Cahit and Saadet's daughter

Feray Akol – Cahit Seyhan's sister

Nesrin and Aykan Akol – Feray's daughter and son

Osman Yavuz – computer geek

Richard and Jane Ford – American expats

Tayfun Ergin – gangster

Cem Koç – chancer

Rafik Bey – grocer

Mustafa Bey – nargile salon owner

Şenol – police computer expert

Prelude

His feet pounded against the dusty road surface to the jagged beat of his heart. Every so often he had to jump a brick or a pile of rubbish, skirt around a new and pristine car that at one time would have made him stop and stare.

But now, at that moment, his existence was only about survival. Physically he had to get away. That was the easy part. There was also getting away in his head, and that was quite another matter. If only she hadn't turned to look at him! Before, when he'd rehearsed the whole thing in his mind, he'd imagined that once she had caught, she'd just fall to the floor. The pain surely would make her drop like a sack of pomegranates. Instead she'd just stood there, turned and calmly looked at him. Try as he might, in the few minutes since he'd left her, he couldn't make that terrible glance anything other than what it had been. Hatred. He knew she had known what she had done. She must have realised that there would be repercussions! Not that her crime and its ramifications made him feel any better now. In a way, all of that was practically irrelevant.

What was relevant was that he felt very differently from the way he had thought he would feel. He'd taken a human life! He'd taken a human life and it didn't feel good. It didn't give him a sense of being a man, of doing what was right, of feeling really honoured or brave or anything except fear, horror and regret. Maybe later, when he wasn't running like a frightened lamb, he might feel differently. Perhaps when he himself was safe . . . He looked up at the tall, blank apartment buildings that lined every street that he ran along and he wondered what, if anything, the unknown people in those apartments had seen. He didn't know the area. That had been one of his advantages. It was also, now, to him, a drawback. Not knowing the area and the people meant that he didn't know, given that someone must have seen him, how that person or anyone else in the district would react. He turned a tight corner into a wider street that looked as if it might be quite important.

It was while running down that wider, more prestigious street that he was passed by a speeding fire engine. As it whipped past his shoulder, sucking his hair in its direction as it went, he found himself screaming.

The darkness and the impenetrability of the smoke was typical of a fire that had taken hold at least twenty minutes before. The three-man team on the high-pressure hose were experienced fire officers who knew how dangerous their situation was.

The blaze had first been reported by a neighbour. A foreigner, he had been panicking when he spoke to the control room. But his shaky, weirdly accented message had been relayed to the station eventually, and the appliance and its crew had left immediately. They'd all known that getting from the fire station to the site of the blaze would take too

2

much time. It was always the same. Unless the fire was on one of the big, broad boulevards off Taksim Square, in the very centre of the city, they had problems. İstanbul was an ancient city. It had been built for ancient forms of transport like horses, carts and sedan chairs. Tiny little streets and alleyways like this one in the district of Beşiktaş were difficult to get to, and even once the appliance had arrived, the logistics of entering some of the tortuously laid-out buildings were a nightmare.

When the officers had arrived, they had been able to see the fire easily from the street. One of the many gawping onlookers had told them that the blazing apartment belonged to a family called Seyhan. They had two sons and a daughter. The young men, at least, had been seen leaving for work earlier in the day. Although the fire officers had to haul the hose up a flight of stairs to the front entrance of the apartment building, they didn't have any further to climb. The Seyhans' apartment was to the right of the stairs leading to the upper floors. The front door was smashed out with an axe. Once inside, had the team not already been wearing breathing apparatus, they would have begun to lose consciousness. The fire, so it seemed, had its origins in a room at the far right-hand end of the central rectangular hall. Dense black and grey smoke curled from the open doorway and across the hall ceiling like tendrils of evil chiffon. Apartment blocks like this were full of plastic foam. It stuffed the chairs and beds of the newly arrived migrants from the countryside – the typical residents of such buildings. Back in their sparse Anatolian villages, these people had rested upon horsehair cushions and mattresses covered with intricate and often very old tapestries. But they had swapped those old things for bright, shiny modern furnishings that looked clean but which, when burnt, gave off fumes that could kill a person who just breathed them in once.

Slowly and cautiously the team moved forward. The smoke in that room was now so dense that not even a scrap of light could be seen coming in from the street outside. The door frames, though thin and now scorched, looked like the edges of a black and ruined mouth. A gateway, the fire officers all knew, that could so easily lead them to their deaths. Even experienced hearts beat faster, the sound of breathing behind masks became short and ragged. Hauling the thick and heavy hose after them, they moved into position. A beat, a moment passed as they all stared into the swirling darkness before them. And then . . .

And then . . . 'Flashover!' Only one of them said it, his words muffled by his mask. But they all knew what it was. The smoke, finally eaten by the strengthening flames, disappeared in a terrible conflagration of red, white and gold. Everything was illuminated: chairs, cupboards, a bed; even the window, once blackened, now burned in shades of bright yellow as the soot on the pane incinerated. The team stood, as they did at moments of flashover, motionless. Temporarily pushed back by the heat as well as briefly awed by the violent actions of the fire (one never, ever became accustomed to such a thing), a half-step back was quickly followed by the activation of the hose and the beginning of the battle these men were duty-bound to win. As they moved slowly forwards, the man at the very back of the team thought he saw something move on the floor just beyond the entrance to the room. At the time, he felt sure it had to be just a low-level flame.

Chapter 1

'That shop always used to sell beer and wine,' Inspector Çetin İkmen said as he slouched gloomily away from the small street corner grocer's shop. 'What does he mean, it's his right not to sell alcohol if he doesn't want to? It's his duty to sell whatever his customers want!'

İkmen's companion, his friend and colleague Inspector Mehmet Süleyman, smiled. Although much younger than İkmen, he had served as a police officer with the older man for over twenty years and so he knew him very well. It wasn't that İkmen had particularly wanted to have a drink. He'd gone into the shop to buy a couple of cans of Efes lager to take home with him for the evening. It was the reason why the shopkeeper hadn't been able to let him have the beer that irked İkmen. He looked up and down the busy Ortabahçe Street and said, 'This isn't some back end of Beşiktaş! This is one of the main thoroughfares!'

His friend raised one of his finely curved eyebrows and said, 'I take it we are talking about . . .'

'People come in to the city from villages in Anatolia to find work, and I have no problem with that,' İkmen said. 'But the owner of that shop only took it over last month and already he's cut out alcohol.'

'If people are practising and sincere Muslims, they can't drink,' Süleyman said.

İkmen lit a cigarette and then said gloomily, 'I thought this area was supposed to be gentrifying. I thought Beşiktaş was meant to be the next Nişantaşı. A place where the middle classes move in, designer shops and bars spring up and massive four-by-four vehicles line the streets.'

Süleyman smiled. İkmen, unlike himself, came from purely working-class stock. In that respect he'd had more in common with the shopkeeper he'd just argued with than he did with his colleague. But Çetin İkmen, unlike the shopkeeper, was not from some village in the far east, up near the border with Armenia. He was an İstanbullu born and bred, and so, although nominally a Muslim, he did not have a problem with alcohol and in fact at times enjoyed drinking it rather more than was good for him.

'I am far from being an enemy of religion,' İkmen continued. 'Anyone can practise his or her religion to his or her heart's content as far as I am concerned. Just don't try and influence me. Let me do what secular people do, and if I end up in hell, then so be it. It's my soul. My business.'

Ever since the Turkish Republic had been founded by Atatürk in 1923, the country had been, officially, a secular state. That hadn't changed. What had altered was that the ruling political party since 2002, those who actually ran the state, derived originally from an organisation with Islamic roots. This, allied with increased migration from the countryside to the cities of people with a more conservative standpoint, meant that religion and its outward symbols was much more visible than it had been. Unlike Turkey in the

1950s and 60s, when Çetin İkmen had been growing up, religion was now a hot topic for discussion; and observance, in some areas, was actively approved. For a secular republican like İkmen, that was not always easy to accept. Although his wife was and always had been a woman of faith, Çetin had been raised to believe that anything not rooted in sound, preferably scientific fact was mere superstition. His colleague, Mehmet Süleyman, though in agreement with the older man in many ways, wasn't so sure. He'd been brought up in a family once part of the pre-republican imperial Ottoman elite, and although he didn't practise it, Islam was still an influence on his life.

'This area is becoming popular with bankers, accountants, PR people and the like,' Süleyman said. 'It's very convenient and there are some nice apartments here. But Çetin, there are still a lot of streets that look as if they've been dropped in whole from one of the eastern provinces. If you remember, when Nişantaşı began to gentrify, there were still some very poor areas until really quite recently.'

'Yes, but if the professional classes are moving in, then why stop selling alcohol? Bankers and media types drink it . . .'

'Not all of them.' Süleyman took his cigarettes out of his jacket pocket and lit up. 'Some of the young professionals in particular are rediscovering religion now. That shopkeeper probably does come from somewhere like Trabzon or Van, but his customers may very well have been raised in very smart Bosphorus *yalıs*.'

İkmen raised his eyes impatiently to the sky. 'What the . . .'

It was at this point that they heard the sound of people shouting. They all screamed out the same thing: 'Fire!'

9

The two men looked first at each other and then in the direction of the sound. And although they couldn't actually see any sign of flames or smoke in the street or on the horizon, they began to make their way towards the rising tide of panicking human voices.

'We will,' İkmen said as he began to break into a some-what breathless jog, 'continue this conversation at another time.'

The fire engine was in the middle of the road. But then because Egyptian Garden Street was so narrow anyway, there wasn't anywhere else that it could be. Amazingly, there was a man in a sports utility vehicle behind the appliance, screaming out of the window and banging his hand down on the horn. Apparently he had to get to a meeting and nothing else in the universe mattered.

Çetin İkmen put his head and his police badge up to the car window and smiled. 'You could back up,' he said. 'We can get the vehicle behind you to move.'

The man, who was very young and very red-faced, gulped, looked down at the floor of his car and hunched his shoulders. This was something İkmen had seen in the narrow streets of İstanbul many times before. Big car, young, inexperienced driver, tiny alleyway. 'Inspector!' he called over to Süleyman, who was talking to one of the fire officers. 'Could you back this car up for this gentleman?'

His colleague, who was also very well aware of this phenomenon, ran over with his hands outstretched for the keys to the ignition. İkmen walked to where one of the fire officers was in conversation with a man with bright ginger hair. The once dusty street was now covered in mud from the water hose, and had to be very carefully negotiated. Officers were still inside the building, where the fire, though no longer raging, had yet to be brought completely under control.

Badge in hand, İkmen introduced himself to the fire officer, who turned away from the ginger-headed man and took the policeman to one side.

'He's American,' he said, as he tipped his head back towards the man he'd just been speaking to. 'He noticed a smell of burning in the lobby. Then he saw smoke coming out underneath the front door of the apartment. It was he who called us.'

İkmen looked back at the tall, rather pallid man and said, 'He looks shaken up.'

'His own apartment is two storeys above the fire,' the officer said. 'He knows most of the people in the block, including the family on the ground floor.'

Süleyman, who was now inside the sports utility vehicle, waved an arm to indicate that the car behind should start to back up. Some builders who had been working on a nearby construction site sauntered over to the back of the crowd in front of the apartment building.

'The family who rent the apartment are called Seyhan,' the officer continued. 'Must've been out when the fire started, as far as we can tell. I don't think that there's anything here for you, Inspector. Of course we won't know for sure until the fire is out . . .'

'No.'

It was İkmen's day off as well as Süleyman's. As they did sometimes, the two men had been spending some time together – drinking tea, playing backgammon, smoking and talking. The younger man was having marital problems, a regular feature of his adult life, and so had welcomed the chance to get away from his family home in nearby Ortaköy. İkmen, of whose nine children only two remained at his home in Sultanahmet, didn't really escape from his apartment when he wasn't on duty, but he was nevertheless often quite glad to get away. In contrast to Süleyman, he adored his wife. Fatma İkmen was a strong, loving and very capable woman. Unlike her husband, however, she was a pious Muslim, and although Çetin was quite happy and content for her to follow her faith, he was becoming increasingly irritated by her almost daily attempts to engage his interest in Islam. Whatever the religion in question, as far as Çetin İkmen was concerned, it was of no interest or concern to him.

'We'll wait until you've extinguished the blaze, just in case,' İkmen said. The car behind the sports utility vehicle was now back on the main Ortabahçe Street and Süleyman had started reversing. The young owner of the vehicle stood on the pavement looking sheepish.

The fire officer shrugged. 'Always happy to have police support,' he said as he looked at the crowd in front of the apartment building, which had kept on growing. 'You can help us push this lot back. But as for the fire . . . What can you say? This Seyhan family are apparently from the east. Could've built a fire to roast their meat on in the middle of the floor. It wouldn't be the first time that's happened. I've known them set fires on floors, in bins, all over the place. They come to the city, never even seen an electric oven before . . .'

12

'But if, as you think, the apartment was empty, that couldn't possibly be what happened, could it?' İkmen asked. 'Would anyone just set a fire and then walk away?'

'Some of them brought up in mud huts can and do,' the officer said gloomily. 'You can make a fire out of wood on a dirt floor with a hole in the ceiling. It's how a lot of them have always lived. Doesn't occur to them that they can't do that here.' He shook his head. 'Bloody peasants!'

A lot of Çetin İkmen also felt irritated by what to him seemed like further evidence of the baleful influence and ignorance of 'them'. He could almost see the family in his mind. The father, flat-capped, mustachioed and unsmiling; the bowed, veiled mother, old before her time; the children, timid if female, while the boys boiled with resentment, struggling to contain their pent-up envy of everyone better off then themselves. On the other hand, the fire officer was generalising, and there was not, as yet, any evidence to indicate how the blaze might have started. Maybe a faulty electrical appliance was to blame? That, too, was not an unusual scenario, even in the best houses and apartments in İstanbul.

İkmen was looking at Süleyman backing the SUV around the corner at the end of the street when the fire chief came out of the building and walked over to his officer. Süleyman had reversed the vehicle at speed. This had prompted some gasps of terror from the car's owner, whose thick hair gel had actually started to melt under the onslaught of heat from his own fear and anger.

'We've found a body,' the policeman heard the fire chief say to the officer in a low, calm voice.

'Just one?'

'I think so,' the chief replied.

İkmen turned and held his badge up for the chief to see. 'Need any help?' he asked.

For a moment the fire chief frowned, and then he said, 'Yes. Yes, actually it might be no bad thing to have a police officer involved.'

Like many Turkish apartment blocks built back in the 1960s, the Mersin Apartments provided a lot of space for their tenants. Apartment A, like all of the others in the building, had three good-sized bedrooms, a kitchen, a big living room and two bathrooms. Arranged around a large central hall, it had the look of a place that had once been very well cared for. Now, although only one of the rooms had actually been subjected to fire, the hall ceiling was scorched where flames had escaped through the open door. The sound of water dripping from ceilings and down walls into the many pools of liquid on the floor sounded lonely and eerie, especially in counterpoint to the gruff voices of the fire officers. And although the scene had now been declared safe from both gas and noxious fumes, there was a very unpleasant smell on the air that İkmen couldn't place.

'I believe this was a bedroom,' the fire chief said as he led İkmen towards a doorway into a deep black hole.

'If we're waiting for forensic examiners . . .' İkmen began.

'It's just to the left of the door. You don't need to go in. Just look.'

İkmen moved slightly forwards. Beyond the door was something so black, so matt in apparent texture that it gave him the feeling he was invading an utterly solid and unyielding place. He quickly pulled his head backwards. The fire chief, who was accustomed to such scenes, said, 'I know, it's a shock. It was a fierce blaze. When we got here, the place was full of poisonous smoke. Then we had what we call flashover. This is when the smoke and the soot ignite and there's a brightness of flame you just wouldn't credit unless you'd actually seen it. Afterwards we get this.'

'A black room.'

The chief unclipped a torch from his belt, switched it on and then gave it to İkmen. 'This should help.'

İkmen shone the beam of light through the doorway and down to his left. There were all sorts of shapes down there. Blackened lumps at eccentric angles, textures of darkness that went from the shiny to the viscous to the granular and the rough.

'I know that everything will just look like charcoal,' the fire chief said, 'but if you look, you'll see a row of sticks. They curve slightly.'

At first İkmen couldn't see anything like curved sticks. Then, as his eyes became accustomed to the light from the torch contrasted against the various grades of black in the room, something that resembled what the chief had told him about came into view.

'There?' He pointed downwards.

İkmen was a short, thin man and so it was quite easy for the burly fire chief to see over his shoulder. 'Yes,' the chief said, 'that's them. Ribcage. Underneath all the soot, the legs appear to be intact. If you get down low you can see the head. It isn't pretty.'

Çetin İkmen bent at the knees and leaned into the blackness.

Above the ribs was something ball-like. Frowning, he said, 'So do you think that this person set the fire?'

'We won't be able to say for sure until the scene has been investigated.'

Moving the torch from side to side, İkmen thought that he had managed to pick out where the body's nose had been. He stood up and handed the light back to the fire chief. 'So the fire had well and truly taken hold when you arrived?'

'Oh, yes,' the fire chief replied. 'Bedrooms, which is what this seems to be, catch quickly. Soft furnishings burn easily. Contained in this room, and to a lesser extent out here in the hall, the blaze wasn't obvious to people passing by in the street. The American who lives upstairs reported it. Smelt smoke in the lobby outside.'

'From your experience,' İkmen said, 'what do you think are the likely causes of the blaze?'

The fire chief shrugged. 'We'll have to mount a full investigation. Faulty wiring, faulty appliances, burning cigarette. Who knows?' He frowned.

İkmen said, 'You don't list arson, and yet you were pleased to see me when I told you I was a police officer. Is there something on your mind?'

The fire chief sighed. 'Come on,' he said as he took one of İkmen's arms in his, 'let's go outside.'

He led the policemen away from the other fire officers inside the building, away from the crowds at the front, to a small, shabby yard around the back. A couple of people in one of the apartments opposite were looking out of their windows to see if they could discern anything of the commotion surrounding the fire, but otherwise the two men were alone. Significantly they could not, it seemed, be overheard.

'There was a fire in a block like this up on Mecit Ali Street just over a month ago,' the fire chief said. 'Started in a bedroom, one victim, just like this. On that occasion the victim turned out to be a girl of fifteen. Her family had only been in Beşiktaş for a year, and the story went that she was home-sick for her old village just south of Van. That, it was said, was why she poured petrol over herself and took her own life. Just like this, the incident happened when the girl was on her own in the apartment, family out and about and no witnesses.'

'You think that the victim here is a girl?' İkmen asked.

'I don't know yet. But if it is . . .'

'You think suicide could be a possibility?'

The chief sighed, took a packet of cigarettes out of his pocket, offered one to İkmen and then lit up. 'You a religious man, are you, Inspector?' he asked.

İkmen eyed the chief very narrowly. If this was a precursor to a discussion about suicide and the possible torments of hell that some believed followed such an act, he was going to have to beat a hasty retreat. But he had to answer one way or another. 'No,' he said gingerly. 'Er . . .'

The fire chief smiled. 'I wish in a way I could be like that too,' he said. 'Secular. But I do believe. Try to be a good Muslim. You know. That said, I don't always like everyone else who calls himself a good Muslim. Can't go along with those Afghans, the Taliban and all that.'

'Well, no, that's just good sense,' İkmen said. 'What killing has to do with Islam is a mystery to all good believers and secular people with understanding.'

'Exactly.' The fire chief sighed once again. What he was trying to say was obviously very difficult for him. 'And to me, Inspector, that means that killing is not allowed,' he said. 'Don't care if it's for religious or political or tribal reasons. Even what some – generally people from the provinces – would call a killing for the sake of honour.' He looked İkmen hard in the eyes at this point. The policeman for his part knew instantly what he was thinking and where his talk was going. 'You . . .'

'The death of the girl on Mecit Ali Street was declared a suicide,' the chief said. 'I've no evidence to say that that wasn't exactly what it was. But she was a bright girl, she was doing well at school and she had a lot of friends. Why would she want to go back to some fly-blown village? Why would she kill herself rather than be clever and popular, as she was? On the day of that fire, one of my men was walking through the crowd when he heard someone say the word "slut". What did that mean? As far as we were told, the girl didn't have a boyfriend. That never came up. Then there was her family. Like a row of stones when I told them what had happened to her. No emotion at all.'

'Shock?'

'Oh, could be, could be,' the chief said as he puffed and then puffed again on his cigarette. 'I tried to find out why that person in the crowd would have called the girl a slut, but I couldn't get anywhere with it. All these migrants close ranks, don't they? But there must have been a reason. Maybe someone saw her talking to some man in the street, or . . .' He coughed and then cleared his throat loudly. 'Inspector, if the body in that apartment in there is a woman or a girl . . .'

'What you're talking about here, Chief, is a possible honour killing, isn't it?' İkmen said. He looked up into the chief's smutted, heavily lined face and smiled. 'Of course I will investigate if you have the slightest suspicion about this death,' he said. 'I will not, I promise you, just let it go.'

Chapter 2

Weeping, he nevertheless arrived at where he had been told to go. A clean shower with good soap and hot water followed. Then new, clean clothes. But they weren't his style, which irritated him. When he put them on and looked at himself in the mirror, the sight of them made him want to tear them off and rip them up. He looked at the stinking pile of fabric that was his old clothes on the floor and had to really control himself. In spite of everything, he wanted to put them on. He looked in the mirror and saw a face that was pure white with black pits where, somewhere, his eyes were sunk. He looked like that American rock star, that freak . . . Marilyn Manson.

What was he doing looking like Marilyn Manson? He was supposed to be a good person, a moral person, not some sexual deviant! The black T-shirt didn't help. It was tight, too, which gave his body the kind of definition he'd seen in magazines he knew he shouldn't be looking at. Shame and anger were followed by more pity for *her*. She who had turned and looked at him through the flames. She whose burning eyes of hatred had shown him that she had understood what he had done and why. What she cannot have appreciated was the utter rightness and necessity of the act.

Stupid girl! Stupid, stupid, wicked girl! How could she not have known? How could she not have appreciated that ramifications were inevitable? And how could he feel sorry for her, and why?

He put his old clothes into a plastic bag, which he then placed on the floor by the door. The new outfit would just have to do. He opened the door, walked out into the street and headed for the tram stop.

Cahit Seyhan and his wife Saadet were just as İkmen had imagined them to be. He was probably about fifty, small and thin, with short grey hair and a large grey moustache. She was maybe ten years his junior, overweight and slow and swathed in many metres of dull, patterned material. Her head, if not her face, was covered. Her abiding expression, like that of her husband, was one of bovine acceptance.

'My sister and her family have just moved into a place over in Fatih,' Cahit Seyhan said. He spoke with a rough accent, which sounded imprecise to İkmen. It made what he said sound sloppy and simple-minded. 'We went to see them.'

'Our son is to marry his cousin Nesrin,' Saadet said.

İkmen just about managed to stop himself from rolling his eyes. What was it about country people and aristocrats and inbreeding? Why did those two particular groups do that? Why did they *persist* in something that would only serve to amplify any pre-existing undesirable traits or sicknesses?

'You've got three children, Mr Seyhan?' the fire chief asked.

They were all standing in the Seyhans' living room, at the

other end of the apartment from the room where the fire had begun. It was a large room, furnished sparsely. Like most Turkish living rooms, it had a sizeable carpet on the floor, although not one of any merit or value. Cheaply turned out in a factory, probably in China, it might very well have been given to the family in exchange for an original rug made by some female ancestor. Equating old with useless, they had probably swapped it for something new and bright, and as the unscrupulous carpet dealer who had almost certainly done the deal with them would have said at the time, brand new was always far superior in a modern home. Apart from that, the Seyhans owned one sofa, a television and several large, tattered cushions that lay around the edge of the carpet in lieu of chairs.

Cahit Seyhan lit a cigarette. 'I have two sons, Kenan and Lokman, and a daughter, Gözde.'

'Where are your children at the moment?' the fire chief continued.

'Kenan works in a restaurant in Sultanahmet. My older son works with cars.'

Things that migrants did, İkmen thought. Waiting at table, cleaning, fixing cars.

'And your daughter?' he asked.

'She was here,' Mr Seyhan said.

İkmen looked at the fire chief, who asked, 'What is the room at the end of the corridor, where the fire started?'

'That is our daughter's bedroom,' Mrs Seyhan said.

Neither of them asked where their daughter was. Neither of them showed even the slightest hint of emotion. İkmen began to feel slightly sick. Maybe, he thought, the fire chief was right. Maybe this girl, Gözde, just like the other girl he'd told him about, had been meant to die.

'Mr Seyhan,' the chief began, 'I have to—'

'Mum! Dad!' A tall, thin man of about twenty-five burst through the door ahead of an agitated-looking Süleyman.

'This man says he is your son,' Süleyman said to Saadet Seyhan as the man threw himself into his mother's arms and then kissed her all over her face.

'Lokman!' she said, smiling as she did so. 'Lokman, my son.'

'Oh well, he was clearly telling the truth,' Süleyman said. He looked over at İkmen, who raised an eyebrow and shrugged. The young man was clearly very dirty, and now that he was in the room, there was a strong smell of petrol too.

'I heard the fire engine,' Lokman Seyhan said excitedly, 'and then one of the boys came into the garage and said that the fire was over in Egyptian Garden. I couldn't believe it was here!' He began to cry. 'Where is Gözde? Where is she?'

'Gözde?' Süleyman asked.

'Our daughter,' Mr Seyhan said. 'She is seventeen years old.'

'Ssh, ssh!' Mrs Seyhan soothed her crying son. 'It's all right, my lion, it will be well, my soul!'

The fire chief said, 'I am afraid to have to inform you that we have discovered a body in your daughter's bedroom. Now of course until tests have been completed we—'

Saadet Seyhan's eyes opened wide and she screamed, momentarily drowning out what the fire chief was saying.

'Mum!' Whereas before she had been comforting him, now the young man comforted his mother, hugging her, kissing her hair, cooing gently into her ears.

The fire chief looked at the dry-eyed Seyhan patriarch and said, 'We don't know if the body is that of your daughter. We don't know how or why this fire started.'

'What does that mean?'

'It means, Mr Seyhan, that we will have to bring in forensic investigators,' the fire chief said.

'Is that why the police are here?' Seyhan asked as he tipped his head towards Çetin İkmen.

'No,' the chief replied. 'Inspectors İkmen and Süleyman were in the vicinity when the fire was discovered. At the moment they are here to assist us in keeping order. A lot of people come to look at scenes like this, for reasons best known to themselves . . .'

In the short silence that followed, Lokman Seyhan looked at İkmen through narrowed eyes. 'I've heard your name,' he said. 'Haven't you been on television? Don't you deal with murders?'

İkmen had been on television in the past five years rather more than he would have liked. He didn't enjoy televised press conferences and he had always hated making statements to the media. But, fortunately or unfortunately for him, he had spent much of his career solving or attempting to solve often very bizarre and disturbing homicides. It was an area of criminal investigation that had always fascinated him and which had for the past fifteen years constituted the major part of his work. Sadly, of late, he was suddenly becoming recognisable.

'The police are here to keep order,' the fire chief reiterated. 'We don't know how the fire was caused or why, and murder doesn't even come into it yet. But you are all going to have to leave this apartment while the investigation is carried out.'

'Leave the apartment?'

'Maybe go to stay with the sister that you mentioned, Mr Seyhan.'

'Or call your landlord,' the fire chief said. 'He should be able to find you somewhere temporary.'

The Seyhans made two calls from Cahit's mobile phone, one to his sister Feray in Fatih district and the other to his son Kenan in Sultanahmet. The latter said that he was coming home as soon as he could, while the former offered the family accommodation for as long as they wanted. Saadet began to open the one cupboard in the living room and had started to remove some items when the fire chief stopped her.

'Mrs Seyhan, this whole apartment is going to have to be examined by the forensic investigators. I can't let you take anything out of here until they have finished,' he said.

'Nothing? Not even tablecloths?'

Not one of them had asked about the missing Gözde since that first time. Now dry-eyed again, the family seemed to have regained their composure, if not their curiosity about the whereabouts of their daughter. İkmen thought about that previous case that the fire chief had told him about and he wondered. Was no one looking for Gözde because everyone knew exactly where she was and what had happened to her?

'What about my medicine?' Lokman Seyhan asked.

'What medicine?'

'Tablets,' he said. 'In the kitchen.'

'What do you take tablets for?' İkmen asked him.

'Diabetes,' he said. 'The doctor gives them to me.'

'Well, obviously prescribed medication will have to be taken,' İkmen replied.

Süleyman took Lokman Seyhan to the kitchen and watched as he opened a cupboard over the sink and took out a packet of tablets. As Lokman turned, however, something on the worktop beside the fridge caught his eye. Fortunately Süleyman saw it at almost the same moment. It was a very small and very pretty mobile phone, and as Lokman Seyhan left the kitchen, he attempted to pick it up and put it in his pocket without the policeman seeing. A very firm hand caught hold of his wrist before he could do so.

'You're not allowed to take anything from the apartment except your medicine, Mr Seyhan,' Süleyman said.

'But it's my phone . . .'

Süleyman took it out of Lokman Seyhan's clawed fingers and peered at its tiny face and minute keyboard. He was, he had to admit, starting to find seeing very small things close up a bit of a problem.

'It's got all my numbers on it.'

'It's pink.' It was. It also, as Süleyman saw when he turned it over, had a little label on the back with the name 'Gözde'.

Süleyman and Lokman Seyhan saw this label at exactly the same moment. The younger man reddened. 'It looked like my phone. Sorry,' he said.

'It is obviously your sister's phone,' Süleyman replied. 'I wonder why she doesn't have it with her.'

'I don't know.'

Lokman Seyhan walked out of the kitchen and back towards the living room. Mehmet Süleyman looked down at the little pink phone and wondered why Gözde's brother hadn't thought that perhaps it might be a good idea to draw such an anomaly to the attention of either the fire officers or the police – given the situation. But he hadn't. What he had done was try to palm his sister's phone without being detected, and once caught, he had clearly lied about why. No Turkish man, much less a man from the back of beyond, would have a phone that looked like a glorified powder compact. And pink? Pink!

It wasn't that he hadn't prepared. He'd practised every day, it was what he loved to do. But his fingers wouldn't do what they usually did. Normally they caressed the keys, loved the feel of the instrument, revelled in the glorious sounds that it made. But hands that still shook, just would not stop shaking, made progress impossible.

Hamid Bey twirled one end of his moustache between his fingers and said, 'Schubert, it would seem, is making you nervous. Why?'

He loved Schubert's *Six moments musicaux*. It was one of the most wonderful pieces ever written for the piano and he'd been perfecting his performance of it for months. How he felt, the way his hands wouldn't work, had nothing to do with Schubert. It had to do with the look she had given him through the orange, gold and bright red flames. Indirectly it had to do with Hamid Bey. It also had very much to do with the fact that he just couldn't remember what he'd done with the petrol can. He'd poured the liquid over her head (she had screamed; he didn't want to think about that) and then he'd put the can down and . . . what? Where had he left it? What had he done with it? It certainly hadn't been with him when he left the apartment building on Egyptian Garden Street. And yet he knew he should have taken it! He knew he would get into—

'Schubert?' Hamid Bey reiterated. 'After all these weeks we've spent together in his company, please don't tell me that we have now all fallen out?'

Hamid Bey left his wicker peacock chair and came over to stand beside the piano. As usual, he stood too close.

'I don't think I feel very well, Hamid Bey,' he said. 'I'm sorry.'

Hamid Bey sighed. The teacher was so close, he felt his tobacco-scented breath on the back of his neck. Then Hamid bent to speak into his ear. Even closer. 'We must put on a good show,' he said. 'Performers are coming from Georgia and Armenia. We must show them what we can do.'

'Yes, Hamid Bey.' Everything inside him cringed.

'Yes.' Hamid Bey remained where he was for just a moment and then he sauntered back to his peacock chair. As he sat down, he said, 'So let's have no more talk of illness, shall we?' He took the baton that he always kept on the coffee table by his side and beat it against one of his fine brown brogues. 'Attend! *Moderato*! Let us begin again!'

He put his shaking fingers back into their starting position on the piano and took a deep breath.

Chapter 3

'People don't think about dental records any more these days,' the investigator said. 'But . . .' He bent down towards the body and moved the charred jaws apart, 'unless this woman was a criminal . . .'

'You're sure it is a woman?' the fire chief asked. It was late. Dark outside. He'd been at the scene of the fire since mid-morning, but although he was clearly exhausted, he was still obliged to oversee the work of the investigation team.

'Yes,' the young man said. Then, peering down into the blackened mouth, he added, 'I can see dental work. Fillings. She's seen a dentist.'

'I'll need to ask the family where thier daughter got her teeth done,' the fire chief said.

'Yes. And as I say, if they ask you about DNA analysis, tell them that unless their daughter blew up a car or something, no one will have that.' He let the jaws go and sat back on his haunches. 'Everyone watches all those CSI programmes from America now and so everyone thinks that DNA is the answer to everything. Some sort of magic process whereby we take a hair sample from a body, the police do something, there's a lot of violence and shouting and then the name of the murderer falls out at the other end. It makes me mad.'

The fire chief, in spite of where he was and his tiredness, smiled. The forensic scientist was right: a lot of people knew a bit about complicated concepts like DNA because of television and the internet. Not many, sadly, knew enough to really understand them.

'I'll speak to the family,' he reiterated.

'Don't tell them that we have any doubts about the fire yet,' the young man said. 'Just ask for the name of their dentist. We'll contact the police.'

'They were here earlier,' the chief said.

'Yes, I know.' He turned away, back to his work once again. 'İkmen.'

'You know him?'

'I know of him,' the scientist said. 'This may well interest him.'

'Murder?'

The investigator shrugged. 'Or suicide,' he said. 'The accelerant was poured over her head. Some of these girls either choose or are compelled to set themselves alight under certain circumstances.'

The two men looked at each other, neither really wanting to say what both knew was in their minds. Eventually it was the chief who broke the silence.

'You think,' he said, 'that the police might find that this girl may have transgressed her family's standards in some way?'

The scientist frowned. 'Let us call it what we both think it might be, shall we, Chief?'

The fire chief took a deep breath. 'A killing or a suicide designed to regain the honour of this family,' he said.

'That's it,' the scientist replied. 'That's what I would say we are probably up against. That is what I will suggest to the police that they look into.'

Çetin İkmen couldn't sleep. Like the chief, he'd suspected right from the start that the fire on Egyptian Garden Street had been set deliberately. The forensic investigators hadn't found any obvious electrical faults in the apartment, no signs of unattended burning cigarettes. What they had found behind the front door in the hall was an empty petrol can. Lokman Seyhan was a car mechanic. How simple could it be? Maybe the girl had been seen out by a neighbour with an unrelated man, or perhaps slightly risqué text messages had been exchanged with a boy down the street. The family got to know or were told and son Lokman was given the task of killing his own sister. Family honour was restored. Simple.

Except that İkmen knew that it wouldn't be anything of the kind. First of all, the body had to be identified as being that of Gözde Seyhan. Once that had been established, hopefully from dental records, an investigation would have to be conducted into Gözde's life, who could have killed her and the possible reasons why. In the meantime, the petrol can would need to be examined for forensic evidence and whatever was on Gözde's telephone would have to be looked at very carefully. Youngsters like the (at present only officially missing) Gözde Seyhan lived their lives on and in their mobile telephones. None of İkmen's younger children had any idea what a conventional address book, made from paper, looked like. Life was becoming ever more dominated by electronics, ever more modern and fast and incomprehensible to a man in his late fifties like Çetin İkmen.

After a while, he left Fatma snoring in their bed and went into the living room. If he wanted to, he knew that he could watch any number of channels on the TV that would entertain him with music, sport, news, drama, soft porn or even midnight cartoons. But he didn't want any of that. He lit a cigarette and then went over to his chair by the window and sat down. Pulling one of the window blinds open, he looked out and across Sultanahmet Square to where the great soaring bulk of the Sultanahmet Mosque made the already dark horizon around it black. Some people, even some avowedly religious types like the fire chief, tended to conflate honour killings with religion. True, such outrages did tend to happen almost exclusively amongst those who followed a religion of whatever sort. The faith was often used as justification for the killing. If a girl was behaving in an 'immoral' way, God was often cited as being the entity who was most offended by this. But the reality was that honour killings, in İkmen's experience, were about saving face.

Human beings were naturally curious. In cities, where lots of things happened and where opportunities existed to expand the mind and experience new ideas, this curiosity was at least catered for. But in small villages in the east, where, İkmen knew, snow could fall for three months of every year almost without let-up, minds could turn to darker pursuits. If, for example, someone saw a neighbour's daughter talking in a slightly flirtatious way to a young man who was not a relative, a campaign of malicious gossip could begin. And if the girl's family did not do something to curb their child, the whole group could be ostracised as people of unwholesome and weak character. Such ostracisation could take the form of simply not speaking to that family, but it could also have financial and other implications. These could include people refusing to do business with the family, not selling them goods, and the withdrawal of offers of marriage. Sometimes curbing the recalcitrant child meant just locking her away, or maybe giving her a very public beating. But sometimes harsher sanctions were required and the child would either be killed or persuaded by her relatives to kill herself. The press was littered with stories of fathers with tears in their eyes putting guns to their daughters' heads, of boys thought too young to attract long prison sentences killing their sisters. And then there were the suicides. Pathetic little notes would often accompany those, from girls so sorry for their 'poor' fathers, brothers and uncles, so mortified by the 'crimes' that had left them with no choice but to end their own lives.

And with increasing migration from the countryside, instances of honour killings in the cities were escalating. Çetin İkmen had been unable to secure a conviction in the three suspected cases he had so far been called upon to attend. Lack of evidence and some apparently iron-clad alibis had meant that he had been unable to take those cases any further. In two of them he had known almost beyond doubt that the girls in question had been murdered in order to restore family honour. In one of those cases some satisfaction had been gained by the fact that the family involved had, shortly after their girl's death, suffered a financial catastrophe that had all but put them out on to the streets. All three families had suffered some level of privation. But like the fire chief, who had failed to gather enough evidence against the family on Mecit Ali Street, İkmen was still irked by his lack of success. There was something else that worried him too, something that he knew he had to consider when it came to the officers working with him. There were people in every strata of society, across all professions, who approved of honour killings. Whether they came from a village background, or were advocates of 'traditional' values, or believed that some religious imperative existed to excuse such behaviour, they were a reality and they were, İkmen knew, present in the ranks of the police. Who approved of such killings and who did not, he didn't know. But he was very sure that, should this case turn out to be what he thought it was, he would soon find out.

No one spoke of anything except practicalities.

'Lokman and Kenan can sleep here,' Feray Akol said as she rolled out two thin mattresses on the floor of a drab, almost empty room. 'One day this will, please to God, be the room that my Aykan brings a bride home to, and then I will be able to take my rest.'

Saadet Seyhan, looking on in a vague daze, said, 'Kenan has gone out. I don't know when he will be back.'

'Men do that,' her sister-in-law said simply. 'Tonight your boys can sleep here in my son's room. You are family.'

It was very obvious to Saadet that Feray was irked. Her face twisted with the effort of holding in her rage. A widow of some ten years, she had come only three days before to İstanbul with her daughter Nesrin from the village where she and her brother Cahit had been born. Her son, Aykan, had

36

been working in the city for two years before he'd managed to earn enough money to send for his mother and sister. Feray had thought that her entry into the city would be like that of a queen. All she had found in reality was a tiny apartment with an antiquated bathroom, an unidentifiable smell in the kitchen and mould in all the cupboards. And now she had to share that very little with her brother and his family. The only consolation was that at least the neighbours were respectable. In Fatih, it was only women from other parts of the city who went about with their heads uncovered. There were no bars, no shops that sold alcohol, no licensed restaurants, and women did not, as far as she could tell, leave their homes and their children to just go out whenever they pleased. In that sense, this part of İstanbul was very much like the village. It made Feray feel as secure as anyone who had just come from a village of three hundred people to a city of twelve million could feel.

Saadet and Cahit lay on the floor of the small living room. As their nephew played some endless shooting game on a console on his lap, they tried to sleep, Cahit with some success, but Saadet couldn't. She told herself that it was because Kenan was still out and she was worried about where he was and what he was doing. But that wasn't really the case. While Aykan shot up aliens or foreign enemies or whoever they were, Saadet buried her head in the cushion that Feray had given her and fought to hold back her tears. If Cahit heard so much as a murmur from her, he would, she knew, beat her black and blue. Eventually she went to sleep. When she woke, however, it was still dark. Aykan was nowhere to be seen and Cahit had moved from her side.

In the corner of the room she heard him talking to someone she couldn't see.

Cahit said, 'I know what you've done, where you've been!'

It was her son Kenan's voice that whispered an answer: 'Don't talk to me! Don't talk to me about *that*!'

Chapter 4

The elderly woman who stared at him from across the corridor looked, Mehmet Süleyman thought, Greek. Dressed in a black cardigan and skirt, her hair hidden behind a jet-coloured headscarf, she was like Zoë, the Greek nanny he'd had as a child. She'd been old back in the 1960s, when Mehmet's mother had first engaged her to look after her two boys. Zoë, he recalled, had been a Phanar, a native İstanbul Greek. In common with the Süleyman family, she had been a relic from a long-gone past. Like the Phanar Greeks, the Ottoman Turkish Süleyman family were a diminishing breed. With no sultanate or empire to serve, as well as no money to speak of, families like the Süleymans were in an unstoppable decline. Nobody in modern Turkey cared that Mehmet's grandfather had been a prince. His own son, Yusuf, admittedly still a small child, didn't even know. Mehmet's own upbringing had been very different. He had known who and what his grandfather had been almost with his first breath.

The old woman turned and muttered something that sounded rough and countrified and was most certainly not Greek. A Kurdish dialect, maybe? As she went back into her apartment, so the door to the apartment he had been knocking on opened.

'Mr Ford?' he asked the tall, ginger-haired man who stood in the doorway. He spoke in English, which, he imagined, would be rather more comfortable for this man.

'Yes?'

'I am Inspector Süleyman of the İstanbul police.' He extended a hand, which the other man shook. 'You reported the fire down in the Seyhan apartment yesterday.'

'Yes.' Richard Ford, an American, was probably in his early forties, Süleyman's own sort of age. 'Is there a problem?'

'No.' Süleyman smiled. 'May I come in, sir?'

'Oh, yes.' For a moment the American looked a little flustered, but then he stepped aside to allow Süleyman in and said, 'Please . . .'

Like the Seyhans' apartment, Richard Ford's was centred around a large square hall. In common with Turkish homes, it had a small mat behind the front door covered with pairs of discarded shoes. Süleyman duly slipped his own shoes off and then followed the American into a big, light living room. In front of one of the two large picture windows at the back of the room he saw a small woman sitting at a computer screen. She looked up, smiled and said, 'Hi.'

'My wife, Jane.' Richard Ford gestured towards a large red sofa and said, 'Please, take a seat.' He looked over at his wife as Süleyman sat. 'This man is from the police,' he continued. 'About the apartment downstairs.'

'Oh, right.' Jane Ford stood up. She was tiny. Short and thin, she wore camouflage combat trousers and a sleeveless red T-shirt. She was, Süleyman reckoned, about ten years younger than her husband.

'Mr Ford,' Süleyman began, 'we do not yet know what started the fire down in Apartment A, but the fire investigators, as well as our own people, are trying to find out. Can you please tell me how and when you first noticed it?'

Richard Ford told the same story he had told to the fire chief. He'd been coming back to his apartment when he saw smoke curling out from underneath the Seyhan's front door. He'd called the fire brigade. 'I'd seen the two Seyhan boys go off to work when I looked out the window at about six thirty. I went out to get bread at around eight,' he said. 'I didn't see the parents or the girl and so I didn't know who might be in there.'

'They have a very pretty daughter, don't they?' his wife said. Much darker than her husband, she had short black hair cut into a pixie style. She too, Süleyman thought, was pretty in her way. 'Is she OK?'

After a not inconsiderable amount of coaxing, the fire chief had eventually managed to get the name of Gözde's dentist from her family. With any luck he or she was now checking the girl's records.

'We heard the firemen found a body,' Jane Ford continued. 'Is that the daughter? Is it Gözde?'

Süleyman couldn't tell them what he, at least officially, did not know. 'The body is as yet unidentified,' he said. 'Mr Ford, Mrs Ford, do you know the Seyhan family? Do you converse or . . .'

'We don't really speak Turkish that well yet,' Richard Ford said with a smile. 'We've been here three years, but . . .' He shrugged. 'The Seyhans came to the building maybe a year after us.

41

His wife nodded in agreement.

'The *kapıcı* told me that they came from somewhere in the east. The mom and the daughter are both always covered.'

'Oh, but we don't have a problem with that,' his wife put in quickly. 'Everyone is entitled to dress how they want, right?'

Süleyman didn't answer, but said instead, 'Some women cover, others do not. The Seyhan family are rural people. Covering of women remains more common in those areas.'

'They have to be fairly well off to be able to live here,' Richard Ford said. 'I know this isn't the best part of town, but . . . I don't know what the men do, but it must pay quite well.'

Lokman Seyhan worked in a garage, his brother in a restaurant; their father apparently drove a taxi that he shared with a friend. Süleyman looked at Mrs Ford. Something she had said had piqued his interest.

'Mrs Ford, you clearly know the girl Gözde's name. Were you friendly with her?'

Jane Ford smiled. 'We exchanged pleasantries,' she said. 'On the stairs, sometimes when she was pegging clothes out in the back yard. She didn't go out.'

'Her family kept her in.'

She shrugged. 'I guess.'

It was not unusual for the daughter of rural parents to be confined to her home. Back in her village, which in Gözde's case was near the city of Kars, she would be more or less confined until her marriage. Girls who went out could possibly be up to no good. And in view of the fact that several people involved in the investigation believed that if

42

the body did turn out to be that of Gözde Seyhan, she could possibly be the victim of an honour killing, that kind of background did make sense.

'Mrs Ford do you know whether Gözde Seyhan had a boyfriend?' Süleyman asked.

A moment of icy silence was followed by a shocked expression passing over Jane Ford's face. 'A boyfriend?'

'Yes.'

Then she turned her head away and a little laugh came from her throat. She no longer looked Süleyman in the eye. 'No! God, no! She was a good girl.'

Süleyman looked over at her husband, who was observing his wife closely.

'She never went out,' Jane Ford continued. 'Never! How would she get a boyfriend! God, no, girls like that are pure. That is essential to them and their families, right?'

Yes, it was right, and Süleyman said so. What was not right, however, was Mrs Ford's response to his questions about Gözde Seyhan. That wasn't right at all, and he felt sure that Mrs Ford was lying. He turned back to her husband.

'Did you see anyone leaving these apartments when you discovered the fire, Mr Ford?'

'Er . . .' Richard Ford looked away from his wife. 'Um, no,' he said. 'People passing on the street – the guy who sells *simit* bread, the lady who takes in laundry at the end of the road.'

'That is all?'

'That's all I remember,' he said. 'Say, Inspector, has the Seyhan girl been seen since the fire? Are they all OK or what?'

Süleyman cleared his throat. 'Mr and Mrs Seyhan and their two sons are staying with family for the moment. Gözde Seyhan is officially a missing person.'

Jane Ford gasped. 'Oh my God!' she said. 'So Gözde *was* in that fire!'

Süleyman, who was accustomed to members of the public making such leaps of logic, albeit understandable ones, said, 'No. We don't know anything of the kind, Mrs Ford. Miss Seyhan is a missing person. That is all.'

'Oh.' Her agitation deflated, or seemed to do so, immediately. 'Oh, I see.'

But in spite of her decreased anxiety, her face looked sad, and flushed. Mr Ford and Süleyman spoke for a few more minutes and then the policeman got up to leave.

As he shook hands with Richard Ford, he asked, 'So what brings you to İstanbul? Do you work here?'

'Yes,' Richard said with a smile. 'I work at the university. I'm a biologist.'

'Oh.' He turned to look at the man's wife. 'And you?'

'Oh, I'm just along for the ride,' she said, 'although I do run a website.'

'A website?'

'It's for people, expats, new to İstanbul. It's called Make the Most of İstanbul,' she said. 'It's just advice about where to go, what to do. Real estate.'

'Ah.' It wasn't the sort of thing that Süleyman or even his half-Irish wife Zelfa would be interested in. But then they were Turks.

'I think new people find it useful,' she said.

'I am sure they do.' Süleyman began to walk back towards

44

the front door. Just before he reached the hall, he turned and asked. 'Oh, one more thing: why live in Beşiktaş? I know that it is becoming more popular now, but this part is not so fashionable. There are many people from villages here still, I think.'

Jane Ford smiled again. 'Oh yes,' she said excitedly. 'And that is why we love it! Village people are so authentic, don't you think?'

The Yıldız family had fallen on hard times. Their apartment building on a road off Kennedy Street, the dual carriageway out of town to Atatürk airport, had developed some serious faults after the earthquake of 1999 and had eventually had to be demolished. Partly because of this and partly because they were tired of the city, Constable Hikmet Yıldız's parents decided to return to their village in Anatolia. This left Hikmet and his brother Ismail, who moved further into the city, to a small apartment in Fatih district. Ismail had, in recent years, developed an interest in reconnecting with his Islamic faith, and so living in a religious district was very good for him, especially in view of the fact that he, unlike Hikmet, was unemployed. His neighbours sympathised and many of them told him when various positions became vacant and encouraged him to apply. But in the meantime, his brother was the sole breadwinner. He was also one of the few officers who lived near to where the Seyhan family were staying. And so Hikmet it was that İkmen chose to make contact with them. He was ushered into the small, crowded apartment by Aykan Akol, Cahit and Saadet Seyhan's nephew. An overweight lump of a man who apparently worked as a security guard,

Aykan waved an uninterested hand in the direction of his uncle and aunt and then left the room.

Constable Yıldız introduced himself, and then asked the couple if they had heard yet from their daughter. Cahit Seyhan responded with a curt 'No.'

'You have no idea where Gözde may have gone, assuming that she did in fact leave your apartment?'

'No.'

It was highly unlikely that Gözde Seyhan had left the apartment to be replaced somehow by some other, unknown woman. But it was possible, and as yet, there had been no word from Gözde's dentist.

Saadet Seyhan said, 'My girl was a good girl. She didn't go out on her own.'

Hikmet made a mental note of her use of the past tense and then asked, 'Why didn't Gözde come with you on the day of the fire? You came over here, didn't you?'

There was a pause. Cahit and Saadet Seyhan were small people who, in spite of the increasing late spring heat, wore a lot of clothes. Saadet reminded Hikmet of his own mother, a woman who also always covered her head and wore voluminous *Salvar* trousers, which she topped with large dresses and many, many cardigans.

'My son is betrothed to his cousin Nesrin,' Cahit Seyhan said. 'We came to visit my sister, her mother, to discuss our children's future. There was no need for the girl to accompany us.'

So Gözde would have been left alone to do housework or washing or to watch the television. Nothing unusual in that for a girl from a village background. Nothing that Hikmet's

46

brother Ismail would find in the least bit out of place. But for Hikmet himself there were mixed feelings. Girls destined for marriage were quite rightly supposed to be pure and cloistered, and that was all very good. But he had been in the city for most of his life and he knew a lot of girls who were not like that at all. İkmen's deputy, Sergeant Farsakoğlu, was a case in point. She was in her thirties and single, and she had a career. What was more, he liked her and several other women just like her that he knew. In fact Hikmet, who was no stranger to the occasional romantic dalliance, was no longer sure whether he wanted eventually to marry a virgin from his village, even if that was what his parents wanted. Ismail would of course go along with what was expected. He had found peace and security in his faith and felt that he wanted to pursue a traditional course when he came to marriage. That was fine – for him.

'As you know,' Hikmet continued, 'the body of a woman has been found in your daughter's bedroom. Were there any women that Gözde was friendly with who may have visited her?'

'No.' Again Cahit Seyhan answered for both himself and his wife.

'Was your daughter unhappy about anything?'

'No. What would she have to be unhappy about?'

'I don't know,' Hikmet said. 'That is why I am asking.'

Cahit Seyhan shrugged. There was very little emotion in that room. The man sat in virtual silence in a pool of grey cigarette smoke, the Seyhan sons were apparently already back at work and the family they were staying with were almost invisible. Only a slight reddening around Saadet

Seyhan's eyes gave any clue to how she might be feeling. But then maybe she had not wept. Maybe she had just not slept.

Hikmet offered Cahit Seyhan his card. 'You can use me as a contact,' he said. 'If you have any questions . . .'

'We don't,' Cahit Seyhan said as he pushed the card away.

'Oh.' Hikmet's boss, Çetin İkmen, would no doubt have said something pithy and appropriate at that point, but Hikmet just felt frozen out and rejected.

When he finally left the family, Hikmet walked out on to a street where every woman he could see was covered. That was by no means unusual for Fatih municipality; what was out of the ordinary was the fact that he noticed it. Back when they had lived in the old apartment, some of the women had covered and some had not. When Ismail had started becoming very religious and had suggested the move to Fatih, Hikmet hadn't really thought too much about it. He spent so little time in the apartment, he hardly noticed where he was. Except that now he did, and he wasn't sure what he felt about it.

It was İkmen's friend and colleague Arto Sarkissian who finally made the call. A pathologist with thirty years' experience, the ethnic Armenian had known the policeman and his family all his life.

'I have just received the body of a seventeen-year-old girl,' Arto said. 'Our forensic investigators tell me she was called Gözde Seyhan.'

'Ah.' İkmen put a hand up to his forehead and sighed. 'The dental records matched with what was left of her teeth?'

'Her dentist has confirmed it.'

İkmen looked out of his window at the darkening sky outside, and then he said, 'OK, Arto. Keep me informed.'

'I will.'

The connection cut and İkmen put his phone down and looked over at his sergeant, Ayşe Farsakoğlu. She was bent over a cardboard file, frowning.

'Ayşe,' he said, 'we will need to find out exactly who that petrol can we found at the fire in Beşiktaş belongs to.'

She looked up. 'Was it arson?' she asked.

'That I don't yet know for certain,' İkmen replied. 'But the body is definitely that of Gözde Seyhan. Any progress on the contents of her mobile phone?'

'No, sir,' Ayşe said as she lifted her office telephone receiver and began to dial, 'but I'll chase it up right away. If this is an honour killing, then we must make an example of the perpetrators.'

She looked both angry and determined. İkmen had wanted to say that she should not allow herself to get too carried away until they actually knew how the fire had been caused. But so many alarm bells were going off in his head that to say so much as a word would, he felt, be extremely hypocritical. And so he let her make her call and kept his counsel.

Chapter 5

'The body the firemen found was that of your sister.'

Kenan Seyhan listened to his father's voice on the end of the telephone line, then he nodded. 'I see.'

'Now the police tell me that they must keep her body for some tests,' Cahit Seyhan said. 'They need to discover how she died.'

'Yes, they do,' his son replied.

'Everything rests in the hands of Allah.'

Kenan Seyhan didn't answer. He had been sitting outside the restaurant where he worked, having a cigarette, when his father had called. Only very reluctantly had he picked up.

'I won't be home tonight,' he told his father. 'Auntie Feray and Mother needn't cook for me.'

'You're going—'

'You know where I'm going!' Kenan said hotly. 'So don't say anything. I'm away from you! Doing what you want!'

'You're not—'

'I'm away from you, aren't I?' Kenan snapped. 'As we agreed!'

His father put the phone down on him and Kenan sighed. As he looked into the distance, he saw the lights that hung between the minarets of the Sultanahmet Mosque blaze into life. They made him, momentarily, frown.

It was nearly ten p.m. by the time İkmen and Ayşe Farsakoğlu arrived at number 14, Star Apartments, Egyptian Garden Street, Beşiktaş. The block was on the opposite side of the road from the Mersin Apartments where the Seyhan family lived. Number 14 was high up on the fourth floor. In addition, this building was less well cared for. There was a lot of litter in the stairwell, and as they had entered, the officers had been observed by a large number of quite dirty-looking children. Standing in front of a blank, scarred front door, waiting for the occupants to open up, İkmen had to keep on pressing the timed light switch on the wall in order not to be plunged into darkness.

They had come, late as it was, to see someone called Osman Yavuz. A mobile telephone number registered to him had been the last one that Gözde Seyhan had called before her death. In fact, assuming that the girl had died between seven and seven forty-five in the morning, the call, which had been recorded as having taken place at 6.51, had occurred only just prior to her demise. İkmen, who had already rung the doorbell once, rang it again. Ayşe Farsakoğlu looked over at her boss nervously.

'If he is out . . .'

'He could be,' İkmen said. He put his ear close up to the door and heard the sound of some sort of cop or cowboy show shooting away on a TV set inside. 'Someone's in.' He banged on the door with his fist and shouted, 'Police! Open up!'

He hadn't wanted to attract attention, but apparently that was what was needed, because as well as several neighbours poking their heads out of several doors, the door in front of him slowly opened too.

'Yes? What is it? What do you want?' The voice was old and reedy and it belonged to a tiny woman whose back was so hunched, her face looked as if it was growing out of her chest.

'Good evening, Aunt,' İkmen said. 'We've come to see a man called Osman Yavuz.'

'Why?'

'Does he live here?' İkmen asked.

The old woman looked around with tiny, hostile eyes, and seeing that many of her neighbours had now gathered outside their apartments, she said, 'Come inside. Too many ears out here.'

As they stepped over the threshold and took off their shoes, İkmen and Ayşe were aware of the scorn with which the old woman regarded them. They also noticed that the apartment where she lived was small, dark and smelt of sour cooking oil.

'Osman isn't here any more,' the old woman said as she led them through into a tiny lounge that was crammed with ancient, creaking sofas. On the sofas, cushions of all sizes and colours were piled up in chaotic pyramids. On top of some of these structures sat a range of various-coloured Persian cats. There were places for humans to sit, just not very many. The old woman walked over to the television in the corner and turned it off. 'American rubbish!'

'Where has Osman gone?' Ayşe asked.

The old woman shrugged. 'I don't know,' she said. 'Maybe back to his mother.'

'You're not his mother?'

She laughed. 'Osman is eighteen!' she said. 'I am his grandmother.'

'So his mother . . .'

'His mother was the wife of my son,' the old woman said.

'Was?'

Her face fell into a purse-shaped collection of wrinkles. 'My son died,' she said. 'Years ago. His wife went back to be with her family in Bursa. What's all this about? Why do you want Osman?'

'We need to talk to him about one of his friends,' İkmen said.

'Who? He doesn't have any friends.'

The old woman, like the officers, remained standing. Her small eyes looked up at them, filled with suspicion.

'We need to speak to your grandson,' Ayşe repeated. 'Why don't you know where Osman has gone?'

'He's eighteen. He's always coming and going. I don't know what he does!'

'We'll need to have his mother's telephone number,' İkmen said.

'She doesn't have one,' the old woman replied. 'Have you tried his mobile?'

'The number is out of service,' İkmen said.

Now the old woman frowned. Suddenly she realised what had happened. 'You have Osman's number already?' she said.

'Yes.'

'How . . .'

'We'll need his mother's address,' İkmen said. 'Can you write that down for us?'

She said that she could, and shuffled off to her bedroom to get a pen and some paper. As soon as she had gone, Ayşe said, 'What about the photographs on the phone? Do we mention them?'

'What? To the old lady?' İkmen shook his head. 'Not even to the boy's mother, if we find her.'

'Mmm.' Ayşe frowned.

'The boy will have to know that we have his phone number, because we managed to trace him through it. But if he knows for sure that we've seen those photographs on Gözde's phone, he might bolt.'

'If I were him, I would,' Ayşe said.

'Depends what he's done – if anything.'

Ayşe lowered her voice. 'Sir, he has naked photographs of that girl on his phone!'

İkmen shrugged. 'We think,' he said. 'She certainly sent them to him. Doesn't mean he asked for them. Doesn't mean he had anything to do with her death.'

The old woman shuffled back in and shoved a piece of paper into İkmen's hand.

'I just hope that he has maybe got a job now,' she said wearily. 'It does no good for men to be lying in their beds doing nothing but sending texts and dreaming. A man without work is a useless thing. What is more, a man with no work is a dangerous thing. They get up to no good . . .'

Mehmet Süleyman was not a great devotee of the internet. It had its uses, clearly, and e-mail was very convenient, but he couldn't sit looking at it for hours on end like some people. The Make the Most of İstanbul site was, however, of interest, peripheral as it was to the suspicious fire in Beşiktaş. Jane Ford, the wife of Richard Ford, the man who had first discovered the blaze, administered the site.

Make the Most of İstanbul provided a lot of information. There were sections covering property, health, education, professional services, shopping and cultural events. There were book and music reviews, and forums for discussion of topics like the upcoming ban on smoking in enclosed spaces. When he came across this, Süleyman looked at the cigarette between his fingers and sighed. Come July, he'd have to go outside the station if he wanted to smoke. İkmen, who always had been and remained a voracious smoker, was currently living in denial about this. But he too, in the end, would have to conform.

Süleyman clicked on another category and found that Make the Most of İstanbul had a 'contacts' section. Part friendship site and part lonely hearts column, it was peopled by men and women nervously trying to build lives in an alien city. Like displaced people everywhere, their aim, albeit unconscious in some cases, was to cling to what they knew, thereby relegating the exotic 'other' in which they found themselves to the periphery, albeit a colourful one.

American male, 34, tall, athletic, Harvard grad. Alone in İstanbul. Wants to meet slim, health-conscious American female, 28–34, for fun, sightseeing and possibly romance.

American male, *American* female. It was so specific. No other kind of Westerner would do. Not a Frenchwoman, not a Briton, not an Australian. And it wasn't just confined to Americans either. Almost everyone, it seemed, wanted to stay in their own ethnic or religious niche. The exceptions, more coyly worded, were no less specific, no less needy.

Professional Spanish lady (40) would like to meet distinguished Turkish gentleman for companionship. Any age group considered.

Any age group . . . He imagined her. Professional, competent, attractive, but forty and therefore willing to take whatever she could get. It was sad, but then loneliness of any sort was never pretty. He lived in a house full of people and yet he was alone. Once again he and his wife were not getting on, and as was his custom, he was beginning to spend his time elsewhere: with Çetin İkmen, at work and, just in the last month, with a certain gypsy woman in what had once been the old Jewish neighbourhood of Balat. Gonca was somewhere in her fifties. A respected artist, she was also a handsome, sexy and vibrant character who made him laugh. He knew it was wrong, but Gonca had been there for him before and she was, especially when he was unhappy, a very hard habit to break.

He came out of the contacts section and began looking at some of the articles that readers of the site had submitted. They had titles like 'Walking in the Princes' Islands', 'My First Ramazan' and 'Street Vendors of Old İstanbul'. He read a few excerpts. He found them informed, earnest, worthy. These were people who obviously cared about where they were and wanted to actively engage with it. That said, he also detected an air of condescension, particularly in the reader submissions. Local 'colour' was not always what these writers believed it to be. Some 'İstanbul customs' were not native to the city at all; rather they had been imported to it from Anatolia by economic migrants. What was more, much of this commentary was quite uncritical. True, to criticise the practices of a country that was not your own was not easy. But even a staunch patriot like Süleyman found some of the very fulsome praise rather difficult to stomach.

He spent another half an hour flicking through various menus, and then he quit and shut down his computer. It was already midnight and he still hadn't eaten anything. His wife, Zelfa, would have prepared something hours before. That was almost certainly in the bin by this time. He took his jacket off the back of his chair, lit up a cigarette and left his office slowly.

Chapter 6

Fire investigation was, the pathologist knew, a very exacting and specific field of study. So when he received a call from a member of the investigative team telling him that the fire at the apartment in Beşiktaş had been set deliberately, he was in no doubt that that was correct. Someone had poured petrol over Gözde Seyhan's head as she stood in the middle of her bedroom, and then ignited her with either a match or a lighter. The theory concurred with his own opinion. The investigator also told him that from the angle at which the petrol had been poured, he was certain the girl could not have done it herself.

Because a volatile accelerant had been used, the girl hadn't stood a chance. The flames had burned upwards, inflicting massive damage upon her head and torso, while her legs, which had attracted rather less petrol than the other parts of her body, were comparatively unscathed. The room had burned as it had because of Gözde's abortive attempts to put herself out. Not knowing that a petrol blaze, unlike an unaccelerated fire, couldn't be smothered, she had attempted to extinguish the flames by rolling on the floor. During the course of this action, she had brushed up against her bed, the curtains and some other fabrics that were scattered around the room. A lot of highly flammable man-made fibres were involved, and so the whole area had ignited and then burned with a ferociousness that would not have happened had Gözde just simply dropped where she stood.

Dr Arto Sarkissian looked down at the blackened remains of the girl and tried not to picture what she had been through that day. But he couldn't. Questions like, had she screamed? Had she even had time to make any sort of sound? kept on running over and across his mind in loathsome waves. Who had done this to her? Who *could* do such a thing to another human being? And why? Çetin İkmen, as well as the fire investigators, was of the opinion that the girl's death was some sort of honour killing. But the doctor had established that Gözde Seyhan was a virgin, and so why anyone would have cause, if that was indeed even a vaguely appropriate term, to kill her was a mystery. But then he knew little of honour killings, and how and why they happened. Rare, if on the increase in the city, they had until recently been recognised as being a rural or tribal phenomenon. Personally, Arto had rarely come into contact with a body strongly suspected to have died as a result of an honour killing, until now. Some people he knew muttered about a perceived rise in Islamic fundamentalism. But Arto, though a Christian himself, always refuted the notion that honour killing was a Muslim phenomenon.

'Every society does it,' he would say to friends who insisted upon discussing such things. 'Muslims, Jews, Christians, Hindus. It's something that's more about the notion of honour in a community, whatever that is, than a religious construct. If a man cannot keep his women "in order", then he loses face. It says far more to me about men than it does about religion. What ghastly control freaks we all are!'

Whatever his opinion, it wasn't going to help Gözde Seyhan. She'd died in agony, her skin roasting, every breath she took feeding the flames that were consuming her ruined lungs.

Hamid İdiz had taught what he liked to call 'pianoforte' for over thirty years. His mother had been a concert pianist, and although Hamid had never attained those dizzy professional heights himself, he had always led a life 'in music', as he liked to put it. From his small apartment on Efe Lane in the fashionable suburb of Şişli, he operated a small but exclusive piano school, which had, he hoped, given several generations of İstanbullu children a greater appreciation of music.

Hamid Bey, as he liked to be called, was an easily recognisable local character in Şişli. Resplendent in English tweed suits, winter and summer, he also sported the kind of luxuriant moustache so beloved by his Ottoman forebears. This he waxed every day and twirled between his fingers obsessively as his often criminally untalented pupils attempted to play. But he was a good teacher and he knew it, and his students, for the most part, liked him. There was, however, another side to his character of which most of his students and all of their wealthy parents were unaware. Hamid İdiz liked to cruise. Sashaying down the middle of the main İstiklal Street in Beyoğlu, his hips swinging provocatively from side to side, he loved to attract like-minded men and take them into tight, dark alleyways. Under such circumstances full sex was rarely a possibility, but a frequently fumbled foray into mutual masturbation or oral sex gave him the high that he, and whoever he was with, needed. Sometimes he would develop a fancy for one of his young pupils, but generally, his adventures in Beyoğlu would mean that he could resist temptation. He did have 'friends', too – men equally as furtive and closeted as himself who would visit for a glass of wine, some classical music and the passive sex that Hamid Bey so enjoyed.

It was two hours before his first lesson of that day when a person arrived he had not expected to see. They kissed, and excited by the spontaneity of the arrival, Hamid Bey went to his bedroom, took his clothes off and exhorted his paramour to, 'Take me!' He closed his eyes, ready for the delicious pain mixed with pleasure that he so craved. But it never came. Instead he felt a sharp, cold pain across his throat, and as blood poured down his chest and on to his nice satin sheets, Hamid Bey choked and then died.

'Well, Osman Yavuz would seem to be on the missing list,' Çetin İkmen said as he replaced his telephone receiver and lit up a cigarette.

Ayşe Farsakoğlu, who was also smoking, pointed at İkmen's cigarette and said, 'Remember the ban comes into force in July.'

İkmen growled, 'Don't remind me.'

As quickly as she had brought the subject up, Ayşe changed it. 'That was Bursa, I take it?'

'A sergeant went to see the boy's mother. She claims not to have seen him for six months. She thought she was at his grandmother's in Beşiktaş.'

'Did the sergeant believe her?'

'He told me he saw no reason not to,' İkmen said. 'Apparently the mother was very forthcoming about the boy. It would seem that trouble follows him.'

'The grandmother intimated that he was lazy.'

'Jobless, lazy and given to random acts of petty vandalism, so his mother told the sergeant,' İkmen said. 'Although whether we can swallow that whole, I don't know. Apparently the widow Yavuz has five other kids, younger than Osman, to take care of, as well as an elderly mother and father. Maybe she just wanted lazy Osman out of the way.'

'Shift him over to her husband's mother.'

'Indeed.'

They both sat in silence for a moment, savouring what would soon be a luxury of the past – the ability to smoke at their desks. Neither or them welcomed the ban, although Ayşe had said that she would probably use its imposition as an excuse to try and give up. İkmen, on the other hand, had stated to everyone that he had absolutely no intention of quitting. 'I won't be told what to do with my own bloody body!' he said to anyone who would listen. 'It's mine and I'll do whatever I want with it!'

'Well we know that whatever else Osman Yavuz may have done, he didn't take Gözde Seyhan's virginity,' Ayşe said. İkmen had spoken to the pathologist Arto Sarkissian earlier, when this fact, as well as the grim news that the fire had been beyond doubt deliberate, had been given to him. Shortly afterwards he had officially opened a murder investigation.

'Gözde must have had some sort of relationship with the

boy,' İkmen said. 'People don't send naked pictures of themselves to strangers, do they?'

Ayşe shrugged. 'I don't know,' she said. 'Gözde was kept inside by her parents. On one level she lived a traditional rural life, and yet she was surrounded by city mores and values, and of course, like a lot of these women, she watched a lot of television. I think that girls like Gözde are often the victims of mixed messages, sir. Mother and father tell her she has to stay in, stay pure, not answer back. TV shows her a world of scantily clad R and B singers, material wealth she cannot even hope to aspire to and lots of attractive men. Maybe she and the boy did meet, somehow, perhaps when she was hanging out washing. Clearly they swapped phone numbers, although whether the boy requested those photographs has to be open to question. Not all of these covered country girls are as innocent in their heads as they would have their parents believe.'

İkmen, who knew his deputy to be a committed feminist, said, 'I can't believe *you* are defending the boy.'

'I'm not,' she said. 'He may well be as guilty as hell. I mean, we all know about sexting, don't we?'

The İstanbul police had dealt with several of these cases over the previous twelve months. Basically young, very naive girls were targeted by unscrupulous men and boys to either send them naked photographs of themselves, usually via their phones, or to 'perform' on short video clips for the pleasure of these males. It was a kind of blackmail. Either the girls did as they were told, or their conservative parents (and the parents of these girls were always conservative) would be told lies about them. Such lies, if the parents were so inclined, could lead to the girls being in mortal danger.

'But I believe we need to be cautious,' Ayşe continued. 'This looks like an honour killing. But it might not be.'

'We need to find Osman Yavuz,' İkmen said. 'We also need to find out who owns the petrol can we found at the Seyhans' apartment.'

'It wasn't Gözde's brother Lokman's?'

'He says not, and none of his prints were on it,' İkmen said. 'We can't prove that it was or wasn't Lokman's can. That said, he works in a garage and so he had easier access to petrol than anyone else. And it was definitely petrol that was poured over Gözde and then set alight.' İkmen frowned. 'Somehow we need to build a biography of this cloistered girl's life. Let's start by seeing if we can dig up any gossip about her. Honour killings can sometimes have their genesis in whispers heard in the bazaar, can't they?'

'The word of a bitter old woman or a man the girl may already have rejected can sometimes cause families to kill or maim a child just to save face.'

'Sadly, that is very true, Ayşe,' İkmen said. 'I want you out in Beşiktaş and over in Fatih where the family live now. See what you can pick up.'

'Sir.' She rose from her seat and began to put her jacket on.

'And take Constable Yıldız with you to Fatih,' İkmen said. 'He has local knowledge.'

Gonca the gypsy made a lot of noise whenever they had sex. Her many children had either left home years before or were playing out somewhere in the street, and her neighbours knew exactly what she did and made no comment or trouble for

65

her about it. Gonca consequently gave full voice to her feelings. But then Mehmet Süleyman loved that kind of spontaneity. His wife, long ago, had been just like that. When things had been right between them.

'Oh!' Gonca threw herself off him and lay back on her huge bed with a smile on her face. 'You know,' she said huskily, 'you have a very good penis. One of the best! I should like to keep it under my pillow and bring it out when I want an orgasm.'

'Just my penis?' He was smiling. Such a statement was typical of Gonca. She was, after all, not just a gypsy, but a very outré gypsy artist. And artists were supposed to be weird.

'Why would I want anything else?' she said as she gave him a cigarette and then lit one for herself. 'A whole man would drive me mad. Even you. But if I could just have your penis . . .' She winked at him, then put her hand on the object of her desire and said, 'Imagine how much fun I could have with it!'

He laughed. 'You are impossible,' he said as he gently ruffled her long black hair.

Her broad brown face broke into a hundred cracks and wrinkles as she smiled. 'I am who I am,' she said, and then she touched the side of his face very tenderly with one thick finger. 'Maybe I would take the whole body if it was you. Maybe.'

'And maybe cats will land on the moon,' he said.

Gonca slipped her legs over the side of her bed and put on her dressing gown. 'Cats are very clever,' she said. 'Don't underestimate them. I'm going to get *rakı*. Do you want some?'

It was the middle of the day, but he wasn't at work and so why shouldn't he indulge in a little alcohol?

'Yes,' he said. Gonca left the room.

He'd made a conscious decision to spend the day with Gonca after his wife had basically kicked him out of his house. He'd willingly taken his son to school and would have stayed at home to be with Zelfa. But she had told him to go. 'When you drop Yusuf at school, just keep on going,' she'd said. 'Get out of my sight!'

She'd lost patience with his infidelities. Not with Gonca – Zelfa didn't know about her – but with other women he had come into contact with. Zelfa was menopausal and had by her own admission lost interest in sex. So he'd gone else-where. Not that he was excusing himself; he knew that what he was doing was wrong. But that didn't mean he was going to stop doing it.

Süleyman switched his mobile phone back on and found that he had one text message. It was from his deputy, Sergeant İzzet Melik, and it said, 'Call me.' İzzet very rarely contacted his superior when he wasn't on duty, and so Süleyman did as he was asked.

'İzzet?'

'Sir, I'm in Şişli,' İzzet said. '2B Ateş Apartments, Efe Lane. I've just got here, and I'm standing next to a bed with a dead naked man on it. His throat's been cut.'

İzzet knew how much his boss thrilled to the chase. Murder and its resolution was addictive, they all knew that. Süleyman had already slipped his shirt over his shoulders and strapped his gun holster underneath his arm as he said, 'I'll be there.'

He put his trousers on just as she came into the room

67

holding two tall glasses of white, cloudy *rakı*. He looked up at her and frowned. 'Sorry.'

'Duty calls?' She took a long gulp from one of the glasses and then a small sip from the other.

'An incident in Şişli,' he said.

'Oh, where the rich people live.' She smiled.

'I have to go.' He stood up, walked over to her, took her head in his hands and kissed her hard and long on the lips. Then he left.

Chapter 7

The Akol family and their new guests the Seyhans lived in an apartment above a fabric shop on Macar Kardeşler Street. It was a rather nondescript sort of place, although the apartment did overlook, if at a distance, the magnificent Roman Aqueduct of Valens.

But Ayşe Farsakoğlu and Constable Hikmet Yıldız didn't go to the Akol apartment. Only that morning, Çetin İkmen had told them that Gözde's death had not been an accident. Other officers had already been in to collect the clothes the family said they had been wearing on that fateful day. News of the murder was out on radio, television and all across the internet. As İkmen had suggested, Farsakoğlu and Yıldız went into Fatih district to listen to what, if anything, people were saying about it, and about the families who lived in their midst. It was Wednesday, market day, and so most people would be out and about.

The two police officers had to do a few things to their appearances before they walked towards the seventeen streets that made up the Wednesday market. Hikmet was out of uniform, and Ayşe had covered her head with a scarf tied into a turban by a female officer back at the station who had a very religious sister. There was no way on earth that she could ever have tied it herself.

'I look like your mother!' she grumbled to Hikmet as she gazed with a critical eye at a pile of cherries heaped up on the back of a tattered old donkey cart. He didn't reply. The truth was that she was indeed considerably older than he was. Not that she looked like his mother in any way. But her anger disturbed him. She was so resentful about wearing the turban. He knew she was a modern, secular woman, but he couldn't really understand why she was *so* angry. She was, after all, only playing a part.

The stall next to the cherry cart was selling plastic bowls, brushes and mops. It stood in front of a small shop that sold Muslim religious artefacts. There were wall hangings depicting the Kaa'ba in Mecca, the most holy place in Islam, CDs and tapes of religious lectures and music by musicians such as the British convert Yusuf Islam. There were *tesbih* prayer beads in every colour imaginable, small prayer mats for travelling and transparent lockets containing drops of water from the sacred Zamzam well in Saudi Arabia. A woman in full black *chador* stood outside, looking through the window at the CDs.

'Can I help you, brother?' an elderly, rather querulous voice asked.

Ayşe was about to answer until she realised that of course he had been talking to Hikmet.

'Sister and I are just looking,' she heard Yıldız say. So now she was his sister. That was OK. Except she knew that amongst the religious people, the word 'sister' did not necessarily mean that one was related. People were brothers and sisters in Islam. It was a graceful and gracious form of address and she remembered hearing it from her few visits back to her father's old village. But it was not her.

70

'So am I your sister now?' she said to Yıldız as the two of them moved through the crowds of bearded men, covered woman and lots of children.

'Ayşe,' he said – she'd told him that he had to naturally call her that – 'you cannot be my actual sister.'

'Why not?'

'Because some people, a few admittedly, know me round here.'

He only lived at most half a kilometre away. And busy as the market and its environs were, there was always the chance that he could bump into someone that either he or his brother knew.

They looked around some more stalls, most of them selling food or household goods, and then went to a small restaurant back on Macar Kardeşler Street, where they sat in the family room upstairs. This too made Ayşe feel like a fish out of water. Going to family rooms above restaurants, which people had been doing since time immemorial, was something she had done when she was young. She'd gone with her mother and her mother's friends, sitting with them as they gossiped away from their husbands. Men could and would enter family rooms but only as Hikmet was doing now, with a female relative or with children. They both ordered mixed vegetables with rice and chips and some cans of Coca-Cola.

'I haven't eaten in one of these places in years,' Ayşe said as she leaned across the table towards Hikmet Yıldız.

He frowned. 'So where do you normally eat?'

'If I eat out at all, it is in Beyoğlu,' she said. 'Sometimes I will stray down to Karaköy.'

71

These were very Westernised, very secular districts of the city, where women could and did eat on their own, if they wished. This place, with its family room, its groups of almost completely covered women and thickly bearded men, was a whole other world.

'Did you find out anything in Beşiktaş?' Hikmet Yıldız asked his superior. Ayşe had been to the street where Gözde Seyhan had died, before coming on to Fatih.

'People had only just heard that the body was Gözde's,' she said. 'There was a sort of subdued atmosphere. People were shocked, I think. All the talk I heard consisted of expressions of sympathy for the dead girl and her family. If Gözde was having some sort of relationship with the boy across the road, then I don't think that was general knowledge.'

'Beşiktaş isn't conservative.'

'Parts of it are,' Ayşe said. 'The Seyhans' neighbours were a mixed bunch.'

'Some foreigners.'

'Americans.' The Ford couple. The wife ran a website for expatriates in İstanbul.

The waiter came then, bringing them their food and drink. It was simple fare but it looked good, and again it was redolent of food that Ayşe had tasted since her very early childhood. It was as she was eating that she heard the two women behind her begin to talk.

'My sister lives across from this family whose daughter died in a fire in Beşiktaş,' the one directly behind her said.

'If the girl was bad, then it was well done,' her companion replied.

Ayşe looked over at Hikmet and put a finger up to her lips to silence him, lest he suddenly decide to talk.

'Oh, I agree!' the first woman said forcefully. 'If she had shamed them, then what could they do?'

Ayşe had expected such attitudes in Fatih. What came next, however, was a surprise to her.

The first woman said, 'My sister does say, however, that the family themselves – not the people who lived here already, but those from over in Beşiktaş who are staying with them – are not as decent as they could be.'

'What does that mean?' the second woman enquired. Ayşe Farsakoğlu pricked up her ears. She was quite anxious to know that too.

'Some immoral behaviour. I can't say,' the first woman said.

'No, of course not,' her companion agreed. 'I wouldn't expect you to.'

Ayşe felt her hackles rise. When the two women had left, she said to Hikmet Yıldız, 'Why do they do that?'

'What?'

She leaned across the table towards him again and said, 'Not talk about sin.'

He shrugged. Some things were obvious, or so he thought. 'They don't want to sully themselves,' he said. 'Talking about sin is bad.'

'Doing it is worse,' Ayşe snapped back. 'Killing young girls for no good reason is pretty bad.'

They looked at each other and saw in each other's eyes their differences of opinion. He could not condone honour killing but he could understand where it came from and why it happened. Her mind was totally closed. He looked away first.

Still staring at his profile, Ayşe said, 'I wonder what kind of "immoral behaviour" the Seyhans indulge in. I'd be willing to wager it does not include the mother.'

There was blood everywhere – all over the bed, on the carpet, up the walls.

Süleyman looked down at the pale, stiff body that lay face down on the bed and said, 'Do we have a name?'

'Hamid İdiz,' his sergeant, İzzet Melik, said. 'A piano teacher.'

There had been a very shiny grand piano in the sitting room.

'Constable downstairs has already turned one student away.'

Süleyman bent down in order to look at the face of Hamid İdiz. Beyond the ghastly shade of blue that tinged his skin, he looked as if he had been an attractive man.

'Who found him?'

'His first student, a girl, rang the bell several times before going to get the *kapıcı*,' İzzet said. 'According to her, Hamid Bey never missed a lesson and was never late. The *kapıcı* concurred with this and opened up the apartment. Hamid İdiz was diabetic, and so of course the *kapıcı* was worried that he might be in a coma.'

'Reasonable.' Süleyman looked around the bedroom. A gold colour scheme had been employed, now sodden with red. 'Do we know how old Mr İdiz was?'

İzzet looked at his notebook. 'Fifty-three, the *kapıcı* said.'

'Did he say anything else?'

They both knew, as all Turks did, that the custodians of apartment blocks usually knew a lot of things about their tenants.

'He said that Mr İdiz was "flamboyant",' İzzet said.

Süleyman picked up a magazine that lay on a chair over by the window and moved the front cover aside with the end of a ballpoint pen. 'What wonderful euphemisms people use for the word homosexual,' he said.

'The apartment's full of queer porn,' İzzet said.

'What fun forensics are going to have!'

'Yes, sir.' İzzet frowned.

'I assume we're waiting on the arrival of Dr Sarkissian?'

'Yes, sir.'

'In the meantime, did the *kapıcı* see anyone arrive before the girl this morning or last night?' Süleyman said.

İzzet shrugged. 'Well, he did . . .'

Süleyman looked at the many bottles of cologne and after-shave on Hamid Bey's kidney-shaped dressing table and said, 'Well?'

'Sir, this is quite an easy-going building,' İzzet said. 'You know how posh they are over here.'

Süleyman did. Aristocrats they generally were not, but Şişli people were nearly always well-to-do, and they guarded their goods and their privacy jealously.

'People come and go without hindrance,' İzzet continued. 'The *kapıcı* only challenges tradesman, police, gypsies.'

'Yes, but he usually knows who comes and goes, even if he is instructed to look the other way,' Süleyman said.

'Yes, well we did get to that,' İzzet said.

75

'Good.'

'And none of Mr İdiz's regulars came to the apartment either last night or this morning. A young man of about twenty-five came to visit someone this morning, and then there was a gypsy last night, but the *kapıcı* got rid of him. All the other visitors were women.'

'Could have been a woman,' Süleyman said as he put on a pair of plastic gloves and then began to look in a small bookcase that was beside the dressing table. 'Go and get descriptions from him, İzzet. Men *and* women. Just because the man was homosexual doesn't rule out his being killed by a woman. His sexuality may very well have been irrelevant to his death.'

İzzet Melik left to go down to see the *kapıcı*. Süleyman riffled through Mr İdiz's many books by luminaries such as Orhan Pamuk, Martin Amis and Iris Murdoch. Mr İdiz it seemed, had liked to read, if not as passionately as he liked to listen to music. His collections of CDs and sheet music were both vast. In addition, all of this material was well-thumbed, indicating that as a teacher of music he was clearly very busy.

Sergeant Melik came back into the room and said, '*Kapıcı* is going to make a list, with descriptions of as much as he can remember.'

'Good.' Süleyman scanned the room and then said, 'Any sign of any sort of diary or appointment book? He was a private teacher; he must have had some sort of schedule.'

'Not yet, sir, no,' İzzet replied.

'Well, then maybe once the doctor has arrived, we should make that our priority,' Süleyman said. 'If nothing else, we will have to contact his pupils to let them and their families know that Mr İdiz is no longer giving piano lessons.'

Inspector Metin İskender looked at İkmen over the top of the very thin and expensive reading glasses he had only recently started wearing. 'My experience of the sexting phenomenon usually involves rings, as in groups of males, targeting one or more lone female,' he said. 'They threaten, exploit, usually blackmail and then move on.'

Metin İskender was much younger than either İkmen or Süleyman. In spite of coming from a very poor background, he had married well and risen through the ranks of the police very quickly. He was clever, arrogant and sometimes charmless, but he was totally committed to his job and he was good at it. In recent years he had been given the task of trying to combat the rising number of crimes perpetrated using mobile phone technology. This had taken him into some very outlandish corners of the human psyche.

'A sexting operation will generally start just with one boy and one girl,' he continued. 'The girl will either come from a very traditional family or a semi-liberal background. She will almost never, in my experience, come from the academic elite or even from the social elite.'

'Because parents in those groups are too liberal about sexual matters?'

'In reality they may or may not be, as you know, Inspector,' İskender said. 'But the sexters dare not take that risk. Traditional girls are much easier to blackmail. So this boy will basically groom the girl by telling her that he loves her, and eventually he will ask her to send him photographs of herself. Clothed at first, but later semi- and then totally naked. He may even ask her to abuse herself on camera.'

İkmen shook his head. 'What can you say? And these men then share the photographs amongst them?'

'Yes. All members of the group can be involved with different girls at the same time. They can all share photographs and videos and sell them on to others outside the group too. These images can end up anywhere – even abroad.'

'So Osman Yavuz could be one of a group?'

'Yes,' İskender said. 'Do you have any idea where he might be?'

'No. His description and photograph have been circulated. His grandmother in Beşiktaş thought he was with his mother in Bursa. But he isn't there,' İkmen said. 'No one seems to know where he is, or rather no one is admitting to having that knowledge. His mobile phone is dead. He's probably ditched that. All we really know about him is that he was lazy and isolated. His grandmother said that he had no friends, and yet if I recall correctly, he spent a lot of his time texting, which—'

'He could have been texting the girl or other members of a sexting ring,' İskender said. 'You know, Inspector, from what you've told me, I have to admit that this Yavuz character does sound suspicious.'

'I didn't know how suspicious until I spoke to you,' İkmen said.

İskender shrugged. 'It's about knowing what to look for. Which brings us to the inevitable question about whether or not the apartment this man shared with his grandmother has been searched.'

'It hasn't, no,' İkmen said. 'Not yet.'

'Well then it must be,' İskender replied. 'And given the circumstances, maybe I should be the one to do it.'

Chapter 8

The other mechanics had tried to break the fight up, but now that Lokman Seyhan had pulled a knife, everybody was standing well back. Only one of the men had noticed that Orhan Bey, the owner of the garage, had disappeared very soon after the fight had begun. The rest of them knew that natural justice had to be allowed to take its course, whatever the result. This was bitter brother-against-brother violence, and it seemed to them to be about something that was deeply personal to both of them.

'You dare to show your filthy face here!' Lokman Seyhan screamed at his brother Kenan. 'Womb-scraping!'

'All you know is how to kill!' Kenan yelled through the tears that ran down his cheeks. 'You kill everything I love!'

Lokman lunged at him with the knife, missing Kenan's face by less than a centimetre. 'Arse-giver!'

'Bringing death in the name of religion! Using Islam to excuse your sadism! Blasphemer!'

'You call *me* a blasphemer!' Lokman laughed. 'You son of a donkey, cock-sucking—'

'Murderer! You are no brother of mine! Pull a knife on me? Kill me too, will you, Lokman? Who is going to be your next victim? Our mother?'

'*Our* mother? You were born of a djinn and a whore and came out of the womb of a donkey!' Lokman lunged again. 'Why don't you fight me like a man, Kenan? Why don't you draw your knife and let's get really busy?'

A usual day for the Beşiktaş Garage mechanics involved some oil changes, tyre replacement and maybe the fitting of a new exhaust. Murder had never been on their agenda. True, men had sometimes had the odd fight that sometimes had involved knives, but when Kenan Seyhan pulled a gun out of his jacket pocket, they all instinctively took another step back.

'Maybe it is for the best that Orhan Bey went to get the police,' the oldest man whispered to the youngest. 'We cannot be party to death!'

Lokman Seyhan, whose face had now turned white, looked his brother in the eyes and said, 'So you're going to shoot me.'

Kenan took the safety catch off and smiled. 'It's an act of revenge,' he said. 'You know all about that, don't you, Lokman!'

Mehmet Süleyman showered and dressed and had already switched on his laptop when Gonca came into the bedroom with his tea. Once he had finished all the work associated with the homicide in Şişli the previous day, he had gone straight back to his gypsy lover for another night of extremely unbridled passion. He'd told his wife that he was staying at the home of his old friend Balthazar Cohen in nearby Fener, knowing that Balthazar would lie for him. But apparently Zelfa had not called. She was adopting an 'I don't care' approach, which was a technique she had employed against her husband before. It had little effect. Only threatening his

82

relationship with his little boy, Yusuf, could hurt Süleyman now. His marriage was over in all but name.

'What are you looking at?' Gonca said as she put his tea down by his elbow and glanced over his shoulder at the computer screen. 'Is that English?'

'It's a website called Make the Most of İstanbul,' he replied. 'It's for expatriates. Mainly for Americans, I think, but other foreigners use it too.'

'What for?'

'All sorts of things.'

'Like what?' She sat down beside him and began to suck one of his ear lobes.

'For restaurant recommendations, real-estate advice, language classes, to make contact with people . . .' Distracted by her now, he took his ear lobe out of her mouth and said, 'I have to go to work.'

'No time for . . .'

'No time for anything except this very nice tea you have brought me, no,' he said.

Gonca pulled a frown. 'Pity.'

He picked up his glass of tea and smiled. He'd become a little worried about her during the course of this their latest affair. Maybe it was because she was now that much older than when he had first met her. 'Gonca,' he said gently, 'I am married.'

'I know!' She said it bad-temperedly, pulling slightly away from him as she did so. 'But you don't love her!'

'No . . .'

'So if you don't love her . . .' Then suddenly she smiled. 'Maybe your wife and I could fight!'

'Over me? I don't think so,' Süleyman said sternly, then turned back to look at his screen. 'Not seemly for a police officer to be associated with such activities.'

'And with gypsies?' she said.

He didn't respond. Gonca did this sometimes, played the 'downtrodden gypsy' card, as he put it. As a working artist, which was her actual profession, she had all the confidence in the world. But as an ageing woman, it was slipping now.

'I think that you just use me for sex,' Gonca said as she got up off the bed and walked over to the window.

He did not respond. Intent upon the screen, his eyes were caught by an unusual lonely hearts advertisement: *Turkish boy, newly arrived from Anatolia. Lonely and innocent. Please would a nice girl call?*

There was a box number after this short, rather pathetic (Süleyman felt) little request. Whether any 'nice' American or European girls had contacted this person's box was moot. Süleyman was willing to bet hard cash that a lot of middle-aged women had. But that, maybe, had been the point. Mrs Ford, the American who ran the site, would possibly know. But then the case with which she had been associated was now solely İkmen's. Süleyman as of the previous day, was working on the murder of Hamid İdiz.

'You know I think that the Turks are colder these days,' Gonca said as, still staring out of the window, she lit up a cigarette. 'Everyone talks about religion now.'

'Some people do.' He closed down the Make the Most of İstanbul website and then switched off the laptop. 'Does it bother you?'

'I like to have my head uncovered in the street,' she said. 'I like to live a free life and take my pleasure where I will.' She looked over at him and frowned. 'I don't want you to get cold like these men I see with their long, long beards!'

There was real fear in her eyes, and despite himself, he went over to her and took her in his arms. 'Why would I do that?' he said. 'Grow a beard? Become cold?'

'I . . .'

He kissed her. 'Gonca,' he said, 'I have a religion. You say that you do not, and that is fine, for both of us. I care about you. I would never make you do anything you didn't want to.'

He stopped short of telling her that he loved her. In truth, he didn't know whether he did or not. What he did know was that he was aroused again, and so, to her great delight, he made love to her up against her bedroom wall, below the window.

When he'd finished, he smiled and said, 'So who's cold now?'

Neither of the brothers would say what the fight was about, and so none of the police officers Lokman Seyhan's employer had called to break up the proceedings could begin to guess what the problem might be. They were all quite junior officers, and once they'd asked the men what the fight was about, they found themselves at something of a loss. One constable weighed the MKEK Yavuz 16 pistol – a standard military service weapon – in his hand, while his colleague asked Kenan Seyhan whether he had a licence for it.

Kenan shrugged his shoulders. 'No.'

'Then why were you carrying it? Why were you threatening your brother with it?'

The garage owner, Orhan Bey, prodded Lokman Seyhan in the chest and said, 'You drew the knife! You've always been trouble! You can go!'

'Orhan Bey, please . . .'

'These are the facts,' Orhan Bey said to the police officers. 'This man,' he pointed at Kenan Seyhan, 'came into my garage this morning, crying. I recognised him as this man's brother.' He pointed to a terrified-looking Lokman Seyhan.

'Orhan Bey!'

'Be quiet!' he snapped. He turned to the police officers once again. The rest of his employees watched in rapt silence. 'I don't know why this man was crying,' he continued. 'I thought that maybe there had been another death in their family. I left Lokman alone with his brother. I am a reasonable man. But then . . .' He threw his arms dramatically in the air. 'Chaos! They are at each other's throats, and then my employee pulls a knife on his own brother! His *own brother*!'

The first constable looked at both of the Seyhan brothers in turn and then said, 'Are either of you going to speak to us?'

Both men looked down at the ground, in silence.

'You speak about another death in the family of these men,' the second constable said to Orhan Bey. 'What was the first death?'

The two brothers looked up, white-faced, but neither of them spoke.

'Their sister died a few days ago, in a fire,' Orhan Bey

said. 'The whole family had to be moved out of their apartment. You people, the police, are involved.' He looked at the two Seyhan men with contempt. 'It's been reported in the newspapers that the girl was murdered.'

'Did Osman have a computer, Mrs Yavuz?' Ayşe Farsakoğlu asked the old woman.

'A computer?' She lowered herself down on to one of her heavily cushioned sofas, pushing two cats on to the floor as she did so. 'Where would he get a computer from? Do I look as if I would have money for a computer?'

In the boy's bedroom, İkmen and İskender were searching through his things for any clue that might connect him to possible sexting rings.

'Do you know if he went to internet cafés?'

Mrs Yavuz shrugged. 'How should I know? He didn't go out much, and when he did, he didn't tell me anything about it. What's all this about?'

Ayşe sat down. A large black Persian cat sprang out of her way and then growled at her.

'Reza!' the old woman shouted at the animal. 'Don't growl! If you growl, I'll have you turned into gloves!'

The cat ran off in the direction of the kitchen.

'Mrs Yavuz,' Ayşe said gently, 'we have reason to believe that your grandson may have been collecting indecent images of girls on his mobile telephone. Now we're not yet sure—'

'Indecent images! Of girls!' Mrs Yavuz put a hand up to her chest and said, 'Allah! No, that can't be right! All he ever did with that phone was send those text things!'

'Mrs Yavuz, I know that this is difficult to understand . . .'

'Sergeant Farsakoğlu?' It was İkmen's voice calling her from Osman Yavuz's bedroom.

'Sir?'

'Can you come in here, please?'

Ayşe got up. The black Persian came scampering out of the kitchen and immediately took her place.

'Indecent images?' the old woman said. 'What indecent images? Have you got my grandson's phone?'

'Excuse me,' Ayşe said, and made her way out of the old woman's sitting room and across the hall into what had been the boy's bedroom. Large posters of Beşiktaş Football Club hung on the walls; underfoot were many brightly coloured T-shirts, seemingly discarded to their fate.

'Sir?'

Inspector İskender was standing beside Inspector İkmen. As Ayşe got closer to the two men, İskender held up a picture. It was of a pretty, smiling young girl with very small, very naked breasts.

'There were a lot of these in a box underneath Osman's bed,' İskender said. 'All laser-printed.'

'Any of Gözde Seyhan?' Ayşe asked.

İkmen held a large cardboard box up for her to see. 'We don't know, he said. 'There are hundreds of images in here. Osman Yavuz was obviously a very busy boy. We need to find where these copies might have come from.'

Chapter 9

Although what he was reading was an account of an intense homosexual relationship, Mehmet Süleyman could identify with the sentiments expressed. Hamid İdiz's private diary, as well as being a very well-written compendium of erotica, was also an account of a relationship between two men that was becoming a great love. There were similarities between İdiz's feelings for his unnamed lover and the intensity that Süleyman himself felt at times with Gonca.

When Beloved takes me, wrote İdiz, *it is the finest pleasure in the whole of creation.*

In the whole of creation . . . When Süleyman had made love to Gonca up against her bedroom wall, he'd had a terrible urge to tell her that he loved her. Was it, could it just be sex? He looked down at the diary again and read in İdiz's careful hand, *Why then do I stray? What kind of person am I? Some boy on İstiklal Street said he'd suck me off and I let him. 20 TL. Cheap little slut!*

Süleyman would go home to his wife. Not that he'd have anything more than harsh words with her. But he wasn't above picking up some tourist, even a local whore. He was good-looking, it was easy. But was it right?

İzzet Melik, who was looking through some of İdiz's

papers at his desk across the office, said, 'Hamid İdiz was apparently involved in some music festival supposed to be held at the Aya İrini in May. Says here performers are coming from Georgia and Armenia as well as from here in Turkey.'

'If you find the names of the people who might be organising it, take a note,' Süleyman said.

'Sir.'

Silence descended yet again as Süleyman read: *Beloved's family are such animals! They call what we do an abomination. But it is so beautiful!*

The image of Gonca's face at the moment of orgasm flashed through his mind. He wasn't concentrating! His Beloved, if that was what she was, kept on distracting him. He turned away from the diary to the deceased man's appointment book. That was very dry and very uninformative. *Friday 5th November – 1 p.m. Halide P, 2.30 p.m. Nurettin O, 4 p.m. Ali Reza Z, 6 p.m. Murad E.* Kids booked in for piano lessons, three boys and one girl.

He looked at the same date in the diary: *Friday 5th November – Beloved stayed the whole night! Could hardly bear to part with him this morning. Bathed him first. Sweet Baby! Halide P, first lesson, silly giggling fool as usual. Nurettin at 2.30 (yawn). Then two proper little tarts if they did but know it! Ali Reza might because he always has a hard-on when he's playing, but Murad E is forever nervous. Every time I so much as pass him by, he shakes and blushes. I do it deliberately, just for the sport. What fun it would be to have a threesome with those two lovelies! Not that I ever will. Not that I ever should.*

The diary appeared to be a very comprehensive account of Hamid İdiz's erotic experiences, including fantasies that quite clearly involved some of his students. Süleyman looked at dates in the current year and found again one entry in the appointment book and another corresponding entry in the diary.

Appointment book: *23rd February – 4 p.m. Ali Reza Z, moved from 6 p.m. to 7 p.m. Murad E.*

Diary:*23rd February – Can't stop looking at Ali Reza's bulge. Think he might have caught me at it today! But then he did smile. Murad E is really bad for me! He's so gorgeous now I just want to rip his clothes off every time I see him! So I've taken to being extra stern with him. I can't afford to have accusations, the police on my doorstep and all of that!*

Süleyman wondered how old these children were and began to feel cold. He thought about his own son, who had just started taking violin lessons with a Mr Reynolds that Zelfa knew from the Irish Consulate, and visibly shuddered. İzzet Melik saw this and said, 'Cold, sir?'

'No, İzzet,' he replied. 'Not cold. We need to find out who these students of Mr İdiz's are. We particularly need to identify two boys known as Ali Reza Z and Murad E, and we need to do it quickly.'

Officers were sent out to every internet café in the Beşiktaş Ortaköy and central districts of the city. Each one clutched a copy of the photograph of Osman Yavuz that his grand-mother had given to İkmen. Cool kids in hip-hop gear joined nerdy boys wearing thick glasses in poring over the photograph of the young man the officers said they needed to speak to urgently. But even as all of that was happening, İkmen brooded. Finding Osman Yavuz would not, he felt, bring them any closer to Gözde Seyhan's killer. Although there was no evidence to directly connect anyone else to the scene of the fire, the investigators had been clear in their assertion that Gözde had not killed herself. That said, İkmen was not convinced of Yavuz's guilt. He had been involved with the girl, although no photographs of her had been found in the box underneath his bed. Clearly he was implicated, on some level, in 'sexting'. But when İkmen looked at Yavuz's photograph – a thin, rather vague-looking boy – he couldn't see murder in him. Perhaps one of his sexting friends had killed Gözde? Maybe the girl had threatened to expose Osman and all the rest of them, irrespective of the cost to herself? Then again, possibly Gözde and Osman had been in love, and when she was killed he just ran away in grief and fear that the police might think that he had been involved in her death. There was still, also, Gözde's own family.

Ayşe Farsakoğlu walked into the office she shared with İkmen and said, 'The Seyhan brothers are still down in the cells.'

Lokman and Kenan Seyhan had been arrested for brawling as well as carrying illegal weapons.

İkmen lit a cigarette. 'Are they saying why they were fighting yet?'

'Depends what you're prepared to swallow.' Ayşe sat down behind her desk. 'But Kenan says the gun is his. An old service pistol, apparently. And his brother admits to carrying a knife. The story they're both sticking to is that they had a dispute over money. Other mechanics at the garage say it was much more personal than that.'

'Meaning?'

'The insults traded included Kenan accusing Lokman of murder and Lokman casting aspersions upon his brother's parentage.'

'Unpleasant.' İkmen rose from his seat and took his jacket off the back of his chair. 'Perhaps I should have a few words with them before they are released.'

'Maybe you should, sir.'

İkmen saw the Seyhan brothers together in an interview room. A burly constable ensured that the two men were just frightened enough to behave themselves.

'Your colleagues at the Beşiktaş Garage have told us that the fight you had with your brother was about rather more than money,' İkmen said to Lokman Seyhan.

Lokman looked first at his brother and then with a snarl said to İkmen, 'Ex-colleagues. Orhan Bey sacked me!'

'So why were you fighting?'

Both Lokman and Kenan looked down at the floor.

'Was it over your sister?' İkmen asked. 'You, Kenan, accused your brother of murder. You were heard to say that Lokman might kill *again*, possibly with your mother as the victim. Did Lokman kill your sister Gözde?'

Kenan kept his head down and then murmured, 'No.'

Lokman, İkmen noticed had begun to sweat heavily.

'Then why did you call him a murderer?' İkmen asked. 'That's a very serious accusation to make.'

'I used it as . . . I was angry,' Kenan said. He looked at

his brother with utter contempt, and then added, 'We have different lives.'

İkmen shrugged. 'Most siblings do,' he said. 'My brother and I live very different lives. But I have never accused him of murder.'

The Seyhan brothers remained silent, their bodies cringing away from each other as they sat in front of the policeman.

'So your brother Lokman did not, you are absolutely certain, Kenan, kill your sister Gözde?'

'I just told you he didn't!'

Both their faces were red, and Kenan as well as Lokman had started sweating.

İkmen smiled. 'Well that's good, then.' He rose to his feet. 'As you can imagine, gentlemen, I have to investigate all and any allegations pertaining to your sister's death. You would want me to do that, wouldn't you?'

'*I* would,' Kenan said.

Lokman looked up at İkmen and asked, 'Can we go now?'

'Your weapons have been confiscated and I am told that you have been processed,' İkmen said. 'I see no reason why you can't leave us now.'

Both men got to their feet while İkmen instructed the constable to open the door and let them out. Just before they left the room, however, he said, 'Oh, but please, for the moment do not leave the city without telling us, will you?'

Lokman's face blanched. 'Are we under suspicion?'

'Why?' his brother enquired. 'Why do . . .'

'Gentlemen!' İkmen smiled again. 'I say this merely because we may need to contact you should we apprehend your sister's killer. It is better that you stay in contact with us in case that happens. I am sure you are as anxious for it to come to pass as I.'

Neither Lokman nor Kenan made any kind of reply. When they left the station, İkmen watched them exchange a few snarling if quiet words, and then go their separate ways.

The Zafir family lived in the fashionable village of Yeniköy. Dr Zafir, who came originally from Jordan, was a physician, his Turkish wife an engineer. It was Dr Zafir who answered the door when Mehmet Süleyman and İzzet Melik called. Once they had explained why they were calling, he very quickly took them through to the family's luxurious living room, where sixteen-year-old Ali Reza Zafir was practising scales on a shiny grand piano. When he saw that his father was not alone, Ali Reza stopped playing and stood up.

'What's the matter?' he said as he looked nervously over at his father. 'Who are they?'

He was a good-looking boy. Slim and angular, he had large downward-slanted eyes that gave him a slightly sleepy and sensual look. His response to the arrival of two strange men was, Süleyman thought, very jumpy.

'These gentlemen, Inspector Süleyman and Sergeant Melik, are from the police,' Dr Zafir said. 'They've come about . . . well, we all read about poor Hamid Bey's tragic death in the papers this morning, and . . .'

'I haven't seen Hamid Bey since last week,' the boy said as he walked over to his father and put his arms around him. 'I always go on Fridays.'

'Yes, we know,' Süleyman said. 'We also know that you were, like quite a few of Mr İdiz's students, due to take part in the Turco–Caucasian Music Festival at the Aya İrini in four weeks' time.'

'Yes. Why?'

'We managed to speak to the Armenian organiser this morning,' Süleyman said. 'Although it won't be easy, he is going to speak to his Georgian counterpart and they will then make contact with other music teachers here to ensure that the Turkish pianists are not disadvantaged in any way. But that is not really what we have come to speak to you about, Ali Reza.'

'So what?'

'May we sit down?' Süleyman asked.

Dr Zafir, suddenly embarrassed at his own tardiness, said, 'Oh, gentlemen, I apologise. We all knew Hamid Bey and so it has been a shock. Please do sit down.'

Süleyman and İzzet Melik sat down on a large brocade sofa with very ornate gold-painted legs. Dr Zafir and his son sat down opposite on a similar piece of furniture.

'I've spoken a little to your father already, Ali Reza,' Süleyman said, 'but now I have to speak to you about a rather delicate matter.'

'What?' The boy's face had paled.

Süleyman was dreading having to say what he knew he must, but all of a sudden the boy's father intervened.

'Ali Reza,' the doctor said, 'Inspector Süleyman has just told me that apparently the police have reason to believe that Hamid Bey was a pervert.'

The boy looked at his father with genuine horror on his face. 'A pervert?'

'A homosexual,' Dr Zafir continued. 'A man who has unnatural—'

'I knew that Hamid Bey was gay,' the boy cut in. All of a sudden he looked a little brighter, as if somehow relieved.

'You knew?'

'Yes.'

Dr Zafir looked at his son with suddenly appalled eyes. 'Why didn't you tell me? I would have taken you away and—'

'He was a good teacher,' Ali Reza said. 'I liked him. Anyway, he never did anything to me.'

'Yes, but—'

'Dr Zafir,' Süleyman cut in. This interview, which he had specifically asked the father to take part in so that the boy didn't feel threatened, had turned into a domestic situation. 'Homosexuality is not illegal in this country. Hamid Bey's sexuality is not a problem for us. What is difficult is that evidence exists that he seemed to have a fancy, shall we say, for some of his under-age male pupils. What I need to know is whether Ali Reza was one of them.'

'What? You mean like did he touch me or . . .'

'Yes.'

The boy shrugged. 'No,' he said. 'Never.'

It was emphatic.

'Did he make suggestions of a sexual nature to you?' Süleyman continued. 'Did he leer at you?'

'Oh, he leered,' Ali Reza said simply.

'What!' Dr Zafir, who had been blissfully unaware of all this, was beside himself. 'If I had known . . .'

'You would have gone mad, like you are now, Father,' Ali Reza said. 'Hamid Bey never did any harm to me. But he was the best piano teacher in the city, and if I'd told you, you would have taken me away from him.' He turned to

Süleyman and Melik and said, 'I want to be a concert pianist one day. Hamid Bey was going to help me to do that. But he never touched me, never made any indecent suggestions. Not to me.'

'My son wants to be a pianist, but he's also going to train as a doctor, aren't you, Ali Reza?' Dr Zafir cut in quickly. Then, to the officers, 'My family has a history of service. It is essential to give as well as to receive in life.'

'Yes.'

'Did Hamid Bey make any such suggestions to anyone else?' İzzet Melik enquired of the boy.

Ali Reza lowered his head a little. 'Well, yes, one boy. Sort of.'

'We are trying to track down a boy who is only referred to in the paperwork as Murad E,' Süleyman said. 'Unlike for you, Ali Reza, there don't seem to be any records, financial or otherwise, for him. Was this the boy that . . .'

'That's the boy,' Ali Reza said. 'Murad something. I didn't know him that well, but sometimes we talked after lessons. He was a good pianist but he was poor, you know. I think he came from Karaköy, somewhere like that, some tenement. Hamid Bey used to teach him for nothing.'

'And what did Hamid Bey get in return for that?' İzzet Melik asked.

'Murad is good, like I say,' Ali Reza said. 'But . . .' He lowered his head again. His father hugged him close.

Süleyman said, 'But what?'

'Hamid Bey leered at me, as I said.' Ali Reza looked up with fearful eyes again. 'But with Murad . . . He, Hamid Bey,

98

would sometimes fiddle with himself, you know, when Murad was playing. He . . . he never did anything else and Murad said that he did it very discreetly. He wasn't supposed to see.'

'But he masturbated.'

'In front of Murad, yes,' the boy said. 'That was what Murad told me.'

'You shouldn't spy on our neighbours,' Hikmet Yıldız's brother Ismail told him.

'I'm not spying, I'm doing my job,' Hikmet responded calmly.

'Don't give me that!' Ismail waved a sharp, thin finger in front of Hikmet's face. 'I'm always here, remember? I see everything.'

'And I'm a police officer and—'

'People in this neighbourhood keep the law!' Ismail said as he walked around their small, tatty kitchen in an agitated fashion. 'People here are pious and good. Their lives, *my* life is ruled by the standards of religion. It is you who are out of step!'

'No I'm not!' Hikmet stood up, looming over his much shorter and thinner brother. 'I pray, I keep Ramazan, I love Allah.'

'Then why do you persecute those who also love Him?'

'Because, my brother, not everyone keeps Allah's laws even when they appear to do so,' Hikmet said. 'Some people hide behind religion.'

'But these people, this family who you believe killed their own daughter . . .'

'I don't say that!' Hikmet shouted. Ismail wasn't a bad man, but he only believed what he wanted to, whether or not it was the truth. 'Anyway, how do you know who I'm watching or what I'm doing?'

'Because I know people! People tell me things! People tell me that you and some glamorous woman police officer were going around the market trying to make as if you don't belong here! Everyone knows the police want to pin it on the Seyhans! They want to make what happened to that poor girl an honour killing!'

'No we don't!'

'Yes you do!'

'Inspector İkmen would never do such a thing!' Hikmet said. 'He is a man of principle!'

'He is a man without—'

'He is my boss!' Now standing right over his brother, Hikmet said, 'I don't know whether the Seyhans killed their daughter or not and nor does anyone else! They are suspects, like a few other people we know about. Everyone who is involved with a murder victim is a suspect! They have to be!'

'Why? The Seyhans are good people. You can discount them!'

They were going around in circles. Hikmet left the kitchen and went out to the back yard for a smoke.

'Yes, that's right!' he heard Ismail say as he took out his cigarettes. 'Pollute the body you were given!'

Hikmet wanted to say 'Since when were you the great puritan?' but he managed to restrain himself. Ismail hadn't always been as religious as he had become since they'd come to live in Fatih. He used to be a drinker before he found religion. In a lot of ways, Hikmet agreed with his brother and with his neighbours: quiet, pious people didn't usually commit crimes. But sometimes they did.

Chapter 10

The woman in the Rainbow Internet Café recognised the picture of Osman Yavuz immediately.

'He comes in at night,' she said. She looked at her watch. 'Around about now. Although not lately.'

'Do you know why not?'

She shrugged. She was a middle-aged, heavily lined woman whose exuberant dress hinted at a past possibly on the stage. 'I don't know,' she said. 'Maybe he got fed up with all the queers.'

The young constable, who had already been into five other internet cafés asking about Osman Yavuz, looked around at the very unflamboyant and distinctly studious men around him and said, 'Queers?'

'Oh, they won't come in while you're here,' the woman said breezily. 'Why would they?'

She looked at him sternly, and not wishing to get involved in any sort of conversation about police brutality towards the gay community, the constable said, 'So what did Osman Yavuz do when he did used to come in here?'

'Well, he sat in front of a screen and went into zombie mode,' the woman said. 'What else do any of them do? I mean, the queers do at least chat each other up.'

'Did he use the printer?'

'Oh yes,' she said. 'They all do that, too.'

'Did you see what he printed?'

'No, but I can guess.'

'What?'

The woman sat back down behind her scruffy desk and lit up a cigarette. 'Porn or bling,' she said. 'Or guns. He's a young heterosexual man; what are any of you interested in?'

'You know this?'

She cleared her throat. 'I don't *know* that that particular boy printed those sorts of pictures for certain. But I think I'm pretty safe in assuming that he did so. A lot of boys are obsessed with sex and power and all that. Boys are. And if they come from poor families, then it's all so much worse.'

'Why?'

She looked at him as if he was an idiot. 'Why?' she said mockingly. 'You ask me why? Because their families tell them that bling and women are wrong, and of course that makes them want them. Basic psychology. Also the rich kids have them and so . . .' She shrugged again. 'It's why I like the queers.' She smiled. 'Don't tend to give a damn what the families think. They do their thing and to hell with society. Much healthier.'

The young constable, embarrassed, changed the subject. 'So this man . . .' he pointed to Yavuz's picture once again, 'was he always alone? Did you never see him with anyone else? A group of people, perhaps?'

'No,' she said. 'That one was a loner.'

The constable looked around the small room, crammed

with computers and people sitting at them. 'Did he use a particular machine, do you remember?'

'No.' She looked down at her blood-red nails. 'You going to have to take some of my computers away, are you?'

'I don't know,' he said. 'I'll have to speak to my superiors.'

'Well if you do need to move anything, you'll have to speak to my son,' the woman said. 'He might be too lazy to get down here very often, but it is his place and so I can't let you have the machines without asking him.'

'You'd better contact him then,' the constable replied. 'Whether the machines are taken away or not, we'll need to come in here and maybe shut the place for a bit.'

It was nearly midnight by the time Mehmet Süleyman arrived at Kürkçüçeşme Alley in Balat. Almost opposite the old Ahrida Synagogue there was a small neighbour-hood baker's shop. Above that was, apparently, the policeman's destination.

'Has this woman lived here long?' İzzet Melik asked as he followed his superior from the car and began to walk towards a very precarious-looking nineteenth-century wooden building.

'I don't know,' Süleyman replied. 'All we have is a name and an address.'

It had been just after he had returned to the station from the Zafirs' place that the Armenian organiser of the Turco–Caucasian music festival had telephoned Süleyman. Looking through the paperwork he had received from the late Hamid İdiz, he had noticed that some of the Turkish

105

teacher's students were also listed under a second name, Izabella Madrid. As far as the Armenian knew, this lady was also a music teacher, and what was more, she taught amongst others a boy called Murad Emin. Could he possibly be the Murad E that Ali Reza Zafir had spoken of, the boy that Hamid İdiz had fantasised about? Luckily it hadn't taken too long to track down Miss Izabella Madrid, teacher of pianoforte, to the rotting apartment above a baker's shop in Balat.

The two policemen crossed the dusty road and walked around the side of the detached building until they came to a rickety staircase up to the first floor at the back. A fat, bespectacled woman of about seventy sat at the top of the stairs eating a pancake and reading a copy of *Hürriyet*. She sat with her legs wide open, which, unfortunately for the officers, gave them a very comprehensive view of her long blue bloomers. As the men began to ascend, the woman said, 'What do you want?'

'Police.' Süleyman flashed his badge very quickly and then said, 'We're looking for a piano teacher. A lady.'

'Think you've got some talent, do you?' the woman said with a laugh. 'Funny time to have lessons.'

'It's a bit of a funny time to be sitting outside reading the paper,' Süleyman responded. 'It's not summer yet.'

'I know.' She folded up the newspaper and then rammed the last piece of the pancake into her mouth. 'So what's it to be then, boys? A nice bit of Chopin or some good old honky-tonk piano?'

She stood up with some difficulty.

'You are Miss Izabella Madrid?' Süleyman asked.

'Yes,' she said. 'Pianoforte teacher, spinster and Jew. Anything else you need to know?'

'Well . . .'

'I hope you boys are going to do something about the death of my old friend Mr İdiz,' Izabella said as her fat face suddenly clouded. 'We can't have musical people getting killed in their own homes. It's a disgrace!'

The whole family was asleep by the time Kenan Seyhan returned to his cousin's apartment in Fatih. He let himself in, but rather than making his way to the bedroom he now shared with his cousin and his brother, he tiptoed into the living room, where his parents were sleeping. His mother was underneath the window, her small, round body wrapped in a tattered grey blanket. Even from a distance she looked uncomfortable and cold. His father, by contrast, lay on a soft mattress covered by numerous clean, new blankets, snoring his head off. Kenan wiped away the tears that had soaked his face for hours now, and bent down until he was kneeling beside his sleeping father. The look of hatred in his eyes as he stared down at the slumbering man was like poison. Spitefully he flicked the side of his father's face with one finger and then bent low to whisper in his ear. 'Wake up, you son of a whore!' he said. 'Wake up so I can kill you!'

A second later, Cahit's eyes flew open. Kenan slapped a hand over the older man's open mouth and hissed, 'I'm going to have to kill you before you kill again! You're not taking anything else away from me!' Then he put his hands around his father's throat and squeezed as tightly as he could.

It was only luck that made Saadet wake suddenly from

her slumbers just in time to save her husband's life. As she pulled Kenan away from Cahit, she whispered, 'Get out, son! Please! I'm so sorry! Leave now! Don't ever come back!'

He left as quietly as he had come. The last view he had of his parents was of his mother's tear-stained face looking up at him with tremendous tenderness, while his father, still choking on the carpet below, stared into his eyes with raw hatred.

'It was me who discovered Murad Emin,' the old woman said as she placed glasses of tea on the small table that stood between the chairs where Mehmet Süleyman and İzzet Melik were sitting. 'That's why Hamid Bey wanted to keep my name on the paperwork. He knew that I, not him, made that boy. Local, see.'

'He lives in Balat?'

'On Çilingir Street,' she said. 'He's a brilliant boy. Went way beyond my talents very early on, and that was why I recommended him to Hamid Bey.'

'Who taught him free of charge,' Süleyman said.

'The Emins are poor,' Izabella Madrid said. 'Hamid agreed to tutor him for nothing because he is so good.' Her eyes narrowed. 'Why are you interested in Murad?'

'Do you have an address on Çilingir Street?' Süleyman asked.

The old woman scowled. 'You gonna tell me why you want it?'

'Are you going to obstruct the police in the course of their investigations?' İzzet Melik put in harshly.

Izabella Madrid looked over at him with an expression of

undisguised disgust on her features. 'Oh, it's like that, is it?' she said.

'Yes.'

Looking now at Süleyman, she tipped her head at İzzet Melik and said, 'He your muscle, is he? Get him to do all your dirty work, do you?'

'Madam . . .'

'Oh, it's quite all right, I understand,' she said. 'Good-looking man like you, nice manners and all the rest of it. You can't go frightening people and all that. We all need great ugly gorillas in our lives from time to time.'

İzzet Melik's face was now darkened with rage. He said, 'Just tell us where—'

'Number 19, Apartment C,' Izabella Madrid said without even looking it up. 'It's above a barber's shop.'

'Thank you.'

'But don't expect the usual type of poor Anatolian migrant, because you'll be disappointed,' she added. 'The Emin family may not have enough money to put proper food on their table, but they are very, very far from ignorant, as you will see.'

Miss Izabella Madrid was not, as Süleyman and İzzet Melik soon discovered, in any way wrong. Apartment C, 19 Çilingir Street housed some very unusual people indeed.

'We're all very upset about Hamid Bey,' Mr Emin said as he led Süleyman and Melik from a dingy hallway and into a room that was light on furniture while being very heavy on people, music and alcohol. 'That said,' he continued, 'I did meet this very nice Argentinian man earlier on today, and so we are actually in the middle of a tango evening.'

Süleyman looked into the room, where he saw an elderly man strumming a guitar to a heavy Latin beat. A young woman who looked like a prostitute drank straight from the neck of a bottle of *raki*, while a dreamy-looking middle-aged woman in clothes that were almost in rags danced with her body pressed up against that of a very beautiful young man. Three old-timers in flat caps adorned with red Communist star badges sat on the floor swaying to the music. The only anomaly in this very outré arrangement in conservative Balat was a white-faced boy who stood at the back of the room looking horrified.

'I do think that Hamid Bey would probably have approved,' Mr Emin said with a smile.

Chapter 11

What Çetin İkmen liked to call the 'computer retards' had descended upon the Rainbow Internet Café and were currently doing the policeman did not know what.

'You know that Inspector Süleyman's wife once told me that in her opinion, people heavily involved in the computer world are likely to be autistic,' he said to his colleague Metin İskender as they stood outside the café in the strengthening morning sun. Inside, various thin, bespectacled men peered at the ranks of computers and the one large and very old printer at the back of the building.

'I don't know about that,' İskender replied. 'What I do know is that the Rainbow is well known as a haunt of gay men.'

'The woman who works here recognised Osman Yavuz,' İkmen said as he lit up a cigarette and then breathed out slowly. 'Not that she's seen him for a week, she reckons. Do you think the computer retards will be able to find out whether Yavuz printed any of his photographs here?'

'I don't know,' İskender replied. 'Maybe if the printer has some sort of distinguishing fault or something. You know, like typewriters used to in the old days.'

'Um.'

'But I think that it's more likely that it's pictures of men's arses that originate from here, rather than anything else,' İskender said. 'This place teems with queers, especially at night.'

All around them the fashionable and lively district of Beyoğlu slowly began to emerge from the excesses of the previous evening and shook itself awake. The Rainbow Internet Café, which was situated in a small alleyway just north of the main thoroughfare, İstiklal Street, was in an area frequently traversed by transsexuals. When the policemen and their computer experts had arrived earlier that morning, several heavily made-up blonde 'women' had hissed appreciatively at them. The pavement where İkmen and İskender were standing smelt of stale beer, piss, cigarette ends and *rakı*. As İkmen looked around, he wondered vaguely whether his cousin, the transsexual Samsun, was hanging around in the vicinity. It often felt to him that the vast extended İkmen family seemed to be everywhere.

After a few moments İkmen's mobile phone began to ring, and he took it out of his pocket and answered it. As he listened to what the caller said, Metin İskender saw his face suddenly pale. By the time he finished the call, İkmen was white.

'I'm sorry, Metin, I have to go,' he said to his colleague as he began to head towards the top of the alley and his car. 'It seems we have another dead body to deal with.'

It had been a strange evening. As he lay alone in the bedroom next to the one he had shared with his wife, Mehmet Süleyman recalled every second.

'Murad, I'm sure you must be mistaken,' Mr Emin had said to his son as he ruffled his fingers affectionately through the boy's hair. 'Hamid Bey would never have done such a thing. You must have thought you saw and—'

'Dad, he was a homosexual! A queer!' Murad Emin cried. 'I told you ages ago! You didn't do anything!'

'Just because old Hamid Bey was a fruit doesn't mean he was a danger to you or anyone,' his father said. 'He took you on and was very generous to us. Anyway, even if he did have a bit of a fiddle, he didn't do anything to you, did he? I mean that mad chap, Crazy Ali, always yelling outside the blacksmith's shop, he wanks himself . . .'

'Dad!'

Murad Emin was, Süleyman could plainly see, far less liberal than either of his parents. Originally from Gaziantep in the far south-east, Mr and Mrs Emin had come to İstanbul in search of a lifestyle that was more easy-going than that of their home. Unfortunately, and in spite of both being university-educated, they had arrived with no money and two small children to support. So Mr Emin, who described himself as 'a committed socialist', had taken the only work he could get at the time, which had been tour-guiding for a rather dubious chain of small, cheap hotels. Currently he was unemployed. His wife, the woman Süleyman had seen dancing the tango with a man who he later realised was her pimp, worked as an unlicensed street prostitute. Intellectual, atheistic and poor, the Emins did not fit into either the educated middle class or the impoverished religious working class. They were, he realised as he talked to the father and his son, unique. They were possibly on drugs as well.

To him they were likeable, but as Miss Madrid had pointed out to Süleyman and Melik when she'd first told them about the Emins, they were very far away from the usual image of the Anatolian peasant.

'Mr Emin,' Süleyman said to the man, 'if your son says that Hamid İdiz masturbated in front of him, then we have to believe that is what happened. Mr İdiz was a very active homosexual, and apart from that, he does allude in his writings to an unrequited fancy for your son.'

'Oh.'

The boy looked at his father with fury on his face and said, 'I told you! Islam proscribes such things! They are unnatural! Sinful!'

Murad Emin, unlike his thin and heavily-lined father, was a well built and attractive boy. His clothes, though not in the height of fashion, were nevertheless well looked after. His hair was attractively styled and he had a clear complexion. His parents must, Süleyman felt, have some care for him and his younger sister.

Mr Emin took Süleyman away from the tango and into his small, spare kitchen. 'What you have to understand, Inspector,' he said, 'is that my son is a very gifted boy.' He waved his thin arms around the room. 'You can see how we live. My wife . . . she has a degree, we both do, and yet she . . .' His eyes filled with tears.

'Sir, I am not here to pass judgement upon what men and women have to do to survive,' Süleyman said. It was very obvious by this time just what Mrs Emin was. 'My aim is only to make sure that Hamid İdiz's pupils are safe, and also, if I can, to find his killer.'

Mr Emin bit down hard on his thin lower lip. 'Miss Madrid, Murad's first piano teacher, spotted his talent,' he said. 'He still used to go to her to practise after school even when Hamid Bey had taken him on. We don't have a piano . . .'

'You say he used to go to Miss Madrid?'

'Murad took a little job at a nargile salon in Tophane. Week nights The owner has a piano. He lets my son practise. It's convenient.'

Süleyman nodded.

'Hamid Bey was so impressed by my son that he wouldn't take payment for his lessons,' Mr Emin said. This reflected exactly what both Ali Reza Zafir and Izabella Madrid had told Süleyman. 'He said that my son could go all the way. Join one of the great orchestras. Get out of this.' He looked around the dank kitchen with sad eyes. 'I knew what Hamid Bey was, what he would sometimes do. My son told me. But he never touched Murad, never hurt him. I would never have tolerated that. Maybe I was wrong in what I did tolerate.'

'Your son, though unhurt, is not happy, Mr Emin,' Süleyman said. 'But no crime has been committed and so my work here is done, with the exception of the fact that at some point I will have to interview your son formally about Hamid Bey. I will have to interview all of his pupils.'

'Of course.' And then suddenly his face brightened. 'Inspector,' he said, 'do you happen to know whether the Turco–Caucasian Music Festival is still going ahead? Murad is so silent these days, there's no point asking him, and his poor mother was so looking forward to it.'

Süleyman said he had some information. Then they had returned to where the tango was happening, and together

115

with İzzet Melik he had looked on politely and in silence. It was only just before they were about to leave that the thing that now haunted him happened. Mr Emin's wife, the prostitute, showed them out. As Süleyman passed, she smiled and whispered, 'Your wife know, does she?'

He felt his face drain. He wanted to ask her 'About what?' but İzzet was with him and he wasn't sure that his deputy had actually heard what the woman had said. Did the Emin woman know about Gonca? Was that what she meant, or was he just seeing connections where none existed? In the lukewarm light of early morning, he really didn't know.

Çetin İkmen didn't have to go far to find his dead body. Propped up on a bench in the corner of the Kaktus Bar on Imam Adnan Lane, it was only a five-minute walk from the Rainbow Internet Café. What was more, the identity of the corpse was far from being a mystery to him.

'He's called Kenan Seyhan,' İkmen told the two constables who had been called in by the owners of the Kaktus when the body was discovered. The customers, a random selection of media types and those of a generally left-wing nature, stood outside in small shocked groups. They had imagined that the man sitting quietly in a corner was just having a little sleep.

İkmen picked up the tall, empty glass from the table in front of Kenan Seyhan and sniffed it. *Rakı*. 'So he'd been drinking,' he said. 'I wonder what else.'

One of the constables said, 'The doctor's on his way.'

İkmen leaned in as close as he could to the body without actually touching it. Kenan Seyhan had not been dead for long. He was still slightly warm and his face had not yet dropped from what looked like an expression of fear into the slack death mask with which İkmen was all too familiar. Even in death, Kenan Seyhan looked haunted. İkmen called through to Ayşe Farsakoğlu and told her to assemble a squad of uniforms to go and pick up Kenan's parents and his brother. At least one of them would have to formally identify the body. At the same time, Lokman Seyhan in particular would need to be questioned about his recent movements. If indeed he was still in town. He and Kenan had had some very serious 'issues', as the Americans put it. Had he somehow killed his brother in this funky lefty bar and then just run away?

It was while İkmen was looking closely at the corpse that he noticed that Kenan Seyhan had a piece of paper sticking out of the top pocket of his shirt. He picked a clean napkin up from one of the nearby tables and wrapped it around his fingers so he could draw the paper out without touching it. Opening it up, he found four statements written on it in child-like block capitals. They made his hair stand on end.

Even if they didn't know his name, all the men in the coffee house knew what Hikmet Yıldız did for a living. No one really liked the fact that he was a policeman, although the oleaginous owner always insisted he accept free tea. It was too much bother to argue.

Hikmet sat down at an empty table over by the door. Like every other coffee house in the country, this one was sparsely furnished with plain wooden tables and chairs, swathed in cigarette smoke and full of dour men. Away from their wives, they all did as they pleased. Some played backgammon, some

117

watched the endless football matches that always seemed to be on the television over by the samovar in the corner. Others talked in low voices, nodding their flat-capped heads in agreement with each other from time to time. They all smoked, with the exception of the small group of ultra-religious Muslims who sat at a table right at the back of the coffee house, drinking tea, telling their prayer beads and debating. Everybody in Fatih was observant, but these men and boys were different; they looked at Hikmet with active hostility. Clearly, he reasoned, they felt he was an enemy, an agent of a secular state of which they did not approve. They wanted, so he imagined, Sharia as opposed to secular law, just like his brother.

He'd only been sitting down for a minute when the oleaginous owner bustled over and put a glass of tea down in front of him. 'Ah, Constable,' he said, over-enthusiastically, 'what a glorious morning Allah has seen fit to give us, eh? Warm, but not too hot.'

'Yes.'

'A fine day for quiet contemplation in one's favourite coffee house.' He smiled. 'I assume, Constable, that you are free from your very important duty today?'

'Yes.' The creepy man had noticed that he was out of uniform. Although quite what he was going to do with his day off, Hikmet didn't know. Being at home with his unemployed brother was depressing. That was one of the reasons he generally started his days in the coffee house – even old men mutely playing backgammon and the mutterings of religious fanatics was better than that. He was wondering whether he might just head on up to Beyoğlu and spend the day in a bar when a group of smart men wearing sunglasses and some very chunky jewellery swept in and sat down at a table in the middle of the coffee house. All the men were young and unknown to him, with the exception of the slightly older character at the centre of everyone's attention. Hikmet instinctively turned his head away so the man in question couldn't see his face. Not that Tayfun 'The Smoker' Ergin would necessarily have recognised one of the many insignificant police constables who had come to arrest him the previous August. He had, after all, been entirely exonerated by the wife he'd almost beaten to death. When it came to the crunch, she just hadn't been able to follow through and put him away. Now, apparently, the couple were divorced.

'Coffee!' Ergin barked at the oleaginous owner. For someone known by the name 'The Smoker', he had a very light, unscarred voice. But then Tayfun Ergin didn't smoke. He was known as The Smoker because he had started his life of crime collecting protection money from nargile salons for an old gangster called 'Lame' Rafik. When the old man died, Tayfun and his gang of thugs took over, and he had been bleeding nargile salons as well as bars across the city for the past ten years. Quite what he was doing in Fatih, where nargile salons were few and poor and bars unheard of, Hikmet couldn't imagine. But it soon became clear that not everyone wanted the gangster in their midst.

Just after the owner had served Ergin and his men, one of the religious types got up and walked over to his table. Prayer beads still in hand, he said, 'Mr Ergin, your interest is noted, but your interference is unwanted. You should go.'

Ergin, who in spite of everything was a good-looking man,

flashed the religious one a dazzling smile. 'Sir, I am both a businessman who enables and a true believer. I seek only to help.'

The owner, now white-faced with apparent terror, attempted to pull the religious man away. 'Brother . . .'

'No! No!' the man with the beads cried. 'He must know we do not—'

'Ssh! Ssh!' The owner, thinking that Hikmet couldn't see him, nodded his head in the policeman's direction, warning of his presence. But Hikmet could see out of the corner of his eye what was happening. He also saw Ergin and his boys smirking as the religious man sat down amid his own agitated fellows. What had the gangster done to upset *them*? What was he doing in Fatih anyway? And what on earth was all that about 'interference' and 'interest'? Was Ergin moving into Fatih? Why?

The religious types left first, followed a few minutes later by an obviously amused Ergin and his entourage. Although Hikmet doubted very much whether the coffee house owner would tell him anything of any use, he did ask him, 'What was all that about?' just before he left.

'Oh, I don't have the slightest idea, Constable,' the creepy one said with a smile. 'I just don't want any trouble in my place.'

Which was true, but there was more to it than that, and both the coffee shop owner and Hikmet knew it. As he left the building, Hikmet Yıldız decided to bring Tayfun Ergin to Çetin İkmen's attention again. The inspector had been after him for years, and if Ergin was up to something new, he would certainly want to know about it.

Chapter 12

'The toxicology and the DNA will take time,' Dr Arto Sarkissian said to İkmen. 'But taking into account the box we found in Mr Seyhan's pocket together with the alcohol he drank, I would say that he died from an overdose of diazepam mixed with *rakı.*'

The doctor had just managed to catch İkmen before he began his interview with Kenan Seyhan's parents and his brother Lokman. Cahit, the father, had already identified his son's body. Now they all had to deal with what Kenan had written in that suicide note.

'I still think it's very odd to commit suicide in a bar,' İkmen said as he drew level with the door to the interview room.

The doctor shrugged. 'I don't know,' he said. 'The Kaktus isn't the sort of place where people stare or pry into what you're doing. He could down his pills without attracting attention. Also, the kind of middle-class liberal types who frequent places like that are unlikely to rob you. And he wanted that note found.'

'True.'

'He was lucky he wasn't sick,' Arto said as he made his way past the policeman and down the corridor, 'but then I don't think he'd eaten for quite some time.'

121

İkmen pushed the door of the interview room open and sat down at the table in the middle of the room beside his sergeant, Ayşe Farsakoğlu. On the other side were the three white faces of Cahit, Saadet and Lokman Seyhan. İkmen expressed sympathy for their loss before he came to the note.

'There are four statements,' he said. 'As far as we can tell from your son's other personal effects, the handwriting is his own.'

'What does it say?' Cahit asked. He looked tense as well as upset and the skin around his eyes was red. 'Tell us.'

İkmen looked down at the photocopy of Kenan Seyhan's suicide note and said, 'The first statement reads: *My lover Hamid İdiz is dead and so I no longer wish to live.*'

No one moved or spoke. Ayşe Farsakoğlu wondered whether the fact that Kenan Seyhan had been homosexual was the reason why those women she'd heard talking in Fatih had alluded to 'immoral behaviour' in the family.

Lokman Seyhan spoke first. 'My brother was queer.'

'Which would now put into context some of those things you said when you fought him,' İkmen said. 'Hamid İdiz had just been found murdered—'

'I was glad of that!' Cahit Seyhan cried. 'I was glad!'

'You knew . . .'

'That pervert seduced my son!'

'They were lovers,' Ayşe Farsakoğlu countered. Inspector Süleyman, whose case Hamid İdiz was, had been made aware of Kenan Seyhan's death and the events surrounding it. It was his opinion that Seyhan was most probably İdiz's unnamed secret lover.

122

Cahit Seyhan looked at Ayşe with fury in his eyes while his wife, now unable to hold on to her composure any longer, broke down and cried.

'The nature of your son's death as well as the contents of his note leave very little doubt that he took his own life,' İkmen continued.

Saadet murmured, 'Allah!'

'So why are we here,' Lokman said, 'if he killed himself? We've identified his body. Why . . .'

'*I fear my father killed Hamid,*' İkmen said as he continued reading from the photocopy. He followed on with the last two sentences Kenan Seyhan had written: '*My family killed my sister Gözde,*' he said, '*Everyone I care about is dead.*'

The room seemed to chill.

'You are here,' İkmen said, 'because in his final testament your son and your brother named you as the murderers of his sister.'

'He was insane!' Cahit Seyhan said. 'He tried to kill me! He put his hands around my throat.' He shoved his wife in the ribs with his elbow. 'You were there. Speak up!'

'Yes! Yes!' Saadet's words came hiccuping through her sobs. 'I was there.'

'And why did he try to kill you, Mr Seyhan?' Ayşe Farsakoğlu asked.

'Well, because he knew that I disapproved of him, and . . . he'd lost his mind, he . . .'

'He turned a gun on me,' Lokman said. 'Your officers saw it. You questioned us yourself!'

'For what it was worth,' İkmen said. 'Maybe the fight was about your sister, Hamid İdiz or both. I know that you drew a

123

knife on your brother, Mr Seyhan. I know that you drew your weapon first.'

'I . . .'

'In my experience,' İkmen said, 'those about to take their own lives rarely lie. Why would they? They are about to cease. All lies and delusions fall away. There is just the person and death.'

'But he was mad!' Cahit Seyhan reared up out of his seat and banged his fist on the table.

Ayşe Farsakoğlu said, 'Sit down!'

There was a moment when he might not have obeyed the command of a woman, but after a few seconds he did, more calmly, regain his seat.

'Your son was not under psychiatric care and so I can't assume that he was insane. I have no evidence for that,' İkmen said. 'What I do know, Mr Seyhan, is that Gözde was exchanging text messages with a boy who lived on your street.'

There was a profound silence. Nobody in that room even seemed to breathe. Ayşe Farsakoğlu felt an eerie shiver run down her spine. And then, suddenly . . .

'You have no evidence that we killed anyone!' Lokman Seyhan thundered. 'You've been at our old apartment for days! If you'd found any evidence . . .'

'Yet.' İkmen held up a warning finger. 'No evidence specifically against your family has come to light – yet. But we haven't finished our investigation. And now we have your brother and his note . . .'

The room fell silent again. It stayed that way for several minutes. Then İkmen said, 'And now that you know, you may leave.'

'Because you've nothing—'

'Because I am not prepared to charge you until I have found what I need to back up Kenan's testimony,' İkmen said. 'When I get you to court, Mr Seyhan, you are not going home. I don't care how clever your lawyer might be. Your son has told me you burned a girl to death, and I take that seriously.'

Lokman Seyhan's face whitened. 'You believe that?'

İkmen didn't answer. He just looked at him. Later, when the Seyhans had gone on their way, Ayşe Farsakoğlu asked, 'Sir, do you really believe that they killed that girl?'

'Poor Kenan only confirmed what I have believed all along,' İkmen said. He lit a cigarette and yawned. 'I don't know how they did it, but somehow they made it happen.'

'But sir, they all have alibis!'

He smiled. 'They do, yes,' he said. 'Ayşe, I am not saying that the Seyhans necessarily did the deed themselves. But it was done at their behest.'

'How do you know?' Ayşe said.

'I don't,' he said. He shrugged. 'My intuition.'

Everyone knew that İkmen had apparently inherited his intuition, or his 'magic' as some liked to call it, from his mother. She had been a witch. A lot of people, including Ayşe Farsakoğlu, still believed in such things. 'Ah.'

'And I'll be honest, I want to prove Kenan Seyhan right,' İkmen said. 'I think it unlikely that his father killed Hamid İdiz, but I do think that he made Kenan's life a misery, and I think that he somehow killed poor Gözde.'

Nowhere in Hamid İdiz's effects could Süleyman find any reference to how or where he had met his 'precious baby',

Kenan Seyhan. They were an unlikely pair, the educated music teacher and the working-class waiter. When shown a photograph of Kenan, Hamid İdiz's *kapıcı* did eventually own up to some recognition. He had been coming to visit Hamid Bey apparently for about a year.

'For pianoforte lessons, I imagined,' the *kapıcı* said primly. 'But he wasn't the young man I saw come the morning when Hamid Bey died. That definitely wasn't him.'

Hamid İdiz, much as he had loved Kenan Seyhan, also had a reputation for cruising, which his journal bore out. This ranged from quick fumbles in the back streets of Beyoğlu right up to taking pick-ups back to his apartment for full sex. Hamid Bey had been a reckless man who could have been attacked by any one of his unknown lovers at any time.

What was clear, however, as Süleyman questioned Hamid İdiz's twenty young pupils, was that all the girls and the little boys had loved him. Aware and suspicious of all and any difference, the older boys had either tolerated him, like Ali Reza Zafir, or seethed with disgust, like Murad Emin. To Süleyman, none of the kids seemed that relevant, although İzzet Melik disagreed.

'There's something not right about that boy,' he said to Süleyman as they both watched Murad Emin and his father leave the station. 'He's certainly not getting those prudish attitudes of his from his parents. And then he brought Islam into it. I wonder who he is getting that from?'

'School, peer group . . .' Süleyman didn't want to discuss it. Murad Emin was an uptight kid from a liberal family. Not unusual. Maybe that was his way of rebelling. He wouldn't be the first, and besides, he lived in Balat, a very conservative

126

area. There was obviously pressure for him to conform to his friends' and their families' religious and social mores. İzzet understood all of this even if he didn't agree with it.

What Süleyman didn't tell his deputy was the real reason why he wanted to put some distance between himself and Murad Emin. The boy's mother, the prostitute, *knew*. Although she hadn't mentioned Gonca by name, she'd said, 'Your wife know, does she?' Know what? He hadn't dared ask her. She had known he was married. How? She could just have been guessing. However, the likelihood was that she did at least know of Gonca and she knew that she was with a police officer called Süleyman. Both women lived in Balat. The Emin woman could have seen him going into Gonca's house and not coming out again until the morning. That happened regularly. But why had she mentioned it? People, particularly poor people, were usually frightened of the police. Mrs Emin had been drunk when he saw her, but even under the influence of drink, surely she would have seen the potential for danger in what she said?

Unless it was a calculated gamble. Like the sort of mental equation a blackmailer might do.

And that was the crux of the matter. His wife knew about his past affairs, but she didn't know about Gonca and how deeply he was involved with her. He didn't want her to. He knew that if she found out, Zelfa, his wife, and his well-connected father-in-law, Dr Halman, would make sure he had as little contact with his son Yusuf as possible. He could hear them in his head now: 'Going with a *gypsy*! A dirty gypsy!'

He told İzzet Melik that the Emin boy was irrelevant. He never wanted to go back to that squalid little apartment again.

İkmen went back to the Seyhans' burnt-out apartment later that evening. It was still taped off in case the investigators needed to come back and either take more samples or view the site again. By chance, the landlord was gazing mournfully at his off-limits property when İkmen arrived.

'If you're looking to rent it, I suggest you ask the police,' the landlord said as he tipped his head towards the blackened door of the apartment. 'Who knows when they'll be finished with it!'

İkmen showed the man his police identification and said he was sorry for the inconvenience.

'You can understand, I am sure, Çetin Bey,' the landlord said, 'that I need to clean the place up. The Seyhans need to take their belongings and I need to get the apartment in order.'

'Mr and Mrs Seyhan have been staying with relatives.'

'I know.' The landlord offered İkmen a cigarette, which he took, and then lit up a smoke for himself. 'So no rent from them and no rent from new tenants. I am out of pocket, I can tell you!'

Some of the people who lived on the floors above passed up the staircase. One of them İkmen recognised as the red-headed American who had reported the fire.

'Are the Seyhans not coming back?' İkmen asked.

The landlord shrugged. 'They say they can't afford this place any more.'

'Did you offer them other properties?'

'Sure! And not just in Beşiktaş,' he continued. 'I have places in Üsküdar and in Tarlabaşı, much cheaper than here, but they wouldn't have any of it.'

'Do you know why?'

'Said they couldn't afford it,' he said. 'Although why . . .' He shrugged again. 'The father and the sons worked. I mean, I have heard that one of the sons has now died and I am very sorry for that. To lose one child is bad . . . such tragedy! But I offered the family other apartments before that, just after the fire. I'm a good landlord, Çetin Bey, I look after my people.'

'I'm sure.' İkmen smiled. Such protestations probably meant that the landlord had some pretty rough property on his books, but that didn't change the fact that the Seyhans had turned down an apartment of their own in favour of sleeping on the floor at Cahit Seyhan's sister's place in Fatih. Of course, there could be an element of taking comfort with relatives after a tragic event, or even of finding an excuse to escape from this landlord. But it was the Seyhans' avowed penury that really interested İkmen. At the time of the fire, all three Seyhan men had been working. With mobile phones, televisions and what İkmen had recognised as some nice equipment in the kitchen, the family had not been hard up before the fire. So what, if anything, had changed in that short space of time?

It was then that İkmen's mind turned to the other families he had come across who had claimed penury in the wake of a daughter's death. Three families, in fact, all of whom had been investigated by the police because they had been suspected of a crime of honour. All three had apparently hit

129

hard times, and in one case, he had actually seen the victim's mother begging in the streets of Sultanahmet. And yet none of these families had been convicted of anything. Unlike Gözde Seyhan, the other girls had not been burnt. One had been stabbed in the street, another poisoned, maybe by her own hand, at home, while the third had been shot whilst pegging out her mother's washing in the back yard of their apartment building. The only apparent connection between these families and the Seyhans, besides all having deceased daughters, was their sudden lack of money. If İkmen remembered correctly, one of the families, a smart bunch from the middle-class suburb of Levent, had actually moved to one of the tattier streets in Fener after their daughter died. And yet the father hadn't lost his rather good job in the Garanti Bank.

After a few more pleasantries with the landlord, if no actual date for when he could reclaim his property, İkmen left. As he drove home, yawning, he contemplated what, he now knew, was going to be a very busy day come the morning. Places to go, people to see . . .

Chapter 13

'How would I know what Tayfun Ergin is doing in Fatih?' Hikmet Yıldız's brother Ismail said. 'Do I look like a man who indulges in criminal activity?'

Hikmet did think about possibly just slipping in his brother's brief foray into shoplifting when he was a teenager, but then thought better of it.

'Ergin was in conversation with some very obviously religious men in Abdullah's Coffee House,' he said. 'I get the impression they didn't really appreciate his presence.'

'Well they wouldn't.' Ismail said. 'Ergin is a criminal and an unbeliever. Why would good men want anything to do with him?'

'They didn't,' Hikmet replied. 'That was just it. They were, I think, telling him to go away.'

'You should have asked the brothers if they needed help.'

Hikmet laughed. 'What, me? Ismail, men like that turn their faces away from the police. Even you must realise that.'

'Well, Abdullah—'

'Abdullah is far too busy trying to buy me with free drinks and obsequious behaviour to be of any use to me as an informant. Besides, I am under no illusion that he actually likes me. He can't stand the police any more than anyone else who patronises his place. He wouldn't tell me what Tayfun Ergin was doing if his life depended upon it!'

Ismail Yıldız continued washing up the breakfast crockery, then said, 'Well I don't know anything, and so . . .'

Hikmet, still sitting at the kitchen table, lit up a cigarette and sighed. He wanted to ask his brother to keep his ears open for any gossip that might come his way about one of İstanbul's most famous gangsters. Ismail, though, just like the men in the coffee house, just like the owner, Abdullah, was not open to the idea of telling the police anything. But then in the normal course of events, why should they? They were pious, law-abiding people who enjoyed living quietly. It wasn't their fault that post 9/11, everyone and anyone of a religious bent was of interest to the forces of law and order, not only in Turkey but across the globe. They were just trying to get through the day like anyone else.

But Hikmet was still disquieted by what he had seen the previous day and was resolved to tell Çetin İkmen about it. As he left the kitchen on his way to put on his boots in the hall, he heard his brother mutter, if slightly resentfully, 'I'll see what I can find out.'

Hikmet smiled. Religious he might be, but Ismail still had the interests of his unbelieving brother at heart.

Mr Burhan Öz was sitting in exactly the same place he had occupied last time İkmen had seen him: the foreign exchange desk at the Garanti Bank in Nişantaşı. While this was slightly unsettling for the policeman, it appeared to be truly terrifying for Mr Öz whose face went a deep shade of grey.

'What?'

İkmen walked over to the desk and smiled at the thin, mustachioed man. 'Don't worry, sir,' he said. 'I do not come bearing bad news. Just a few questions.'

'About Suzan?'

Suzan Öz, Burhan's eldest daughter, had apparently ingested a bottle of weedkiller while her family were out. This had happened only eight months earlier, and so İkmen was not surprised that the father appeared to still be so raw.

'Not directly,' he said. 'Could you please go and tell your manager that the police need to speak to you?'

The bank allowed İkmen to use a small office at the back of the building. Mr Öz, his hand shaking around a hastily lit cigarette, sat down and looked across an empty desk at the man who had quizzed him at great length eight months earlier.

'My daughter is dead. She took her own life. There is nothing more to say,' Öz said.

'I know.' İkmen smiled. 'But Mr Öz we do have some outstanding issues. Things we have to clear up before we can indeed close the case of your daughter once and for all.'

'Like what?' His eyes shifted nervously. Because İkmen remained convinced of this man's guilt, his discomfort pleased him.

'Your finances,' he said.

'That's none of your business!' Öz said. 'My finances have nothing to do with Suzan's death!'

'Mr Öz, when Suzan died,' İkmen said, 'you and your family were living in a small but smart apartment in Levent. Within days of your daughter's death you had decamped to a much less prestigious apartment in Fener. I am also aware of the fact that your son dropped out of Boğaziçi University.'

133

'History didn't suit him,' the other man snapped.

'Then why didn't he just change courses?'

Burhan Öz put his head on one side. 'My family had problems,' he said. 'After our daughter's death.'

'Of course, but for your circumstances to reduce so dramatically . . . I believe you had a car?'

'My financial situation is my own affair!' Burhan Öz exploded. He ground his cigarette out violently in the ashtray on the desk. 'It has nothing to do with Suzan! Why should it? Why do you want to know about my money?'

It was a fair question, but not one that İkmen could easily answer. That two other families whose daughters had died in what had at first been deemed to be suspicious circumstances were also currently financially embarrassed was not something he could disclose. Suzan Öz's death had been declared a suicide and the case was officially at an end. Basically he was in Öz's hands to tell or not tell him the truth, or even tell him nothing. Burhan Öz, now tight-lipped and guarded, chose the latter course of action.

But İkmen didn't give in to defeat easily. When he got back to his car, he was joined by Ayşe Farsakoğlu, who had been speaking to a few of the Öz family's old neighbours in nearby Levent.

'The rumour is that the father fell on hard times due to a family obligation back in his native Kars,' she said. 'Although whether that information came directly from the family or not, no one could tell me.'

'And yet if that story is true, why did Mr Öz just flatly refuse to tell me anything?' İkmen replied. 'Family obligations are something everyone can understand. Why keep that information from me?'

Ayşe shrugged.

'I don't even know what these families being in reduced circumstances might mean,' İkmen continued. 'All were originally suspected of honour killing, all were subsequently exonerated due to lack of evidence. But then . . .'

'Sir, if you are implying that these families may have paid someone to kill their daughters, surely that doesn't work in terms of satisfying honour,' Ayşe said. 'Surely for honour to be restored, the family themselves have to kill the recalcitrant girl?'

'I agree,' İkmen replied. 'But Ayşe, remember that things have changed in this country in recent years. It used to be that an under-age son could be detailed to kill his sister or his mother and then, if caught, receive a reduced prison sentence because of his age. That doesn't happen any more. Now we have life sentences for this sort of offence. The stakes, and the risks, are high. Anyway, provided that those people who matter to the family in question believe that they did in fact kill the errant daughter, mother or whatever, where is the harm? If no one really knows who pulled the trigger or set the fire, lies can be told and honour can be satisfied.'

Ayşe frowned. 'But who would do such a thing?'

'Money is a very powerful persuader,' İkmen said.

'In the east, girls are locked in rooms with guns or rat poison and encouraged to take their own lives, poor things.'

'Here in the city it's difficult to lock people in rooms for days or weeks on end without attracting unwanted attention,' İkmen said. 'But given the lack of evidence in the Seyhan case, as well as in these older examples like that of Suzan Öz where the families concerned seem to have suddenly hit hard times, I have to wonder whether money is changing hands for murder.' He put his key in the car's ignition and then glanced across at Ayşe, who looked incredulous. 'I know it's a terrible notion, for which I have no evidence. But I haven't got anything else,' he said. 'Osman Yavuz, Gözde Seyhan's boyfriend or whatever, is still missing, and so far we only have a few anecdotes about him from the internet café he frequented. Nothing places any of Gözde's family in that apartment at the time of her death, and yet who but her family would want to kill her? Really?'

'I . . .'

'Ayşe, I'd like you to check out Burhan Öz's story about supposed obligations in Kars. Try and discover what those obligations are or were.' He put the car into first gear and began to move off. 'If he was lying, then we'll look into the Seyhans' finances, and those of the other families.'

'Yes, sir.'

'If you remember correctly, the Seyhans came originally from a village near Kars. Maybe that could be significant.'

The old Mercedes pulled smoothly out into the teeming Nişantaşı traffic to the sound of only a very few, very high-end car horns.

'I had to come and see you. I've been feeling so guilty!'

Tiny Jane Ford, the American woman and wife of Richard from the Mersin Apartments in Beşiktas, wrung her hands dramatically. Even though İzzet Melik, who had been down at the front desk when Mrs Ford arrived, had explained to her that Inspector Süleyman was no longer involved with the Gözde Seyhan case, she had insisted upon seeing him as opposed to waiting for Çetin İkmen. As he led her up the stairs and along the corridor towards Süleyman's office, İzzet pondered miserably upon the possibility that the American woman rather fancied his boss. Most women did. İzzet knew that the enforced celibacy that he endured year after dismal year was very far from being the lot of his superior. What a flat stomach, a perfect nose and gorgeous manners could do!

But this time, İzzet was wrong. The American woman sat down in front of Süleyman and, without so much as a seductive smile, said, 'It's about Gözde Seyhan. I lied.'

Süleyman put a cigarette into his mouth and then lit up. 'You lied? How?'

Jane Ford took a deep breath and said, 'I told you about my website.'

He recalled it. Tour details, property, restaurant guides, lonely hearts. 'Make the Most of İstanbul.'

'Yes, well there are discussion groups on the site. I take part in some of them myself,' she said. 'They're fun and . . . I got to know Gözde a little bit. As I told you when you came to the apartment, I sometimes saw her out with the washing in the yard, taking trash in and out.' She sighed. 'There was a boy. A geeky kid who lived in a block just down the street.'

As Süleyman recalled, İkmen had discovered that Gözde had been sending naked pictures of herself to a local geeky boy called Osman Yavuz. He was currently missing. 'Go on.'

Jane Ford waved the policeman's smoke away from her

137

face with her hand but without any comment. 'I saw how she looked at him and how he looked at her,' she said. 'I got on the forums about it. That girl all cloistered away like that. It bothered me!'

'And what did your correspondents on the forums suggest?' Süleyman asked, knowing via the terrible sinking feeling in this stomach what was about to come next.

'Well, that I intervene,' she said.

'In the face of what I remember you describing as your love for the authenticity of Turkish village life? Wasn't that somewhat hypocritical on your part?'

'But I wanted to . . .' Seeing that neither of the men she was speaking to was looking at her with any degree of sympathy, Jane Ford became quiet.

'What did you do?' Süleyman asked.

She took another deep breath and said, 'I helped them exchange cell phone numbers. I gave hers to him, his to her.'

İzzet Melik, standing beside Süleyman's desk, looked down at his boss and raised his eyebrows. Süleyman, he could see, was furious, if very, very controlled.

'You didn't think that interfering might not be a good idea?' he asked.

'They were in love. I could tell,' she said. 'It—'

'Mrs Ford,' Süleyman interrupted, 'Gözde Seyhan has died in a manner my colleague Inspector İkmen still believes may be of a type known as an honour killing. Now—'

'I know what an honour killing is!' Jane Ford said contemptuously. But her eyes were filled with fear. 'You don't think . . .'

'But surely you came here because you think that Gözde

may have been killed by her family after you put her in direct touch with a boy?' Süleyman said. 'Mrs Ford, you interfered. The girl is dead; the boy, an Osman Yavuz . . .'

'That's him.'

'. . . is missing,' the policeman continued. 'Did your husband know about this?'

There was a moment of hesitation, which told Süleyman that Richard Ford probably had known about, if not approved of, his wife's matchmaking attempt. But Jane Ford denied any involvement from her husband.

'I don't know where Osman is,' she said. 'I swear.'

'I hope not,' Süleyman said gravely. 'Because if you do and you conceal that information from us, we will take action against you. You must tell us immediately if he contacts you.' And then suddenly and violently he snapped. 'You stupid woman! How can you possibly tell anyone about Turkish life and culture when you don't have any idea about how this society works? You are utterly ridiculous!'

Kenan Seyhan was buried in a far corner of the great Karaca Ahmet Cemetery in Üsküdar. In common with many migrants from the countryside, the Seyhan family wanted their son buried on Anatolian soil.

Only the men of the family attended: Cahit and Lokman Seyhan, Aykan Akol, as well as a distant great-uncle who lived in Ümraniye. In this, as in so many other aspects of their lives, the Seyhan family conformed to the norms that had applied back in their village. The women, Saadet Seyhan, Feray Akol and her daughter Nesrin, remained in the Fatih apartment with the windows closed.

For a long time they sat in overheated, stuffy silence until the young girl, Nesrin, said, 'It's so hot, can't we—'

'Grief can weaken,' her mother Feray cut in sternly. 'An open window can bring chills, influenza and death.'

'We've had enough death,' Saadet said softly underneath her breath.

'But I'm hot!'

The girl was fat and red, not unlike her greasy great lump of a brother. Saadet looked at her with contempt. She had never wanted to allow her son to marry Nesrin. She was doughy, lazy and uneducated, and Lokman would soon tire of her. As soon as he got her pregnant, he'd be off on other romantic adventures. He would be bitter; Nesrin, neglected, unhappy, would probably get still more fat and lazy. Saadet had never wanted it. Lokman and Nesrin had been Cahit's project, and look what he had done to make sure the intended wedding went ahead! She felt tears come into her eyes, which she held back with some difficulty.

Feray Akol put a gnarled, calming hand on her daughter's neck and said, 'The heat will pass, my soul. One must endure, there is no choice.' Then she looked across at Saadet and frowned. 'Do you know yet when you might claim your daughter's body?'

Saadet shrugged. 'No.' Her sister-in-law couldn't even bring herself to say Gözde's name. Bitch! 'The police want to keep it while they investigate,' she said. 'Because they say that Gözde died suspiciously.'

Feray scowled. 'Sons of whores! What do they know? What evidence do they have to say the girl died suspiciously?'

'They have . . .' Saadet stopped. She knew the police

140

couldn't have much physical evidence, certainly not against her or her family. But she also knew that Inspector İkmen, if no one else, was not letting go of the notion that the family were somehow involved. When she looked at Feray and Nesrin and even at Cahit, her own husband, that knowledge made her feel better in a strange, painful sort of way. Only Lokman was exempt, but then he was her son and she loved him, her last surviving beloved child.

'They have nothing!' Feray said.

Saadet, silent again, knew what nothing felt like and found herself almost feeling sorry for İkmen and his colleagues.

Chapter 14

A long, languorous puff on a nargile water pipe was a very pleasnt way to spend time after work and before going home. From the interview that Süleyman had conducted with Murad Emin and his father back at the station, İzzet Melik had discovered that the boy worked at the Tulip Nargile Salon in Tophane five nights a week. There, as well as serving customers with pipes and drinks, the boy also used the resident piano to practise. He was, according to everyone they had spoken to who knew the boy, very gifted.

But İzzet didn't go to the Tulip for either the music or even the water pipes. Not really. He went to observe the boy, because if he didn't, no one else would. Süleyman was convinced that Murad Emin had nothing to do with the death of his old teacher, Hamid İdiz, but İzzet wasn't so sure. The boy had come across to him as a very different creature from his liberal parents. There was something stiff and puritanical that did not, to İzzet, totally chime with what could be just normal teenage piety. Back in his home city of İzmir, he'd come across the odd youngster who had been either heavily politicised in a right-wing nationalistic fashion or indoctrinated into fundamentalist Islam. İzmir was a pretty liberal place and so he hadn't encountered that many. But what he had experienced there had stuck, and Murad Emin was striking familiar chords with him. How Süleyman couldn't see that too, İzzet didn't know. Apparently he was taken up with the notion of İdiz's many lovers, including the deceased Kenan Seyhan and his family, as possible murderers of the piano teacher. He had almost entirely forgotten about Murad. It was strange for him to be so fixated on one line of investigation. İkmen, who had been instrumental in discovering Kenan Seyhan's suicide, was very sceptical about Kenan's contention that his own family had killed İdiz. He was of the opinion that Kenan had been lost in both his grief and his bitterness when he wrote the suicide note to that effect. The Seyhans had not apparently approved of either their homosexual son or his well-heeled lover, but there was no evidence to connect them to his death.

The Tulip Nargile Salon turned out to be one of the more ornate smoking places in Tophane. Situated behind the Nusretiye Mosque, the collection of smart salons, rough shacks and outdoor gardens that made up the Tophane nargile quarter were of variable levels of comfort and opulence. The Tulip, with its dark wood-clad walls and its menu that included not just pipes and drinks but also food, was at the upper end of what was on offer. After a brief look inside, İzzet went in and sat down on a purple velvet sofa behind a shiny black grand piano. No one was playing, but that, he imagined, was where Murad Emin practised and possibly entertained the punters too from time to time. Other customers included two men who, like himself, were in their late forties and who sported long, drooping moustaches.

144

They both puffed, with disappointed expressions on their faces, on pipes that İzzet recognised as being *tömbeki*, natural leaf tobacco. As strong as death and twice as lethal. When the waiter came up to ask İzzet what he wanted, he chose a much softer option.

'Apple tobacco,' he said, 'and coffee, medium sweet.'

The three girls sitting over in the corner, giggling, were probably, he thought, smoking apple tobacco. The mustachioed middle-aged men would feel he was letting the side down. But İzzet didn't care. Even though he looked as if he would like it, İzzet hated *tömbeki*. True, some of his attitudes and preferences did reflect those of a typical macho Turkish man, but a lot of them didn't. A fanatical football fan he might be, but İzzet Melik was also a fluent Italian speaker with a passion for Venetian art and architecture.

When his pipe arrived, he took the mouthpiece out of its cellophane wrapping and slotted it into the end of the pipe. He sucked hard, then leaned back and allowed the spicy tobacco to drift into his lungs and around his tired body. It had been a very long day. The American woman, Jane Ford, had almost driven his boss to distraction. But then he could understand that. What had the stupid woman been doing, encouraging a simple village girl in a forbidden and ultimately doomed romantic adventure? And with a boy that İkmen said could very well have been a sexter! Not that Mrs Ford had known about that. But still, to interfere in such a way in a new and, to her, alien culture . . .

His coffee arrived and İzzet sipped it with a small, satisfied smile on his face. It wasn't always so bad being single. He

145

could please himself when he wasn't at work, with no wife to demand his presence at dinner or children to insist he help them with their homework. It was dull but uncomplicated. And who, after all, needed complication? Rumour back at the station had it that Süleyman was once again seeing the gypsy woman he'd had an affair with some years before. Gonca the artist was older, but very striking. She was also sexually athletic and, it was said, as hot as a hearth for Süleyman. That thought did make İzzet jealous, but only because of the sex. Like an itch he couldn't scratch, İzzet's libido was perpetually unsatisfied, his lust for Ayşe Farsakoğlu totally unreciprocated. He wished he hadn't entertained such thoughts as he felt the gloom of his separateness settle around him. But then, suddenly, something absolutely wonderful happened. The grand piano behind him began to emit sounds, music of sublime beauty.

In spite of the fact that he prayed assiduously, went to the local mosque whenever he could and behaved modestly at all times, Ismail Yıldız was not trusted by everyone in the streets around his home in Fatih. His brother was a police officer, so what did he expect? Not that his neighbours necessarily had anything to hide. They generally didn't. But there had been a considerable amount of police activity in the area ever since the Seyhan family had come to live with their relatives the Akols on Macar Kardeşler Street. The Seyhans were still under suspicion of killing their daughter, but in spite of the fact that rumours were now circulating about one of their sons being homosexual, they appeared to be quiet, pious people. The locals liked that.

Ismail went to the grocery shop to get some food for himself and his brother. The owner of the shop was an old acquaintance who was a little bit more light-hearted than most. Rafik Bey had been one of the few local people who had actively welcomed Ismail and Hikmet Yıldız into the area after they moved from their earthquake-damaged flat. A couple of heavily veiled women came in and bought tinned goods, while Ismail riffled in the freezer for chicken pieces. Once he'd found two suitable joints, he went to the shelves to pick up rice, paprika and tarragon. The women left as soon as he arrived at the counter. Rafik Bey added up the cost of the shopping on an old pocket calculator and showed him the total. Ismail handed over a twenty-lire note and waited for his change. As the shopkeeper held the money out, he said to Ismail, 'How are you?'

Ismail took the proffered notes and put them in his wallet. 'In good health,' he replied. 'If Allah would see fit to grant me a job, I would be better . . .'

Rafik Bey shrugged. 'But your brother is working. One must be thankful.'

'Oh, I am grateful every day for Hikmet's work,' Ismail said. 'I wish he wasn't in that particular job, but . . . All I want is something simple. Waiting, factory work, anything. If I had work, then my brother would respect me, listen to me even! Maybe if I worked he would move away from the path of the unbeliever that he treads now. I would do anything to help to save his soul.'

'Your brother doesn't believe?'

Ismail hung his head. 'He is almost an atheist.'

Rafik Bey gasped. 'Oh, that is terrible. What a sin! You know if I needed help here I would think of you, but I don't.'

'It's OK.'

Ismail put his shopping into a plastic bag. He was about to leave when Rafik Bey, who had watched him with a serious, slightly troubled expression on his face, called him back.

'Ismail Bey!'

Ismail turned. 'Yes?'

'You did say *any* sort of work?'

'Yes.'

'Mmm.' Rafik Bey frowned. 'Listen, I can't promise anything,' he said, 'but if you do mean anything, I can ask around.'

Ismail's eyes lit up. 'For a job?'

'For some work, yes,' Rafik Bey said. 'It won't be well paid, or glamorous. But I know people, good people. Not loved by the police, but . . .'

It could be something to do with the local mosque! Then again it could just as easily be something a little shady. Rafik Bey was a good man, who prayed and fasted and read his Holy Koran with love, but he did have the odd business interest that was only barely legal.

But Ismail Yıldız smiled. He was jobless. 'I'd be interested whatever it is,' he said. 'Count me in.'

Rafik Bey took Ismail's mobile phone number and said that he would keep in touch.

İkmen looked out of his office window and saw, to his surprise, that it was dark. Looking down at his watch, he discovered to his horror that it was half past eight.

'Ayşe, you should go home,' he said to Sergeant Farsakoğlu as she put down her telephone. 'It's late.'

148

That he was still working long after he should have gone home too was not something that either of them alluded to.

'Police headquarters in Kars think that the family of Burhan Öz live or lived in a village ten kilometres outside the city,' she said. 'Öz is not an unusual name, so it might not be them. But they have records for a Burhan Öz, born 1954, in this village. Apparently his mother was convicted of theft from a local farm in 1967.'

'Burham Öz must be in his early fifties now,' İkmen said. 'So the date would fit. Anything else?'

'A sergeant and a constable from Kars are going out to the village tomorrow to see what they can find,' Ayşe said. 'I've told them what Öz has claimed and they'll see if they can unearth any evidence for it.'

'Good.' İkmen leaned back in his battered leather chair and lit a cigarette. 'Ayşe, are you aware of any rumours regarding Tayfun Ergin?'

She sat down on the edge of her desk and took her cigarettes out of her handbag. 'The Smoker?'

'The nice man who provides such good protection for bars and nargile salons, yes,' İkmen said sweetly.

Ayşe lit a cigarette and then breathed out slowly. 'No. Why?'

'Constable Yıldız came to me earlier today, rather concerned that he had seen Ergin in one of his local coffee shops.'

'In Fatih?'

'Yes.'

'Doesn't seem like the sort of place he'd want to be,' she said. 'Tayfun likes his *rakı*.'

149

'That's what Yıldız thought,' İkmen said. 'But then he heard Tayfun in conversation with some of the locals. According to Yıldız, Tayfun was made less than welcome, but he got the impression that he may be involved in some sort of business venture up there.'

Ayşe frowned. 'In Fatih? What?'

'I don't know,' İkmen replied. 'Maybe he's moved into protecting religious artefact shops. Maybe he's producing fake Zamzam water. The mind reels.'

'But he isn't our concern. Not at the moment.'

'No, but Yıldız was right to pass the information on.'

'Sure.'

'We are in and around Fatih a lot now, so I would urge you to keep Tayfun in mind,' İkmen said. 'He's a nasty bastard, and although I have no great affinity with the religious men and women of Fatih, I bear them no ill will. If Tayfun is putting the squeeze on the local imam, I want to know about it.'

'Of course.'

Ayşe zipped up her handbag, said good night to İkmen and left. The inspector knew that he would have to make his own way home soon, but still he lingered. Even though his wife was a woman of great faith, he had a lot of problems with religion. An absolute atheist, he deplored the 'superstition' that led people of all faiths to despise other religions as well as irreligious people like him. Sometimes things done in the name of religion, like honour killings, made him want to scream at every person of faith that he knew. *Darwin!* he wanted to yell at them. *Evolution! Darwin! For the love of life, use your rational minds!* But he had never and would never do such a thing. Instead he worried about some imam

150

he didn't even know and what a moron like Tayfun Ergin might theoretically do to him.

İzzet Melik watched out of the corner of his eye as the pianist, young Murad Emin, took a bow. He had no idea of the titles of the classical pieces the boy had played, but they had all been beautiful and brilliantly executed. The Tulip had certainly filled up with customers since Murad had begun his recital.

İzzet called for another cup of coffee, and one of the boys came over to put more charcoal on his water pipe. He noticed another man, about his own age, sitting opposite, smoking *tömbeki*.

'Boy's good,' İzzet said as he tipped his head back towards the grand piano.

The other man grunted his agreement.

'Been playing here long?'

The man shrugged. Then he narrowed his eyes. 'I don't know. Why?'

İzzet, aware that he had probably been coming over rather police officer-ish, said, 'No reason.'

He didn't want Murad to know he'd been asking questions about him. He wanted to keep a low profile just in case the boy recognised him. Apart from anything else, Süleyman didn't want him to have anything more to do with the lad. Murad Emin was a closed book as far as he was concerned. İzzet disagreed with this, even if his reasons were somewhat vague. But then he saw Murad come out from behind the screen in front of the Tulip's kitchen and frowned. Not at Murad, but at the person he was with. Now that, he felt, did not add up in terms of what they thought they knew so far.

151

Chapter 15

For once, he hadn't been able to surrender to the sex. All he could think of was the Emin woman. It did not render him impotent, but it was a good thing that Gonca didn't necessarily want full sex all the time. He'd given her the pleasure she demanded, but as for himself . . . Well, for the moment, that didn't seem to matter too much. At least not to him.

'Baby, I'm not pleasing you?' Gonca said as she looked down at his unaroused body with deep disappointment.

'No! No! No! It's not . . .'

She began to move down his torso, kissing his chest, his stomach, his hip bones.

'*No!*'

He knew where she'd been heading, but for once he didn't want to feel the pleasure that her mouth could usually bring.

Gonca, confused, shrugged. What type of man wouldn't want *that*?

'I . . .' He couldn't explain it himself. He was still completely intoxicated by her, and in the past, he had always been able to lose most if not all of his anxieties in her thick, willing flesh. But not this time. Maybe his encounter with

Mrs Emin, who apparently 'knew' something, was just too real. In spite of everything, he didn't want to have his son denied to him. Zelfa and her father could do what they liked, but he couldn't risk losing Yusuf.

But what did Mrs Emin really know? Without asking her, he could never be sure. The woman was a prostitute who drank and probably took drugs; her knowledge about him could consist of anything and nothing. She could very easily have mistaken him for someone else. Unless he asked her, he would never know. But he knew he couldn't face that. He knew he never wanted to go into the Emins' tawdry and, to him, frightening apartment ever again. As things stood, his wife knew he was going somewhere, but he'd been very careful never to give her any opportunity to find out where. He wanted it to stay that way.

'Mehmet . . .'

He turned to look into her dark, painted, beautiful face and smiled. Such a fascinating, endlessly surprising woman she was. One day he would arrive to find her throwing horse-hair at one of her now very collectable collages; the next she would be deep in philosophical conversation with a wandering sheikh from Iraq – her smoke-scarred voice drawling, like as not, in whatever language the cleric spoke. He lightly touched one of her breasts and she groaned.

'Please!' she said. 'Please!'

Maybe it was the pleading tone in her voice. Gonca didn't often beg for anything. But Mehmet began to feel different, less distracted, more involved. He moved his head down and licked her breasts slowly and sensuously. In less than a minute he was able to forget what had been in his head

154

earlier, and he was also able to ignore his insistently ringing mobile phone.

Out in some of the distant villages of Anatolia, where honour killings were sometimes ignored or even approved, the families involved would convene in what some described as 'councils'. These councils would generally consist of the intended victim's male relatives (father, grandfather, brothers, uncles) as well as, sometimes, 'concerned' friends and neighbours. Women were barred from these proceedings, although evidence existed to suggest that sometimes mothers and sisters knew what was about to take place. Maybe these females just chose not to acknowledge what was happening. Maybe they were simply grateful that they were not in the firing line.

Çetin İkmen rubbed the side of his head to help work away the slight ache that was building up inside, and then switched on his lamp. His wife and children had gone to bed hours ago, leaving him reading the literature that Metin İskender had lent him about honour killing and the connection between the seclusion of women and the sexting phenomenon. A female relative's chastity was important to these people. In fact, he had to admit, it was important to most men. Even his most liberal Western friends admitted to sneaking feelings of dislike for the boyfriends of their daughters. But that was a world away from actually killing anybody. There was also something deeply worrying and unpleasant about an environment where sexting could flourish. How many young people, he wondered, were involved in that distasteful and desperate practice?

The Rainbow Internet Café had failed to give up any more of Osman Yavuz's secrets. Even Mehmet Süleyman's information about the Ford woman and how she had given Gözde Seyhan and Osman Yavuz each other's telephone numbers wasn't actually pushing the investigation any further forwards. The Yavuz boy was still out there somewhere, doing who knew what. İkmen, like Süleyman, had no doubt that Mrs Ford had been telling the truth when she said she didn't know where the boy was. Silly woman! She'd ended up feeling guilty and afraid that she'd be sent to some hell-hole jail straight out of a horror movie. And she hadn't even really done anything wrong! Not really. Someone else had burnt Gözde Seyhan to death, although he was pretty sure that it had been done because of her relationship with Osman Yavuz. What had she said to him during that final call she had made just minutes before her death? Had she known she was about to die? Had he tried to get to her apartment but then, seeing the flames, simply run away?

İkmen didn't know whether Osman had actually loved Gözde or not. How could he? But if he hadn't loved her, if he had just been an awkward, geeky sexter, then that was very sad. To die effectively for love, without having actually been loved, was truly tragic. But then how many girls who were killed for 'honour' were actually in love? He suspected not many. Honour was about so much more than purity. It was about a family not being able to look their neighbours in the face if their daughter was perceived to be bad in some way. In some places, all a girl had to do to get a reputation was go out of the house! Then it would start. The old and bitter would gossip, the holier-than-thou would

156

sniff and then suddenly that family would not be able to buy food in the grocer's, or do business in the coffee shop. It was an appalling situation – for everyone. It was also something that had rarely been seen in İstanbul until the mass migration from the countryside that had started at the beginning of the 1980s. Like many İstanbullus, İkmen often found himself conflicted with regard to the Anatolian migrants. On the plus side, they worked hard and did the jobs a lot of the locals would never even have considered. On the minus side, they were not 'like us' in any sense. Unlike Mehmet Süleyman, Çetin İkmen was not from any kind of 'good' family, but he was still local, and there were profound differences between him and his family and the migrants. That was not, however, to underestimate the latter in any way. Now, 'they' had mobile phones, just like everyone else. They had computers, accessed the internet and knew about social networks and interest groups. The city had had its effect upon them too.

And so if the sophisticated city was indeed acting upon people like the Seyhans, whether they liked it or not, in every aspect of their lives, then why not in the sphere of 'honour', too? In some parts of İstanbul, it was not difficult to get a girl killed. It was just a question of hard cash and how much you were willing to part with. Recent cases of suspected honour killings involved families that now seemed to be poorer than they had been before. Yet if these families were indeed contracting out their honour killings to others, then who? Established gangsters, both domestic and foreign, were unlikely to bother themselves with such 'cheap' work. After all, why kill some little girl for, at most, a couple of thousand lire when

157

a criminal rival or the inconvenient wife of an industrialist could net a quarter of a million US dollars? But then maybe it was just strutting wannabe enforcers who were doing this.

When Süleyman had called him earlier to tell him about Mrs Ford, he'd also said that he was planning to pull in an informant he had who was a rather elderly rent boy on İstiklal Street. The late Hamid İdiz had used such people quite extensively, and there was a chance that the piano teacher's murderer had been one of them. The character Süleyman called 'Flower' would, possibly, have a view on that. İkmen too would have to spread his net wider. Whether any useful information came back from Kars about the Öz family or not, he was going to have to pry around in the seedy world of the small-time enforcers for a while. They would, after all, sell their rivals down the river for sometimes as little as the price of a shot of *raki*. One of them, once, had been Tayfun Ergin.

Süleyman always answered his phone, even if he was off duty and at home. İzzet Melik looked down at his own phone once again and then put it in his pocket. He'd left the Tulip over half an hour ago and had been trying to contact his boss ever since. But to no avail.

İzzet lit a cigarette and blew smoke out on a sigh. Süleyman was, in all probability, with the gypsy woman. It had been a bad day when he'd taken up with her again. If he occasionally picked up a dancer or a tourist, nobody apart from his wife cared, because it never seemed to distract him. He got on with his work with no problem. But with the gypsy, things were different. It was said that she couldn't keep her

158

hands, or anything else, off him. How flattering that had to be to one's vanity. And Allah, did the inspector have vanity! İzzet had always liked and admired Süleyman, but he had never been impressed by either the preening regard he gave to his own appearance or his delight at his role as a fantasy figure for women. The sergeant was no prude, but it wasn't seemly for a police officer to behave like that, and besides, it took Süleyman's mind, if infrequently, off his job. Hamid İdiz, the music teacher of Şişli, had been murdered, and Süleyman was apparently blithely choosing which lines of inquiry he wanted to pursue. İdiz's pupils *were* legitimate avenues for exploration. Just because they were children did not exempt them, not as far as İzzet was concerned. And now that he'd seen Murad Emin together with Ali Reza Zafir at the Tulip, he had a nagging feeling that there was more to these boys than had at first met the eye. For a start, they both worked at the Tulip, and so what Ali Reza had told Süleyman about them only meeting for brief words after their music lessons was wrong. Also the boys, when İzzet had seen them, had been exchanging hostile, if muted words. He had no idea what said words might be about, but the look of the two boys together had made him uneasy and he had wanted to tell Süleyman about it.

İzzet tried to call his boss one more time before he just gave up and began to walk towards the Karaköy tram stop. He'd seen the gypsy, Gonca, once and he had to admit that he'd been struck by the force of her presence. Now he imagined his superior with that woman in his arms and it made him scowl.

Chapter 16

Everyone knew Flower. Short, middle-aged and fat, with wiry black facial hair, his appearance belied his behaviour, which was frequently beyond what anyone would agree was outrageous. Süleyman's wife, who had seen him several times over the years in and around İstiklal Street, described him as being 'as camp as Christmas'. To Süleyman himself, this appellation did seem rather sacrilegious coming from a Christian woman, but he knew what she meant. Flower was someone you met away from other people, in a darkened room. Not that the Yerebatan Saray, the Byzantine cistern underneath the streets of Sultanahmet, was exactly a darkened room. But it was sufficiently anonymous and dimly lit to give both the policeman and his informant a measure of security.

The Yerebatan Saray had been built by the Byzantine Emperor Justinian in AD 532 to store water for the city during times of drought. A complicated series of pipes and aqueducts, some still extant, ensured that water could be carried to every part of İstanbul. Now a ghostly tourist attraction, where Justinian's great water tank with its soaring classical columns could be viewed against a background of classical music and softly phasing coloured lights, it was a place that Flower's compatriots in Beyoğlu would not often care to go.

'This is all very well for the odd tourist pick-up,' he said as he wrinkled his nose in very obvious disgust, 'but one does not generally troll across the Golden Horn. Not enough backpackers, too many imams.'

'The district has changed,' Süleyman said. 'Although there are still hotels and pubs, and I think you will find that backpackers can still be found.'

'Oh, I'm sure they can,' Flower replied. 'Although all the ones I've come across in recent years seem to be on cultural or religious quests.'

'Not so much sex and drugs.'

'Sadly not.' They walked down one of the many wooden walkways that criss-crossed over the metre or so of water that remained in the cistern. Carp made fat by all the scraps from the little café at the entrance to the cistern swam languidly beneath their feet. Then the music began, not loudly or intrusively, although it prompted Flower to say, 'Why is it always Vivaldi in these places?'

Süleyman, amused, shrugged. 'I've no idea. But we must talk about Hamid İdiz.'

They continued on as if moving towards the two columns in the north-west corner of the cistern, known as the Medusas. Each was supported by a large carved head at its base, providing a very good site for numerous tourist photo opportunities. Süleyman and Flower turned away from this and went right into a long corridor of columns lit by phasing lights of blue, red, yellow and green. Once they had gone about as far away from other people as they could get, Flower stopped, leaned against one of the handrails and looked down into the water below.

'Hamid İdiz gave the impression of being a very joyful queer,' he said. 'I liked him. He'd sashay up İstiklal dressed to kill and he wouldn't give a damn. He'd size up all the trade in the back streets and then make his pick and pay whatever was asked without any argument. Being from that class, your class, Mehmet Bey, he felt that haggling was beneath him.'

'Did he like young boys or—'

'Mehmet Bey, dear,' Flower said with obvious forced patience, 'no one wants to be tossed off by a grandfather. Well, there are some. If that wasn't the case, I'd have no business. But Hamid liked young men, and what he paid for was some hand relief or a bit of oral. A furtive fumble in a disused shop doorway, that sort of thing. It turned him on.'

'Did he ever have any trouble with any of the boys?'

'Well of course he did! Who doesn't?' Flower laughed. 'We've all been ripped off, dear. But I don't think that Hamid İdiz was any more sinned against than the rest of us. He liked to drink at the Kaktus and would eat at Rejans if he could. He wasn't one for gay clubs and bars. As I'm sure I don't have to tell you, it all goes off in the toilets and half the punters are trannies.' He wrinkled his nose in disgust again. 'Hamid wasn't into that. Al fresco fiddling was his thing. That and the big romances he had from time to time.'

'With whom?'

Flower shrugged. 'Who knows? We weren't joined at the hip, Hamid and me. All I know is that every so often there would be "someone". Usually a younger man, sometimes a lot younger, and sometimes a bit on the rough side too.'

'Do you know if he liked violent men?' There was no evidence for this in the piano teacher's diary, but then maybe that wasn't really his thing and he left it out. Some people who loved a violent partner were, on one level, ashamed of it.

'I don't know,' Flower said. 'I doubt it. Hamid was very particular. I can't imagine him dealing well with black eyes or blood up the walls. What I do know is that he was a bitch in bed.'

Süleyman thought he knew what this meant but he asked Flower about it anyway.

'He liked to be fucked,' Flower said baldly. 'And you and I both know that there are plenty of takers, of all types, for that sort of action, don't we?'

There was more than a little twinkle in Flower's eye. Süleyman looked down into the carp-filled water below. The fish were so used to humans, they followed them around and literally begged for food. Of course he knew about passive gay men and how they were regarded. At least since Ottoman times, they had been viewed as the only true 'sodomites.' The men who penetrated them were different. They were real men, not homosexual at all. They could use a man like Hamid İdiz and go home to their wives or girlfriends with absolutely no anxieties about their sexuality. They, so hundreds of years of tradition dictated, were entirely hetero-sexual. It wasn't something that Süleyman actually agreed with, but he said, 'Yes. Yes, we all know about that.'

'In Hamid's mind, these men he had relationships with

164

were his romances,' Flower said. 'He called them "darling" and "baby" and other nauseating things.'

Süleyman thought about Kenan Seyhan, and wondered whether with him, Hamid İdiz had at last found his one true love. In part at least, Hamid's death had caused Kenan to take his own life.

Some German-speaking women began to walk towards them, clanking as they moved with numerous cameras and tripods. Süleyman and Flower went still further to the right and into a series of columns only touched on one side by the lights.

'That said, he was a contradictory old bugger,' Flower continued. 'As soon as he got some "darling" or "honey" or whatever and was floridly in love, he'd have to treat himself to a casual tart, apparently just for the hell of it.'

'He'd go to İstiklal for some al fresco sex?'

'Oh no, he did that all the time anyway,' Flower said. 'No, he'd actually pick up or meet some boy or young man, take him home and let him fuck him. It really excited him. He told me once that he often came before any of them even got anywhere near his arse. Fancy that.'

'Indeed.' But Süleyman knew exactly what Flower was talking about, exactly how Hamid İdiz was and why. He himself was married, he had Gonca, and yet it still wasn't enough. There were still girls and women, faceless entities in retrospect, all the time. Women he'd flattered and sometimes paid, just for their looks or their ability to make him come. 'Do you know who any of these men are?' The twenty-five-year-old man the *kapıcı* had said had come to the building on the day that Hamid İdiz died was still unaccounted for.

'No. Hamid and I were not close. They were just men, boys, whatever. This city is full of queers, darling. You know that.'

Süleyman did. He also knew that quite a lot of them, particularly in the more working-class areas of the city, were very closeted. Finding out the names of Hamid İdiz's conquests was going to be difficult. But then the forensic evidence was still being assessed, and provided whoever had killed Hamid İdiz had a criminal record, there was just a chance he could be traced from that.

'So you couldn't point me in any particular direction?' Süleyman asked.

'No. Or rather I could do, but . . .' Flower threw his hands in the air in a theatrical gesture of frustration and said, 'Oh, take me to the café, I am gasping for a coffee!'

He began walking very quickly towards the exit.

Süleyman, in hot pursuit, caught hold of his shoulder. 'Flower . . .'

Flower stopped and put his hands on his hips, a very acid expression on his face. 'Yes, Inspector?'

'What do you mean? *Can* you point me in the right direction or *not*?'

Through the Vivaldi, the echoing sound of a woman's laughter bounced off the damp, vaulted walls.

Flower looked suddenly nervous. 'Look, you are a policeman and I know that you protect such people and—'

'What? Who? What people?'

But Flower remained silent. People were walking towards them now, and Süleyman was aware that he must not lose this moment, whatever it may or may not mean. 'Flower,' he said, 'imagine I'm not a policeman if it helps. But whether

I am or not, you can tell me anything with absolutely no danger to yourself. I know you laugh at what you call my Ottoman ways, but as an Ottoman gentleman I give you my word that this will go no further.'

There was a beat, and then Flower sighed and said, 'You should be looking at the religious types. Those who persecute the queers. Mehmet Bey, this sort of crime is still happening. Look to those bastards for Hamid İdiz's killer; I think you will find him amongst their number.'

In spite of the fact that most Fatih people, if pressed, would have expressed support for Cahit Seyhan and what remained of his family, not many actually wanted to engage with him or his relations. He'd lost a daughter in a suspicious fire and a son to what some said was suicide. There was something wrong with the Seyhan family and no amount of outward piety was managing to sway the good people of Fatih. When Ismail Yıldız went to his local grocery store, everyone was talking about it.

'Kenan Seyhan was a sodomite,' he heard one man say. 'And so to take his own life could be considered an honourable act. Given his nature.'

'Suicide is never right,' another older man said gravely. 'To end one's own life without allowing Allah to determine one's natural span is an abomination.'

A young lad, little more than a boy, who stood at the older man's side said, 'The daughter was bad too. Girls who die like that have always known men.'

Whether the men knew that Ismail was the brother of a police officer or not, they stopped their conversation as soon as they saw him. He didn't know any of them and so busied himself deciding what he was going to prepare for dinner that night. Eventually he decided that he would roast some aubergines with garlic and olive oil. The men left just as he took the ingredients up to Rafik Bey at the counter.

'The aubergines are good today,' the shopkeeper said. 'I think that you and your brother will be pleasantly surprised.'

'I hope so.'

He handed over a ten-lire note and waited for his change.

'Oh, that work I was telling you about,' Rafik Bey said as he took a handful of notes out of the till and handed them to Ismail, 'I spoke to someone who said he would be interested in discussing it with you. Can you be at the Gül Mosque for sunset *adhan*?'

'Yes.' Although Ismail was unsure. In spite of the fact that he would be meeting this stranger at a mosque, he was still a stranger.

'He wants to meet you at the mosque because he is a good person,' Rafik Bey said, as if reading Ismail's mind. 'You know that, don't you?'

Ismail took his change with a frown on his face. All this seemed a bit too cloak-and-dagger for him, the brother – if reluctantly – of a police officer. 'How will I know this man?' he asked. 'How will I find him?'

Rafik Bey smiled and tapped the side of his nose conspiratorially. 'He will know you,' he said. 'Have no fear of that.'

It was halfway through the afternoon when Çetin İkmen got back to his office. The days were beginning to heat up a little now and he was sweating.

'Well,' he said to Ayşe Farsakoğlu as he slumped down behind his desk and lit a cigarette, 'what a deeply unpleasant morning that was.'

Ayşe smiled. Her superior had spent the morning, to use his own words, 'down among the sub-gangster wannabes, the pitiful gangland fan-boys'. He had a sad little contact in the form of a crippled man-boy called Ali, who had reached the dizzy heights of playing court jester to the Tayfun Ergin gang. Basically he got rebuffed by the various women other members of the gang dated, and Tayfun and his heavies laughed. In return for this humiliation, Ali was given food and lodging above one of the bars that Tayfun protected. Although hardly the brightest star in the sky, Ali knew what was happening to him and was not forgiving. His occasional involvement with İkmen was his way of getting his own back.

'I met a friend of Ali's,' İkmen said, 'a boy of at most nineteen who apparently amuses members of the Karabey gang up in Edirnekapı with his hilarious impression of a human ashtray.'

Ayşe winced.

'Believe me, I tried to take the boy to hospital, but he wouldn't have it. Still glamoured, it would seem, by old Hakan Karabey and his whores, his jewels and his explosions of mindless violence,' İkmen said gloomily. 'Why do these kids still want lives like this? We shot Hakan's son last autumn. The shock of it killed his wife. What's to like?'

'The whores, the jewels and the mindless violence, I imagine, sir,' Ayşe replied. 'Little boys with big guns.'

'Yes, little boys who will be stopped by our big boys – in the end.'

Ayşe smiled. One of the things she really admired about İkmen was his unfailing belief in the power of good. Evil might have its day, but good would triumph in the end. At least that was what he always said to her. 'So did you find anything out?' she asked.

'I found out that Ali's friend rather approves of honour killings, like his boss Hakan Karabey,' İkmen said. 'But I don't think he has actually performed one. I don't think he's mentally capable. Ali, on the other hand, is against such killings and was very open to the idea of keeping his ear to the ground amongst his fellow gangster fans. He said he'd never heard of or even imagined such a thing as payment for honour killing. He said that Tayfun certainly wouldn't bother himself with such a venture, and I am inclined to believe him.'

'But on one level Ali loves Tayfun . . .'

'Yes, I know, but the amount of money that could ruin someone like Burhan Öz or Cahit Seyhan is just about what Tayfun spends on bottled water,' İkmen said. 'No, I think that if what we are looking at is a business, then it is small scale. It's fan-boys, baby gangsters . . .'

'Religious nutcases? I don't mean people in al-Qaeda. I mean those on single-handed disorganised missions to rid the streets of sin.'

'But they wouldn't take money,' İkmen said. 'It would destroy their credibility. If indeed anyone is taking money. Oh, of course talking to Ali did also give me a chance to check out Constable Yıldız's assertion that Tayfun might be moving into Fatih.'

Ayşe lit a cigarette and sat down. 'And is he?'

170

'It seems he is putting out feelers,' İkmen said. 'He's finding out who controls what and what that business might be worth.'

'I wonder why he's bothering with a district that seems to have so little to offer someone like him.'

İkmen sighed. 'There is money in religion: artefacts, and shops that sell them. There are many coffee houses in Fatih, too. But yes, it is quite limited when you think of what Tayfun does elsewhere. Any news about Burhan Öz?'

'Kars say that if he is the same Burhan Öz, born 1954, from the village of Gazimurat, then he hasn't been seen out there for years and neither have his family.'

'So we will need to access his bank account records,' İkmen said wearily. 'He would have got almost nothing for that old car of his, so I imagine that it was the family's savings that went. The son couldn't carry on at university and the rent was only partially covered by Burhan's wages, hence the move. Two thousand lire is all that stands between most middle-class people and complete ruin, and I don't suppose the Öz family are any different. Do you know if the Seyhans came from the same village?'

'No, they didn't,' Ayşe said. 'Twenty kilometres away. Out east it might just as well be twenty thousand.'

Chapter 17

Mehmet Süleyman had only been mildly interested in what İzzet Melik had told him about the boys Murad Emin and Ali Reza Zafir. It was unexpected that Ali Reza also worked at the Tulip Nargile Salon and that the two boys seemed to know each other rather better than either of them had let on to the police. But the inspector, so he said, didn't feel that it actually meant anything.

'Maybe they didn't own up to their friendship because it is or was rather more than that,' he said with a slight twinkle in his eye. İzzet mused upon the fact that everything Süleyman seemed to say had some kind of sexual connotation. That gypsy was ruining him!

'If you think that the boys need watching, then I have no objection to that,' he continued. 'But I don't want you approaching them. There's nothing to connect either of them to İdiz's death and I don't want their parents getting the idea that we're harassing their children.'

'No, sir.'

'Personally, I still think that there is virtue in trying to pursue Mr İdiz's admittedly many lovers,' he said. 'Although how that might be achieved, I don't know. With so many men in this city unforthcoming about their sexual preferences, it will be difficult. I'm wondering if we need to put someone on the streets, undercover . . .'

İzzet knew that such an operation would most certainly not involve him, for which he was very grateful. There were, he felt, some virtues in being overweight and ugly. Maybe Süleyman himself would have to do it if no one else would volunteer. In spite of his age, he was pretty enough to be queer.

'There's something else too,' Süleyman said, cutting across İzzet's thoughts.

'Sir?'

'My informant was of the opinion that attacks by religious zealots on the gay community are increasing. Now I don't know if the figures we have bear this out . . .'

'Queers don't always report it when they get beaten up,' İzzet said.

'No, they don't. But some do, and so I'd like to look at those offences and maybe pull in those who have a history of this sort of crime.'

'You think that a religious type could have killed İdiz?'

'It's possible,' Süleyman said. 'I mean, I know that Cahit, the father of Hamid Bey's lover Kenan Seyhan, couldn't have killed him, in spite of what his son believed, because we now know he was working at the time of İdiz's death. But that type of religious person is a possibility.'

'What type, exactly, do you mean?'

'The type that could well murder a daughter for the sake of honour.'

'Inspector İkmen still thinks that the Seyhans killed their girl?'

'Yes, he does,' Süleyman said. 'There is a type of person, whatever their religion may be, who takes its tenets to the ultimate extent. Ignorant, without ambition but often secretly envious of others who are successful in the world, they use religion as a reason for their existence and a prop for their own sense of self-importance.'

'You're talking about Anatolian villagers,' İzzet said. Originally from İzmir, Turkey's third largest city, İzzet gave the lie to his macho-man image by being very much a son of that traditionally cosmopolitan Mediterranean city. Village or small-town Anatolia was not for him.

'Some of these people would have a rural background,' yes,' Süleyman said. 'But not all. I am not talking about hard-line religio-political fanatics. Not *jihadis*, not al-Qaeda. They're far too clever to bother with a couple of men kissing behind an antique shop. They play the numbers game and anything less than mass slaughter will not do. I think we are, or may well be, looking for a nasty, hate-filled loner. Could be a neighbour, a local shopkeeper, anyone who has been offended by Hamid İdiz's presence. He may not ever have even spoken to the man.'

The two of them spent the morning looking at the faces and records of men in two discrete categories: those accused of 'lewd' acts and those responsible for attacks on men engaged in such practices. Some they knew and some they did not. At one thirty, Süleyman went out to a prearranged lunch appointment with some officers from the Iraqi police force who were visiting İstanbul, and urged İzzet to stop for a while and eat before he looked at any more records. İzzet did stop, but he didn't go out to eat. He got in his car and drove over to Tophane and the Tulip Nargile Salon.

He knew that neither Murad Emin nor Ali Reza Zafir would be working, because it was a weekday and the boys were both at school. But then that was the point. He wanted to find out what he might pick up about them in their absence. As he sat down on one of the Tulip's purple velvet sofas, he looked around at the handful of smokers. A couple of young business types in suits smoked very fragrant pipes, probably rose or strawberry tobacco; there was also one middle-aged woman and a young boy in what looked like a butcher's apron. As soon as İzzet sat down, an elderly but fit-looking man came over to him and asked him what he wanted. He ordered a pipe with apple tobacco and a glass of tea.

When the man came back, he inserted a plastic mouthpiece into the top of the pipe in order to get it going. He then handed İzzet his own, new mouthpiece and was about to leave him to it when İzzet said, 'I heard a boy play that piano here last night. It was excellent. Do you know anything about him?'

'Oh, that's Murad,' the man said with a smile. 'Yes, we are very proud of him. You know he's entering an international music competition soon.'

'Really? It's very unusual to have music in a nargile salon. I've never come across it before.'

For a second the elderly man's face clouded, and then he said, 'You know sir, I do not presume to guess what your opinion is about the smoking ban the government are putting in place in July, but it is worrying for businesses like mine.'

'You own this place?'

'It is my honour.' He smiled. 'Young Murad came to us through another boy we employ here as a waiter at night,' he said. 'They both take piano lessons, but Murad, well, he is special, as I know you have appreciated. This old piano was in one of the storerooms out the back for years, but when the other boy said that Murad had nowhere to practise, I let him use it. Out the back at first. But then, when I discovered how good he was . . .' He shrugged. 'Sometimes one has brainwaves. If in the future I can only allow my customers to smoke nargile outside my salon, then I must offer something inside that is more appealing than just tea, coffee, sherbet and *börek*. At first I thought that might be computers but my customers did not seem nearly as interested in them as my staff.' He laughed. 'But the piano . . .'

'And so the boy plays.'

'Exactly!' he said. 'The boy plays beautifully and my customers absolutely love him.'

With a small bow, he left İzzet to his pipe and went to the back of the salon to tend the samovar. Although the owner hadn't mentioned Ali Reza Zafir by name, it wasn't too much of a stretch to assume that it was he who had introduced Murad to the Tulip. The boy's employment constituted what İzzet felt was a rather creative way of dealing with a situation that could spell the end of nargile salons like the Tulip. The complete ban on smoking in enclosed spaces could kill the trade stone dead, and so, he imagined, a lot of nargile salon owners were having to think hard about what they might need to do next.

Relishing the experience of smoking indoors while he

could, İzzet didn't rush his pipe. Süleyman, entertaining the Iraqis alongside their boss, Commissioner Ardıç wouldn't be back for hours. The closet queers and the queer-bashers on the computer system could wait a little longer. But after a good half an hour's almost constant sucking on the pipe, he was satisfied. After paying his bill, he rose to leave.

He was turning to retrieve his jacket from the back of the sofa when he casually glanced over towards the back of the salon. The owner, who appeared to be looking down into his open till, was not alone. As well as two leather-clad heavies that İzzet didn't know, there, large as life, was the well-known gangster and extortionist Tayfun Ergin.

There had been no large withdrawals from Burhan Öz's bank account at the time of his daughter's death, or at any other time come to that. There had not been anything much to withdraw from. The Öz family savings, such as they were, amounted to just short of thirty lire.

'And yet,' İkmen said to Ayşe Farsakoğlu as they made their way along the corridor towards the pathologist Arto Sarkissian's office, 'his outgoings have not increased either. In fact his rent, since he moved from Nişantaşı, has gone down. He doesn't have a car any more and his son is no longer at university. He should be rolling in money.'

Ayşe Farsakoğlu, who had also been privy to İkmen's conversation with Öz's bank manager, said, 'But sir, he is drawing a lot of cash.'

'Exactly!' İkmen said. 'More than he ever has before. It's going somewhere, isn't it? Unless they're all eating out every night . . .'

It was frustrating that they hadn't found a massive withdrawal from Burhan Öz's bank account. It would have given them some leverage to reopen the other two suspected honour killing cases. But then what had İkmen expected? If these families were indeed paying an individual or a gang to kill their disobedient girls, they were going to be very careful about both how the job was done and how payment was made.

İkmen and Ayşe turned a corner and found the Armenian doctor waiting for them at his office door. As usual, İkmen and Arto embraced and then all three of them went inside and the doctor closed the door. As the two police officers sat down, he said, 'I've had a whole sheaf of DNA results through from the Forensic Institute. There's one in particular, from the Seyhan fire, that we should discuss.'

'Oh?'

'Mmm.' The doctor put his spectacles on and then looked down at a rather untidy heap of papers on his desk.

'DNA material was removed from the corpse, later identified as Gözde Seyhan, on the day of her death,' the doctor said. 'As you know, this is quite routine where any doubt about the identity of a corpse exists. We always look at dental records, and this time, of course, they did confirm what we suspected quite independently from the DNA. However, what the forensic team also did once Miss Seyhan's parents were at the crime scene was take swabs from both Cahit and Saadet Seyhan for comparison.'

'Yes.'

'Well, the results show that although Saadet is most certainly Gözde's mother, there is no way that Cahit Seyhan can be her father.'

179

For a few moments İkmen and Ayşe Farsakoğlu sat in stunned silence. They had both met Saadet Seyhan, who to all intents and purposes was a very pious, rather nervous middle-aged woman. But her youngest child was not her husband's and so she had to have been involved with another man in the past. This raised questions about whether Cahit had known and, further, whether Gözde's paternity and not her telephone relationship with Osman Yavuz had been the reason behind her murder.

'Arto,' İkmen began, 'do we have any forensic evidence that could connect the Seyhans to Gözde's murder?'

The Armenian shrugged. 'Their DNA is all over the apartment, because they lived there,' he said.

'The petrol can?'

Arto looked down at his paperwork again. 'DNA was retrieved from two strands of hair. It is human but it does not match that of Mr or Mrs Seyhan or either of their sons. As you have probably deduced, it doesn't match any of the DNA records we have on file either.'

'So our potential killer is a person with a clean record,' İkmen said. 'Great.' He lit a cigarette and then put his head down and looked at the floor.

'Sorry.'

'But sir,' Ayşe said, 'we've been exploring for some time the possibility that the Seyhans may have employed a third party to kill Gözde. All this means is that rather than suspecting that they didn't do it themselves, now we know that.'

'I know.' İkmen forced a small, wan smile. 'But I hoped that somehow they might be directly implicated. I hoped for a miracle, I know. Now we have to look for an unknown murderer who is not on our DNA database and who we may never find.'

'We have Burhan Öz and those other two families whose finances we need to check out. We're not done,' Ayşe said. İkmen was, she could tell, descending albeit temporarily into gloom. 'We'll get them. We have to.'

'And the fact that Cahit Seyhan was not Gözde's father may give you a way in that did not exist before,' Arto Sarkissian said.

'We can't tell him!' İkmen said. 'We don't know whether he knows. If he doesn't . . .'

'You speak to her, on her own,' the Armenian said. 'Who knows, if her husband or her son did order Gözde's murder, perhaps the fact that you know about her infidelity may make her break down. Don't forget, Çetin, Kenan Seyhan told you in his suicide note that his family killed his sister. Unlike the statement he wrote about his lover Hamid İdiz, he did not merely "fear" that his father had killed his sister; he clearly wrote that his family had murdered her.'

'That's not enough to prosecute . . .'

'I know, you need more,' the doctor said. 'But you've now got something in addition to whatever you had when you woke up this morning. It's a possible motive.'

'Yes, but why now? Why kill Gözde now?'

'I don't know,' Arto said. 'Maybe Cahit only found out just recently.'

'And why not kill his wife as well?'

Again the Armenian shrugged. 'Who knows? But this could be significant. Even the unknown DNA on the petrol

181

can could be significant. Just because we don't have a match now doesn't mean that one will not appear at some time in the future. Crimes from thirty, forty years back are now being solved because of this technology.'

İkmen looked up and frowned. 'I don't want Gözde Seyhan to wait thirty years for justice. That girl's awful death demands a solution! She deserves that much and we owe her it!'

When Süleyman returned to the station, he and İzzet worked on a list of men they wanted to talk to with regard to Hamid İdiz's death. The following morning they would assemble a squad of officers and make a start on finding the most furtive gay and bisexual men of İstanbul, as well as those who sought to hurt them.

İzzet had not told Süleyman about his visit to the Tulip Nargile Salon, and so the superior officer did not know about the sudden appearance of Tayfun Ergin. Although he suspected that Ergin might well be providing 'protection' for the salon, İzzet did not know that for certain. What, if anything, Ergin might have to do with Murad Emin, Ali Reza Zafir or the death of Hamid İdiz was also very much open to question. Ayşe Farsakoğlu had told him that there was some evidence that Ergin might be moving his organisation into Fatih, but that was hardly germane to what İzzet and Süleyman were doing.

On his way back to his small flat in Zeyrek, İzzet found himself stopping off in Balat, opposite the Ahrida Synagogue. After a few moments' contemplation of the high wall that separated İstanbul's oldest synagogue from the street, he walked across the road and up the steps to the flat belonging to the piano teacher Miss Izabella Madrid. He reasoned that Murad Emin had by this time probably gone to work at the Tulip as opposed to having a lesson with the old woman. He was right.

'I've just made myself some *latkes*,' Izabella Madrid said as she led him into her living room. 'Do you want some? Do you know what they are?'

İzzet sat down in one of her overstuffed armchairs and, ignoring her apparent rudeness in a way he hadn't done before, said, 'Potato cakes. And yes, that would be nice.'

'Great big lump like you needs to keep your strength up,' she said as she went back into her kitchen.

Latkes! He hadn't had those for years. Just the smell of them frying on the stove made him think about İzmir. A little bit of home.

When Izabella came back, she was carrying a huge plate of great oily shredded potato cakes. 'So where is the beautiful Inspector Süleyman tonight?' she said as she placed the platter and a fork on İzzet's lap.

'Oh, he's er . . . he's at home,' İzzet said.

'With his wife or Gonca the gypsy?' the old woman asked as she settled herself down with a much smaller plate of *latkes*. Then, seeing the look of shock on his face, she said, 'Ah, everyone knows, İzzet Bey! This is Balat, not some polite Bosphorus village. The great gypsy queen pleasures the Turkish prince. We all know this and I, for one, don't judge.'

But İzzet was still shocked. Even the gorgeous, glutinous pepperiness of the *latkes* couldn't distract him from what she'd just said. 'The inspector doesn't want anyone to know!

He needs to keep it a secret because if his wife finds out she may stop him from seeing his child,' he blurted. He'd never, in a non-professional capacity, gossiped so much about another person who was not related to him. But then, in spite of their differences, he did care about Süleyman.

'But people *do* know, İzzet Bey,' Izabella said. 'The gypsy loves him and so her face glows and she speaks of him often. What can I say? Are you enjoying your *latkes*? Are they good?'

'Yes, very good,' he said. 'Some of the best I've ever had.'

'Good.' They both ate in silence for about a minute before she looked up at his still rather blanched face and said, 'So what did you come to see me about, İzzet Bey? I'm old, I'm fat and I'm as bald as a grease-wrestler's chest underneath this wig; what on earth do you want with me?'

İzzet had had no actual plans to see Izabella Madrid when he'd left the station half an hour earlier. He'd thought very little about her since his last visit to her flat. But for some reason that he only half understood, he needed to know more about the boy genius Murat Emin. It wasn't just because, of all Hamid İdiz's pupils, it was only Murad and Ali Reza Zafir who had been subjected, albeit in a very mild way, to his lust. None of the other pupils they had interviewed had expressed any unduly strong feelings about their old teacher. In addition, no motives, as yet, had come to light amongst the other youngsters. Eventually he said, 'I want to know about Murad Emin. I know he's a very good musician, but I want to know what he's like. Understand?'

'You've been to the Emin apartment,' the old woman said. 'You've seen how they live.'

'You know I have.'

She shrugged. 'How would you deal with that? I don't mean all the Communist utopian stuff the father spouts; there's nothing wrong with that. I mean the fact that the mother is on the game, both parents are junkies . . .'

'Both?' He'd imagined that the mother was, but the father too?

'Yes. Emin senior could get a job if he wanted; he's an educated man,' she said. 'But he's on drugs all the time! He steals to get money, which he then spends on heroin, in the same way that his wife sucks the cock of the world to get money for her gear. Their kids have no smart shoes, no computers, no holidays. Murad loves his parents, and is also very loyal to his little sister, but I know he doesn't respect them.'

'How?'

'We talk, or we used to.'

İzzet put a large lump of *latke* in his mouth and chewed thoughtfully before he said, 'You used to talk?'

'Before he went to Hamid Bey for lessons,' she said. 'Chatting all the time in those days. But now?' She shrugged. 'He's still clever, lovely little Murad, don't get me wrong, but there is a hardness about him too.'

'A hardness?'

'As I said to you with regard to your beautiful superior, I do not judge, nor do I moralise,' she said. 'But Murad I think these days judges people by . . .' She paused, deep in thought for a moment. 'I think that, like a lot of boys who

185

come from migrant families, Murad has taken on a rather strict moral code.'

Both İzzet and Mehmet Süleyman had observed this in Murad Emin. What İzzet was a little surprised about was that the usually straight-talking Miss Madrid was being suddenly so coy about it. But then she was from a minority, albeit one that he knew rather better than she would have guessed, but a minority nevertheless that might find the notion of religious fanaticism or radicalisation difficult to express.

İzzet said it for her. 'I wondered when I was at the Emin flat what Murad's allusions to Islam might mean.'

He looked at her with meaning in his eyes, but she turned away from him quickly. 'Well, he wouldn't have learnt anything like that from Hamid Bey,' she said. 'Religion, it wasn't his—'

'I fear that Murad may be getting his religion from unsavoury sources,' İzzet said. 'I know you probably don't know anything about that . . .'

'I don't.'

'But tell me, does he refer to little religious sayings or blessings or things that allude to judgemental—'

'He has talked about his gift coming from Allah,' she said. 'We've had the fact that he wants to be the greatest Muslim pianist and composer. Wants to do it for Allah.' She sighed and looked across at him. 'Murad always used to hug me when he left at the end of his lessons. Now he doesn't. I'll be honest, at first I thought that maybe Hamid had made him homosexual. But it wasn't that.'

'What was it?' İzzet asked.

She looked suddenly much older as her face folded into

a crushed shape. 'He couldn't touch an infidel,' she said. 'Still can't. He told me he still respected me, but he couldn't touch me any more.' She put her plate down and then rubbed her arms with her hands as if she was cold. 'Made me feel dirty.'

İzzet's face flushed. He wasn't a religious man, but he hated the idea of Islam being twisted and abused to make good people feel bad.

'Murad is a tough boy,' Izabella continued. 'He's come through a lot in his short life. I also think that at heart he is a good boy, but . . . I used to be able to read him to some extent, but not now, not now.'

She had no idea about who the boy socialised with or where. She knew he worked at the Tulip, but that was all she did know. When he finally got up to leave, İzzet asked her, 'Do you think that Murad might have been capable of killing Hamid İdiz? The new Murad, I mean, not the lad that you first discovered?'

She helped him put his jacket back on, then said, 'I don't know. I like to think not, but . . .' She walked around to face him and smiled. 'So you liked the *latkes*, then?'

'There were many Jews in İzmir when I was growing up,' İzzet said. 'One of them was my Italian teacher.'

'Oh, good.'

'Another was my mother's father.' He smiled.

'What? A great big Turkish macho man like you?' She looked very closely at him, then said, 'Mmm. I can see it, just.'

'We all have our secrets, Miss Madrid,' he said as he opened her front door and stepped outside. 'Mine is very small and rather nice, because it means that I can appreciate *latkes*.'

'Let us hope that whatever young Murad holds inside himself is equally benign,' she said. 'If nothing else, I know he cares about this Turco–Caucasian music competition. He won't jeopardise that, I do not think, for anything. Don't worry, Sergeant Melik, I will watch the boy, I will care for him.'

'Thank you.'

'Oh, and about your boss,' she said.

İzzet frowned.

'It will all be well for him in the end, with Gonca.'

'What do you mean?'

'I mean that, powerful as she is, her people won't tolerate this love she has for Süleyman.' Izabella Madrid smiled. 'Her father still lives, and the day will come when he will put a stop to it. The gypsies favour their own; we all do. We are all human.'

Chapter 18

Cahit Seyhan went to work early that morning leaving his wife asleep on the floor of his sister's living room. Saadet woke as soon as her son and her nephew came into the room and put the television on. This was nothing unusual, and so she did as she usually did and left as quickly as she could to go to the bathroom. As soon as she locked the door behind her, she heard her sister-in-law Feray snort with frustration back in the hall. She always hated Saadet getting into the shower before her. As if she couldn't bear to wash after such a dirty person. But Saadet ignored her.

Once washed and dressed, it was time for someone to go down to the baker's on Macar Kardeşler Street and buy bread for the day. None of the men would do it and Nesrin, Feray's daughter, was far too lazy to even get out of bed. Feray herself was now in the bathroom, and so Saadet put her coat and her headscarf on and let herself out of the apartment. Of all the chores she'd had to do since arriving in Fatih, going to get the bread was her favourite. It gave her, albeit briefly, the feeling that she was still an ordinary housewife, with her own apartment and family, and not what she really was, a grieving mother and unwelcome guest in her sister-in-law's home.

189

She walked out of the apartment building into bright sunlight. All around her, other women in various degrees of covering passed by clutching bread, and sometimes bags of tomatoes, cheese and olives too. The usual breakfast ritual. The baker, a small toothless man in his sixties, handed Saadet her order of three loaves and she in return wordlessly proffered the correct amount of money in payment. It was as she left the baker's shop that everything suddenly became strange and frightening. A man she had never seen before bundled her into an old Fiat car, and yet another strange man drove her away.

'You're not eating your breakfast,' Hikmet Yıldız said as he watched his brother Ismail stare into space over his untouched bread, butter and tomato. 'If Mother was here, she'd make you eat it.'

'What?'

'Your breakfast,' Hikmet reiterated. 'Eat it!'

'Oh.' Ismail looked down at his plate for a second or so, and then began staring into space again.

'Allah!' Hikmet had taken the trouble to prepare breakfast that morning because Ismail had got in so late the night before. He'd gone to the mosque for sunset *adhan* and then apparently moved on somewhere else afterwards. Hikmet neither knew nor cared where. 'I have to go to work now,' he said as he put his police cap on his head and then bent down to put his boots on. 'I'll be back at about six.'

As he walked across the kitchen, adjusting his gun holster as he went, Ismail said suddenly, 'Don't go.'

Hikmet turned and looked at his brother with an expression

190

of exasperation on his face. 'Ismail . . .' But then he saw that his brother had tears in his eyes, and so he sat down beside him at the table and said, 'What is it? What's happened?'

'Oh, Hikmet,' Ismail said in a terrified voice that was only just above a whisper, 'I've done something, I've agreed to do something so terrible!'

Çetin İkmen pointed at the mobile phone Saadet Seyhan had taken out of her handbag and said, 'Please make that call, Mrs Seyhan. I do not want your family to worry about you.'

He'd had her taken off the street and brought to the station so that he could question her, but he did not want her family to know what she was really doing. With a distinct tremor in her voice, Saadet told her nephew that she'd decided to do all her shopping early and in one hit. There was some argument about the bread and how they'd all been waiting for it, but that was, apparently, quickly defused.

'I will not detain you for very long,' İkmen said once the call was over. 'But Mrs Seyhan, there is a matter I have to discuss with you, and in the absence of your husband.'

Saadet Seyhan's face turned white. İkmen wondered whether she had guessed what he was about to say. So he said it quickly, watching as her eyes if not her voice told him it was true.

'I don't want or need to know who Gözde's father was,' İkmen said. 'I am not judging you, Mrs Seyhan. All I want to do is find out who killed your daughter.'

She didn't speak. She just sat opposite him, her headscarf pulled down low over her eyes, which leaked silent water. Ayşe Farsakoğlu, who was sitting beside İkmen, said,

'Mrs Seyhan, we need to know whether your husband was aware that he was not Gözde's father. We understand you might not know this, but . . .'

'Cahit does not know of my shame,' Saadet said in a voice that was just a little above a whisper. İkmen looked at Ayşe and raised an eyebrow. He had thought that Saadet might try to deny the DNA evidence, but clearly she was either beyond that point, or just wanted the relief that came with telling a long-held and burdensome secret. 'If he knew, I would be dead.'

'As well as your daughter?'

Saadet looked up from underneath her headscarf, her eyes glittering with both tears and hatred. 'If you think I'm going to say that my husband killed Gözde, then you are very much mistaken!'

'If he did, you should tell me,' İkmen said calmly. 'If you loved your daughter, then you should want justice for her.'

'I have just lost my son . . .' She broke down, crying into a handkerchief she took from her pocket.

İkmen looked at Ayşe again, anxious. He didn't want to offend this woman, to push her too far. That way would lead, he felt, only to silence on her part.

'Mrs Seyhan,' he said, 'I accept that you are heavily burdened. Your son Kenan has died, you are obliged to live with your husband's relatives . . .' He took a deep breath and continued. 'We know that Gözde was exchanging texts and photographs with a boy. We know that! We have your daughter's phone. Your son Lokman tried to conceal it from us, but we have it. Mrs Seyhan, your daughter was having some kind of relationship with this boy. I believe it was entirely devoid of actual sex, but—'

'Gözde was a good girl!'

'Yes! Yes, I believe that she was,' İkmen said. 'Which is why her death is so tragic. Mrs Seyhan, we need to find who killed your daughter and stop him from doing anything like this again. Any feelings that you may have about the rightness of punishing girls for having perfectly natural feelings towards boys you have to put from your mind! You yourself—'

'I know what I did!' Saadet said, not crying any more now, her face twisted into an expression of deep shame. 'I know what I did.'

'We have no intention of informing your husband or anyone else about Gözde's paternity,' İkmen said. 'That is something for you and you alone. But I must impress upon you the absolute necessity of telling us anything you believe might lead us to her killer, even if that person is—'

'You are convinced that Cahit and Lokman killed Gözde, aren't you?' she said. 'You have it fixed in your mind that they cannot possibly be innocent!'

'Yes,' İkmen said, 'I do! I have this fixation because I cannot find anyone outside of your family who might have had a motive.'

'What about this boy you say . . .'

'The boy is, admittedly, missing. But we are looking for him.'

'Well, he could have killed Gözde! He could have ruined her and then—'

'Mrs Seyhan, Gözde was a virgin when she died,' Ayşe Farsakoğlu cut in. 'As you said yourself, she was a good girl. She did not deserve to die.'

193

Saadet Seyhan looked down at her hands as she descended into silence.

'If you know anything . . .'

'I know nothing!' She looked up sharply and then reiterated, 'Nothing!'

'But if you did . . .' İkmen's words tailed off, cut short by the furious, almost violent expression on Saadet Seyhan's face.

'I have lost a son,' she said softly but with barely suppressed rage. 'I have lost a daughter and a home, and now you come for my other son and my husband?'

She stood up, scraping the chair furiously against the concrete floor as she did so. 'I want to go,' she said. 'You have to let me!'

'Yes, but . . .'

'I know nothing. Nothing!' she said. She walked over to the door of the interview room and then turned to look at İkmen. 'Let me out.'

'Mrs Seyhan, if your family employed a third party to kill your daughter . . .'

'Let me out!' she screamed. 'I have lost everything! I cannot lose anything more!'

There was a slight catch in her throat as she appeared to realise what she had said, but İkmen, now up on his feet, laid it out for her just in case she had not fully understood.

'I know you cannot bear to lose anything or anyone else,' he said as he began to unlock the door for her. 'But spare a thought for how Gözde felt when her skin was melting off her bones, when her hair was on fire, when she could no longer breathe because her lungs had collapsed.'

She just looked at him, shaking, and then she shot through the door as if fired from a cannon.

'I will catch whoever did this!' İkmen called out after the rapidly retreating woman, 'And I won't care who it might be!'

When he went back into the interview room, he looked across at Ayşe, who said, 'She isn't going to crack, is she?'

İkmen sighed. 'No,' he said, 'and who can blame her. However . . .' He walked over to the table and sat down once again. 'She was unfaithful to her husband many years ago and there must have been a reason for that. Lokman is another matter, but if Cahit is the man I think he is, then maybe given time she may reassess what she thinks about him.'

'You mean, if Cahit did order Gözde's death . . .'

'Given time and some thought, she might just break,' İkmen said.

'You're still convinced that the Seyhans did it, are you, sir?'

'Oh yes,' İkmen said. 'I still don't know how, or whose hand actually poured the petrol over the poor girl's head, but people knew about Gözde and Osman Yavuz. The American couple, the Fords. And if they knew, so did others.'

'If only we could find Yavuz!' Ayşe said with a tired sigh.

'If only indeed,' İkmen reiterated. Then a thought came into his mind that caused him to frown. What if the Seyhans had also killed Osman Yavuz?

A visit to a very respectable address in the pretty Bosphorus village of Yeniköy had been followed by a brief foray into the lower depths of the broken-down district of Tarlabaşi.

Both closeted gay or bisexual men and those who persecuted them lived at every level of society. The boy they had just been to talk to had known Hamid İdiz, although he claimed never to have indulged with him in the al fresco sex that the piano teacher had loved so much. Hamid had been, so the boy said, far too 'out' and obvious for a lot of people.

'Some guys feared he called too much attention to, well, us,' the boy had told Süleyman and İzzet Melik. He'd spoken in a soft voice so as not to wake his elderly mother.

Süleyman had asked the boy whether he thought that maybe one or more of these disapproving men could have killed Hamid in order to silence his clearly very free and easy mouth. But the boy said he didn't think that was the case. 'Hamid Bey was way over the top a lot of the time,' he said. 'But he would never deliberately have put anyone apart from himself in harm's way. He was a kind man for all his wild behaviour.'

When Süleyman and İzzet got back in the former's car, the sergeant said, 'Sir, about all these homosexuals and people who hate them . . .'

'Yes?' Süleyman fired up the engine and began to drive off. Their next port of call was a flat in Hasköy.

'Well, none of them are going to own up to doing him in, are they?'

'No. It's what they can tell us, possibly, about others. Frightened people say things, even about their nearest and dearest sometimes. And both the closeted men and the thugs are frightened of us.'

'I'm still not content that we've explored every angle with İdiz's pupils,' İzzet said.

'You mean Murad Emin and Ali Reza Zafir?'

'Tayfun Ergin was at their place of work, the nargile salon, the Tulip,' İzzet said. 'Ergin provides protection.'

'For many, many nargile salons in the city,' Süleyman said. 'What's that got to do with the boys?'

Süleyman turned the car left on to the teeming Tarlabaşı Boulevard, where, as usual, every other car was sounding its horn. He pulled a face. Another wretched traffic jam! He should have taken a chance and tried threading his way through the back streets of Tarlabaşı.

İzzet said, 'Ergin may have nothing at all to do with the boys. He was probably just collecting his protection money from the owner of the Tulip. But word is he's moving into other areas of business, and I just felt uneasy that he was around those kids.'

'That's your paternal instinct coming out.' The car in front very briefly stopped dead, and Süleyman, incensed, threw his hands in the air and said, 'What?'

'Sir, I think that Murad Emin has been radicalised,' İzzet said. 'All that religious stuff, and apparently he won't let Miss Madrid touch him any more, because she's an infidel, so he tells her.'

Now that the car in front had started moving again, Süleyman had his hands back on the steering wheel. 'You've seen Izabella Madrid?'

'You said that I could watch the boys . . .'

Sighing, Süleyman moved the car forward by centimetres. 'I don't know what this fixation is that you have with these boys,' he said tetchily.

İzzet, for his part, wanted to say that he couldn't understand why Süleyman was so set against even considering the possibility that one or other of the boys, probably Murad Emin, had killed Hamid İdiz. Was it because he didn't like working in Balat, where his mistress lived? He had to squash down a sudden urge to tell Süleyman that everyone knew about Gonca and that he might as well own up to her, at least with his colleagues. But he found that he just couldn't do it. Whether it was because he feared the volcanic response any allusion to Süleyman's private life usually engendered, or whether he just felt bad being the bearer of such unwelcome news, he didn't know. But he said nothing.

'If Murad Emin is being radicalised, then you need to pass that on to counterterrorism,' Süleyman said.

Appalled at his superior's rapid escalation of a perceived threat from a teenager, İzzet said, 'Sir, I don't think he's planning to bomb the Topkapı Palace. He's still involved in his music, still keen to win this Turco–Caucasian music festival.'

'So what are you saying?'

'I'm saying that in view of the fact that Murad Emin is seemingly being radicalised in some way, I don't think we can discount him as a suspect in the Hamid İdiz case,' İzzet said. 'The fundamentalists hate queers. Some of these queer-bashers we've seen today . . .'

'Exactly,' Süleyman said. 'Some of their past profiles include luring homosexuals via sexual temptation into places where they can hurt or kill them. We know these men are capable. Murad Emin is a young kid and an unknown quantity. As I say, hand him over to counterterrorism. Maybe there's a computer in his bedroom on to which he's downloaded jihadist material.'

İzzet did not answer. His eyes fixed on the slow-moving boot of the car in front, he wondered why Süleyman was so adamant about Murad Emin. He also recalled that Murad did not possess a computer, because his parents spent all their money on heroin. Living with them was enough to turn any young man's thoughts to other, albeit even more destructive ways of living.

Chapter 19

İkmen had never met Constable Yıldız's brother Ismail before. He knew that he was a rather religious young man, but he hadn't known that he was unemployed.

'My brother hasn't worked for a long time, Çetin Bey,' Hikmet Yıldız said to İkmen. 'But he is a good person, always looking for a job.'

'I would never have even listened to such a suggestion if I hadn't been desperate for work,' Ismail Yıldız said. 'Honestly!'

He was scared. Scared of being in the station, scared of being in the presence of one of his brother's superiors. It wasn't surprising. The people he usually associated with had little contact with the police, and often, little time for them too.

'Mr Yıldız,' İkmen said with a smile, 'what suggestion do you mean? Did someone . . .'

'Last night my brother met with a man who he had been told had some work for him,' Hikmet said.

'Who told him, er, you?' İkmen said as he switched his attention between the two brothers.

'A grocer called Rafik Bey,' Hikmet said.

'He won't get into trouble, will he? I don't want him to get into any—'

'Ismail!' Hikmet turned to his brother and said, 'If this story is to be told, then it must all be told. Rafik, by knowingly putting you on to this man . . .'

'Cem.'

'. . . this Cem, has broken the law,' Hikmet said. 'Do you understand?'

Ismail Yıldız put his head down as if he were a scolded child. When Hikmet was satisfied he would say no more, he continued.

'Çetin Bey,' he said, 'last night, after sunset *adhan*, this Cem took my brother to a coffee house near the Gül Mosque and made him a business proposition.'

İkmen looked at Ismail Yıldız, who was now so nervous he was shaking. 'I didn't do it!' he said. 'I only told him that I would because I thought he might kill me! People like that do!'

'This Cem works as some kind of broker for someone else he would not name,' Hikmet continued. 'What he does, so he says, is to match people up.'

'Match people up?'

Hikmet, in spite of himself, began to smile. This could be, it had to be, the breakthrough that İkmen had been looking for! 'If you have a daughter who is disgracing herself with a boy, or a wife who is being unfaithful, then Cem, or rather the people he recruits, can help you,' he said. 'Sir, this Cem matches up what he calls "nice, pious, poor men" with families who want rid of a woman who is disgracing them. If the assailant is seen, there is no direct connection back to the family, no forensics – these men have clean records – and very little risk. All the families need is money.'

İkmen felt every hair on his head stand up and a long, rapid shiver went down his back. Could this be how Gözde Seyhan had been murdered? Could it possibly have dropped into his lap, just like that? He said, 'Let me get this straight: this man recruits basically good but poor men, with no criminal history, to kill girls and women for money?'

'Some money, yes,' Hikmet said. 'But not a lot. He sells the idea on the basis of religious duty. He knows that there are a lot of people in Fatih who come from villages where honour killing has been accepted for years. He also knows that a lot of the men are poor, desperate and angry.'

'I would never have done it,' Ismail reiterated. 'I only said I would!'

'Mmm.' İkmen frowned. Hikmet was disappointed; he had imagined that the inspector would have been much more pleased about this than he seemed. 'Didn't this man know that you had a brother in the police force?' İkmen asked.

Ismail shrugged. 'I don't know,' he said. 'He didn't say anything about it.'

'Does Rafik Bey the grocer know what Constable Yıldız does for a living?'

'Er . . .'

'Yes, he does, sir,' Hikmet said. 'I sometimes go into his shop to buy cigarettes. He knows I am Ismail's brother.'

İkmen rubbed his chin, then said, 'Because it occurs to me that recruiting the brother of a police officer to do such a job is, or could be, rather stupid.'

'Ah, well, I, er . . .' Ismail Yıldız looked sheepish.

'Well?'

'When I asked Rafik Bey about possibly finding me some

work,' he said, 'I did say that I would do anything. I would! Just not . . . Well, I was angry that day.' He looked over at his brother. 'Hikmet's lack of faith is painful for me sometimes. I feel as if he mocks me and I also imagine that it is worse because he is working and I am not. I have felt for a while that if I worked, I might be able to bring him back to Allah once again, that he would see me as a person and listen to me.'

'I would—'

İkmen cut his constable short with a wave of his hand. 'And you told this Rafik Bey all this, did you, Ismail?'

Again the head was down and the expression was one of embarrassment. 'Well, yes, I, yes . . .'

At last İkmen smiled. 'Well then maybe,' he said, 'if you are at odds with your brother and his world, whoever these people are may well believe that you would do this terrible thing. You don't know whether they had a potential victim in their sights, do you?'

'Cem said they might do,' Ismail replied. 'He said he'd let me know.'

'Well, keep in touch with him.'

'He said he'd call me.'

'Then you must wait for his call.'

'Sir, you don't intend to use Ismail in some way, do you?' Hikmet asked. 'I mean, he is my brother.'

'Who is in need of work,' İkmen said. 'I have work for him, Constable Yıldız.'

'Yes, but it might be . . .'

'Dangerous? Yes, it might,' İkmen said. 'But then maybe he should have thought about the prospect of danger when he went to meet this unknown Cem character.' He looked sternly now at Ismail. 'You know that if you do this, you may well be condemned by some who call themselves religious, don't you?'

'He does know that, yes,' Hikmet said. 'We talked about it, and Ismail . . . He doesn't hold with honour killing, not really.'

'No!'

İkmen looked at the two young men. Both had come to İstanbul as infants from some back-of-beyond village in the east. Their parents had taken well to city life until the earthquake of 1999 had sent them scuttling back to the countryside. Quite what the boys had picked up about traditional country ways and traditions İkmen didn't know, but he was pretty sure at least that Ismail had a somewhat ambiguous attitude towards honour killing. Clearly it did horrify him, otherwise he would never have told Hikmet about Cem and his business proposal. İkmen, though, was concerned that if Ismail acted as an undercover agent for the police, those he mixed with in Fatih would reject him. But he had explained that. Now, for the moment, he had just one other thing to ask Ismail: 'Do you know of a man called Tayfun Ergin?'

'The gangster?'

'Yes. Do you think he might be behind the man called Cem who gave you this job?'

Ismail thought for a moment, going back over his long and very tiring conversation with Cem, then he said, 'I don't know. He didn't mention him. He didn't mention anyone by name. I just don't know.'

* * *

She had known that this would happen. Her nephew, Aykan Akol, was a troublemaker. He liked nothing more than watching a scene he had precipitated unfold before his eyes. He'd told Cahit that Saadet had not come back with the bread but had gone off shopping on her own instead. The fat pig had had to wait for his breakfast. Now her husband was whipping her with his belt and roaring accusations at her, while the hated nephew stood behind the door, sniggering.

'What man did you go off to see, you whore?' Cahit roared as he laid into her bare back with his belt.

'No one! Cahit, I swear . . . !'

'Why should I believe you? Eh? Why?'

'Because I'm telling you the truth!' she said as she tried to protect her face from his belt and his fists. Once she'd left the police station, she'd made sure that she'd done some shopping in order to lend credence to her story. Had anyone seen her get into that car? No one she knew had been on the street when she went down to the baker's. But maybe someone had been watching her from across the road, from up in an apartment, from almost anywhere.

'Slut!' Cahit pulled his fist back and smashed it into her mouth. She heard the crack before she felt any pain. She put two fingers into her mouth and pulled out a broken, bloodied tooth. The sight of it, the blood, the tooth or both, made her want to scream. It had a different effect upon her husband. He was panting with the effort of it all, and looked satisfied, as if the blooding of his wife had sated his rage, if only temporarily.

'Slut,' he reiterated. Now no longer hysterical, he added in a calm voice, 'You will never leave this apartment again. Understand?'

Oh, she understood all right! He was locking her away, just as he had tried to lock Gözde away, just as his own mother had been incarcerated back in the village. She had been a legend. People had said of her that she was so good, she never so much as saw the light of day. Poor woman. As Saadet watched her husband nurse the fist he had broken her tooth with, she had an overwhelming urge to tell him about her daughter. She hadn't thought about that, hadn't allowed herself to remember it, for years. But now that İkmen had reminded her, she suddenly could not get Gözde's real father's face out of her mind. A soldier from İstanbul, just passing through the village, a conscript at least five years her junior. But he'd been so polite, so kind, helping her to carry water from the well. He'd been good-looking, too. He, the man whose name she hadn't even known, had passed on those fine features to her pretty daughter. Her pretty dead daughter, born of the gentle lovemaking Saadet had experienced only once with her soldier. Oh, she wanted to tell Cahit so much! She wanted to hurt him so badly! But all she actually said as she bowed her head in his direction was 'Yes, Cahit.'

He left the room without further comment, locking the door behind him just to make his point. So now she was confined. Locked in an airless apartment with a husband, a sister-in-law and a nephew she hated and who hated her. Her niece she didn't hate; she was just fat and lazy and useless. Only Lokman, her one remaining son, had a place in her heart. But would he help her? Would he let her out in defiance of his own father? It was unlikely and utterly unthinkable should she decide to tell him the truth about his sister's real father. Her son could, she knew, even kill her. But then if she did get out of the Akols' apartment, she didn't have anywhere to go.

Saadet sat down on the floor, took a handkerchief out of her sleeve and held it up to her mouth. A front tooth! Her bully of a husband had knocked out a front tooth! But then who but she would ever see it? No one. She wasn't going out again; it didn't matter. Locked away, she would cook and clean and do what her sister-in-law told her. Cahit would beat her, and occasionally he would force himself on her. Saadet, overwhelmed, began to cry. She couldn't live like that, she just couldn't, not after Gözde, not after Kenan.

Only that policeman, only İkmen, could help her now. But she'd passed up the chance he'd given her only hours before to tell him everything and make a new life for herself. She'd not been ready, she'd been too afraid. And now that time had passed and Cahit had made her his prisoner. The only way she could make things right was to somehow leave the apartment. But how she was going to do that, Saadet just didn't know.

He slipped into the Rainbow Internet Café almost without her noticing. The skinny loner boy the police had been so interested in. He sat down at a computer beside a bunch of trannies, who were so caught up in giggling at something on their machine, they didn't even see him. But the woman with the blood-red nails and the flamboyant dress sense did. She took out the card one of the inspectors had given her and went into the alleyway behind the café to make the call. Fifteen minutes later, Osman Yavuz was being led away into

208

a police car amid the screams and squeaks of the gang of transsexuals.

'I didn't kill Gözde!' the boy said as İkmen and İskender looked at him across the table with still, fathomless eyes. Osman was and always had been completely unnerved by policemen. 'I loved her!'

'Then why did you cut and run when you found out she was dead?' İkmen asked.

'Because I knew you'd think it was me!' Osman Yavuz was not a very impressive boy. Skinny and spotty, he was also pale and very, very nervous. And he smelt bad, giving the distinct impression that he hadn't washed for some time.

'Why would we think it was you?' İskender asked. 'What makes you imagine that we'd think you were so important?'

İskender had a way with a put-down that İkmen found both impressive and unnecessarily cruel. This boy, whatever he may or may not have done, was clearly a nothing in the great city of İstanbul; he hardly needed reminding of that.

Osman Yavuz just hung his head, so İkmen took a different tack. 'Osman,' he said, 'why did you think we'd even know of your existence? Your relationship with Gözde was a secret, wasn't it?'

'Yes.'

'So how would we know about you, then? How would that work?'

The boy looked up. 'Because of her phone,' he said. 'I watch *CSI*, I know what forensics can do with phones even if they're really badly damaged.'

'Just the phone?'

'Well, there was, er . . . there was the American lady who

209

lived in Gözde's building,' Osman said. 'She, er, well she sort of . . .'

'She knew about you and Gözde, yes, we know,' İkmen said.

'She gave Gözde my phone number and she gave me hers,' he said. 'I used to go for English lessons to Mrs Ford, a long time ago. She doesn't do that any more. Gözde called me first. It had to be that way, because if I called her, her dad or one of her brothers might pick up and then she'd be in trouble.'

'What about the photograph?' İskender asked. 'Tell us about that.'

'The photograph?' He knew exactly what the younger, arrogant policeman was talking about, but he needed to buy some time in order to marshal his thoughts. The photographs, all of them, had been madness!

'The photograph of the woman you say you loved, naked, sent to your phone,' İskender said harshly. 'Tell us.'

Osman took a few moments to breathe and then he said, 'It was Gözde's idea . . .'

'Oh, it's always the girl's idea, of course!' İskender, overly familiar with far too many sexters, their habits and excuses, was immediately losing his patience.

İkmen put a calming hand on his arm. 'Go on, Osman.'

Though shaken, the boy did manage to regain his composure and continued, 'Of course I loved that she did that. But she wasn't a bad girl and I didn't suggest it to her! We never did anything wrong. I only met her three times, and only around the back of her building where the washing hangs. Her parents and her brothers were out and Mrs Ford

210

called me over because she said that Gözde was alone. We kissed once. Once!'

'How did you meet or notice Gözde?' İkmen asked.

'I saw her in the street many times.'

'Did she know that you were watching her?'

'No, but later on, when we began to talk and text, she said that she'd noticed me too.' He leaned forward and rested his arms on the table. 'We were in love.' İkmen at least saw that the boy's eyes were full of tears. 'You know that her family killed her, don't you? Because of me.'

He began to sob. Ever since he'd learned of Gözde's death, he had, so he said, been living rough in the great Karaca Ahmet Cemetery in Üsküdar. Living on food and alms begged from visitors, he'd mourned for his lost love every day.

'Why do you think Gözde's family killed her?' İkmen asked. 'Why would they do that?'

'Because of us,' Osman said. 'Because they must have found out about us! Gözde was happy. I spoke to her on the day she died and she was happy because I had told her that somehow I was going to get her out of there and take her away.'

'You didn't think of asking her father for her?' İskender put in slightly sarcastically.

Osman Yavuz laughed, but without any mirth. 'Me? Even getting over the fact that I have no job, Cahit Seyhan would never have considered me. They come from a village where all the families marry each other all the time,' he said. 'Her brother was to marry his cousin and Gözde was supposed to marry some old man her father had picked out for her. I didn't stand a chance.'

'So you had planned to run away together?'

'Yes. If we could. We had no choice.'

İskender, frowning, said, 'But to go back to that photograph ... Did you share it with anyone, Osman? There were a great many printed photographs of other women in all sorts of states of undress in your bedroom at your grandmother's flat.'

İkmen had almost forgotten about those. Osman Yavuz's face went very white and then he put his head down in his hands.

'The truth, Osman, if you please,' İskender said with what İkmen felt was an unnecessarily smug expression on his face.

Chapter 20

In the past, the only people who admitted to crimes they had not committed were, in general, mentally ill. Confused and frightened, they frequently responded to routine inquiries by the police by owning up to things they had not done. But the late 1990s and now the twenty-first century had seen the rise in certain quarters of the fundamentalist or glory-seeking admitter. Together with his boss Mehmet Süleyman, İzzet Melik had spent most of the previous afternoon questioning a known queer-basher and recent religious fundamentalist they had picked up in the district of Sütlüce.

Oh yes, but of course he'd killed Hamid İdiz! The man was a queer and this 'soldier of faith' had done the whole world a favour by cutting his throat like the pig he had been. They all knew he hadn't done it. His wife, an enormous woman who clearly loved her husband but was also exasperated by him, tried to remind him that they had been at her mother's house in the city of Edirne when Hamid İdiz had been killed, but to no avail. And so, because the man was adamant, they'd had to take him in and question him. What a waste of time!

Now it was late, and as İzzet locked his car and began to walk towards the bright lights of the Tophane nargile joints, he hoped that Murad Emin and Ali Reza Zafir had finished their shifts and gone. He was in luck. The Tulip was full of locals and this time some tourists, but the piano was silent, and only the man he knew as the proprietor and a few middle-aged men were now serving. İzzet ordered his usual, an apple tobacco pipe and a medium-sweet coffee, and began to think about what he might do next.

If Murad Emin, at least, was being radicalised, then how was that happening? His home was out of the question, as were his music lessons. School was a possibility, but Süleyman had already contacted them and their opinion of the boy was very high. He was an excellent student without, they felt, any overt religious feelings or opinions. But what the boy was expressing had to come from somewhere, and so far İzzet could think of few places where this could happen. When Murad was not at school or at his music lessons, he was at the Tulip. Although the nargile salon didn't seem like the sort of place where those of a radical nature would meet, he knew that appearances could be deceptive. He also knew that on some level, the gangster Tayfun Ergin had an interest in the place, and as Inspector İkmen had only just found out that very day, Ergin was possibly part of a new business that was being set up in Fatih. This 'company', so İkmen had discovered, made its money by providing people willing to kill to families who wished to dispose of an inconvenient daughter or wife. Honour killings to order. Just the thought of it made İzzet wrinkle up his brow in disgust. What kind of creatures would do such a thing?

His coffee and nargile arrived. How to proceed to find out more about the Tulip, its staff and customers was what exercised İzzet now. Puffing on his pipe, he dismissed the idea of revealing his profession to the owner. There were apparently computers on the site somewhere, although as the proprietor had told him, they were no longer held for the benefit of customers. Staff used them, which could mean that Murad and Ali Reza and maybe other kids too were being radicalised on line. There were *jihadi* and other radical sites all over the internet. Like the mobile telephone, the internet could be a fantastic thing, but it could also be an instrument of such darkness too! Words like 'sexting' and 'grooming' in the context of preparing a young person for sexual assault were terms that hadn't existed until the twenty-first century. But to just ask to use the Tulip's computers out of the blue was not a good idea. To İzzet himself it sounded suspicious, and if other Tulip staff members were either radicalising or being radicalised it would set off all sorts of mental alarm bells. For the time being he would just have to continue to observe, to get to know a few people and gain their confidence.

Later, two middle-aged men came and sat across the table from İzzet and began talking about football. They both supported the local team, Beşiktaş while İzzet was vociferous in his support for his beloved İzmir team, Altay SK. But it was a good-natured exchange, and what was more important, it brought in other customers and members of staff. The owner, İzzet discovered, was called Mustafa Bey. He supported Galatasaray and he also thought that women shouldn't go to football matches. Women, he said, shouldn't really leave the house.

*　　*　　*

215

'Get out!' she hissed. It was dark and her lover was deeply asleep, but Gonca could see that someone else was in her bedroom too. Someone familiar and yet unwanted, leaning over her bed. She got up as quietly as she could, pushing the weighty bulk of the unwanted man before her. As she closed the bedroom door behind her, Mehmet Süleyman murmured just the once and then apparently descended into a deep slumber once again.

The kitchen was about as far away from her bedroom as she could get, and so Gonca took the intruder through several bedrooms filled with sleeping children and confronted him there.

'What do you want, Şukru?' she said to the middle-aged man who stood in front of her. 'What do you mean by breaking into my house? My bedroom?'

Şukru spread his arms wide and said, 'May a brother not see his sister once in a while? However eccentric she may be?'

Şukru was a few years older than Gonca. A large, dark father of eight who in his youth had been both a wrestler and a trainer of dancing bears. Now he made his living as so many gypsies did since the break-up of their largest community, in Sulukule, by moving from one unsatisfying casual job to another. The gypsies in İstanbul were not what they had been. State legislation to first stop their women dancing in makeshift bars up by the city walls, then to take away the bears and finally to dismantle Sulukule had rendered many of the men jobless and bitter. Şukru was lucky that he had a famous artist for a sister who was also very generous, and he knew it. But he was also a man

216

who possessed traditional gypsy values. In addition, he had come on this occasion as an emissary from their father.

'People are saying that you love that policeman,' he said as he tipped his head in the direction of Gonca's bedroom. 'Is it true?'

She sat down at the kitchen table and lit a long black cigarette. 'Yes.' She said it simply and quickly, because the truth needed no embellishment.

'Ah.' Her brother sat down opposite and took a cigarette for himself. 'You know that he is married, that he is—'

'I know he is married, I know he is not one of my kind, I know that he is a policeman and so an enemy of my people,' Gonca said. 'You can tell our father that I know all that.'

Şukru would never have come of his own volition. Their father, who claimed that he was over a hundred years old and had fathered over a hundred children, had sent him. He was very prominent and powerful within the gypsy community, and this visit was all about him.

'Gonca, you can take lovers,' Şukru said as he lit his cigarette and began to puff. 'We have always known that is what you do, but—'

'I married men from our community twice,' Gonca said. 'Twice, Şukru! Two useless lumps of flesh who neither worked nor looked after the children they sired! Now I am beyond all that; I want something for myself!'

'But if you love this man, then—'

'Then that is my business!' she said.

'Gonca, he's a married man!'

Contrary to what most non-gypsies believed, the people of Sulukule as well as in other settled gypsy communities

217

were very morally proper. Gonca, with her wildly eccentric and very collectable collages, with her legions of lovers and her clear delight in the sexual act, was an exception. Everyone, including her father, knew it.

'It has been said that you intend to marry this man,' Şukru said with obvious concern in his voice. 'Is that true?'

She shrugged. 'If I want to marry him, then I will,' she said. 'If not, then . . .'

She shrugged again, trying to seem casual about it, even though that was very far from the truth. She was besotted by the policeman; she would have stuck her head in a fire if he had asked. If he suddenly said that he didn't want to see her again, she'd kill his wife first, then him, then herself. She had it all planned. Never had she felt anything like this in her life. She was going to cling on to it with every gram of strength that she possessed.

'But you can't marry him,' Şukru said. 'He is a policeman. They will never allow it, not to one of us!'

She looked at her brother, who she could see was the image of herself, and then she looked down at the table. What the police authorities would make of Mehmet Süleyman marrying her had not occurred to her. Now at Şukru's prompting she did think about it. It was not a comfortable notion.

'And that he is married is not right!' Şukru said. 'Need I go on, Gonca? Need I even get to the part about how different you are from him?'

She put her head down still further and then shook it, making her floor-length hair shudder and sway towards her brother as she did so.

'You know what can happen if you marry out, don't you?' he said.

She knew, but she didn't make any sort of movement to indicate that she did. The punishment for marrying out was well known and did not need to be reiterated.

'Father is not happy, but he is content for you to take lovers like this, as you know,' Şukru said. 'But love? Even when children cannot result from such a union, it's still not right, Gonca. We cannot have that man in our family. You cannot take him away from his people.'

She looked up at him with disgust. They were all quite happy for her to have a policeman as a lover while she could potentially find out information from him, while they could whisper in her ear periodically, as they did, that she should think about blackmailing him. 'So I can fuck his brains out, but I cannot love him?'

'Sister, you—'

'What?' He was halfway across the table now with his fingers at her throat. 'Don't want to think about your sister with a cock inside her? Oh, you are a hypocrite, Şukru,' she said. 'You who take so readily the money that the world outside the gypsy city gives me!'

He loosened his grip on her neck and stood up. 'I come as a messenger from the family,' he said. 'I come for all of us.'

'To come into my bedroom and frighten me half to death!'

'No,' he said as he once again leaned down on to the table and took her by the throat. 'No. To tell you, Gonca, that if you do not give this man up and stop this stupid pining for something you cannot have, you will be killed. You and your policeman both. That way, if in no other, his family and ours may regain some honour, some dignity and some self-respect.'

He left then. Gonca, no longer angry or confident or defiant, sat at the kitchen table shaking and drinking *rakı* on her own until dawn broke. Only then did she return to her bedroom and look down at the sleeping body of Mehmet Süleyman. Then, and quite at odds with her usual way of expressing herself, Gonca very quietly cried.

They'd asked him why he'd gone back to the Rainbow Internet Café and were amazed at the mundanity of his answer.

'I had to pick up my e-mail,' Osman Yavuz had told İkmen and İskender towards the end of his interview. 'It had been ages. I was worried.'

'About what?' İkmen had asked him. 'What on earth could be that important that it caused you to risk your liberty?'

'I needed to know if I had any messages,' he'd said. 'If you're not on line, then you just don't exist, you know?' It had sounded so limp, so bloody stupid. Which it was.

What had also been stupid was the sexting. He'd never got Gözde involved in that; he'd never shown her picture to anyone. But the fact that he had shared pictures of other girls in the past with friends and acquaintances meant that the police didn't believe him. They wanted to know who else he'd shown Gözde's picture to, and he just couldn't tell them, because it had never happened.

'You have not convinced me, at least,' Inspector İskender had said, 'that you did not abuse that girl's trust, that you did not in fact kill her when she threatened to tell her parents that you forced her into providing that photograph.'

'I didn't kill her, I loved her!'

'Then why did you make her send a naked photograph of herself to you?' İskender said. 'What were you going to do with it if you didn't share it with your friends? Use it to masturbate?'

'No!' Osman felt his face flush at the word, and yet he *had* used pictures to gain relief, just like all the other nerds he knew around and about İstanbul. He'd even, to his shame, used that picture that Gözde had sent him. But why not? In spite of what the American woman had told him, in spite of what he had told his love, he was never going to actually be with Gözde. They were never really going to run away together and live happily every after. That never happened in real life. Something, usually parents, always got in the way. 'When my grandma told me that the Mersin Apartments were on fire, I knew,' he said.

'Knew?'

'That it was Gözde,' he said. 'That they had killed her. I ran into the street and I saw that it was the ground floor that was alight and I knew!' He put his head down and sobbed.

İskender looked at İkmen, who appeared to be genuinely sorry for the boy.

'Osman,' the older man said gently, 'we will have to know the names of the people you shared photographs with.'

The boy continued to weep.

'Osman . . .'

'Osman Yavuz,' Inspector İskender said tartly, 'we need to know who the other men you exchanged photographs with were, and we need to know that now!'

'But I . . .' Osman Yavuz raised his tear-stained face and

looked into the hard features of his interrogator. 'They were just people I met at the Rainbow sometimes. Anyway, I told you, I never showed any of them that picture of Gözde.'

'The fact that you shared lewd pictures at all is appalling and against the law!' İskender roared.

'But I don't know who they are!' Osman wept. 'We meet, we talk, I don't know their names! Not all of them!'

'Well then, we'll have the names that you do know!' İskender slapped a pen down on the table in front of the boy and said, 'Get writing!'

But when it came to it, Osman couldn't. He couldn't think straight, much less remember the names of people he hardly knew. They'd just been boys swapping pictures they'd taken off their dad's phone, their elder brother's BlackBerry. Nameless nerds, just like him. Because he couldn't remember, and because they still did not entirely believe his story about Gözde, the police decided to detain him. Osman sat in a small, cold cell and tried not to cry when he thought about what his grandma might say.

Chapter 21

Ismail Yıldız paced back and forth across the small kitchen he shared with his brother Hikmet, nursing his silent mobile phone in his hands. Hikmet, who was trying to eat his breakfast in something resembling peace, said, 'Will you sit down, Ismail? You're making me dizzy.'

'I just want him to ring,' Ismail said. 'Cem. He said that he had a girl lined up. Why doesn't he just call me?'

'Because he isn't ready yet,' Hikmet said as patiently as he could. 'We wait for him, remember? You can't force anything. If you do, it will look very suspicious and he will back off. Remember what Çetin Bey said.'

'Yes, I know, but . . .'

'I understand that you're scared,' Hikmet said. 'Going under cover is always frightening, but you won't be alone. You'll have the whole team at your back. As soon as we've found out who this Cem is and what he's doing, we can pull him, and hopefully the others he works with too.'

Ismail sat down at the table and watched Hikmet shell and then eat a hard-boiled egg. 'Do you really think that he works for that gangster? Tayfun Ergin?'

'I don't know,' Hikmet replied. 'Ergin has been active in this area lately. It's possible.'

'Oh.' Ismail put a nervous hand up to his lips, his face white with tension and lack of sleep.

Hikmet laid a hand on his brother's wrist and said, 'It will be all right.'

'*İnşallah.*'

But Ismail was not convinced. He'd asked his brother the same set of questions almost continually ever since they'd left the station the previous afternoon. It was because he was scared, because he wanted whatever was going to happen to happen quickly and be done with. But there was no hurrying something like this. A link had been made with a man who apparently arranged honour killings for money, and it was now up to this man, Cem, to take the process to the next level. What Hikmet didn't tell his brother was what İkmen had told him, which was that he was half expecting Cem and his 'business' to be entirely chimerical.

'This man has to know you're a police officer,' İkmen had confided to him. 'It could so easily be a feint, a distraction, even a wind-up.'

'My brother is known as a very religious man, Çetin Bey,' Hikmet had countered. 'Maybe in this fashion they seek to distance him from me?'

İkmen had accepted that that was possible. He'd sent his officer and his officer's brother home to do what they were doing, which was to wait.

'Hikmet, if something goes wrong . . .'

At that very moment Ismail's mobile began to ring.

In his panic he almost dropped it. 'Allah!'

With terrified eyes he looked over at his brother, who said, 'For heaven's sake, answer it!'

With fingers that sweated and shook so much he could barely control them, Ismail Yıldız eventually managed to push the receive button and then said, 'Yes?'

There was a tense second before Hikmet saw him take a deep calming breath and then say, 'Oh, hello, Mother, how are you?'

Cem, whoever he was, was not going to call when Ismail or anyone else wanted him to. As Hikmet had known right from the start, this was going to be a waiting game.

The American woman, Mrs Jane Ford, had expressed little surprise when Osman Yavuz's name had been brought up by Mehmet Süleyman. But then the young man had told İkmen that Mrs Ford had, once upon a time, been his English teacher. Later, in his cell, he'd told İkmen that she'd been something else to him, too.

'I didn't want you to think that I was close to him,' Jane Ford told İkmen when he and Ayşe Farsakoğlu visited her at her apartment. Her husband was at work and so she was alone, working on her Make the Most of İstanbul website, when they called.

'Why not?'

Mrs Ford looked him straight in the eye and said, 'Osman and myself . . . well, look, I had a little bit of a fling with the boy. So unserious, so much an aberration! This was before he became besotted with Gözde. I was glad when he got so stuck on her! What was I thinking! So I helped him to meet her. She was sweet and he was all sexed and romanced up!'

According to Jane Ford, she had in effect wound the boy up sexually and then just let him go. The sexting, which had

followed her desertion of him, was now a little more understandable. Nevertheless, İkmen left the Fords' apartment in
a dark and gloomy mood. Looking at his watch as he got
back in his car, he said to Ayşe, 'It's midday. Let's get some
lunch.'

Because this was İkmen and not someone like Inspector
İskender, who really appreciated good food, they didn't end
up having their lunch at a restaurant or even at a café. He
drove down to Tophane and selected a nargile salon at
random. It was called the Peace Pipe. 'You can get a sandwich here,' he said as he looked with a cursory eye over the
menu. 'If you like that sort of thing.'

Ayşe ordered a cheese sandwich and a coffee and agreed
to join İkmen in an apple tobacco nargile. She liked water-
pipe smoking but she had also agreed to join him in order
to prevent him from getting a *tömbeki*. His smoker's cough
was quite bad enough without a massive hit of raw leaf
tobacco.

As they waited for their order to be brought to them, İkmen
said, 'Is it just my suspicious mind, or do you think it possible
that Mrs Ford might be a suspect in the Gözde Seyhan case?'

Ayşe furrowed her brow. 'Mrs Ford? Why?'

'She was in the vicinity, her own apartment, when the fire
that killed Gözde began,' he said. 'She'd had an affair with
the boy the girl was seeing, the girl the boy was besotted by.'

'But she said that her fling with Osman was just that, a
fling, an aberration.'

'She tells us.' He shrugged. 'It's just a thought. I'm putting
it out there because it's in my head and because the woman
lied.'

'No one wants to be even remotely connected to a murder, sir,' Ayşe said. 'I think that self-preservation kicks in with most people. That and panic.'

'Mmm.' Ayşe's food, the nargile and their drinks arrived and İkmen fitted his mouthpiece into the pipe and fired it up. As usual, he wasn't eating. 'I do wonder, though,' he said, 'how an older woman like Mrs Ford would take the news that a lover, albeit a discarded one, had taken up with a young and pretty girl.'

Jane Ford was not much older than Ayşe who now looked down at her sandwich with apparent rapt attention. 'I don't know.'

'I'm just thinking it might have injured her pride,' İkmen said. 'Inspector Süleyman had a look at her Make the Most of İstanbul website, you know, and found it very informative. He also told me it was rather sad, too. There are a lot of lonely foreigners in this city, and not a few of them take up with us. Apparently they find us rather alluring.'

Ayşe smiled. Time was when she had found Mehmet Süleyman 'rather alluring'. She still did, although these days she had that well and truly under control.

'And on the basis that not every lonely heart is single, Mrs Ford clearly found her own way around her loneliness very close to home.'

'Poor Mr Ford.'

'Indeed.' İkmen cleared his throat. 'But my point is, Ayşe, that we have to be open to possibilities here. Mrs Ford was in the Mersin Apartments when the fire began and she did have a potential motive to kill Gözde Seyhan. Discarded or not, Osman Yavuz had been her lover.'

'But she helped him contact Gözde Seyhan!'

'Maybe in the hope that he'd get over her, reject her, that her parents would put a stop to it? I don't know,' İkmen said. 'But the DNA the forensic institute discovered on the petrol can we found in the Seyhan apartment has to belong to someone.'

'How do we obtain Mrs Ford's DNA, unless . . .'

'I can't arrest her on a hunch,' İkmen said. His face fell and he sighed. 'But who am I kidding? I know it was the Seyhans. Saadet was so close to cracking yesterday. If only . . .' He leaned forward and squinted at something or someone apparently behind Ayşe's shoulder. 'Isn't that Cahit Seyhan?'

She turned and looked over her shoulder. The thin, shambling figure of Cahit Seyhan had indeed entered the establishment next door to the Peace Pipe. Unnoticed, İkmen and Ayşe watched him sit down and order a pipe from a waiter at an establishment the owner of the Peace Pipe told him was called the Tulip.

As sure as the sun rose in the east, it was certain that one day Mehmet Süleyman and İzzet Melik would come to a point where one would say an unwanted thing to the other. It had all started out with İzzet telling his superior about his most recent foray into the Tulip nargile salon.

'If I can get the confidence of the punters as well as the staff, I know I can get in to look at their computers without arousing suspicion,' he said.

'And yet you will have to do it while neither Murad Emin nor Ali Reza Zafir is working,' Süleyman replied. 'It seems like a lot of effort for what I still believe is a non-existent case. But then if you choose to do this on your own time . . .'

For several minutes, in spite of İzzet's inner fury at his ideas still being dismissed in such a cursory manner, they talked of other things. Then İzzet, unable to keep quiet any longer, said, 'So much radicalisation happens on line these days. Young boys like Murad, like Ali Reza are very vulnerable to these messages and—'

'Oh, will you please stop it with these two boys! On and on!' Süleyman said. 'There are other suspects, you know, other people with real issues against poor old Hamid İdiz.'

It had been at that point that İzzet had exploded. It had been at that point that he had taken that irreversible step over into his superior's private life.

'Why do you want to avoid Murad Emin?' he cried. 'Is it because he lives so close to where your mistress the gypsy lives?'

They were both standing by this time, but now İzzet took a step back. Süleyman's face was so dark with blood it was almost black. İzzet inwardly reminded himself that he was no slacker when it came to defending himself. He also decided that since there was no way back from what he had said already, he might as well continue.

'Inspector, everyone knows about you and Gonca the gypsy,' he said. 'I know, the men in the squad room know, Inspector İkmen knows, all of Balat is abuzz with it! Miss Madrid the music teacher told me that people all over the city have heard about it!'

Süleyman was like stone. Nothing moved except for a very

slight rise and fall of his chest as he breathed. But his eyes burned into İzzet's face.

'I've told no one,' İzzet said. 'That I promise you. But you have to accept that people know, that there's no point trying to pretend.'

Still the inspector did not respond. İzzet had not expected that and now found that he didn't know what to do next. Should he reassure Süleyman that everyone was basically on his side? Or should be really stick the knife in and tell him what Izabella Madrid had told him about how Gonca's people were unlikely to let the situation between them develop still further?

'If you really are avoiding Murad Emin in case you are seen by people the gypsy knows who may talk, then you can stop doing that,' İzzet said. 'There's no point.'

Süleyman tried to put one foot in front of the other, then gave up and resumed his seat once again. The world, or so it seemed, knew! In spite of everything he had done to keep it quiet, it was common knowledge. And because it was common knowledge, Murad Emin's prostitute of a mother had known! Of course she had! All at once he felt humiliated and stupid and frightened. If everyone knew, what about his wife? He hadn't been home for days; he had no idea whether she knew about Gonca or not. The fear that she did and that she would as a result take Yusuf away from him robbed him of his breath.

'Inspector?' İzzet had bent down to look carefully at his superior, who had suddenly gone from being very red in the face to very, very white.

Süleyman knew that İzzet was concerned. For all his

macho-man posturing, the sergeant was a good person who he knew respected him. It must have taken a lot of courage for him to tell his boss what he had. But Süleyman was still furious. How dare İzzet even breathe the gypsy's name within his hearing; how dare he bring such humiliation down upon him! As soon as he could find his voice he looked at the sergeant and said, 'Just go. Don't argue with me. Just leave.'

İzzet Melik left. It was the end of his shift anyway, and so, albeit with a very heavy heart, he made his way out of the station, into his car and over to Tophane and the Tulip nargile salon.

That night, he raped her. He'd done it before, but not for many years. He'd done it just before she met her lovely soldier out in the fields, Gözde's tender father. Then, as now, Cahit had put his hands over her mouth to stop her screaming as he forced himself into her. Saadet cried because she was both humiliated and hurt. She thought about her soldier and about her poor dead Gözde and how much the girl had looked like the man who had been her real father. The thought of him helped her to some extent to bear what Cahit was doing to her. He was a beast, he always had been! That his daughter had not been his and that neither of his sons had really taken after him was a judgement upon him. Even Lokman, for all his macho swagger, was not like him. Sometimes she could see the hatred in her son's eyes when he looked at his father. But then Cahit deserved no less.

She looked up into his cragged, straining face as he pushed himself into her for the last time and wished with all of her soul that he would die. As far as she knew, she was still able

231

to bear children, and he, her pig of a husband, had deliberately forced himself upon her without using contraception. What a terrible thing it would be to become pregnant again at her age. By her hated husband, the beast, the murderer. Saadet closed her eyes, as much to blot out the word in her head as to hide Cahit's sated face. He got off her and she heard him zip his trousers up. He'd never, even when they were young, made love to her naked. There'd never been the freedom to do that in his parents' house, which was where they had lived when they were first married. A house always full of people and animals. Only her soldier had ever made love to her naked. They'd found a spot underneath some olive trees, where he had undressed himself and then her. He'd kissed and caressed her body for what had seemed like hours before they'd had intercourse. After that, aroused again, she'd mounted him. He'd told her how beautiful she was and she'd even hoped that he would just throw his uniform into a ditch and offer to run away with her. But he hadn't. He'd been a very patriotic boy. But he still cried when his company moved on to the next village. She had seen him do it.

'You should be honoured that I still want to relieve myself with you,' she heard her husband say as he sat down on a chair to lace up his boots. 'I could get that anywhere I wanted.'

'Then why don't you!' Saadet found herself saying, more vehemently than she knew could be healthy for her. 'You used nothing, I could be pregnant!'

Cahit smiled. 'I need a son to replace the unnatural thing that Kenan became.'

232

'We can never replace Kenan!' Saadet began to cry, although with rather more fury than grief. 'We can no more replace him than we can replace Gözde!'

'That little slut!' Cahit grimaced and then spat on the floor. 'You give me a boy, woman, or I'll kill you!' He began to walk towards the door, which he unlocked with the key he'd had in his pocket. 'In the meantime you can stay in here and make my baby. That will keep you in where I can know where you are!'

With a head full of hatred and a heart full of grief, Saadet began to cry and scream as she heard Cahit lock her into that tiny, airless room once again. With every fibre of her soul she hoped that he hadn't made her pregnant. She looked down at her belly and began to pound at it with her fists, but then as quickly as she had attacked herself she stopped. Killing whatever might be nascent within her wasn't the answer. Getting out was what she had to do; there really was no other reasonable option. Inspector İkmen had asked her for the truth many, many times, and now at last she was ready to tell him. It would, she knew, be beyond anything he had ever heard before. The wickedness of it!

But first she would have to get out – somehow. She got up and stood on a chair to look out of her one solitary window. At three floors up it was much too high for her to either climb out or jump. She'd have to find some other way. She thought about the only times she was ever allowed out of that room, to go to the bathroom, and about the people who supervised her. There was her husband, his sister, her nephew and her niece. There was also, occasionally, Lokman. Now if she could somehow get to speak to him alone . . .

Chapter 22

The owner of the Tulip nargile salon, Mustafa Bey, had been, so İzzet learned, a taxi driver.

'But you know how it is, İzzet Bey,' he told İzzet as he placed a confidential arm around his shoulder, 'one becomes tired of the streets, of trying to negotiate this madness that we call our city.'

'Absolutely.' İzzet had told Mustafa that he was a wrestling coach. It was what his older brother did for a living and was something that the whole Melik family had always been extremely enthusiastic about. Earlier he'd suddenly come across the boy, Murad Emin, who had walked over to serve him. The boy had not seemed to recognise him. That or he had chosen not to acknowledge him. Whatever the reason, İzzet had a very strong feeling that even if Murad did recognise him, he wouldn't tell his employer that he was a policeman. If İzzet was right, Murad would just want to keep his head well and truly down. Ali Reza Zafir, his friend, did not appear to be at work.

Mustafa knew his wrestling, and for a while he and İzzet talked about the modern sport, discussing moves and holds, and the great festival of oil wrestling that took place every year in the city of Edirne. İzzet was not entirely sure where

235

the conversation was going and how he might turn it to his advantage when Mustafa began to talk about wrestling in days gone by.

'People just don't talk about the golden days of the Ottoman sport any more,' he said sadly. 'I mean, my great-grandfather saw Alico wrestle. He was only a child and Alico was at the end of his career, but he saw him. I don't suppose any of the lads that you train even know who Alico was, do they, İzzet Bey?'

İzzet admitted that his 'lads' most certainly did not know who Alico, once the Sultan's champion, or any of the other wrestlers from the late Ottoman period were.

'All they do, the young people, is talk on their mobile phones and sit in front of the computer all day long,' Mustafa said gloomily. 'If they would get a book out and look these things up, then they might actually learn something.'

İzzet had a sudden flash of inspiration. 'But Mustafa Bey,' he said, 'you and I both know they won't do that.'

'More's the pity!'

Assuming the identity of a grumpy middle-aged man with little time for youth was not difficult for İzzet Melik. His own teenage children were hundreds of miles away with his ex-wife in İzmir. Whenever he saw them they treated him like a rather inconvenient stranger and were indeed much more interested in talking to their friends on their mobile phones or on social networking sites. 'Unless information is on a computer screen, they just won't pay attention,' he said.

'Oh, I know!' Mustafa agreed. 'These boys who work here, whenever they're not serving, they're out the back on those computers! On the net! My customers are adults, they can't be bothered by such things. But the boys . . .' He threw his arms up in despair. 'I only keep the wretched machines because I don't think the boys would come to work if I didn't have them. They must be "on line" all the time. Tell me, İzzet Bey, are you a slave to these machines?'

İzzet said that he wasn't. In fact he went further and said that although he knew how to use a computer, he didn't actually possess one of his own.

'Probably very wise,' Mustafa said gloomily. 'If you had one, your lads would be forever on that instead of practising their holds.'

'I agree,' İzzet said. 'Although with regard to what we were talking about before, it would be nice if the boys could look up information on famous athletes like Alico.'

'That's true.'

'I mean, if it were on a screen, they would look at it, wouldn't they? Assuming of course that such information is on the net . . .'

'Oh, it's all there,' Mustafa said. 'Everything's on the net. A lot of it is rubbish and some of it is incorrect, and of course it's all very basic. But you can go and look up Alico, Mehmet of Kurtdere or anyone you like on my machine if you want to.'

'What . . .' İzzet's natural instinct had been to say *What, now? Thank you very much.* But he restrained himself. To seem too eager, especially when Murad Emin was around, might be seen as suspicious. He did not, after all, want to inadvertently jog the boy's memory of him. Looking at the computers and hopefully seeing some evidence of who might have been viewing what was for another day, when Murad was not working. 'That's very kind of you, Mustafa Bey,' he said. 'I may well take you up on that kind offer at some point.'

Mustafa shrugged. 'It's nothing,' he said. 'The things are on all the time; just go in and look up whatever you want. All the kids do it. Why not you?'

'Why not indeed.'

As İzzet left the Tulip later on that night, he saw the light from the two computer screens seeping through the curtains at the back of the salon. He also heard the muffled sounds of young male voices coming from the same direction. He would, he decided, come back again at lunchtime the following day, when Murad Emin would be at school, and take Mustafa Bey up on his offer of some time on the internet.

Mehmet Süleyman had telephoned his wife in a fog-like daze. He'd been so convinced that she would know about Gonca that he could feel his ears actually cringing away from the telephone as he spoke to her. But his wife, though cold, had clearly not heard anything about the gypsy. She was a woman with a famously hot temper who would, he knew, have been completely incapable of keeping such a scandalous example of his infidelity to herself. She'd just asked him where he was staying and he had told her that he was going to be lodging with a friend for the time being. She did not ask him what gender said friend might be. But then she was, or professed to be, totally uninterested in her husband as a person.

He went over to Gonca's house. As soon as she saw him park his car outside, the gypsy hustled her children out of

238

the house and into the yard and the street. Some of them viewed him with resentment as they passed, but that was nothing new. He was a man their mother was fucking who was not their father – and he was a policeman into the bargain. They met in the kitchen, where they kissed, and then she took him by the hand and pulled him into her bedroom. He had planned to at least broach the subject of everyone apparently knowing about their affair, but Gonca had other plans. She undressed him slowly, licking his face, his chest, his balls before pushing him down on to her bed and climbing on top of him. That first, desperate coupling was followed by many others as she gave and received pleasure as greedily as she had done the very first time they had met. He loved it. Even though it made him feel guilty for the conversation he knew he was going to have to have with her about their relationship, he couldn't stop himself being aroused and then satisfied by her. Watching her come to orgasm as he held her down on the bed and made love to her, he wanted so much to tell her that he was in fact *in love* with her. But he didn't. And when they'd finished that time, she did not attempt to arouse him again but instead turned to him with a serious expression on her face and said, 'My darling, we must talk about something. It's something very bad.'

The dead of night in their little quarter of Fatih was indeed as dark and as quiet as the grave. Those of a religious nature, Hikmet Yıldız was discovering, were very predictable and conservative in their personal habits. Unless it was Ramazan, everyone went inside early and closed their doors behind them. Summer was a little more liberal, with groups of sleepless young children playing in their yards or in the street, their veiled mothers watching them intently from dark doorways. But even then the noise was not great, not like the constant rows and screams and blaring music they had endured back in the days when the Yıldız family had lived in their rackety old apartment block. Hikmet rather missed it now that his nights were punctuated by a stillness that he personally found a little spooky. The faithful were sleeping the sleep of the just and would only be disturbed in order to attend to their devotions.

Hikmet lit a cigarette and thought about his brother sleeping, or trying to sleep, with his mobile phone on his pillow. Ismail wasn't dealing with his new-found 'job' at all well. He'd got himself into this situation with the mysterious Cem all on his own. Now Hikmet, for reasons that were not just about his brother and his security, was helping him to extricate himself from it, and hopefully assisting in the solution of a terrible crime as well. To honour kill for money was a notion almost beyond belief. But on a purely practical level it made a lot of sense. To use a service whereby a complete stranger committed a murder for you was, he felt, simple genius. None of Gözde Seyhan's family had been anywhere in the vicinity of the family's apartment when the girl burnt to death, yet someone had killed her, and the most likely candidate for that was some sort of proxy. The girl had been seeing a boy; she had apparently, poor kid, been very happy.

Hikmet had only seen Cahit Seyhan, Gözde's father, once. A thin, dried-out, ratty man who looked as if a strong gust of wind would knock him over. He had what Hikmet considered to be the close-together eyes and spiteful expression of a bully. The type that would use cultural norms and religion as excuses to victimise and harass others. After all, it wasn't as if Hikmet didn't have respect for religion; he did. His parents were very religious, kind and peace-loving people who would rather die themselves than take a life, whatever the reason. Unfortunately the world was not always like his parents.

Hikmet started to drift off to sleep at about two o'clock. Less than half an hour later, the sound of his brother's ringtone, a weird cheep-cheeping bird-like sound, woke him, and within seconds Ismail was in his bedroom, his phone pressed to his ear.

'It's him,' he said, his eyes shining with terror through the darkness as he held a hand over the mouthpiece. 'Cem!'

'He *will* kill you,' Gonca said. 'Şukru never makes idle threats.'

'Then I will have him arrested,' Süleyman said. 'People who kill police officers go to prison for life.'

'No, no, you don't understand!' she said. She'd been struggling to make him understand for some hours and he still didn't seem to get it. 'It isn't just my brother. It isn't even *all* my seven brothers. It's my whole family. You are not one of us, you can never be one of us. You have to go.'

They were still in her bedroom, still in her bed, but neither of them was naked any longer. She had started it, covering herself up when she had first spoken to him after their hours of lovemaking. Now he was covered also. It seemed more appropriate.

'Gonca, you and I have been seeing each other on and off for years,' he said. 'Your children know, they can't avoid knowing, and so I assumed that your extended family had to be aware of my existence too.'

'They were, they are,' she said, her eyes cast down now. 'Yes.'

'So what has changed?' he asked. He was truly baffled, and quite rightly so.

Gonca said nothing. How could she tell him that she loved him? That was not and could never be realistic. Besides, she didn't know what his response would be. Would he be horrified that a mere mistress had fallen for him? Would it make him angry, or even worse, would it hurt him that her love for him had ruined what they had?

He put a hand on her arm and said, 'Gonca, I don't want to lose you. We have . . . we have some good, er, times together, you and I.'

She knew that he had difficulty articulating just what their relationship was, but she was aware of the fact that he most certainly did not consider her just a cheap lay. They were far too close for that. But she chose to misinterpret what he said, hoping it would silence his puzzled questions.

'We have good sex,' she said.

'I like to think that we don't *just* have sex.'

'But what else is there?' She glanced up into his eyes, which now looked even more confused than they had done before. 'We don't talk, do we?'

'Yes we do!' He sat up and pulled her chin around so that she faced him full on. 'You know we do! And even if we didn't, what business, suddenly, is this of your family?'

242

'They don't like it. If it carries on, my brother will kill you.'

'Yes, but I don't—'

'Don't try to understand, just go!' she said. She was very close to tears, which she did not want him to see.

Mehmet Süleyman played around with the idea of telling her how he felt, but then rejected it. He knew how she was when she was adamant; he also knew that threats made by members of İstanbul's gypsy community were not to be taken lightly. He'd worked on a few cases in the past that had involved gypsies, and he had come to regard them as people of utter conviction. If Gonca's family wanted him dead, then he would die, life sentence or no life sentence. A life would be sacrificed to prison in order to safeguard the family's honour. Another form of honour killing. As he looked into Gonca's dampening eyes, he wondered how, when and where they might try to do it. After gazing at her for a long time, he said, 'I'll go then.'

She shook free of his hand and turned away. 'Good.'

He wanted to carry on and tell her that he didn't want to go, but he didn't do that. Instead he asked if he might have a shower, a request that Gonca acceded to. And so he washed and then, after getting his things together, he left. It was five o'clock in the morning when he got into his car and began to drive off to who knew where. Now that his marriage was basically at an end, he had nowhere to go and no one to talk to about what had just happened. Once again he was rootless, and once again he faced the prospect of returning to his parents' home in Arnavautköy with his tail between his legs. The lack of knowledge about what had just happened hit him again, and he began to feel tears of fury rising up behind his eyes. He had been dismissed, frightened off and chased away, and he didn't like it.

Chapter 23

The girl was called Sabiha; she was sixteen and she was
going to be alone in her parents' apartment in the Çarşamba
district of Fatih that evening after seven.

'The family want it to look like suicide,' Ismail Yıldız
told his brother Hikmet, Çetin İkmen and Ayşe Farsakoğlu.
'That is what Cem told me.'

They had all met up at the small restaurant underneath
İkmen's apartment. Meeting at the station might have alerted
the mysterious Cem to the fact that Ismail Yıldız was not
quite who he appeared to be.

'What did you tell him?' İkmen asked.

'I told him I'd do it,' Ismail replied. It was a warm morning,
but he was trembling and blue with cold. Rarely, if ever, had
İkmen seen someone so scared. 'The family will leave a key
underneath the doormat outside the front door.'

'How will you do it?'

'I said I'd burn her.' He winced as he said the words.
'Like you told me, Çetin Bey.'

'He was happy with that?'

'He said the family did not expect to live in their apartment again. They didn't care what happened to it. Cem said
I'd get two thousand lire.'

'I wonder what his cut is?' Ayşe said bitterly.

'Considerably more, I imagine,' İkmen said.

'What are we going to do?' Ismail said. 'What—'

'Well you, Ismail, are going to go to a garage and purchase some petrol,' İkmen said. 'Can't have a fire without accelerant.'

'Yes, but . . .'

'What are the arrangements for after the murder?' İkmen asked. 'What are you supposed to do then?'

'I wait for Cem to call me,' Ismail said. 'Once he knows that the girl is dead, that the fire is set and I'm away, he'll call me. Then I will arrange with him to collect the money.'

'Will he watch the fire, do you think?' Hikmet Yıldız asked.

Ismail shrugged. 'I don't know!' Turning to İkmen again, he said, 'What are we going to do?'

'Well, you're going to set fire to an apartment and then run away,' İkmen said.

'Allah!' Ismail Yıldız wrung his hands until they went purple.

'You get to have some pyrotechnic fun, while we get to rescue the girl,' İkmen said. 'We call the fire brigade and get her out.'

'Yes, but . . .'

'We'll only take her out once the fire officers have arrived,' İkmen said. 'In a body bag. We don't know where this Cem might be hiding. But he'll have to have some sort of confirmation that you've done what you said you would. So, whether he is *in situ* or not, we have to give him that proof.'

'What will you do with this Sabiha?'

246

'We'll take her to a safe house,' Ayşe Farsakoğlu said. 'Poor child! What will be left of her life after this?'

'Cem told me she has a boyfriend,' Ismail said. 'A neighbour. The girl's brother told their father. That's why the family want her dead.'

'Yes but having a boyfriend can mean a lot of different things,' Ayşe continued. 'Maybe they are in love, but then maybe the two of them just looked at each other one day; you know how it can work with these people.'

'These people' included, Ismail knew, him. She'd meant religious, pious, very moral people – just like him. He could understand why Sabiha's parents might want to put her to death, even if he could in no way approve of such an action. But the way this female colleague of Hikmet's was looking at him now made Ismail Yıldız feel humiliated and low. She looked down on him and people like him. She had no love for piety or religion, and although he disapproved completely of honour killing, he found that because he could relate to the reasons why it happened, he felt conflicted. There was no way in the world that he was going to kill Sabiha; he was going to do exactly what the police told him. But he was not comfortable with that, and there was no sense in which he ever would be.

'If you arrive at the apartment in Çarşamba at eight tonight,' İkmen said, 'we will be there to meet you.' Then in response to what appeared to be yet another question coming from Ismail he said, 'You simply enter the apartment – we will have replaced the key underneath the mat – and then set the fire. We will all be waiting for you to do that. Don't worry, we won't really let you burn the apartment down.'

247

'You will be . . .'

'We're police officers, Ismail,' İkmen said with a smile. 'You leave the details about how we're going to run this operation to us. All you need to remember is to take the petrol you will buy this morning to the apartment at eight o'clock tonight, set the fire, run away and then wait for Cem to contact you. As soon as he calls you, you call us.'

'But what if he double-crosses me?' Ismail asked. 'What if he gets me to do the job and then just disappears with all the money?'

'Oh, I don't think that will happen,' İkmen said.

'Why not?'

'Because he'll want to use you to kill again,' İkmen said. 'You know we all complain about the escalating violence in this great big dirty city of ours, but finding someone who is prepared to kill in cold blood, even for money, is still rare. Also, you have no criminal record. He'll want to hang on to you, possibly employ you again. By this act you will become a valuable commodity.'

Although he smiled, İkmen felt suddenly troubled. What, he wondered, had Cem seen in Ismail Yıldız that made him think that he could kill? Maybe it was nothing apart from lack of a criminal record and his financial need. But then maybe it wasn't.

Cahit had gone out and taken his awful sister Feray and her daughter Nesrin with him. She'd heard him talk about shopping, and the two women had giggled excitedly. Her husband was going to buy them things, things he'd never even thought to buy for her. He was doing it to hurt her, Saadet knew that. Once Cahit and the women had gone, her jailers consisted of her nephew Aykan and her son Lokman. It was the latter who unlocked the door and brought her a breakfast of bread, cheese and olives at just after nine. He put it down on the floor in front of her in a way that was both contemptuous and embarrassed. He didn't seem to notice her broken, bloodied mouth. Or if he did, he didn't say anything about it.

'It's your—'

'Lokman, my soul, please close the door behind you and sit with me,' Saadet said. She sat down on the floor and gestured for him to join her.

But he remained where he was and said, 'I have to get back to cousin Aykan.'

Saadet wanted to say all sorts of cruel things about how the computer-addicted Aykan was unlikely to even know that her son had left the room. But she didn't. Instead she said, 'I don't know what your father has told you about me . . .'

'He said you went out whoring yesterday,' Lokman said. 'He said that you must be punished now.' There was still embarrassment on his face, but there was also a small smile now for his mother. It was clearly fighting to overcome the contempt that his father had tried to instil within him.

'Lokman,' Saadet said sternly. 'You know me. You know your own mother wouldn't whore.'

She could see that he knew that. His eyes glistened. 'But then where did you go yesterday? Where did you go?'

'I went shopping.'

'You were hours! No one, no neighbours, saw you, and you were hours!'

'Lokman, I am a covered woman who is unaccustomed to this district,' Saadet said. 'Why would anybody notice me? I went shopping! I admit I was out far too long, but I needed to walk and to think. Son, I have lost all my children except for you. Allah has seen fit to take Gözde and Kenan from me.'

For a moment his face seemed to harden. He had never liked Kenan, even when they were children. But he had loved his sister, and now the mention of her name caused him to suddenly soften. He sat down on the floor in front of his mother and pushed her plate towards her. 'Eat.'

Saadet ignored the plate. 'Lokman, I need to know something and I need to know it now.'

'What?'

'Why did you try to hide your sister's mobile telephone from the police?' she asked. 'It troubles me, makes me wonder if you had some hand in Gözde's death. Or rather in covering it up.'

He gazed over at her with straight, damp eyes. He looked for a moment as if he were about to choke, but then he cleared his throat and said, 'Gözde was seeing a boy from up the road. I knew about it. They cared for each other.'

Saadet felt her heart jump. What it meant if Lokman knew, she couldn't imagine. 'Did you tell your father?'

'No! No! I didn't tell anyone! I took the phone so that no one, not even the police, would ever know, ever besmirch my sister's name!' Lokman said. 'Kenan knew because Gözde told him herself; she didn't trust me enough. Kenan would have told no one. Afterwards, he believed that me and Father had ordered Gözde's murder!'

250

'Yes, I know. We all ended up in the police station, didn't we.'

'How could he do that?' Lokman said. 'How could he . . .'

'He could do it, Lokman, because your father did kill your sister,' Saadet said baldly. 'Kenan knew.'

Lokman frowned and then shook his head. 'No,' he said. 'No, that's not right, Mother. Father was here with you and Auntie Feray, Nesrin and Aykan when it happened. He couldn't possibly—'

'Your father arranged it,' Saadet said. 'I didn't know until we arrived here that day and I could do nothing about it! I didn't believe it at first. Even when we went back to our burnt-out apartment, I didn't believe it. But then the fire officers said that they'd found a body and I knew. I cried in your arms, remember, Lokman? Your father told me that he paid someone . . .'

'Who?'

'I don't know!' Saadet said. 'Do you think if I knew that I'd be sitting here now? If I knew who killed my daughter I'd be fighting to get past you to get out of here. I don't know his name. I would know his face, though. I need to get out to tell the police.'

'Tell the police about my father?' He looked shocked and horrified.

'Your father killed Gözde!' Saadet said. 'He paid every *kuruş* we have so that it could be done! Why do you think we are so broke? Why do we not even try to go back to our apartment?' She lowered her voice just in case her fat lump of a nephew might somehow hear her. 'Your father has ruined everything, Lokman! He must be brought to justice! Think about it!'

251

Stunned, Lokman looked down at his own hands as they lay limply in his lap. Still he said nothing.

Saadet, desperate, leaned forward and tried to look into his face. 'Last night, Lokman,' she said, her throat drying against the words that she had to spit out now, 'your father raped me. I am so sorry to have to tell you this, my son.'

Not so much as a tiny flicker crossed his features. Whether he was shocked or not, she just couldn't tell.

'I need to get out of here and tell the truth,' she said. It was her final attempt to reach him, which could, she knew, also be her last chance. 'You have to help me, Lokman,' she added. 'If you do not, I will die in here. If not by your father's hand, then by my own.'

He looked up at her then with what to Saadet was an unknowable expression on his face.

Sleeping in his car had not been an option. When he left Gonca's house in the early hours of the morning, Mehmet Süleyman drove out to the beautiful village of Yeniköy, where he parked up beside the Bosphorus. There he sat, sleepless and eventually red-eyed, until the sun came up and he went to get a takeaway coffee from a small local *büfe*. Tired, depressed and still bewildered at his lover's behaviour, he eventually managed to wake up enough to drive to the station, where he found that İzzet Melik was already waiting for him.

'Sir,' the sergeant said as soon as Süleyman entered his office, 'sir, I was at the Tulip nargile salon last night, on my own time, and I got into conversation with the owner. We got on well and . . .' He stopped and stared at his superior with a frown on his face. It was very rare that Süleyman

252

looked anything less than immaculate, but this morning he was positively shabby.

Süleyman lit a cigarette, which he then waved at his inferior. 'Carry on,' he said. 'I'm not going to shout at you for going on about Murad Emin and Ali Reza Zafir. I'm not going to shout at you about anything.'

İzzet was relieved. Although he hardly dare admit it to himself, he had been worried in case his boss railed at him. They had not, after all, parted on anything like good terms the previous evening. Süleyman had been furious that İzzet had had the temerity to so much as breathe a word about his gypsy lover. Now he appeared subdued. It made İzzet wonder about what might have happened in the intervening twelve hours. Had Süleyman thought about what had been said and come to the conclusion that he had put İzzet and all his colleagues in a difficult position? Or had he maybe spoken to her, the gypsy, about it? Had they, she and he, argued about it, maybe? Had the gypsy's family finally taken a hand in their business as Izabella Madrid had suggested? Süleyman did after all look more miserable than İzzet had ever seen him look before.

'Sir, we have absolutely no reason, as far as I can tell, to think about any of Hamid İdiz's other students. In terms of his murder, I mean. But these boys . . . or rather Murad Emin . . . I went, as I told you, to see his old piano teacher, Miss Madrid, again, and she is worried about him. Murad has changed in the last year, and not for the better.' Seeing that Süleyman was about to speak, possibly to raise some sort of objection, he went on, 'I know that Mr İdiz could still have been murdered by someone he just picked up somewhere.

But sir, there is something wrong about this boy. Also, at the Tulip nargile salon, the boys play about on computers. They may just play games, Google women's breasts. The owner of the place seems to think that what they do is quite innocuous, but I don't know.'

Süleyman leaned back in his chair and rubbed his eyes. 'You say you have an easy relaitionship with the owner?'

'He offered me the use of his computers any time I wished,' İzzet said. 'I approached him in the guise of a wrestling coach; you know that is what my brother does. The owner of the Tulip is a great enthusiast. Offered to let me look up stuff about all the old Ottoman wrestlers on the net. It sounded fascinating.'

'And did you take him up on this offer?' Süleyman said.

'No. I felt it was too soon, and also I need to know what I'm looking for before I do that. But I will do it when, with your permission, sir, I go to the Tulip for a lunchtime smoke.'

'Of course.' Süleyman sighed. 'With my blessing, İzzet. Did either of the boys, Murad or Ali Reza, see you at the Tulip?'

'Murad did,' İzzet replied. 'But he didn't acknowledge me in any way. I don't know whether he recognised me or not. But if he did, I don't think he said anything about it to his boss.'

Süleyman frowned, 'Mmm. Yes. All right, İzzet, get over there at lunchtime.'

He didn't say anything more. İzzet did think about maybe tackling him on what appeared to be a change of heart with regard to Murad Emin and Ali Reza Zafir, but then thought better of it. He had paperwork to catch up on, as well as, later, a bit of research prior to his visit to the Tulip. After all, if he was going to try and find out what the boys were looking at on the computers, he needed to know how best to do that. A visit to a friend of his in the computer support team was therefore a necessity. He sat down at his desk and switched on his own system in a silence that was very intense. What on earth could have happened to Süleyman?

For his part, Mehmet Süleyman sat and smoked and inwardly berated himself for a fool. İzzet had always had a point with those two boys, Ali Reza and Murad. They were the only pupils of Hamid İdiz who had reported either seeing him masturbate or hearing about it. Ali Reza had not, apparently, been too disturbed by it, but Murad had. The boy had been upset and, in addition, had expressed some views that would point towards an antipathy towards homosexual people. And yet because of that one remark from the boy's mother as they were leaving, that might or might not have referred to Gonca, Süleyman had chosen to ignore Murad. He had *chosen* to do that! Paranoid beyond belief that his wife would somehow find out about the gypsy, he had avoided anyone he thought might know about her for months. Even İkmen, he now realised, was from time to time kept at arm's length. And then, as it had transpired, everyone apparently had known anyway! İzzet Melik had many faults, but lying was not one of them, and so Süleyman knew that it had to be true.

He glanced across at his sergeant as he worked away diligently at his reports, and just the look of him made Süleyman feel ashamed. Murad Emin could well have killed Hamid İdiz, and both he and, most importantly, İzzet knew it. Thanks be to Allah for İzzet, the clear-sighted, noble, honest man! Süleyman wondered how he could possibly have allowed himself to let his own needs override his sense of justice. Murderers had to be caught, for the sake of everyone in the city, even the country. If in doing that his wife became aware of his infidelity with the gypsy, then so be it. Even the loss of his son, that dear, adored child, was not worth the danger that a killer on the loose represented. A killer could, after all, attack almost anyone once that first murder had been committed, even Mehmet Süleyman's own beloved child.

The Antep Apartments were in a small street not far from the Sultan Selim Mosque. A shabby 1960s concrete block that was typical of that part of the Çarşamba district, it had one large front entrance and a small back exit that was accessed by a concrete yard. At the back of that was a low wall, and beyond that a patch of waste ground where lots of little boys kicked plastic footballs about. In common with most areas where migrants from the countryside had settled, the streets teemed with people and life was lived very much out in the open. Women, though veiled, sat on their doorsteps, watching their children play and laugh and squabble amid the dust of the street. Men stood in small flat-cap-wearing groups on street corners, smoking, eating *börek* and discussing football.

'This is not, İkmen, the sort of place where one passes unnoticed,' said Commissioner Ardıç, Çetin İkmen's boss, as he viewed with some distaste the domestic scene that was unfolding around their car. 'These types . . .' he waved a swollen, dismissive hand in the general direction of the street,

256

'know their own, and they do not generally take kindly to outsiders.'

Like İkmen, Ardıç was a city man born and bred, and like a lot of city people he did not have a great deal of time for unreconstructed migrants from the countryside. He routinely referred to the quarters where they lived as 'ghettos', and he viewed their often very separate lives as products of entirely their own making. That İstanbullus did not sometimes readily accept them was to Ardıç unthinkable. İstanbullus could not, apparently, do any wrong.

'We can't just arrest this family,' İkmen said. 'If we do, this Cem character will just disappear.'

'So what is your plan?' A small child, a girl in a cut-down adult dress with dirty hair and a sore on her lip, was looking at the men in the car with open curiosity. Ardıç, who viewed the urchin with disgust, tapped his driver on the shoulder and said, 'Will you do something about that child? Shoo it away or something!'

But İkmen very quickly put his hand on the driver's shoulder too, holding him into his seat. 'Actually, sir,' he said, 'we should maybe go now. I don't want to call further attention to us. I just wanted you to see where this oper-ation is going to take place.'

'Oh, very well, if you say so.' Ardıç shrugged. The car began to move slowly away from the kerb and towards the end of the road. 'So this plan that you have . . .'

'According to Constable Yıldız's brother, the family will leave the apartment at seven o'clock tonight,' İkmen said. 'A team of plain-clothes officers will follow them and keep them under surveillance at all times. Sergeant Farsakoğlu has already made contact with the *kapıcı* of the building and is at this moment in his apartment, where I will join her at six o'clock this evening.'

Ardıç frowned. 'She's a striking woman, Farsakoğlu. How did she get in there without attracting attention?'

İkmen smiled. 'It is really quite amazing what a set of dreary old clothes, no make-up and a very unfashionably tied headscarf can do,' he said. It was true. The timid lady visitor to the apartment building's caretaker had been almost unrecognisable as Ayşe. 'We cannot just occupy that building once the girl's parents have gone, because we have to think about this Cem and where he might be. Maybe he will be watching to see that Ismail Yıldız does what he will hopefully be paid to do.'

'Clearly we have to apprehend this character,' Ardıç said. 'Honour killing for money! Whatever next? But then that is your rural type, isn't it, that—'

'The aim of the operation is to secure the safe passage of the girl out of the apartment, to apprehend this Cem person and, ultimately, to take the girl's family into custody,' İkmen interrupted. He knew that their driver was a 'rural type', and was anxious not to let Ardıç offend his sensibilities. Try as the commissioner might to treat everyone equally and with some respect, İkmen knew that he just did not either understand or trust those migrants from the countryside who had not integrated into city life. The driver, he felt, fell into that category.

'You've contacted the fire department?'

'Yes,' İkmen said. 'They will expect a call from the *kapıcı* once the fire has been set and Ismail Yıldız has left the building.'

'How are you going to manage that?' Ardıç asked.

İkmen smiled. 'Oh, our colleagues at the fire department have told us how to create a very small, very noxious blaze, sir,' he said.

'Contained, I trust.'

'Of course. Sir, this is largely acting.'

'Mmm.' The commissioner eyed him narrowly. 'You're rather good at that, İkmen. But that said, your face is somewhat familiar to the public due to your various media appearances.' İkmen had, from time to time, been on television to give out statements on behalf of the İstanbul police. He had also, more recently, appeared on several news programmes in the wake of his very successful undercover operation in London, where he had almost single-handedly saved the life of the British capital's mayor.

With a sigh, İkmen flicked his own moustache and said, 'This will go, and with a suit that is actually ironed . . .'

'Oh, of course,' Ardıç said without a hint of irony in his voice. İkmen in smart clothes without his moustache *was* unrecognisable. 'Just make sure that the vast horde of plain-clothes officers I have allowed you to use in order to support this operation know who you are.'

'Yes, sir.' İkmen smiled again, but then very quickly frowned. The scene of the operation was going to be over-seen by a large team of men and women who would be communicating with İkmen and Ayşe Farsakoğlu inside. They would be looking for a man fitting the description of Cem that Ismail Yıldız had given them and making sure that none of the local people got to know what was really going on. And then there was the girl . . .

Ardıç had some misgivings about that too. 'This girl,' he said, 'er . . .'

'Sabiha.'

'What if she does not believe what you tell her?'

The plan was for İkmen and Ayşe to take the key that her family would leave underneath the doormat and let themselves in.

'Oh, she will believe us,' İkmen said. 'It will break the poor kid's heart, but she'll believe us. She'll have to.'

The driver took them out of the tangle of the small streets of Çarşamba and drove back to the station along the western shore of the Golden Horn. Maybe it was being close to the water and the open sky above, but only once they were near to the Horn did Çetin İkmen feel as if he could breathe easily again.

Chapter 24

Both originally İzmir men, İzzet Melik and his computer support friend Şenol had a lot in common – with the exception of computers. Şenol understood them, while İzzet just got by. In discussion with Şenol about the computers at the Tulip nargile salon, it soon became apparent to İzzet that he didn't know enough to even start to find out what Murad Emin and Ali Reza Zafir might have been looking at. And so Şenol, in the guise of a sports fan friend (which he was not) went along with İzzet when he drove to Tophane for his lunchtime smoke.

Because the Tulip was all but empty when they arrived, İzzet found it easy to engage the owner in conversation. As ever, it was about wrestling, and this time Mustafa Bey absolutely insisted that İzzet and his friend look at all the websites devoted to the Ottoman heroes of the sport on one of his computers. For a while he looked at the sites with them, getting ever more enthusiastic as he found information about more and more arcane and obscure Ottoman wrestlers. İzzet was, he had to admit, rather taken with it himself. But for poor Şenol, feigning interest in something he personally found mindless was almost an act of will too far. It was therefore with some relief that he watched the owner go to take in a delivery of tobacco and serve a few customers.

'You enjoy yourselves, take your time, İzzet Bey,' Mustafa said as he left the back room to go back into the salon. 'There's no hurry.'

But of course there was, and Şenol started the second machine up as quickly as he could once the owner had gone. İzzet largely left him to it.

'You know what we're looking for, don't you?' he said as Şenol looked from one machine to the other and then back again, pressing keys and pushing buttons as he went. 'Evidence that someone has visited extremist *jihadi* sites,' he added. 'Anything extreme, violent, anti-Western, anti-democratic.'

'Insane interpretations of Koranic scripture,' Şenol said. 'All that stuff.'

Mustafa was busy with the tobacco supplier, a small hunchbacked man whose complexion was very similar to the leaves he was now holding up for his customer to see. From what the owner said, it seemed very likely that he was going to personally try the product before he committed to buying. An old man who could have been his father turned up and said that he would prepare a pipe for the three of them to share. Then another man, possibly again some sort of relative, poured some tea from the samovar for the tobacco man, Mustafa and his father, then set about serving the few customers in the salon. So everyone was occupied. İzzet, though still very much on the alert, told Şenol to take his time. There was no great hurry, and so care could be taken. Şenol lit up a cigarette, and the light from the two screens

262

bounced against the surface of his pale blue eyes. İzzet, also smoking now, began looking at the two large stacks of DVDs under the table that the computers stood upon. The first one he found was *Bambi*.

When Sabiha's brother Emir had got married back in their old village, he had stayed on to work on their uncle's farm. Emir's absence had made Sabiha very sad. He had been a nice brother, generous and kind. He had even liked Sami, which was amazing given what everyone else said about him. Sami was Sabiha's guilty secret, a neighbour who was also her boyfriend. He was a year younger than Sabiha; he was also a little simple, although not, as some said, brain-damaged. Just a bit slower than others in some ways. Sami had not been slow to respond when Sabiha had kissed him. Emir had told Sabiha that he believed she and Sami should be married. But she knew that she could never tell her father about Sami. He would not approve, especially if he knew what Sami had done. Because Sami had not just kissed Sabiha. Every time she thought about the pain and also the pure pleasure of having him inside her, Sabiha glowed with excitement.

'Why are you going to Sultanahmet this evening?' she asked her mother. Her parents, especially her mother, almost never went out after six o'clock. 'Why can't I come?'

Sami and his family were away, staying with relatives in the east. So it wasn't even as if Sabiha could organise a secret little tryst while her parents were out.

'Your father has business,' her mother said as she folded the tea towels into the airing cupboard.

'What business?'

Her father was a cook at a small restaurant in Kumkapı. He worked for a family of Armenians who, he always said, treated him very well.

'Is Father looking for a new job?'

Her mother didn't answer. She just kept on folding the tea towels, her face very straight, not looking up at her daughter. Sabiha gave up trying to speak to her and flung herself down on the sofa. It had been an odd sort of day so far. Her father had left early to go to work because, he said, he was doing the lunchtime shift as opposed to his usual evening slot. He wouldn't say why, just like her mother would not be drawn about where he might be taking her for the evening. Sabiha couldn't believe that the two of them were actually going out, as in, to a restaurant or a bar (they didn't drink), or to anywhere that wasn't quiet and pious and somewhere that her mother would immediately dislike. That said, perhaps her parents *were* going out for a romantic meal together after all! If she had secrets, then so could they.

Sabiha looked over at her mother and said, 'You know, Mum, I think you're really pretty. I mean it.'

Her mother deserved to go out. She was just as pretty as the free and easy secular women who went out in places like Beyoğlu and, to a lesser extent, Sultanahmet all the time. This time her mother did look up at her and smiled. But then just as quickly her smile fell into a cloud of tears, and with a face contorted by grief she ran out of the room. It was turning out, Sabiha thought, to be a very odd day.

'I have done what you asked, Şukru,' Gonca said as she stitched a hank of white horsehair on to her canvas. Some strange woman who 'thrilled' to her art up in Cihangir had commissioned it. A collage to represent gypsy life past. Few had horses these days, and no one still had bears.

Her brother, once a master of bears, walked into her studio and smiled. Gonca always knew that he was near, even without looking at him. They were, and always had been, practically twins. 'What do you want, Şukru?'

He sat down in an old wicker chair that she kept over by the sink and looked at her. Her face, though still very beautiful, was pale from lack of sleep and the absence of make-up. Her eyes, he could see, were clearly puffed around the edges, where, presumably, she had been crying. To get rid of the policeman had been difficult for her. But then Şukru knew that it would be. Some years before, his wife had died suddenly and violently in a road traffic accident. He knew the pain of a love suddenly curtailed.

'How are you?' he asked.

For the first time she took her eyes off her canvas and looked at him. 'How do you think I am?' she said. 'Eh? How do you think?'

Şukru took in a deep breath and then looked down at the floor. In spite of the fact that he knew that what had been done had been for the good name and honour of his family, he still felt sorry for her. 'How was he, your policeman? When you told him?' he said.

'Oh, overjoyed!' she said. 'Ecstatic! Just delighted to be told to go for no apparent reason!'

'Yes, but . . .'

'But did I tell him that I loved him? That *that* was the reason he just had to go? Of course I didn't!' she said bitterly.

'Would you have done that, Şukru? Would you have broken the heart of the person you loved?'

She was crying now. He hadn't seen her cry since they were children.

'No . . .'

'Then why would I, eh? Why would I?' she said. Finally at the end of both her strength and her patience, she stuck her needle into her canvas and leaned back against the stool behind her. 'I wish I could just curl up and die!'

'No you don't.'

'Don't you tell me what to feel!' she screamed. She was weeping so hard she was choking. 'Don't you dare do that, Şukru!'

She called him names. Vile and abusive names that would have made a lesser man than him blush. She had loved that policeman so much! The force of her hatred and her passion was enormous. But Şukru just let her scream it all out in his direction. Better that than at their father. He, old as he was, was likely to kill her for less. Only when her fury had finally burnt itself out and she was lying on her studio floor sobbing into her hair did he even attempt to go over to her.

'Gonca . . .' He wasn't going to say that he was sorry, because he wasn't. What had been done was what had to be done. He put a hand on her shoulder and felt her body flinch underneath his touch. He pulled away and then sat back on his haunches, waiting for whatever she was going through to stop. He wasn't going to leave her like this.

After about ten minutes of almost silent crying, she raised her head and looked at him. Her eyes were even more puffy now, and her face was bright, bright red. Şukru felt how

266

badly women suffered for love, even old women like his sister. Barren and wrinkled and no longer as slim as a whip, Gonca still had such presence, such dignity and even beauty. But she mourned the leaving of her lover, because as Şukru knew only too well, she would be terrified that he had been her last. After a few moments of heavy breathing she said, 'Go, and do not come back until I send for you.'

'Gonca . . .' She had never been this upset before, not even when her first husband ran away with a girl half her age.

'Just go,' she said quietly. 'I will recover, Şukru, because I have to. I have children.'

'Yes, but . . .'

'Just go!' Her eyes were black with fury, the pupils glittering like tiny chips of malignant jet.

Şukru stood up, and with a shrug began to walk towards the studio door. Just before he got there, he turned and saw his sister, now sitting up on her haunches, snarling at him like an animal. 'I keep this family, I love this family,' she said with pure hatred in her voice. 'But I will never forgive you or this family for doing this to me. To kill love is a sin. It is a sin against people, against nature and against God!'

Three of the DVDs had Murad Emin's name written on them in marker pen. İzzet assumed that it was in the boy's own handwriting.

'I can't find anything exactly untoward on here,' Şenol said as he scrolled through various menus and did other seemingly arcane things. Out in the salon, Mustafa, his father and the tobacco supplier were having a very therapeutic smoke.

From what İzzet could hear of their conversation, the leaf tobacco was extremely mellow and satisfying.

İzzet looked at his watch and realised that he and Şenol had been ensconced in the small back room with the computers for over an hour. Soon Mustafa Bey would be wanting to join them again for more tales of the exploits of famous Ottoman wrestlers.

'Şenol?'

'Yes?'

İzzet passed one of the three DVDs over to him and said, 'Can you have a look at this?'

'OK.'

İzzet went back to looking through the crack in the door to make sure that they were undisturbed. He heard Şenol slide the disk into the computer, and then he heard what sounded at first like Arabesk music. But the singer's words were not in Turkish, or in fact in any other language that İzzet could speak.

'What . . .'

'Something in Arabic or Farsi up on the screen,' Şenol said as he looked very intently at one of the computers. 'Do you . . .'

'No,' İzzet said. 'Italian, some French and English. You?'

'I can only really speak German, a little English,' Şenol said. Then there was a sound like a muffled scream, and Şenol's eyes widened. 'Allah!'

'What is it?'

Reluctant though he was to leave his post and risk possible discovery, İzzet ran over to his friend and looked at the screen over his shoulder.

'I could so easily have lived without seeing that,' Şenol said with a distinct quaver in his voice. 'My life would have been so much better without that image.'

İzzet could only agree. As he watched the headless body of some poor soul twitch on the ground in front of the hooded men with machetes who had just executed him, he wondered what kind of person would want to do or even see such terrible things.

Chapter 25

Çetin İkmen looked at his own clean-shaven face in the bathroom mirror and frowned. He didn't like his face without its
moustache. Hairless it seemed to highlight what he felt was
a weak chin. He put a hand up and touched the rough skin
that now seemed to shout at him from his left cheek. On the
few occasions when he had done this in the past, he'd never
liked it. He would, he knew, be growing another moustache
again as soon as the operation in Çarşamba was at an end.
Like the suit that Fatma was ironing for him in the kitchen,
it wasn't right, not for him. He was mustachioed, crumpled
and stained; it was who he was. He was also, now that he
was alone, deeply worried about what they were about to do
that evening, and not just because he had already considered
all the things that could possibly go wrong.

İkmen was not, and had never been, convinced that this
man Cem had anything to do with the death of Gözde Seyhan,
the whole reason for his investigation into honour killing.
The girl had lived a long way from Fatih, where Cem appeared
to be based, and although the Seyhans had had relatives in
that district at the time of Gözde's death, they hadn't had
strong connections with the area. Cem could be involved in
some way with the gangster Tayfun Ergin, who was by all

271

accounts moving in on some businesses in Fatih. But that was in no way certain. Honour killings in the city had increased in line with the recent heavy migration from the countryside. Some people denied this, but to İkmen it was obvious. And just as people became more sophisticated when they came into contact with new and more challenging situations, so crime in the city evolved from what it had once been out in the country. For an outraged father to kill his daughter in the middle of the city was not easy. One could not count upon the silence of long-term and loyal neighbours and friends, the police were more sophisticated and more punitive over such matters, and disposing of a dead body in a built-up area was fraught with danger. To contract that murder out, even at a price poor people would struggle to pay, made sense. And yet İkmen was not convinced that Cem had killed Gözde. There was a feeling about what Ismail Yıldız had told him about this man and his operation that made İkmen think that he'd never done anything like this before. Chillingly, the possibility of several people making money out of this phenomenon was not lost upon Çetin İkmen. Where a need existed, real or perceived, so people would appear to fill that need. Sadly the need was real, and it was, apparently, increasing.

'Murad's probably on his way home now,' his father said as he smiled and tried to look at the officers through half-closed eyes. 'School, you know. He's been to school.'

It was almost as if he was trying to remind himself where his son had been. But then by anyone's standards, Mr Emin was way off his head on whatever he'd taken earlier that day.

'We need to speak to Murad,' Süleyman said sternly. He had two constables and İzzet Melik at his back, and in his pocket three appalling extremist DVDs with Murad Emin's name on them.

'There's his mobile . . .'

'We need to speak to your son in person,' Süleyman said as he pushed past the boy's father and entered the apartment. The sharp smell of burning cannabis resin hit his nostrils immediately, but he ignored it and motioned for the other officers to follow him in. 'We'll wait.'

'Oh.'

Süleyman waved in Mr Emin's face the warrant he had just obtained to search the premises, and then told İzzet and the constables to go and look in the boy's room. Mr Emin, dismayed and agitated now, joined them. Süleyman himself went into the litter-strewn room that passed for the family's living area. There he found, half clothed, Emin's wife.

'Oh,' she said when she saw him, her eyes clouded by the smoke from the joint that she was holding, 'what can I do for you? I can give you a hand job for—'

'No thank you!' He stomped over, took the joint out of her hand and threw it into an ashtray. He was furious. This woman, this broken, degraded, filthy addict, had made him, albeit unconsciously, look away from her son, a boy who at the very least was besotted with extremist propaganda.

He looked over his shoulder to make sure that no one was listening to him, and then he hissed, 'Last time I was here, you said something about did my wife know. Did my wife know what, exactly? About whom?' He put a hand up to her

273

throat and squeezed just a little. 'Well? What did you mean by that? Speak!'

Finally, terror at what he might do to her broke through the drugs and she said, 'About us!'

'Us?' He had expected her to say something about 'the gypsy', but instead she was talking about 'us'. 'What do you mean? I don't know you! You are nothing to me! What?'

The woman took a breath, pushing his now slightly slackening hand away from her throat. 'It was about six months ago,' she said. 'In a bar, down İstiklal Street.'

'What? What was in a bar, where . . .'

'You were alone,' she said. 'We went out the back. You gave me ten lire.'

He didn't remember her or the occasion, of course he didn't, but he knew of other instances like it.

'I remembered you because you were much better-looking than my usual punters,' she said. 'Class.' Then she added crudely, 'Nice clean cock.'

'You were . . .' He took his hand away from her and sat down in the chair opposite. In a room at the front of the apartment he could hear his officers taking things apart. He'd paid her for some kind of sexual favour – he dared not ask – but he didn't recall her at all. He didn't recall any of the women that he just paid and took when he felt the need from time to time. So like the dead man, Hamid İdiz! Addicted to sexual thrills even when he was involved with women that he cared for or even loved! What was wrong with him? He put his head in his hands, then heard her say, 'I won't tell anyone. About us.'

He looked up into her watery, bloodshot eyes and said,

'There is no us. I do not recall you, madam. Not one little bit.'

He had no doubt inside that she was telling the truth, but he could not admit it. To continue to deny her story was the only way forward, even though he knew that she wasn't lying. Heavy footsteps coming down the hallway alerted him to the presence of others, and he moved as far away from the woman as he could get.

It was İzzet Melik. 'Inspector,' he said gravely, 'I think you ought to come and see what we've found.'

Süleyman stood up and left the room. Both he and İzzet Melik were standing in the hallway when the boy, Murad Emin, appeared in the open front doorway. As soon as he saw them his face whitened, and dropping his heavy school bag on the floor in front of him, he turned and began to run.

'Get after him!' Süleyman yelled at the constable who, in response to the commotion, was looking out from the boy's bedroom door.

Ayşe Farsakoğlu put a hand underneath her scarf and scratched her head. She wasn't used to wearing anything on her head, and so having some hot flap of cotton tied up underneath her chin was irritating. But to take the headscraft off was not an option, even though she was indoors. The *kapıcı*'s wife was a very traditional woman who had all but covered her face when Çetin İkmen had joined them in the small caretaker's apartment. Ayşe looked over at her boss, who appeared so strange in his smart ironed suit and shaven face. Not only did he look very different, he looked extremely uncomfortable too.

'That family are good people,' the *kapıcı* said as he eyed the two officers with suspicion. 'They come from Diyarbakir. I come from Diyarbakir.'

No one had told the *kapıcı* or his wife why the police were so interested in Sabiha's family. They knew only that they were under surveillance, and that once the inspector and his sergeant were in the apartment, they would be left with a constable who would make sure that they didn't say anything to anyone that they shouldn't. The only fact they possessed was the one that pertained to the fire department. At some point a fire crew would arrive at the apartment building and go into the 'good' family's place. There would be a lot of noise and a lot of confusion. But they were not, under any circumstances, to take what they would see at face value. Nothing was going to be as it might seem.

Ayşe looked at her watch and then said to İkmen, 'It's seven, sir.'

'OK.' He got up, walked over to the *kapıcı*'s door and put his eye up to the spy-hole. The *kapıcı*'s apartment had not been chosen as a base only because of what its tenant did and who he was; it was also strategic. The front door was directly opposite the front door of the girl's apartment. İkmen looked at the dingy green door opposite, poised for any sign of movement.

'Would you like some more tea?' the *kapıcı*'s wife asked Ayşe Farsakoğlu for probably the fifteenth time since she had arrived.

'Oh, er, yes,' Ayşe said. 'That would be very nice.'

The woman was unhappy enough at having her domestic routine interrupted, at having a strange, unrelated male in

276

the place. Better to let her do what she probably did each and every day, which was to boil up the samovar and serve tea, in a seemingly unending stream.

'Would your, er, would, er, *he* . . .' The woman tipped her head towards Çetin İkmen.

'Oh, no. Thank you,' Ayşe said. 'He, er, he's busy.'

'Right.' She went into the kitchen and Ayşe heard the sound of tea glasses clinking in the sink.

The *kapıcı* looked at İkmen with a mixture of distaste and understanding. The inspector had his head pressed against the spy-hole, but still he was able to smoke a cigarette. That was impressive. What wasn't so good was that he clearly had some sort of issue with the family of the *kapıcı*'s old friend from back in Diyarbakir. A good man with a good wife and good children. Why the police should be so interested in such people, he couldn't imagine. He was sure – in fact he had actually told the inspector – that it had to be some sort of mistake. Not that the policeman had done anything more than smile rather oddly at that.

The *kapıcı*'s wife came back into the living room and handed Ayşe a tiny tea glass on a gold-rimmed saucer. It was probably her best, most fancy set, reserved only for guests. It reminded Ayşe of her own parents, who had also, long ago, come to the city from the countryside. Keeping up appearances had been important to them too. She looked over at İkmen just in time to see one of his shoulders convulse.

'Sir?'

'They're leaving,' she heard him say.

Ayşe took a sip from her glass and then put it down on the small table beside her. Çetin İkmen watched with one curious eye as a middle-aged man and woman, both thin, both covered in heavy, drab clothing, closed their apartment door behind them, looked at each other for a moment and then left.

She looked down into the small bowl her son had put in front of her and observed the tiny portion of food in it with great distaste. If Cahit did indeed want her to get pregnant again, he was not doing his bit in terms of her welfare. Three slices of aubergine, some mashed tomatoes and one slice of bread was hardly what Saadet would have called a meal. But she didn't say anything to Lokman; she still didn't have any way of knowing what might or might not be on his mind. She had opened her heart to him; now it was up to Lokman how he responded.

'Eat,' he told her as he stood in the doorway. Outside in the hall, beyond her makeshift prison, life continued, with television noise, people's voices, the clank of food pots against the top of the cooker. 'If you don't eat, you won't have any energy.'

Lokman left, closing and locking the door behind him. Energy? For what? All she did was sit and contemplate her supposed 'crime', and the ways she might be punished for it, such as another assault by Cahit. Saadet felt her body go cold. She hadn't loved him for so long, she could no longer recall when or even if she had ever loved him. There must have been a time, possibly when her poor dead Kenan was born. That had been a nice time, when she had been young, the village had been comfortable and familiar, and they had had everything any of them could want. By the time Lokman arrived two years later, things had changed. Cahit found work in the fields hard to come by, they were poor and often hungry, and for several years she couldn't conceive. Only when the soldiers arrived and one beautiful one gave her a chocolate bar and her Gözde, did another little life light up her own. For a while.

Saadet began to eat, to the sound of laughter from her hated sister-in-law's living room.

Murad Emin had run down the stairs outside his family's apartment, into the street and off towards the Golden Horn. One of the constables had warned the boy and then raised his pistol as if to shoot him, but Süleyman had pushed the weapon down and said, 'He's a child!'

The other constable, now in hot pursuit, nevertheless found it hard to gain on the boy. Süleyman and İzzet Melik followed on in the former's car, while back at the apartment, the boy's parents stood at their front door looking shell-shocked and confused.

Murad Emin ran very quickly but without any fully formed plan about where he might go or what he might do. That the police had finally come was enough to keep his feet hammering against the pavement, pushing him ever further away from the young but clearly less fit constable behind him. If the officer knew the area, he was sunk, but if he didn't, Murad could, he knew, confuse him very easily by darting back into the tiny streets of Balat, which in this part of the district were on a hill. He'd known when he'd seen the big, ugly cop at the Tulip that he was in trouble. He should have listened to his own heart then and just left. He glanced at the

Golden Horn once before he turned off on to an uneven little track beside a coppersmith's workshop. Still with the sound of the constable's laboured breathing behind him, he turned first right, then left, then left again, which brought him to a tiny alleyway between two very large and dilapidated houses. Miss Madrid always said that these houses had once belonged to prominent Jews, although Murad wasn't at all sure about that. According to Miss Madrid, everything that was good and beautiful and clever had been made by or thought up by Jews. He could still hear those heavily shod feet somewhere behind him, and so he powered up the steep track between the houses as fast as he could. If he could get to the top of the hill, he could hide out in the derelict houses up by the church of St Mary of the Mongols and then take some time to think about what he might do next. The return of the police had come quickly and had taken him by surprise. Now he was going to have to do what he should have done before, which was to find someone who wasn't Ali Reza Zafir to take care of him while he decided what to do next. He had hoped one day to contact al-Qaeda or the Taliban and go off maybe to Afghanistan to fight. But he didn't know how to do that, and now he was alone and penniless and wanted by the police. Murad grunted with pain as he pushed himself up to the top of the hill and then looked around for the familiar entrance to the little group of derelict houses.

Chapter 26

'My parents would never do such a thing! You're lying!' the girl said as she pushed away from Ayşe Farsakoğlu and pulled her headscarf tightly across her face.

'Sabiha,' Ayşe said as she squatted down beside the girl, a man is coming here to kill you. He's doing it at the request of another man, who has been paid by your parents to murder you. I know it's a lot—'

'My parents would never do that, they love me!'

Ayşe put a hand on the girl's shoulder, which she shrugged off immediately. 'I know that it is truly awful to think about one's parents in this—'

'They have no need to kill me!' Sabiha cried. 'I haven't done anything wrong!' But she turned her face away as she made this denial, and Çetin İkmen saw her.

'Sabiha!' Ayşe pleaded. 'Please listen!'

'I haven't been with boys or . . .'

İkmen looked down at his watch. Seeing that Ismail Yıldız would very soon be with them, he sat on the other side of the girl and said, 'Now listen, I don't know what, if anything, you may have done with a boy or boys. What I do know is that your parents have been told, apparently by your brother, that you have been having some sort of relationship with a man.'

281

Sabiha was a pretty, narrow little thing. She creased her pale brow and said, 'My brother? Emir?'

'If that is your brother's name, yes,' İkmen said. 'The man who has been enlisted to kill you, a man who very fortunately came to us and now works for us, told me just that.'

'Yes, but Emir . . .' Her eyes began to fill with tears. 'Emir said that he liked Sami, that—'

'Sami is the boy you have been seeing?' İkmen asked.

'He's a neighbour, he . . .' She looked up into İkmen's eyes with a pleading expression on her face. 'Emir? You are sure it was Emir?'

'Unless you have another brother . . .'

'No.' She began to cry. Ayşe put a hand on her shoulder, which this time she did not resist. Suddenly she burst out, 'But I trusted him! How could he?'

'I don't know,' Ayşe said, biting her tongue in order to stop herself from talking about men and how treacherous they were. Such blatantly feminist rhetoric would not play well with a headscarved girl from the countryside, however 'bad' she may have been.

'Sabiha,' İkmen said, 'we have to catch this man who made the arrangement with your parents to have you killed. In order to do this, we have to make it look as if you have indeed died. But be assured that we will protect you at all times—'

'But my mother and father,' she cut in, her face now red with crying and anxiety. 'What will happen to them?'

İkmen looked across at Ayşe, who just shrugged. He knew he couldn't and wouldn't lie to the girl. 'They will be arrested,' he said.

'Arrested!'

'Sabiha, they are trying to have you killed,' Ayşe said.

'Yes, but arrested! My mother and my father . . .' She took her mobile phone out of her pocket and began to dial a number. İkmen grabbed it and pressed the cancel button.

'I can't let you warn them, Sabiha,' he said as he put the phone into his own jacket pocket. 'I'm sorry.'

Crying still, the girl said, 'But what will happen to me? If I've no mother or father? If I've no brother to care for me? What?'

Neither Ayşe nor İkmen had answers for her. She would be taken temporarily to a safe house for her own protection, but then . . . 'Very soon the man who was employed to kill you will arrive,' İkmen said. 'Sabiha, my dear, we must get ready. We may have only one chance to find and capture the evil person who is behind this wicked trade. We need you to help us.'

The Emins didn't have a clue about where their son might have gone.

'He goes to school, he works at some nargile place,' his father said. 'There's Hamid Bey . . .'

'He's dead.'

'Oh yes, right. There's Miss Madrid . . .'

'These are all people and places we know about!' Süleyman said impatiently. If Murad Emin had any sense, he wouldn't be hiding out with any of them. 'Don't you know who your son's friends are, Mr Emin?'

Mr Emin looked over at his wife, who shrugged and carried on smoking her joint.

283

'I've no idea,' he said. 'Murad's a close sort of a boy.'

'A close sort of a boy who looks at violent *jihadi* DVDs at work and has pictures of the dead bodies of infidels underneath his bed!' Süleyman roared. 'Mr Emin, I am coming around to the opinion that your son could very well have been involved in the death of his homosexual piano teacher, Hamid İdiz.'

'Oh, no, he always liked—'

'We've always made sure that Murad met all sorts of people from all over the world,' the boy's mother said. 'This is a house of liberal values, some would say immoral—'

'Your son clearly moves to a different rhythm from your own,' Süleyman cut in sharply. He looked around the dirty, neglected apartment and then went over to the boy's school bag and opened it. 'Maybe the answer lies in here,' he said.

As he bent down to pick the bag up, İzzet Melik whispered in his ear, 'What about Ali Reza Zafir, sir? They knew each other from İdiz's lessons and they both work at the Tulip.'

Süleyman looked into the bag, at tattered exercise books, a sweat-stained gym shirt and a load of leaking pens, and then nodded at his sergeant. 'OK,' he said, 'let's go.'

They'd lost Murad Emin in the rat-trap streets of Balat; they had no choice but to follow all and any leads that they did have.

İsmail Yıldız did not look like a killer. He was a shabby, sheepish-looking man who held the petrol can he had brought with him limply in his left hand. He passed it without comment over to İkmen, who poured the liquid on top of

284

the great bundle of rags he had constructed in the aluminium dustbin the *kapıcı* had brought in from the back yard. İkmen told Ismail to open one of the front windows ever so slightly so that passers-by might see and smell the smoke. Then he threw a match into the dustbin and told Ismail to run.

'What happens now?' Sabiha asked as she watched the flames from the dustbin shoot up and almost touch the living room ceiling.

İkmen watched for a few seconds, until the smoke reached the window and began to make its way outside. Then he took his mobile phone out of his pocket and pressed a key to bring up a pre-programmed number. In less than five seconds, someone answered.

'We're "go" here,' he said into the instrument, then he looked at the two women in front of him and smiled. 'Not long now,' he said.

Ayşe looked at the girl Sabiha as she shivered and went white in the light of the ever-rising flames. The two women moved out of the room and into the hall.

Dr Zafir was in a jocular mood. 'Oh, you're in luck, Inspector,' he said to Süleyman as he let him and İzzet Melik into his very smart apartment. 'Ali Reza is with us this evening. Often he works at his little job in the nargile salon, but not tonight.' He called the boy. 'Ali Reza!'

A small blonde woman sat on one of the large sofas in the lounge: Zafir's engineer wife. She greeted the officers warmly and then offered them tea, which they accepted. She called for the maid to make the drinks while she smiled very prettily and they all waited for the boy.

'Dad?' The boy, standing at the bottom of the apartment's grand staircase, looked at the police officers and then at his father with concern on his face.

Dr Zafir went over to his son, put his arm around his shoulder and brought him into the room. 'The officers want to ask you something, Ali Reza,' he said. 'No need for alarm.'

'We need to know whether you've seen Murad Emin,' Süleyman said, getting straight to the point. He saw the boy look at İzzet Melik. 'We know that you work together at the Tulip,' he said. 'We know that you know each other better than you would have had us believe.'

Dr Zafir brought his son over to his mother and sat the boy between them. His face expressed concern and he said, 'What are you implying, Inspector?'

'I'm implying nothing,' Süleyman said. 'I'm saying as a statement of fact that your son and the Emin boy sought for reasons best known to themselves to conceal the extent of their friendship from us. I don't know why. The fact is that we need to speak to Murad Emin urgently, and so if your son knows where he is . . .'

'Why do you want to speak to Murad?' the boy asked. 'What has he done?'

'Why do you think he's done anything?' Süleyman countered.

Ali Reza looked up at his parents and then down at the floor.

'Well?'

Dr Zafir looked at Süleyman with daggers in his eyes. How dare this mere public servant speak to his son like that!

The boy looked up and sighed. 'Inspector, I haven't seen Murad since last night, at the Tulip.'

'You were working together.'

'Yes.'

'You haven't seen him today? This evening?'

'No.'

'My son has been here with us since four,' his father said. 'He finished school at three and then came straight home on the bus.'

'I wasn't feeling too good,' Ali Reza said.

'Why was that?'

'Oh, Inspector, the boy—'

'It's all right, Dad,' Ali Reza said with a smile. He turned to Süleyman. 'Actually, I have been meaning to say something before, but . . .' He lowered his eyes. 'Working with Murad has become a bit of a trial lately.'

Dr and Mrs Zafir both frowned.

'In what way?' Süleyman asked.

'He makes me nervous,' the boy said. 'With his opinions about people and . . . He doesn't like unbelievers.'

'People who are not Muslims?'

'Yes.' He looked up with strained, bloodshot eyes.

'Well, Ali Reza,' Süleyman said, 'we did gather that for ourselves when we interviewed Murad.' He looked at İzzet Melik, who nodded his agreement. 'We got the impression that this was nothing new.'

'It isn't,' Ali Reza said. 'It's always been annoying and upsetting. I thought that we were friends.' He looked genuinely hurt. 'I tolerated it for a while because he was my friend, but then it went further.'

287

'What do you mean?'

'He started getting into all the *jihadi* stuff,' Ali Reza said. 'DVDs. He got them from those bearded crazy men you see on the street over where he lives. Then photographs and websites he was told to go on and . . . I think he may even want to join the Taliban or something.'

His mother put a hand up to her chest and murmured, 'Allah!'

Süleyman leaned forward in his seat and looked the boy hard in the eyes. 'Now tell me the truth, Ali Reza,' he said. Do you think that Murad could possibly have had something to do with Hamid İdiz's death? You have nothing to fear; just tell me the truth.'

'I don't know,' the boy said, a little sulkily, Süleyman thought. 'Why should I? Murad is no friend of mine, not any more.'

İkmen had his mobile phone on vibrate, but he still took it out of his pocket to look at it. He didn't trust technology and was anxious to be right there when Ismail Yıldız called. Now that the fire officers were inside the apartment, the whole street, including a strangely subdued *kapıcı*, were out and about and seeing what they could see. Usually the most vocal of people, whipping up people's emotions and spreading gossip whenever anything happened in the buildings they cared for, this *kapıcı*, on this occasion, was virtually silent.

Now divested of her dowdy clothes and horrible head-scarf, Ayşe Farsakoğlu was in charge of the scene, while Çetin İkmen, still in his uncomfortably smart suit, stood behind the crowd and out of sight. Ismail Yıldız had headed home as soon as his job was done, and was now awaiting instructions from Cem. None of İkmen's officers had reported seeing anyone answering Cem's description in or around the scene. Yet he would have to somehow verify what had happened, which could mean that he would either come by himself in the near future or maybe send someone else to check it out.

As the body bag containing what İkmen knew was in fact the live body of the girl Sabiha was carried out of the building and into the street, and Ayşe yelled at her officers to keep the weeping locals at bay, one such weeping local raised his mobile phone in the air and took a picture. Some people, it appeared, were rather less distrusting of electronics than İkmen.

Chapter 27

You couldn't trust Gonca the gypsy's kids.

'Oi, you!' one of them called out to Izabella as she walked past the Church of St Mary of the Mongols. 'In them derelict houses. There's that boy you teach the piano, the one whose mum sells her snatch!'

Izabella Madrid wasn't shocked. 'Sells her snatch, does she?' she said very calmly. 'Is that the same as trading your arse? Better? Worse?'

For a moment the child, a boy, looked confused, and then he said, 'My mum's an artist and she makes more money then you! Her boyfriend's got a gun!'

'Yes, he's a policeman,' Izabella said.

'My mum can have anyone she likes!'

He ran away laughing. Izabella resisted the urge to shout out something really obscene about his mother and just smiled to herself instead. Then she looked at the derelict houses. They'd been in that state for years. Kids had always played in them, although not generally serious sorts like Murad Emin. She hoped he hadn't been chased into the old buildings by the gypsies' kids or other 'rough' types.

Izabella went into the first house, which was really just two walls and half a ceiling, and called out the boy's name.

There was no reply. The sky was darkening and the place was taking on a distinctly spooky character. Not that Izabella was easily frightened. She was, she always told anyone who asked her, about threats both physical and supernatural, far too old and too ugly to be really afraid of anything. But that wasn't altogether quite true, and when she went into the next house, which had the benefit of a back wall, she did feel just a little shudder pass through her body.

'Murad!'

Her voice echoed around what had once possibly been the home of a man of substance and his family; a merchant, a jeweller or a pharmacist. It was very strange that Murad should be in such a place, if indeed he was. The boy worked most evenings at the Tulip nargile salon.

'Murad, it's Miss Madrid,' she said. 'Gonca the gypsy's children have gone now; you can come out.'

Gonca's tribe were not generally vicious or bullying, but they were completely wild and totally without religious direction. A pious boy like Murad would be a prime target for such carefree rolling stones, particularly in view of the fact that he had a mother they could all make fun of. Poor Mrs Emin. A junkie like her husband, although rather more degraded inasmuch as she was the one who sold herself for their heroin. With what she earned, the Emins could probably have afforded to pay for Murad to have piano lessons with Hamid İdiz, but their 'gear' had, as always, come way before their children. Murad had in recent times become a rather more haughty and challenging boy than he had been, and Izabella found the Islamicisation of almost his every utterance wearing and incomprehensible. But she was sure that given time and increased wisdom he would come to a rather more balanced and peaceable interpretation of his religion. He was, after all, a clever boy.

She knew that she wasn't alone when something moved towards the back of the building and a rat ran out and across the front of her shoes.

'Murad?'

She had begun to walk over towards the place from which the rat had come when suddenly the boy stood up and ran towards her.

'Oh, Miss Madrid!' Murad Emin said as he raced into her somewhat startled embrace. 'You've got to help me!'

She said that she would, of course she did; he was crying by this time. But his race into her infidel embrace gave her pause deep down inside. The Murad she knew just didn't do things like that, not any more.

It was gone eight o'clock when Saadet heard Cahit and her nephew Aykan leave the apartment. Cahit wanted to show him, so he said, a new coffee house. But he didn't take Lokman, and Saadet knew why. She knew the signs. He was going to a brothel and he was taking that great fat lump of a nephew with him, because where else would Aykan get sex?

Cahit had been a hypocrite almost from the start. The first time she'd seen him coming out of the brothel back in the village, he'd told her he'd only done what he'd done for her sake. A decent woman like her wouldn't want to have to pander to his baser urges, would she? He wouldn't expect it of her. He was doing it for her! But then, for a time, he'd been at the brothel more than he'd been at home. Saadet had spoken nervously to his mother, who had beaten her for telling on her husband but had put a stop to it. As a punishment, Cahit had made Saadet do what the whores had done. Then they'd moved to the city and he'd started going to brothels again.

She heard the door shut behind them and settled in to listening to the television from the next room. Nesrin and the hated Feray were in there, rotting their brains with soap operas and American sitcoms they couldn't possibly appreciate. Saadet thought about Gözde and how much she had loved the American series *Friends*. She'd wanted so much, she'd told Saadet one day, a nice apartment with friends just like Rachel. At the time, Saadet had smacked her for her 'looseness'. Now the thought of it made her want to cry with shame. Whatever that girl had done had been nothing compared to what had been done to her, what Saadet had *allowed* to be done to her! But she did not allow herself the luxury of tears. She was a terrible, terrible woman who deserved absolutely no compassion, not even from herself.

She heard Nesrin laugh her silly high-pitched laugh and wondered how, if at all, she could persuade Lokman to defy his father and not marry her. Nesrin wasn't a bad girl – she wasn't like her mother – but Saadet knew that her son could do so much better. The boy would be bored with her after just days, and then they would both be unhappy. She thought about her soldier and about how some of the sexual things she had hated to do with Cahit she had loved with him. As she closed her eyes she could see herself, young and naked, her body straining towards his under the full sun of a summer

294

morning. She was aware of the fact that the front door of the apartment had opened and closed once again, but she thought that it was probably because Lokman had now gone out too.

So she was very surprised when less than a minute later Lokman opened the door of her prison and looked down at her. She could only hope that he wasn't going to hit her.

He whispered, 'Auntie Feray has just gone out. Nesrin is dozing. If you want to go, now has to be the time.'

'But Lokman . . .'

'Sssh!' He put a hand over her mouth and then raised her up from the floor so he could speak to her. 'I don't know what the truth is,' he said softly. 'But if there is a chance that Father killed Gözde, then that cannot stand.'

She looked into his eyes as he took his hand away from her mouth. 'Lokman . . .'

'I'm doing this for Gözde,' he said. Then he added almost grudgingly, 'And because Father shouldn't rape you, it's wrong.'

'Send it to him,' İkmen said to the terrified boy who had just taken a very bad, very shaky photograph of the body bag being loaded into an ambulance. He'd tried to get the fire appliance into the shot as well but had only managed to photograph one rather anonymous open door.

The boy sent the photograph to the man, apparently called Al, who had given him twenty lire to take it for him.

'Where and when did you meet this man?' İkmen asked. There was a tall, broad constable at his side now, who the boy looked at with fear.

'I don't know. Maybe twenty minutes ago?' the kid said. He was no more than fifteen, spotty and geeky. He'd no doubt spend his twenty lire on computer games. 'He said there was a fire.'

'Which he wanted photographs of?'

'He wanted photos if they brought a dead body out,' the boy said.

'Did he say why?'

'No.'

İkmen didn't ask the boy why he had agreed to perform such a gruesome task for someone he didn't know. The kid was dressed shabbily; it was obvious. He asked him where he'd met the man, and the boy pointed to a small alleyway on the left that passed beside a grocer's shop.

'What did he look like?' İkmen asked as he looked down at the boy's phone to see whether 'Al' responded to what had been sent to him.

'Oh, he was old,' the boy said.

'And by old you mean . . .'

'Thirty-five,' the boy said, 'maybe even forty.'

Even the constable, who was no more than twenty-five himself, smiled.

'I see,' İkmen said. 'Ancient. And was he short? Tall? Fat or thin? Dark or fair?'

The boy looked up into the sky, as if that might suddenly and magically improve his memory, then he said, 'Well . . .'

İkmen's phone began to ring, and he put it to his ear immediately.

'It's me,' Ismail Yıldız said.

'Yes? And?'

'Cem has just called,' he said. 'He wants to meet me at the nargile salon at the Royal Tombs on the corner of Divan Yolu and Babıali Street.'

'When?'

'As soon as I can get there,' Ismail said. 'I'm leaving home now. I'll take a taxi.'

İkmen reckoned it would take Ismail about ten minutes to get from his home in Fatih to the Royal Tombs in Sultanahmet. It would take İkmen about the same amount of time to jump in his car and go over there.

'I'll be there,' he said. 'But if you get there before me, keep Cem with you for as long as you can.'

'Yes, Çetin Bey.' Ismail cut the connection.

İkmen told the boy to give his details to the constable at his side, then he went over to Hikmet Yıldız and told him to follow him to his car. Hikmet was in plain clothes, but İkmen chose two uniformed officers to accompany him as well. Arresting this Cem, an unknown quantity, could be quite straightforward or it could be problematic. He had no idea.

Just before they headed off towards Sultanahmet, Ayşe Farsakoğlu came over to the car and said to İkmen, 'Sabiha's family are apparently returning to the apartment.'

'Well I'm off, hopefully to meet Cem,' he said. 'Play along with them until I've secured him.'

'Yes, sir.'

He drove off in the direction of the Royal Tombs in Sultanahmet.

* * *

Ali Reza Zafir had no idea about where Murad Emin liked to go when he wasn't either at his piano lessons or at work. İzzet Melik had been obliged to tell the owner of the Tulip nargile salon who and what he really was when he and his colleague had found those extremist DVDs. Now, with Süleyman, he returned to the salon, but the boy wasn't there and no one had any sort of idea where he might be.

As they left the Tulip, İzzet said, 'I think he's probably still in Balat.'

He hadn't gone back to his parents' apartment. A constable had been left there with Mr and Mrs Emin, and he said that Murad had most definitely not been seen.

Süleyman was still not happy about going back to Balat yet again, but he said, 'You may be right. We should check it out.'

'With junkies for parents, the kid can't have that much money, even though he does work,' İzzet said. 'And Balat is a very good place to hide out. Lots of nooks, crannies and ruins.'

They got into Süleyman's car and headed for the Atatürk Bridge. As Süleyman pulled out into the horn-hooting traffic, he said, 'You know, İzzet, I'm not sure that I understand the relationship between Ali Reza and Murad Emin.'

'Relationship?'

'I don't mean that they're lovers or anything like that,' Süleyman said. 'I think they are or were friends, very good friends. But there's something else too. A feeling of . . . indebtedness?'

İzzet frowned. 'What do you mean?'

'I'm not really certain,' Süleyman said. 'Maybe it has

something to do with their piano-playing. When we first met Ali Reza he said he wanted to be a concert pianist. But from what I can gather, it is Murad who has the musical genius.'

'You think Ali Reza might be jealous?'

'It has to be possible,' Süleyman replied. 'And yet surely if he was *that* jealous, he would have informed on Murad's interest in terrorism when he first found out about it. Clearly he didn't do that, even though he claims that it bothered him. The boys have to be rivals in this upcoming Turco–Caucasian music festival. Why not get Murad out of the way?'

'He'll be out of the way now,' İzzet replied.

'Yes, but why not off him sooner?' Süleyman asked. 'It's not like Ali Reza is some sort of street kid who will attract reprisals. He could have got rid of Murad at any time. Why didn't he?'

Chapter 28

Cem was the invisible man. As the boy back in Çarşamba had told him, İkmen saw that he was indeed about thirty-five, medium height, medium build, not particularly dark and not particularly fair either. He wore dull, rather rumpled clothing, typical of a manual labourer from the country. He had a small, nascent moustache and a flat cap that sat as if dropped directly down from heaven on the top of his head. Ismail Yıldız, in his loose cream shirt and baggy *şalvar* trousers, looked positively exotic in comparison.

While İkmen and Hikmet Yıldız watched, the two men greeted each other and Ismail ordered tea. Neither man smoked or did much beyond say a very few words to each other until their drinks had arrived. İkmen put his radio to his ear in order to hear their conversation. Ismail Yıldız had worn a wire to record his every encounter since he'd left the girl Sabiha's apartment. The two men chatted about this and that, the weather and the pollution in the city, until İkmen heard Ismail say, 'So, brother, you have called me here to talk about the job and also, I hope, to pay me. The job was satisfactory?'

There was a pause, a slight smirk even, then a very light and youthful voice said, 'The job was done well.'

'The girl . . .'

'The girl is where her parents wanted her to be,' Cem said.

'Did you have any . . . problems?'

'With the girl?'

'Yes.'

'No.'

There was a pause. İkmen had not discussed in detail what Ismail was supposed to say to Cem about how he had killed Sabiha. In the silence between the men, he winced.

'What's the matter?' Hikmet Yıldız asked him.

'I should have briefed your brother more comprehensively about how he would kill the girl,' İkmen said. 'I . . .'

'No problem getting in,' Ismail said. 'Luckily she had her back to me and so I just grabbed her from behind.'

'Dangerous to pour the accelerant over her at such close quarters.'

'I pushed her to the floor,' Ismail continued. 'She knocked her head as she fell, which stunned her, and as she lay there I poured it on to her and then lit a match. It was all over in seconds.'

İkmen, hidden in the darkness of the night amongst the royal gravestones, made another painful face.

'What do you mean, she died immediately?' Cem asked, clearly shocked.

'Well, no. No, she didn't *die* immediately,' Ismail said. 'There was writhing around and some screaming and . . .'

'You seem very cool for a man who has just taken the life of another,' Cem said.

'Ah! He is not convinced, I don't think,' İkmen said to Hikmet Yıldız. 'This could be a problem.'

302

'My brother is very imaginative,' Hikmet said by way of at least some level of comfort for İkmen. Although even Hikmet was worried now. If Cem just upped and walked away, they would not have nearly so strong a case against him as either an outright confession or the exchange of money could demonstrate.

'I took the life of a bad woman,' Ismail said with some rather unexpected confidence. 'How would you expect me to feel? This is pious work. I am elated.'

'Well, yes, of course!' This time it was Cem who was clearly wrong-footed.

'Good boy,' İkmen murmured. 'Good, Ismail.'

'Of course you are,' Cem repeated.

'Such necessary work is an honour and a pleasure.'

'Yes.' There was a pause while Cem drank his tea and Ismail Yıldız looked straight ahead with a small smile on his face.

'So, um,' Cem said eventually. 'If more such opportunities were to come along . . .'

'I would be delighted to oblige,' Ismail said. He lowered his voice a little and added, 'But, as we agreed, a man must eat, and . . .'

'Of course.'

Sometimes, İkmen felt, it wasn't easy being a Turk. Unless one was talking about the desperate, hand-to-mouth criminal fraternity, common courtesy precluded any rapid route to discussion of money. Even the city's most hardened gangsters winced away from it. Negotiations were always lengthy and frequently, at least to start with, oblique.

'I may well contact you again, when another opportunity arises,' Cem said.

'Is that likely?'

Cem smiled. 'I have, shall we say, a few people to see.'

They both went back to drinking their tea and quiet contemplation. Much as İkmen knew that Ismail could not hurry this meeting, he moved his feet agitatedly. He looked at Hikmet Yıldız, who was watching his brother intently. Cem was a completely unknown quantity; he could refuse to pay Ismail, he could attack him, he could even be armed. Guntoting was not unknown even in very populous areas like Sultanahmet.

Ismail Yıldız smiled. 'Well, Cem Bey,' he said, 'I am afraid that I really have to go now. My brother will return home soon and I want to be there for him. I don't want him asking any questions.'

'No.'

Cem did not move to take anything from either his jacket pocket or his trousers. Did he even have any money to give to Ismail? İkmen began to feel his heart pound.

Ismail, still smiling, said, 'And so, Cem Bey?'

'And so . . .'

'Cem Bey,' Ismail persisted. 'As I said before, a man must live . . .'

Had İkmen been closer to the men, he would have seen a twinkle in Cem's eye as he said, 'Ah, so you don't do what you do just for the sake of a place in Paradise?'

Ismail looked down at the ground. 'Were I a rich man, that would be my pleasure,' he said. 'But you sought out a poor man with no job. I am pious and observant, as you know, but . . .'

'It's OK,' Cem said with a small chuckle in his voice.

'You are of course quite right, and I have to thank you very sincerely on behalf of the girl's family for a job well done.'

He put his hand into his jacket pocket and pulled out what looked like a very heavily stuffed envelope.

'Right, that's it!' İkmen said. Hikmet Yıldız beside him used his radio to call the constables still in the car on Divan Yolu. Then he drew his pistol and followed his superior up into the tea garden and nargile salon above. Cem looked confused as İkmen approached him. He barely noticed Hikmet Yıldız come in behind him. In vain he tried to take back the packet, but Ismail had now passed it over to İkmen.

'Hello, Cem,' İkmen said with a smile. 'Police. We've been dying to meet you.'

Inspector İkmen was out, apparently. Not off duty and at home, but out.

'He must be working somewhere,' Lokman Seyhan said to his mother Saadet as he sat down beside her. They were in the waiting room at the front of the station together with all the other people who wanted to see this or that officer or just simply talk to the police.

'Do they know when he will be getting back?'

'No.'

Saadet took one of her son's hands in hers and said, 'You should go back to the apartment. If your father finds both of us gone . . .'

'I don't want to go back to him if he killed my sister,' Lokman said. Then he sighed. 'I don't want to marry Nesrin.'

'Why didn't you say?'

'To him?' Lokman said. 'He'd made up his mind. You know how he is!'

Saadet lowered her head. Yes, she knew how Cahit was when he made up his mind about something. Poor Lokman, the only thing she could not forgive *him* for was his treatment of his brother Kenan. That had been cruel and heartless; that had been just like his father. But she said nothing. A man sitting next to Lokman lay down on the bench and immediately began to snore.

'If Father did arrange for Gözde to be killed . . .'

'I swear to you that he did!' Saadet said, looking around her all the time in case anyone might be listening.

'Mother, you had better be very sure of your facts . . .'

'I saw the killer with my own eyes,' Saadet said.

Lokman sat back in his seat as if deflated and said, 'How?'

'We passed him when we left the apartment on our way over to Fatih, on the day of Gözde's death,' she said. 'Your father pointed him out to me. He made sure that I knew, that I felt pain, that I felt responsible for bringing such a bad girl into this world.'

It had taken Lokman Seyhan some time and thought to decide what, if anything, he believed about his mother's story. All afternoon and half the evening he had considered it, raking the facts she had told him over and over in his mind. To be truthful, he hadn't believed her when he unlocked her room, let her out and helped her to get past his sleeping, snoring cousin, Nesrin. But he'd heard his father rape his mother the night before and he knew he couldn't let her go through that all over again. Cahit had taken his cousin Aykan to a brothel, and Lokman knew that although his father would

306

be what he described as 'sorted out' there, he'd still want his wife when he got home. A whore was just for a hand job or a blow, depending on how much money you had, but a wife was for intercourse and babies, and Lokman knew that his father wanted to have more children. He had after all, as Cahit Seyhan put it himself, 'lost' two of his children, who now needed to be replaced. Since they had left Fatih, Saadet had told Lokman a lot more about his father and Gözde and how she had died. He was now sure that his mother was right. But he was still anxious about what the police might say and do. He was angry too, and not just at his father.

'Why didn't you do anything?' he asked his mother as the door of the station opened and shut. It was not Çetin İkmen, but some man who just went up to the front desk and wept. 'Why didn't you try and save Gözde? You could have told me or Kenan or—'

'Oh, and you would have believed me?' Saadet said.

'Kenan would . . . he did,' Lokman said. 'Remember his suicide note?'

'Yes.' Of course she did. But Kenan had only guessed, that, or he'd worked it out for himself. He hadn't *known*, inasmuch as she had never told him. She had been too frightened of Cahit to speak to anyone, even the son, whom she knew would believe her and who would have helped her to spirit Gözde away. What a coward she had been! Afraid of a beating, afraid of giving up her own life for her young daughter. 'I am not a good person. I am weak,' she said at length. 'I cannot bring Gözde back, or Kenan, but I must try to put some of it right now.'

Lokman looked at her without the great affection he had once felt for her but with a new respect nevertheless. 'I'm staying with you,' he said. 'We'll get through this together. We don't have anyone else.'

Süleyman had already decided to pay a visit to Murad Emin's piano teacher, Izabella Madrid, when he and İzzet Melik came across Gonca the gypsy. She was walking past the Church of St Mary of the Mongols and she had her youngest boy, Rambo, who was about twelve, with her. She did not look happy, and was shouting at the boy in the Roma language she used when she was alone with her family and friends. He, in turn, swore at her in Turkish and then, before anyone could stop him, ran over to Süleyman and said, 'Shoot her with your gun! Go on! Shoot the old witch!'

Rambo had always been a handful, but now that he was on the edge of puberty, he was taking on some of the characteristics of a monster.

Süleyman, hideously embarrassed, especially in front of İzzet Melik, said, 'Now, Rambo, that is no way to speak about your mother.'

'She treats me like a kid!' the boy said, and imitated his mother's voice: 'Oh come home now, Rambo, it's dark!'

'You shouldn't play in the derelict houses up here!' Gonca said as she made herself look at her boy and not at her lover. 'Junkies take drugs in them! They're full of needles! What do you want, eh, Rambo? You want to get AIDS?'

The boy rounded on her furiously. 'I won't get AIDS!' he shouted at her. 'But you will! You fuck everything, you do!'

Aware that they were losing what could be valuable time

in the midst of this 'domestic', İzzet Melik put a hand on Süleyman's arm. 'Sir . . .'

'Rambo!'

'It's true,' he said. 'You're no better than that boy's mum who sells her snatch for gear.'

'I don't sell myself!' Gonca said as she finally looked at Süleyman and felt her heart jump inside her chest. Then she said to her son, 'What woman? What do you mean?'

Rambo looked at Süleyman and İzzet Melik and said, 'The woman whose boy goes to the old Jewish woman who teaches piano.' He prodded Süleyman's chest with his finger. 'She knows you.'

It had to be Izabella Madrid, the woman they were on their way to see. 'How do you know that, Rambo?' Süleyman asked.

'What's it worth?' the boy answered arrogantly.

Before Süleyman could answer, İzzet Melik pushed himself forward and took the boy by the scruff of his neck. 'A fucking good smack if you don't tell us!' he said.

Furious that her son should be manhandled by anyone except her, Gonca flew at İzzet and tried to prise his hands off Rambo, but without success. 'Don't you—'

'How do you know Miss Madrid?' İzzet persisted. 'Come on, you little sod, tell me!'

It wasn't often that Mehmet Süleyman felt ineffectual, but this was one of those rare occasions. He just stood while İzzet shook the boy and Gonca tried unsuccessfully to get Rambo released.

'Well?'

'I don't know the Jewish lady or the boy! I hear things,

that's all. See them about,' Rambo said. He was trying to keep a defiant expression on his face but he was in reality really quite scared of someone as bulky, rude and seemingly without limits as İzzet. 'The boy was hiding out in the derelict houses. The old woman come past and I told her he was in there.'

'When?'

'I dunno, couple of hours ago.'

İzzet began to loosen his hold on the boy and said, 'So did she go in to look for him? Did she?'

Süleyman was looking over İzzet and Rambo's heads at Gonca, who had now given up trying to rescue her son and was gazing back at the man she loved with tears in her eyes. To meet him unexpectedly like this was killing her. And yet she knew that it would not be the last time that something like this was going to happen. İstanbul, all twelve million people of it, was still at heart a collection of villages.

At last Rambo spoke again. 'Yes, she looked for him and she found him.'

'Oh?'

'Yeah,' he said. 'I see them go off back down in the direction of the old synagogue. She had her arm around him. The silly boy was crying.'

İzzet let Rambo go and looked across at Süleyman. 'That doesn't sound very much like the Murad Emin that we know,' he said. 'We'd best get down to Miss Madrid's, sir.'

Chapter 29

The girl Sabiha's parents denied everything. They were, they said – or rather the father said for both of them – horrified that their daughter had apparently perished in a house fire. So far they hadn't actually seen either their apparently ruined apartment or their dead daughter, but they had been devastated by the scene outside their block. Did they know a man called Cem? No, they didn't. They knew no one by the name of Ismail Yıldız either.

Cem, whose surname was apparently Koç, said very little. He was clear on the fact that he didn't want a lawyer, but that was all.

'You were recorded handing a sum of money comprising two thousand Turkish lire to a man called İbrahim Yıldız in the Royal Tombs nargile salon earlier this evening,' İkmen said. 'What was that for?'

Cem Koç turned away and stared at the smudgy grey wall of the interview room.

İkmen looked at Ayşe Farsakoğlu and lit up a cigarette. Cem wrinkled his nose in very obvious disgust.

'The law, for the moment, permits me to smoke, and so I shall,' İkmen said. 'If you don't like that, Mr Koç, I'm afraid there's nothing I can do about it.'

311

Resolutely silent, Cem Koç continued to stare at the wall.

'Mr Yıldız is claiming that you employed him to kill a young woman called Sabiha Şafak,' Ayşe Farsakoğlu said. 'This was at the request of her parents, who, Mr Yıldız claims, wished to dispose of Sabiha because she had besmirched their honour. There was a young man involved, it was alleged.'

Still nothing. İkmen frowned. On tape at least, Cem Koç had admitted no liability for the procurement of Ismail Yıldız's services as a paid assassin. It had been alluded to, but no direct reference had been made to murder, and the girl had not been named. There was the money, and the fact that the key to the Şafaks' apartment had been left ready for Ismail to let himself in. But there was also a lot of the brother of a policeman's word against that of Mr Koç. In his head, İkmen could hear Ardıç's fury. He could also imagine how difficult life could now become for Ismail Yıldız, who did, after all, have to go back to live in Fatih near this man Koç and, no doubt, Koç's friends too.

'Mr Koç,' İkmen continued, 'does the name Tayfun Ergin mean anything to you?'

If he could give Koç an 'out', allowing him to name and shame his boss – if indeed that was the case – that might help.

Not a flicker.

'We think,' İkmen said, 'that some people in this city are using honour killing as a way of making money. Can you imagine such a dreadful thing? Making money out of the misfortune of having a daughter or a wife who has dishonoured her family? How cynical! How opportunistic!'

312

He felt rather than saw Ayşe look at him. She knew precisely what he was doing. Spiritual cop, secular cop. She slipped very easily into the role. 'And what of the girls?' she said. 'Sabiha Şafak, then over in Beşiktaş, Gözde Seyhan burnt like a Roman candle. We're also looking at some poor girls who have died mysteriously even further back than that.'

They both saw that Cem Koç was about to speak. He stopped himself, then did let himself utter. 'I know your name,' he said to İkmen, 'even if you don't look the way you do on the television. You're not concerned with honour! You are a man without God or tradition!'

'Oh, and you are?' İkmen asked. 'A man who gives two thousand lire to another man in a nargile salon for, it would seem, no apparent reason? What's that about?'

'I've not done anything.'

'Anything what?' İkmen said. 'Anything illegal, immoral, what?'

'I . . .' And then as if suddenly realising he was talking when he should be silent, Cem Koç shut up. He folded his arms across his chest, looked back at the wall and closed his mouth tight shut.

Izabella Madrid's apartment was dark and silent when they got there. There was no television set banging away in the background and there certainly wasn't anyone at the piano. İzzet Melik looked at Süleyman, whose face was as troubled as the sergeant's mind.

'You're worried.'

'I'm not comfortable,' Süleyman said.

The baker who owned the shop downstairs had told them that he'd seen Miss Madrid come home with one of her students a couple of hours before. They'd gone into the apartment, and according to the baker, they had not left since.

'What choice do we have?' Süleyman said. He withdrew his gun from the holster underneath his jacket and with his free hand hammered his fist on the door. 'Miss Madrid! Miss Madrid, it's the police. Open up!'

Only silence washed back at him from inside the house. He looked down into the street below and was relieved to see that Gonca had finally done what she'd been told and gone home. She'd seen the look of panic in Süleyman's eyes when Rambo had told him about Izabella Madrid and Murad Emin. The boy, she deduced, had to be a problem at the very least, possibly violent and dangerous. She had flown after her lover and his deputy and in the face of Süleyman's entreaties had begged him not to go, pleading with him to send İzzet Melik on his own. The man from İzmir had rolled his eyes in despair at that point. Also at that point, Süleyman had rounded on her. Telling İzzet to go on ahead and wait for him outside the Ahrida Synagogue, he had looked her hard in the face and said, 'I used you. Your insane behaviour forces me to finally tell you the truth. It was just sex, Gonca. You're good, I'll grant you. But you're also old and I'm glad you finished it. Now I can find a woman of my own age.'

Then he'd walked away from her. At first she'd raced down the hill after him, hurling abuse. But once they had got near to the synagogue, her steps had slowed and she had just stopped and stared at him. Now, mercifully, she had gone.

'Miss Madrid!' İzzet yelled. 'Open up!'

314

Still nothing happened. After a few moments, Süleyman told İzzet Melik to stand on the other side of the door, then he counted them both down to zero. They kicked in the door and stood back behind the walls on either side to look within. While Süleyman covered him with his pistol, İzzet took his torch out and shone it into the dark little apartment. From the front door they could see right through to Miss Madrid's small living room. Straight as a ramrod she could be seen sitting up on a tall wooden dining chair. Her face was pale but not nearly as pallid as that of Murad Emin, who sat by her side. He was shaking and he had a gun up to her head.

'Do you have any idea when Inspector İkmen will be able to talk to me?' Saadet Seyhan asked the officer on the front desk. İkmen had apparently re-entered the station at some point, but now he was busy.

'No.' The officer didn't even look up at her. Some newspaper or other was far more interesting.

'Sir!'

'I've told you!'

'Please!'

Now he did look up and pointed to the back of the room where Lokman was reclining half asleep on the bench. 'Go back to your son!'

'Sir, I have urgent information for Çetin Bey!' Saadet said. 'Please! Please!'

'Inspector İkmen is a very busy man,' the officer said. 'He'll see you when he can and not before. Sit down or I'll have both you and your son thrown out!'

As time had gone on, Saadet had become more and more

desperate. She wanted to see İkmen, to get it over with, to have Cahit in custody before he fetched up at the station demanding that she and Lokman go home with him. İkmen had definitely returned from somewhere; she'd heard one of the other officers at the desk say so. But ever since then he'd been 'busy'. It was pitch black outside now and she knew that Cahit had to be back from the brothel by this time. She feared what he was thinking, what he was imagining she and Lokman might be up to. More than anything she wanted to protect her last remaining child, even if he was Cahit's son.

Before she left the desk she said, 'I have urgent information for the inspector. About a case he wishes to solve. I can help him!'

'Can you?' The officer put his paper down and looked at her, for the first time, with just a small smile on his face.

'Yes,' she said. 'Yes, I can! It's about—'

'You know we have a man who comes in here every day with "urgent" information for Inspector İkmen,' the officer said. 'It's always about either Communists, aliens or the ghost of some Byzantine emperor.'

Saadet began to feel herself shrink. But she said, 'I am not mad.'

'That's what he says,' the officer said, and then he roared at her, 'Sit down and wait your turn!'

Lokman, who had been asleep until then, looked around him with glazed, shocked eyes.

'It's my own stupid fault,' the old woman said as she looked at the two policemen at the end of her hall. 'I should have got rid of that gun years ago.' She shrugged. 'It was my father's, he was very fond of it. I kept it on the piano. Just in case.'

'Just in case?'

'Just in case someone should try to rob me,' Izabella Madrid said. She looked over at Murad Emin, whose sweaty hand now held that gun, and added, 'You know my father fought in the War of Independence, with Atatürk. Fought the Greeks, the British, the French. That weapon came through all that with him. I reckoned that if it could protect him, it could protect me. But the world turns and things change and what do you know, now I'm going to be killed by it.'

She seemed very calm. But then as Süleyman had frequently observed, quite a few elderly people were calm when faced with their own mortality. 'Is it loaded?' he asked.

'Oh yes,' she said. 'I always made sure of that.'

'Murad, son,' İzzet Melik said, 'we just want to talk.'

'No you don't,' the boy said. 'You want to arrest me.'

'What for?' Süleyman asked. 'Why would we want to arrest you?'

Murad Emin didn't answer.

'If it's about the DVDs we found at the Tulip, then we do need to talk,' Süleyman said. He didn't mention that he thought that Murad could have killed his old piano teacher, Hamid İdiz. He didn't want to alarm the boy, not in this position. 'Watching that stuff isn't good for you, Murad. The people who do those things are sick.'

'No they're not, they're good Muslims!' the boy said. 'If the infidels will not change their ways, then they have to be killed.'

'No they don't,' Süleyman said.

'What do you know?'

'I know that the Koran is a sacred and noble text that exhorts Muslims to care for others, to refrain from killing and to be understanding of and kind to unbelievers, whoever they are,' he said.

The boy did not reply. So many kids like this, radicalised by shrill clerics, evil videos and toxic pamphlets, hadn't even read the Koran. They just took in the bile of others to plug the gaps in their own sad, lonely or unfulfilled lives. Murad Emin, a musical genius, did not entirely fit that profile. But he was still angry, unstable and armed.

'Miss Madrid has only ever had your best interests at heart, Murad,' Süleyman said. 'You don't want to hurt her. Put the gun down and let's talk.'

'Why should I do that?' He pushed the muzzle of the pistol still further into the old lady's temple.

'Because at the moment we have a situation that is not too serious,' Süleyman said. 'But if you pull that trigger, if you kill somebody . . .'

'How do you know that I haven't done that already?' Murad said. 'Have you thought about that? Have you wondered whether I may have killed someone else?'

Süleyman hadn't wanted to even get near to any sort of discussion about Hamid İdiz, even though he thought that Murad might very well have killed him. Talk of İdiz would agitate the boy whichever way one looked at it. If he had killed him, he would be worried about what might happen to him now. If he hadn't, then there could be more talk about 'unbelievers' and also no doubt about 'sin' and 'perversion' too.

318

'Murad, this can be fixed,' Süleyman said. 'You are a very talented boy. This can all—'

'With both my parents on the gear, my mother on the streets and absolutely no future? Who cares whether I can play the piano? I'm not like Ali Reza! I'm nobody!' Murad's face turned bright red. 'There is only one way for me, and I have chosen that way.'

Süleyman looked at İzzet Melik, who was, he felt, thinking the same thing as he was. The boy was going to kill not Miss Madrid, but himself. In the 'war' that existed only in the twisted acts of violence that he glorified, Murad Emin was preparing himself to go to Paradise.

'You know that it isn't true, don't you?' Süleyman said.

'What isn't true?'

'That people who kill themselves, for whatever reason, go straight to Paradise,' he said. 'It's a lie.'

'No it isn't,' the boy said without so much as a flicker of doubt.

'Yes it is,' Süleyman said. 'Think about it. Why would we be created just to be destroyed? Why have earth at all if our time on it is not useful, philanthropic and joyful?'

This was not an argument that he'd just picked out of his head. It was something he had asked the extremists he had come across many times over the years. Their various replies were now summed up by Murad Emin.

'Life is total obedience,' he said. 'Joy is a sin.'

Süleyman, at least, had just resigned himself to a long night of tension peppered with philosophical discussion, when he heard the sound of feet on the stairs up to the apartment behind him. He had called for uniformed back-up just before they went into the apartment, but he knew, or at least he hoped, that couldn't be them. He had instructed them specifically to stay back until he told them otherwise. But footsteps there were, and although he wanted to look around to see who might be approaching, the fact that the boy had heard a noise he didn't understand meant that Süleyman had to try and keep eye contact with him.

'Who's that?' the boy asked. 'Keep back! Keep back!'

Süleyman watched the old pistol push against Izabella Madrid's head again. 'It's nothing, Murad, nothing at all!'

'Yes it is!' the boy said. His eyes were bright now, wide and bright and staring. He took the gun away from the old woman's head and pointed it out in front. 'Tell them to—'

'Get back!' Süleyman yelled. 'Whoever you are, get back!'

'Mehmet, I—'

The gun went off with such force that the boy completely lost his hold on it. It flew out of his hand, hit the floor and skidded to a halt beside İzzet Melik's heavily shod feet.

The old woman screamed, Melik picked the gun up and Murad Emin collapsed in a fit of shuddering, screaming fury. Over at the door, Süleyman bent down to cradle Gonca the gypsy in his arms.

'I came back,' she said as she tried to staunch the blood that was pouring out of her abdomen, 'to tell you that you are a bastard.'

Chapter 30

Saadet Seyhan finally got in to see Çetin İkmen just as news about the shooting in Balat was coming through. İkmen had taken a moment away from his so far fruitless interrogation of Cem Koç in order to find out what was happening. He had been very surprised to see Saadet, especially in company with her son Lokman. He had barely shut the door of the interview room when she said, 'Çetin Bey, it was my husband, Cahit Seyhan. Kenan was right, Cahit killed Gözde!'

İkmen frowned. 'You're sure?'

'Well, he didn't actually kill Gözde himself,' she said. 'It was a sort of arrangement, you know, a . . . you know, a business thing . . .'

'My mother believes, Inspector İkmen,' Lokman Seyhan said, 'that my father paid a man to kill my sister.'

'Your mother believes?'

'I have come around to the idea that she could be right,' Lokman said. 'Although I knew nothing about it at the time.'

'My son knew nothing. Nothing!' Saadet continued. She was tired and cold and hungry, but she was so elated to finally be in İkmen's presence, finally able to get some justice for Gözde, that she was almost in tears. 'But I did. I knew what evil that husband of mine would do! May Allah forgive me!'

'Do you know who this man was?' İkmen asked. 'The one your husband employed to kill your daughter?'

'If you mean do I know his name, then I don't,' she said. 'But I did see him once, Çetin Bey. I cannot and will not ever forget his face.'

'Well if you could give us a description . . .' He also thought it might be a very good idea to get Saadet Seyhan to have a look at Cem Koç. 'Mrs Seyhan, there is another—'

Ayşe came through the door without knocking.

'Sergeant . . .'

'Sir, may I speak to you?' she said. She looked upset. 'It's urgent.'

İkmen excused himself to the Seyhans and went outside into the corridor. 'What is it?' he asked her. 'What has happened?'

'That shooting in Balat,' Ayşe said. 'Inspector Süleyman and Sergeant Melik were there!'

İkmen felt sick, but he put a calming hand on Ayşe's shoulder and said, 'Are they OK?'

'I don't know!' Then she broke down. She liked İzzet Melik a lot and would miss him badly if he were to die. But for Süleyman to die was impossible for her to contemplate. Long, long ago they had been lovers, and she still had a lot of feelings for him.

İkmen took her gently over to the side of the corridor, out of the way of the increasing human traffic. 'Ayşe, you must try to be calm,' he said. 'Tell me what you know.'

'But I don't . . . they . . .'

'Tell me anything you know about the incident,' İkmen said. 'Anything.'

She took a deep breath to calm herself as much as she

322

could and said, 'All I know is . . . a woman has definitely been shot. I . . . Officers have taken her to the Jewish Hospital in Balat.'

'Officers?'

'I don't know which officers,' she said. 'No one seems to know! No one knows if anyone apart from the woman has been hurt.' And then her calm façade broke down again and she cried.

'Ali Reza?' Light from the many spotlights in the kitchen ceiling illuminated the boy dressed for the street and carrying a rucksack. He looked round at his mother, who stood in the kitchen doorway, blocking his exit. Sleep-sodden, her hair tangled into what looked like a nest on the top of her head, Mrs Zafir said, 'What are you doing? It's the middle of the night.'

'I thought I might go out for a walk,' Ali Reza said.

'In the dark!'

'Why not? It's not raining.'

She walked forward and grabbed hold of his rucksack. He tried to stop her, but his mother was too quick for him.

'Don't!'

She unzipped the bag and looked inside. There were a lot of clothes, as well as Ali Reza's asthma inhaler and also his passport. Mrs Zafir pulled that out of the bag and held it up for him to see. 'What's this for?'

Ali Reza looked down at the floor and said, 'It's my passport.'

'I know *what* it is,' she said. 'What I want to know is *why*.'

The boy shrugged. He had been planning to get some food and drink for the journey, but that was probably out of the question now.

Mrs Zafir looked closely at her son. 'Was it the police? Did they upset you coming here and asking questions?'

Well of course it was the police! They were the whole reason he was going. But he wasn't going to tell her that. 'No.'

'Because I know you've been very upset and unsettled since Hamid Bey died,' she said. 'But Ali Reza you still have the competition to think about. That's very important to you.'

'I wasn't going to leave or . . .'

'Then why the passport?' his mother said as she once again held the document aloft. 'Ali Reza, I'm your mother, you must tell me the truth. I'm not going to move from here until you do.'

And that was, Ali Reza felt, a shame. Because what would have to happen next was not what he wanted to happen. He loved his mother, but she wouldn't budge, so there was going to be no choice. No choice at all.

'OK,' he said. 'I'll tell you.' He smiled. Then, knowing exactly what her reply would be, he said, 'Can I have some hot chocolate, please?'

She sighed with what he knew was relief. She felt she'd cracked him. 'Mummy's special? Of course,' she said. His mother did make the absolute best hot chocolate in the world. He'd miss that. For a moment he thought that maybe he ought to let her make it for him one last time, but then he decided against it. She went over to the refrigerator and leaned inside

324

to get the milk. Ali Reza picked up the heavy chopping board that was on the preparation island beside him and brought it down on her head with all his force. Mrs Zafir dropped to the ground without a murmur just as the boy's father entered the kitchen to find out why his wife hadn't come back to bed.

Once Dr Zafir had managed to wrestle his son to the ground and disarm and disable him, he checked his wife's neck for any sign of a pulse. But there was nothing.

News travels fast in small, tight-knit communities. As soon as Gonca's brothers and father knew what had happened, gypsies came from all over to wait outside the Jewish Hospital in Balat. They neither cried nor spoke but just stood in a large, silent group, waiting. Gonca was not their most moral or noble sister but she was a famous woman and a generous member of their community. Only her father and three of her brothers were allowed inside while the doctors performed the operation that could save her life.

İzzet Melik, whose job it was now to stay at the hospital and monitor the situation, introduced himself to Gonca's family. Her brother Şukru, at least, already knew who he was.

'You work with Inspector Süleyman,' he said.

'Yes.' İzzet did not expand upon that and neither did the gypsy. 'This is an excellent hospital. Your sister is in very good hands.'

'The Jews are good at medicine,' Gonca's ancient walnut-coloured father said.

İzzet did not respond.

'What I want to know,' Şukru said from beneath his thick, lowering brows, 'is what my sister was doing when she got shot.' He looked up at İzzet Melik and asked, 'Do you know?'

'No.'

'Really?'

He didn't, not really. As far as he was concerned, Süleyman had managed to dismiss Gonca long before they arrived at Izabella Madrid's apartment. How the gypsy had got past the squad cars that had pulled up shortly after he and Süleyman had got there, İzzet didn't know. She must have hidden on the stairs somewhere to wait for Süleyman. But then surely she must have heard what was going on in the apartment?

'You will have to speak to your sister,' İzzet said, 'When, *inşallah*, she recovers.'

'Where is Inspector Süleyman?'

İzzet was far from comfortable with all this and was rather pleased when a young nurse asked them if they would all move out of the corridor outside the operating theatre and into the waiting room. But Şukru persisted. As they walked into the waiting room he said to İzzet, 'Well?'

İzzet kept his gaze down. He said, 'Inspector Süleyman has arrested the person who shot your sister. He is obliged to question that individual now.'

'Not be with the woman he sleeps with?'

'Şukru!' The old man put a hand on his son's arm and said something to him in their own language. Şukru instantly lowered his head and sat down. Gonca's father went over to İzzet and said, 'I know where my daughter was shot. The old Jewish teacher's place. How is Miss Madrid?'

326

'Unhurt,' İzzet said. He was much happier talking to the old man than to any of the brothers, especially Şukru. He had no desire to discuss his superior's private life. If he was honest, he was completely sick of hearing about Süleyman's romantic associations.

'Good.'

'The doctors here checked her out and she was OK,' İzzet said. 'She'll be at the station now. We have to try and find out why the person who shot your daughter was threatening Miss Madrid.'

'You don't know?'

'We're not sure,' İzzet said. 'But the assailant will be questioned and we will find that out.' He added, 'As for your daughter, sir, I believe she was simply in the wrong place at the wrong time. We have no reason to believe that she knew or had any involvement with the assailant.'

He had been trying to reassure the old man, but the gypsy didn't look very comforted when he said, 'You know my grandson, my daughter's youngest boy, says that his mother was arguing with Inspector Süleyman outside the Church of St Mary of the Mongols. She pursued him down the hill towards Miss Madrid's place.'

That was exactly what had happened, exactly what young Rambo must have seen.

'Do you know why they were arguing, Sergeant?'

'No, I don't,' İzzet said. In a different and softer way, the old man was asking the same questions as his son. He was not going to get an answer either. 'You'll have to ask your daughter,' he added again, 'when, *inşallah*, she comes through the surgery.'

* * *

327

Murad Emin refused to say a word. His father, barely conscious admittedly, sat by his side, and Süleyman was assisted by an officer from the Juvenile Police Directorate. But the boy was choosing to be completely dumb and it was driving Süleyman mad. If Gonca were to die, he wanted to know why; he had a right to that, as did her family! But because Murad was legally a minor, he would not be pressed to speak until he came up before one of the psychologists over at the directorate's headquarters in Üsküdar. While arrangements for transportation across the Bosphorus were looked into, Süleyman went to speak to Izabella Madrid.

'Some nice boy came and gave me a glass of tea and a packet of cigarettes,' she said as he sat down beside her in the little room she'd been given to wait in. Then she frowned and said, 'How's Gonca?'

'Still in surgery.' He looked down at his hands, then fished in his pockets for his packet of cigarettes and his lighter. 'She'll fight.'

'Of course she will,' the old woman said. 'That's how she is.' She watched him light his cigarette and then lit up one of her own. She said, 'She fought to keep you, didn't she? Then her family took a hand.'

He looked up sharply at her. She smiled.

'Balat is a village, Inspector,' she said. 'Different races and faiths we may be, but we all know each other. Something you should know . . .' She'd thought about what she was about to say at some length that night and decided that whatever happened, it needed saying. 'Gonca's family wanted you gone because the Queen of the Gypsies, as I call her, loves you. Everyone knows it.'

He was truly shocked. He put his cigarette into his mouth to stop himself from screaming. *She* loved *him*.

'They can't have that, the gypsies. Not love, or worse still, marriage, between one of them and one of us, whoever we are.' She laughed. 'They are tighter than the Jews in that respect.' She looked at his face. 'You didn't know? Well, she would never have told you. But I think that you should know now.'

She fell silent and they both smoked while he chastised himself bitterly for never having told Gonca that he loved her. Now it could quite possibly be too late. Izabella Madrid had known that when she'd told him what was now tearing at his soul. Gonca loved him!

The old woman, at least, knew better than to leave him with that knowledge with nowhere for his mind to go. 'What of little Murad Emin?' she asked. 'Has he spoken to you?'

Süleyman cleared his throat, dragged a tired hand through his hair and smiled at her. 'Miss Madrid,' he said, 'I need to know how Murad came to be at your apartment earlier this evening. How did he get from being your pupil to being your jailer?'

She told him how she had found Murad, upset and frightened, in the derelict houses at the top of the hill. 'He said his father was raging because he couldn't get his fix. He was frightened. I said he could come home with me,' she said. 'I wasn't happy about it, but . . .'

'Why not? Murad was a good pupil, wasn't he?'

'Yes, but as I told Sergeant Melik,' she said, 'all that radical religious stuff he was coming out with, I didn't appreciate it.'

She looked at him accusingly, or maybe he just thought

that she had because he felt so guilty. He should have listened to İzzet when he talked about Murad Emin! But of course he had been too caught up in trying to prevent anyone from finding out about Gonca. Idiot.

'He only picked up the gun and put it to my head when he saw you and Melik running down the street towards my apartment,' she said. 'He looked out the window, and next thing I knew I was a hostage!'

'So he just planned to stay . . .'

'Until the morning, yes,' she said. 'Then he'd go back home. That was what he told me.'

'Did he try to telephone home, do you know?'

'No.' She shook her head. 'I don't know Mr Emin that well, but I do know junkies, and I knew that if he was raging, he wouldn't even be aware whether the boy was in or out. The mother?' She shrugged. 'Does she know what year it is? Poor bitch is either being screwed or sticking needles into herself. What does she know?'

She had remembered him, Süleyman thought gloomily. She'd remembered him because he'd been so clean! What other terrible degraded creatures did she provide relief for? He really dreaded to think. And now was not the time.

'Murad possessed violent jihadist DVDs and still images,' he said. 'Really disgusting things.'

'Such things can be bought on the streets. Has he done anything else?'

'I don't know,' Süleyman replied.

She put her cigarette out and then lit up another. 'Do you think he had anything to do with Hamid İdiz's death? Do you think Murad could have done such a terrible thing?'

330

'I don't know,' Süleyman said. He finished his cigarette and got up to go. 'I'll have to interview you formally at some point. But I just wanted to make sure that you were all right.'

She smiled. 'I'm an old soldier, Inspector. Don't worry about me. Interview me whenever you want. I'm not going home. Can't really face it. And anyway, if I'm here, hopefully someone will tell me what happens to Gonca.'

'Of course.'

'She's a wild and sometimes difficult character, but I like her,' she said.

Süleyman left. As he closed the door of the interview room behind him, he saw a constable leading Ali Reza Zafir, in handcuffs, along the corridor. Dr Zafir, his father, was following, and he was crying.

Chapter 31

Because both Ali Reza Zafır and Murad Emin were under-age, the decision was taken to send them, under separate transport, to the Juvenile Police Directorate in Üsküdar. Neither boy had spoken a word since being brought into the station and it was now going to be up to the psychologists at the directorate to try and find out what they could. Süleyman prepared to take Murad to a waiting area at the back of the building to await transport. Ayşe Farsakoğlu, much happier since she had been told that Süleyman was alive, was given the job of escorting Ali Reza. She didn't know anything about him, apart from the fact that he had been charged with the murder of his own mother.

Süleyman cuffed Murad in the interview room and then, escorted by a constable, took him out into the corridor. Çetin İkmen was out there with a middle-aged woman and a young man. Saadet and Lokman Seyhan. As the two officers' eyes met, they smiled briefly at each other. It had been a very busy and terrible night.

'If you don't recognise our suspect then you don't recognise him,' İkmen said to Saadet Seyhan, who looked downcast and disappointed. 'It is no good to anyone if I try and convict someone who is innocent.'

'No. I'm sorry, Çetin Bey, I just didn't know the man.'

'It's OK.'

Süleyman turned Murad Emin around to face him and then straightened the boy's shirt. He was tired and sweaty and looked more like an abused child than someone who had just shot a defenceless woman.

'But Çetin Bey,' Saadet said to İkmen, 'are you still going to bring my husband in for questioning?'

'Of course,' İkmen replied. 'But I do have to warn you that—'

'That's him!' She shouted it so loudly that Süleyman looked up from what he was doing and stared at her.

Saadet Seyhan was pointing in his direction. Her face purple with rage, she screamed, 'I'd know him anywhere! Bastard!'

'But that is Inspector Süleyman,' İkmen began, 'you know him . . .'

'I know the young man too!' Saadet screamed. 'That young man there! He killed my daughter Gözde, may his soul be damned to hell!'

Süleyman looked at Murad, who for the first time since he'd been in the station smiled and then spoke. 'She's mad,' he said simply. 'Poor old madwoman.'

İkmen looked at Saadet Seyhan and said, 'Are you sure? Would you be willing to sign a statement . . .'

'It's him!' she said. She tried to fling herself across the corridor at the boy, but her son caught her and pulled her back. 'It's you!' she yelled at Murad Emin. 'Bastard! You know what you've done! You know what my husband paid you blood money to do! Where are you taking him?' she asked İkmen. 'Where is he going?'

334

İkmen assured her that he would tell her what was going on just as soon as she went back into the interview room with her son.

'I want to make a statement!' she said. 'About him! That boy!'

'And you will,' İkmen said as he hustled the pair back into the interview room and shut the door behind them.

He came over to Süleyman and the boy. 'So this is . . .'

'Murad Emin,' Süleyman said. 'The Balat gunman.'

İkmen looked the boy up and down for a moment, then said, 'It must be a night for juveniles.'

'I'm taking this one down to be transported to Üsküdar,' Süleyman said.

'Well there's another one down there too,' İkmen replied. 'With Sergeant Farsakoğlu. I've no idea what it's about. I'll get as much as I can from the Seyhans and then—'

'I didn't kill their daughter. Why should I?' the boy said.

'I'm not speaking to you,' İkmen said and turned to Süleyman. 'Everyone all right? The Balat incident . . .'

'No officers hurt. One civilian woman injured,' Süleyman replied. He didn't say who. Now was not the time.

İkmen nodded, then turned away and walked back towards the interview room. Süleyman pulled Murad Emin beside him and told him to get walking. As he moved, he watched the boy closely for any signs of guilt or panic. But there weren't any.

Ayşe tried not to smile when Süleyman came into the room, but it wasn't easy. She was glad he was alive, even if he had not been interested in her for a number of years. It was

335

said that the person who had been shot over in Balat was his gypsy lover, that outrageous artist who Ayşe envied so very much. But she still hoped that the gypsy lived, in spite of that.

'Inspector . . .'

Süleyman turned Murad Emin around in order to sit him down. He and the boy were directly opposite Ayşe Farsakoğlu and her charge, Ali Reza Zafir. It took Süleyman a moment to recognise the other boy, but when he did, he said, 'This is the boy?'

'Charged with killing his own mother,' Ayşe said.

He was about to say something in response to this when the boy at his side said, 'You killed your mum! Why?' In spite of the fact that it was a chilly early morning, Murad Emin was sweating. 'You lunatic!' he said. 'Why?'

Ayşe Farsakoğlu said, 'These kids know each other?'

'Oh, yes,' Süleyman said. 'These two certainly know each other.'

He wanted to ask Ayşe how and why Ali Reza had come to kill his own mother, but he suspected that she was just an escort and so wouldn't know. The boy was nothing to her. His sudden, almost hysterical laughter, though, spooked everyone. In that cold little concrete room with only darkness outside, it sounded like something from a madhouse.

Süleyman felt Murad Emin's body shake beside him. He put a hand on his shoulder as if to steady him, but the boy was beside himself. 'What have you done?' he screamed at Ali Reza. 'You would have been all right! You . . .'

'And you,' the other boy said very, very calmly, 'what are you doing here, Murad? Violent DVDs, is it? Not very clever, that. Not very bright. We didn't need that rubbish. You should have listened.'

'That'll be enough.' Süleyman looked at both boys when he spoke. 'Save it for the psychologist.'

A truck pulled up outside and Ayşe waited until the officer driving it and his escort got out. 'This is for us,' she said to Ali Reza as she pulled him to his feet. 'Come on.'

One of the officers outside opened the door and told Ali Reza to walk towards him. Before he did, Ali Reza looked at Murad Emin and smiled. 'It's all going to come unravelled now,' he said, then he laughed his spooky mad laugh again, touched his nose conspiratorially and said, 'Leopold and Loeb, baby, Leopold and Loeb!'

Murad Emin, his previous calm demeanour now totally exploded, screamed, 'No! No, it wasn't like that! Not for me! It was never like that for me!'

Gonca survived the surgery to remove the bullet from her abdomen. But the surgeon who had performed the operation did not give her a very high chance of survival. She'd lost a huge amount of blood and her stomach, liver and spleen were all badly damaged. When Süleyman, now accompanied by İkmen, did manage to get to see her, she was in a coma and attached to a life support system.

İkmen now knew the circumstances of the shooting, although he could not agree with his colleague about the apportionment of blame. 'She came after you,' he said as he put a hand up to his much taller friend's shoulder. They both looked down with grave faces at the immobile woman in the bed. 'It was the boy who shot her, not you.'

They didn't stay long. The gypsies were now camped outside the hospital, and neither of the officers wanted to give the medical staff any more problems. As the two men left, Gonca's brother Şukru came up to Süleyman and said, 'If she dies, you will need to explain yourself. If she doesn't, you will keep away from my family.'

Süleyman wanted to tell him that Gonca loved him, and that Şukru didn't understand. But instead he just nodded his head and said nothing. İzzet Melik had told him that the gypsies wanted explanations. And who could blame them? Now was just not the time.

When they got back to İkmen's car, he lit up cigarettes for both of them and passed one over to Süleyman. 'I've managed to charge Cem Koç with attempting to procure the services of a paid assassin,' he said. 'Not exactly how Constable Yıldız's brother would describe himself, I don't suppose.'

Süleyman said nothing. Gonca in a coma had looked like a person he barely knew. Scrubbed of make-up, dressed in white, her amazing hair rammed into a paper surgical cap, she had looked alien, frightening and old.

İkmen put the car into gear and began to drive off. 'I expect it will be said that we set Koç up, but whatever happens he will be put out of business and at least the girl he tried to kill is safe.'

'What about her parents?' Süleyman said in a dead voice, thick with anxiety and lack of sleep.

'When they came back to the apartment, they were of course shocked and horrified for all the world to see,' İkmen said. 'There's nothing on paper to connect them to Koç.'

338

'What about the money?'

'The money Koç gave to Ismail Yıldız was taken from his own account,' İkmen said. 'The family had not yet paid. Maybe I should have given them the time to do that.'

'But then Koç might have slipped through your fingers.'

'He may yet do so.' They drove from the hospital and over the Golden Horn on the Atatürk Bridge. It was a fine day, with lots of gulls hovering over the bright, clear waterway. But neither man noticed the day too much. Neither of them had slept for over twenty-four hours, and now they were obliged to attend the Juvenile Police Directorate over the Bosphorus in Üsküdar.

'And the girl?' Süleyman asked.

'Sergeant Farsakoğlu has had her taken to a refuge in İzmir,' İkmen said. 'Whether she'll stay there . . .' He shrugged. 'Constable Yıldız's brother is going to have to endure a lot of questioning.'

'You don't doubt that he was telling the truth, do you, Çetin?'

'Not at all,' İkmen said. 'He's a genuinely good religious man. He was shocked that religion should be used in the service of such barbarity.'

'Where on earth did Koç get such an idea from?' Süleyman asked.

'Well, that we don't know yet,' İkmen said. 'Cahit Seyhan, the father of Gözde, our burning girl of Beşiktaş, is doing what so many seem to do and refuses to speak.'

İkmen had had Cahit Seyhan picked up just after Saadet Seyhan had given her statement to the police. The next step was to question Murad Emin, but that had to be done by

339

staff at the Juvenile Police Directorate. It would either be another study in silence, or a very interesting and probably disturbing experience.

As they passed in front of a massive hoarding showing an advertisement for a new home-grown TV police series, İkmen said, 'Sometimes even I just occasionally hanker for the methods of the past.'

'You mean . . .'

'Cahit Seyhan is the sort of man who beats and rapes others in order to establish his dominance. That's how he operates, how his mind works. Perhaps a beating . . .' But then he laughed. 'Did I really say that? I must be exhausted.'

Dr Zafir had never met Mr Emin before.

'Our sons know each other,' the doctor said to the thin, grey man who sat with him in the waiting room at the entrance to the police station. 'I'm here because I don't know where to go.'

'No.'

Dr Zafir didn't want to say 'because my wife has died' or been killed or murdered or however one expressed such a thing, because he really didn't want to think about that. And so he ploughed on with 'They share a love of the piano.'

Mr Emin looked up and smiled. He'd lost a front tooth, somehow, the previous day and so he looked even more dishevelled and desperate than usual.

'My son described your son as a genius.'

'Oh, he's that all right!' Mr Emin said, and then his face darkened. 'Yes.'

'It's good for boys to have shared interests. I . . . I have a friend, you know, we started school together, college, university, medical school . . .'

'You're a doctor?'

'Yes.' He almost dismissed it. Then suddenly the anxiety rolled in again, as it did, on a vast, heart-thumping breaker. 'Our boys are in so much trouble! So much trouble!'

Mr Emin had no idea what Dr Zafir's son might have done, only that he had been arrested. 'They say Murad has broken some law to do with terrorism,' he said. Then he shrugged. 'Pictures and film of al-Qaeda and such-like. A lot of fuss. Don't get me wrong, I don't like it.' He leaned forward in his chair and took a soggy roll-up out of his pocket. He put it in his mouth and lit up. 'Same for your boy, is it?'

'My son killed his mother.' It came out stark and emotionless, just like that. Then all of a sudden, and quite unbidden Dr Zafir began to cry.

Mr Emin watched him. Part of his mind couldn't bring itself to believe what the other man had just said. That a boy known to Murad would actually kill his mother! How had that happened, he wondered and to someone as rich and exalted as a doctor? But then education didn't mean as much in the modern world as it had, as Mr Emin knew to his cost. Anyone could fall from grace at any time, anyone could slip off the radar. He looked at Dr Zafir and wondered whether he might be persuaded to part with some heroin for a small consideration.

Chapter 32

The boy walked into the room. From behind the two-way mirror that allowed İkmen and Süleyman to see what was about to happen, it was dimly lit and vaguely eerie. The psychologist, a woman, introduced herself as Hatice. She and Murad Emin sat down in soft chairs that had been placed opposite each other. Over in the corner sat a constable, and next to him was a television and DVD player. Hatice asked the boy how he had slept and whether he'd managed to eat anything. Murad replied in the affirmative to both of those questions. She talked about nutrition and the importance of eating the right food, and Murad said that as well as a physical necessity it was also a spiritual duty for a Muslim to look after his body.

'I've never smoked or drunk alcohol,' he said. 'I wouldn't.'

'But he quite happily worked in a nargile salon,' İkmen said to Süleyman. He whispered, even though none of the people in the next room could possibly hear either of them.

'Mum and Dad have always been on the gear,' Murad said.

'Heroin.'

'Yes. I don't want that life.'

'What kind of life do you want, Murad?'

'A clean, good life, dedicated to my religion.'

Hatice smiled. 'That sounds very nice. There's nothing wrong with a life of abstinence, prayer and contemplation.'

İkmen rolled his eyes up at this and Süleyman sighed. The chairs they'd been given to sit on were small and hard and he was very uncomfortable.

'But why the DVDs?' Hatice asked. 'The DVDs of violent acts committed in the name of religion by people whose only function is to distort and then kill for their own pleasure.'

'Al-Qaeda are heroes,' Murad said. 'They're right. Americans and other infidels kill Muslims, they take their lands, they drink and dance and commit abominations, their women are uncovered and they're whores.'

'What, all non-Muslim women?'

'Yes!'

'Look at his eyes,' Süleyman said to İkmen. 'They're shining. It's as if he's having some sort of ecstatic experience!'

He was right. Murad Emin's eyes were bright with fervour, and now he was also smiling. 'Yes, they're all whores.'

'So what about Muslim women who choose not to cover themselves?' Hatice said. 'Women like me.'

She was modestly but fashionably dressed and her head was not covered.

'You? Well you seem OK, I think,' Murad said.

'Oh, so not all uncovered women . . .'

'Even if women are covered and they meet men, they are still whores,' Murad said. 'And that's it really, that's the thing about women: you can't always know just from looking at them whether they are real whores or not. My mum never

344

covers herself, even though I wish that she would, but she isn't a whore.'

Süleyman looked at İkmen and said, 'He's changed his tune. Yesterday, when he was holding a gun at old Miss Madrid's head, his father was on the gear and his mother was on the streets. Do you think he's trying to come across as crazy?'

'I don't know,' İkmen said. 'He's been accused of being the person that Cahit Seyhan employed to kill his daughter Gözde. Saadet Seyhan is absolutely certain he is the one.'

'Murad,' Hatice said, 'can you tell me how you feel about women?'

The boy frowned. 'What do you mean?'

'Well, do you like women? Do you have fancies for girls that maybe you'd like to talk to or go out with or—'

'No! Mixing of the sexes is a sin!'

'Who says so?'

He didn't speak at all for a moment, then he said, 'It's my religion. It's wrong. I don't want to talk about it.'

Hatice smiled. 'That's OK,' she said. 'Now what about men? Do you have male friends, Murad?'

He looked down at his hands, and İkmen thought that his face coloured just a little. 'Not really.'

'What, not at school? Not at the nargile salon? Your piano lessons?'

'I don't go to a proper piano school any more,' he said. 'Hamid Bey died and now I go to Miss Madrid.

'Ah, Miss—'

'I don't want to talk about her, she's a Jew,' Murad said in a way that was not panicky at all, just straightforward.

Hatice smiled again and said, 'I don't suppose you do.' Then she said, 'But you do know a boy called Ali Reza, don't you, Murad?'

He raised his chin a little as if trying to shut his own mouth from the inside, then with a tiny affirmative he admitted that he did.

'Because he knows you,' she said.

'He tells lies about me!' Murad said.

'Like what?'

'Well, like . . .' He was red again, red and hot and flustered.

'Does Ali Reza call you a homosexual?' Hatice said.

The boy got up in an apparent fury, only to be told to sit down by the constable, who was now up on his feet in front of Hatice.

'No one calls me homosexual!' Murad shouted. 'Homosexuality is a sin, I'd never do it!'

'Well, let's see what your friend Ali Reza has to say about that, shall we?' Hatice said as she went over to the television and put a DVD into the player. 'I had some time with him earlier today. Like this session, it was recorded.'

İkmen looked at Süleyman, who said, 'I thought we were supposed to be observing both the boys' sessions?'

İkmen shrugged. 'Who knows?' he said. 'This is the Juvenile Directorate. It's a mystery.'

Murad Emin sat down. The DVD, after a splutter, began to play.

'Murad hates women because he wants to fuck men,' Ali Reza Zafir said. He was sprawled in the chair that Murad Emin was sitting in now, looking casual, cocky, almost relaxed. 'He doesn't want anyone to know. He hides behind his religion. He's guilty.'

'That's not true!' Murad Emin wailed at the screen. 'He's lying!'

But Hatice silenced him. 'Watch and we'll talk later,' she said. 'This is what I want you to hear, Murad.'

There was a pause, and then the image of Ali Reza Zafir on the screen said, 'I wouldn't put it past Murad to hurt or even kill a woman.'

'And yet it was you,' the screen psychologist said to him, 'who killed your own mother.'

'That was an accident.'

'You hit her over the head with a very heavy chopping board. What kind of accident was that?'

There was a pause. Ali Reza Zafir looked up at the camera in the corner of the room in a very deliberate fashion and said, 'Murad killed our piano teacher you know. Hamid Bey.'

'No. No! No! No!'

The psychologist switched the DVD player off and looked at a stricken Murad Emin.

'Did you kill Hamid İdiz, your piano teacher?' she asked.

'No!' the boy was almost in tears now. 'No, I didn't!'

'Murad, I have to remind you,' she said, 'that we have taken a DNA sample from you, and if that matches DNA found at the scene . . .'

'I did not kill Hamid Bey!' Murad wailed. 'Do whatever you like! I did not kill him, I would not kill him.'

'Why not? You very freely stated in front of police officers that Hamid İdiz's homosexuality offended you, that he sometimes masturbated in your presence . . .'

'I . . . I didn't kill him,' the boy said. He paused, then asked her, 'What else did Ali Reza say?'

'What about?'

'He shrugged. 'I don't know. Me.'

'That was all Ali Reza said about you,' Hatice said. She looked down at a piece of paper on her lap. 'Now we must address the most serious allegation against you, Murad.'

İkmen looked at Süleyman and took a deep breath. They were getting, hopefully, to Gözde Seyhan.

'An allegation has been made that you, under the direction of the girl's father, killed Gözde Seyhan,' Hatice said. 'You poured petrol over her and set her alight at her home in Beşiktaş. You did this, it is alleged, for money.'

The boy said nothing.

'The allegation has been made by someone who the police at headquarters deem to be reliable,' Hatice said.

'An old woman,' Murad said. 'She shouted at me. I'd never seen her before.'

'The dead girl's mother.'

'Yes.'

Hatice leaned forward. 'Murad,' she said, 'we also have forensic evidence from the scene of Gözde Seyhan's murder that does not, as yet, relate to anyone known to us. Principally there was a petrol can at the scene that yielded some samples, hair . . .'

'They won't match me!' He said it in a very childish and petulant way. But then he was only fifteen.

'We will see,' Hatice said. She looked at her notes again and asked, 'Murad, who or what are Leopold and Loeb?'

The boy didn't answer, but Çetin İkmen, behind the two-way

glass, visibly paled. 'Leopold and Loeb?' he asked Mehmet Süleyman. 'Why is she asking him about Leopold and Loeb?'

Süleyman shrugged. 'I imagine it's because when the boys were being transferred . . .'

'Your friend Ali Reza referred to Leopold and Loeb when you were waiting to be transported here from police headquarters,' Hatice said. 'Can you tell me what that means, Murad?'

'Can Ali Reza?'

'I'm asking you,' she said.'

For the first time in the interview, Murad Emin looked completely away from her and then shut his eyes.

Behind the glass, Süleyman said to İkmen, 'What are Leopold and Loeb? I don't understand.'

'I don't know much,' İkmen said. 'But I do know that Leopold and Loeb were famous murderers back in the early part of the twentieth century. There were, some reckoned, homoerotic overtones to the crime.'

'Where did it happen?'

'In America. Alfred Hitchcock made a film about them,' İkmen said.

'So what . . .'

'If my memory serves me correctly,' İkmen said, 'Leopold and Loeb were very young when they killed. They were young and they killed entirely without any motive beyond the desire to commit the perfect crime.'

'Which of course they didn't achieve.'

'No,' İkmen said. 'But if I'm right, what let them down was their insatiable desire to talk about what they'd done. In effect they gave themselves and each other away.'

*   *   *

349

It was becoming very clear to Ayşe Farsakoğlu that Cem Koç was not in fact a religious man. He lived in Fatih, his family were good Muslims and he did, in general, abstain from loose behaviour and alcohol. But he was no saint. He was also not, to Ayşe's way of thinking, a real sinner either. His crime was his relative poverty and the fact that he could apparently close his mind to the terrible agonies the girl Sabiha would have gone through had she really been set on fire. But neither of the girl's parents had, as yet, admitted to seeking her death. That made things difficult, but not, as Ayşe knew, impossible.

'I completely accept that you have no connection to the gangster Tayfun Ergin,' she said as she looked up at the man sitting opposite her. 'Although what he's doing in Fatih . . .'

'Gangsters are everywhere these days!' Cem Koç said nervously and completely oblivious to the irony of a criminal complaining about other criminals. 'I've heard it said that Tayfun Ergin is trying to provide protection to the coffee houses where the Faithful sometimes meet. But they don't want him. They don't need his kind.'

'So you didn't get the idea to set up your contract killing business from Tayfun—'

'I didn't get it from anywhere!' Cem said. 'I didn't get it! Such a thing does not exist!'

Ayşe Farsakoğlu looked over at the other officer in the room, a constable, with whom she shared a smile.

'The girl's parents are, they say, totally ignorant of any kind of need or arrangement to kill her.'

'Yes, because no one wanted to do that, only that man . . .'

'Ismail Yıldız? Did he make the whole thing up?'

'Well, yes . . .'

'Well no, actually,' Ayşe said with a smile this time at Cem Koç. 'Sadly for you, Mr Koç the girl's brother in Diyarbakir has confirmed Mr Yıldız's story.'

'The girl's brother?' His face reddened. 'Ah, yes but if he was in Diyarbakır . . .'

'The police in Diyarbakır began questioning Mr Emir Şafak yesterday,' she said. 'You know, Mr Koç, he admitted that he and his parents had sought his sister's death for some time. He told them how grateful his father had been to meet you.'

Cem Koç lowered his head towards the table.

'He named you, Mr Koç,' Ayşe said. 'He said that you knew his father from the Gül Mosque, that you often talked of this and that after your prayers.'

'No, he's—'

'He named you!' Ayşe said. 'If you want to see a copy of his statement . . .'

'No! No.' Cem Koç put his head in his hands, and for a few moments Ayşe left him alone with his misery.

Then she said, 'Cem, we know you intended to earn money from the death of Sabiha Şafak. The best thing you can do now is to tell us who else, if anyone, is involved.'

Cem stayed completely still with his head in his hands for some time. At last he murmured, 'You set me up. I've seen the cop shows from America. With that Yıldız man you set me up.'

'No,' Ayşe said calmly. 'We did not, Mr Koç. You approached Mr Yıldız. We were just fortunate that he came

351

to us. Had he not, then you would be facing a much sterner charge. Now . . .'

'Oh.' Cem Koç raised himself up from the table and wiped his weary eyes with the back of his hand. He sighed, looked up at the ceiling and then appeared to make a decision. 'I met a man in a nargile salon, over in Tophane,' he said. 'We got talking. He told me that he'd had this difficult daughter who had dishonoured him. He said that he'd managed to rid himself of her with no risk to himself because . . .' He faltered here, but Ayşe did not help him. 'He'd paid, he said, six thousand lire to have her killed. Some very ordinary lads, under-age, had done it. The father was proud of it.'

'And you thought . . .'

'I couldn't kill anyone! I couldn't! But . . .' He shrugged. 'I've got debts. I kept on thinking about it. I didn't speak to anyone, but . . . I thought if I could just find someone who could do such a thing. Rafik Bey at the grocer's shop is a friend. Everyone goes into his shop to buy things but also to talk. I said that if he heard of anyone who really needed money and was up for anything . . .'

'Rafik the grocer didn't know what you would want this person to do?'

'No! No,' he said. 'I told him I had a new business. I said it was a little outside the law. He said he was OK with that. Only me and that . . . man knew.'

'How did you know that Ismail Yıldız wouldn't just come to us?'

'He did!'

'But why did you think he wouldn't?'

Cem Koç thought about this for a few moments. 'I don't

352

know. I just *felt* that he was genuine. He was so bitter at his brother, the police officer. He wanted to prove himself, to be a man somehow.'

'Ismail Yıldız is not under-age,' Ayşe observed.

Cem Koç shrugged. 'But he was willing to take the risk anyway. He said so. What could I do? He was there, and he was willing.'

'Where did you get the two thousand lire to pay Mr Yıldız with?' Ayşe asked.

'A moneylender,' he replied. 'I was trying to be clever, trying to cover my tracks. I borrowed the money and then when the Şafaks paid me . . .'

'How much?'

'Six thousand lire, like the man in the nargile salon had told me,' he said. 'I reckoned that was the going rate.'

'For a bespoke honour killing?'

He shrugged.

'Do you know, Mr Koç, whether this type of "trade" is something that many people do?'

He looked up. 'I don't know,' he said. 'How would I? I met one man in a nargile salon who told me about one killing. I just went by that.'

'How did you meet the Şafaks?' Ayşe asked. 'How did the subject of Sabiha's death arise?'

'Her father and I go to the same coffee house,' he said. 'We talk. He said that his son had told him that his daughter was bad. He was distressed. I told him I might be able to help.'

'For a price.'

'Yes. But he was happy with that, he . . .'

'And are you now ashamed of what you did?' Ayşe asked. On some level Cem Koç had to approve of honour killings, otherwise nothing on earth could have made him procure someone to perform one.

'I don't think that bad girls should dishonour their families,' he said.

'Yes, but do you think that—'

'I think that their families should do it really,' he said. 'But everyone is so afraid of being caught. You, the police, you're so much better these days, aren't you?'

Ayşe felt sick. She had revised her opinion of Cem Koç during the course of this interrogation. He was just sorry that he had got caught. He didn't have a scrap of feeling for Sabiha Şafak. To hell with what his financial needs might be!

'Do you know the name of the man you got this idea from in the nargile salon in Tophane?' she said coldly.

'No.'

'What was the name of the salon?'

'I don't remember.'

Ayşe sighed. 'Well then, Mr Koç,' she said, 'do you think you might recognise this man if you saw him again?'

'I might do,' Cem Koç replied.

'Well, let us see if we can get a description from you, shall we?' Ayşe said. 'Let's start with that.'

Chapter 33

It was almost midnight by the time İkmen and Süleyman were ready to interview Cahit Seyhan. He was brought from his cell to the interview room in a state of bleary-eyed exhaustion. The officers, by contrast, though both had now gone for what seemed like an eternity without sleep, were buoyed up by some information that was hopefully going to make their interrogation of Seyhan a whole lot easier.

'Right, Mr Seyhan,' İkmen said as he sat down opposite the man. 'One last time, did you pay to have your daughter Gözde murdered? We know you are not as well off as you were . . .'

'I did not kill Gözde,' Cahit Seyhan said emphatically. 'No.'

'Right.'

Süleyman sat down next to İkmen and opened up a cardboard file.

'So, Mr Seyhan,' İkmen continued, 'can you please tell me why both your wife and a man called Cem Koç who you met in the Tulip nargile salon in Tophane say that you did?'

Cahit Seyhan growled and then threw a limp, dismissive arm into the air. 'My wife is a liar!' he said. 'I want to have more children with her and the bitch denies me!'

'Yes, there is also a rape charge,' Süleyman said.

'She wants to have me put away so she can run around with men!'

Both İkmen and Süleyman ignored this.

'I don't know any man called Koç!' Cahit Seyhan said.

'Well you told him all about the arrangement you had come to with what you described as "some under-age boys",' İkmen said. 'Koç has identified you.'

'I was—'

'Murad Emin, who is a waiter at the Tulip, is under-age,' İkmen said. 'Murad Emin, Mr Seyhan, who your wife identified as the person you yourself pointed out to her as being Gözde's killer! Was it your idea, or did it come from the boy?'

'We know that people, particularly in the countryside, sometimes employ under-age boys to perform honour killings because their age will preclude them from long prison sentences,' Süleyman said. 'Whose idea was it? Yours?'

'I don't know this Koç man! I don't know him!'

'How did he know you, then?' İkmen said. 'He described you and then we got him to look at hundreds of photographs, and he picked you out!'

Cahit Seyhan looked around the room as if trying to find some sort of way out. İkmen lit a cigarette and the room began to take on a vague and diffuse greyness.

Süleyman, who also lit up, now said, 'If you tell us everything and name everyone involved, we can make sure that your cooperation is noted.'

'What, do some sort of deal?' Seyhan looked suddenly eager and even a little hopeful.

'No,' İkmen said as patiently as his growing anger would allow. 'We don't do deals. We'd make sure that your cooperation was noted. That's all.'

Cahit Seyhan looked down at the desk for a long time before he spoke. He had been betrayed by his wife and his son. Why Lokman had turned against him, he couldn't imagine! They surely had to have a duty to him above anyone else. Now more than at any other time he regretted coming to the city. Had they stayed in the village, Gözde would have remained pure, Kenan would have married and Lokman and Saadet would never have had the courage to betray him. But they were no longer in the village; they were in a place that he didn't understand, an evil place that was going to destroy him.

'I liked the music at the Tulip,' he said at last. 'The piano.'

'You conversed with Murad Emin because of the piano,' İkmen said.

'I spoke to both the boys,' Cahit Seyhan said. 'They offered to help me out. With Gözde.'

'They?'

'Ali Reza took the money,' Cahit Seyhan said. 'He planned it, but Murad did it. He wanted to. He said it was his duty. Ali Reza I think was only in it for the money. I find that really unsettling. To kill only for money. That cannot be right. How does one clear one's conscience when money is involved?'

He stared down at the desk with an expression of frozen hopelessness on his face. İkmen looked over at Süleyman and let his next lungful of smoke out on a sigh. He was shattered, relieved that Seyhan had finally confessed but also totally baffled by the man. Süleyman, for his part, could think only about the two boys.

'Leopold and Loeb were a couple of very talented, very intellectual boys who lived in Chicago in the 1920s,' İkmen said. It was morning now, and Murad Emin had, at İkmen's request, been transferred back to police headquarters. 'In 1924, they killed a fourteen-year-old boy called Bobby Franks. They did it both for the thrill of the thing and also to see if they could get away with it. They didn't, mainly because neither of them could keep their mouths shut. They wanted the world to know how clever, how daring and how wild and crazy they'd been. They got put away for life. But then that's how young people are, isn't it, Murad? Young people just have to open their mouths.'

Murad Emin, pale from lack of sleep, remained silent and unmoving.

'We would not have paid you half the attention that we have had you not alluded so vehemently to your own piety,' Süleyman said. He was very well aware that it was İzzet Melik and not him who had pursued Murad Emin with such vigour. But he put that embarrassing thought to one side. 'And now that Mr Seyhan, Gözde's father, has confessed to procuring her death via you and Ali Reza Zafir, there is really no point in maintaining this ridiculous silence now.'

'Mr Seyhan has confessed, Mrs Seyhan has identified you and when the forensic material comes back from the laboratory you will have run out of places to hide,' İkmen said. 'Now you tell us everything.' He looked briefly over at Süleyman and then went back to the boy once again. 'Tell us everything about the murder, about your part in it and about Ali Reza.'

The boy looked up with wide, terrified eyes.

'Tell us *everything* about Ali Reza,' İkmen said. 'Everything.'

Murad Emin began to visibly shake. The psychologist Hatice, who had been standing over in the corner of the interview room, went outside and came back in with a blanket and a drink. She put the blanket around the boy's shoulders and placed the drink down in front of him.

'Drink some tea,' she said. 'I know that this is very hard, Murad.'

He looked at her through eyes streaming with tears.

'But you must trust us,' Hatice said. 'We are all here not just because we know what you did, but because we know what you didn't do. You didn't kill Hamid İdiz, did you, Murad?'

He reached forward with a hand that shook so much, Hatice had to bring the tea glass up to his lips for him. İkmen and Süleyman looked on as the psychologist made the boy drink and then wiped his face with her handkerchief. 'Murad. Please.'

At first his voice was not much more than a whisper. 'No.'

'No, you won't tell us anything, or no—'

'No, I didn't kill Hamid Bey,' Murad said.

'Do you know who did?' İkmen asked.

Hatice, now squatting down beside the boy, put her arms around his shoulders, which, for a very pious boy, did not seem to trouble him. He nodded his head.

'Was it Ali Reza Zafır?'

359

The unmoving silence that followed made Çetin İkmen think for a moment that maybe there was another, unknown killer out there somewhere, another crazy kid they had yet to apprehend. But then the boy said, 'Yes.' He sighed, and it was as if an invisible membrane had burst, allowing a free flow of words and deeds and horrors. 'He wanted to see what it was like. I'd told him how horrible the girl's death was. How when I'd set her on fire she'd turned and looked at me through the flames, her face melting down into a scream!'

He put his head in his hands and began to sob, huge, wet, dammed-up tears. He'd been carrying that around, unable to express it. He had tried to tell his friend about it, but he'd just laughed.

'I couldn't bear the thought of her face! But . . . Leopold and Loeb, he was obsessed with them.' He shook. 'He said it could be our business,' he whispered once he'd recovered himself sufficiently. 'He could make a lot of money and do what he wanted and I could do the work of the righteous! We could be together!' He looked up at İkmen and Süleyman and said, 'But I couldn't do it, not again. I told him, but he just laughed!'

'And so he killed Hamid İdiz?'

'He said that he could do it better than me,' Murad said. 'He said no one would ever suspect him!'

'He was right,' Süleyman said. 'We didn't.'

'Tell us how he killed Hamid Bey,' İkmen asked.

'He thought I wouldn't care because of how Hamid Bey was. My love for Ali Reza was different. Pure. We didn't . . .' Murad took a sip from his tea glass before continuing. 'Hamid Bey was attracted to both of us, we knew that,' he said.

'But he never hurt us or did anything to us. Ali Reza went to visit him. He dressed up. Made himself look older and available. Make-up and . . . He told me that Hamid Bey was very excited. He . . . he went to the bed and he . . . Ali Reza cut his throat from behind.'

'Ali Reza told you that?'

'He did.'

İkmen lit a cigarette while he watched the psychologist attempt to comfort the boy. He was glad that she was doing it and not him. In spite of Murad's youth and his lack of privilege, it was still hard to summon up any sympathy for this boy. He'd set a living girl on fire for the sake of a twisted idea of morality, a pathetic obsession and, he supposed, some money.

'How much money did you make for burning the girl?' he asked.

'Ali Reza gave me a thousand lire.'

İkmen looked at Süleyman and raised his eyebrows. 'So a nice five-thousand-lire profit for Ali Reza.'

'The money wasn't important.'

İkmen pulled a cynical face. 'No.'

'What did you do with it?' Süleyman asked.

With an almost disinterested simplicity Murad said, 'My parents took it. They take everything.'

'How?'

'I went home afterwards and they went through my pockets,' the boy said. 'They do that when they're desperate for the gear.'

'Didn't they ask you where you'd come by such a large amount of money?' Süleyman asked.

The boy looked at him pityingly, and in truth, Süleyman himself had been instantly ashamed of his naive question. 'They're junkies,' Murad said. 'They don't care.'

Only now did Çetin İkmen's pity for Murad manifest itself. Where else but to an avenging God could such a boy turn? 'Your clothes must have smelt of petrol when you left the apartment in Beşiktaş,' he said. 'What happened to them?'

'Ali Reza has an aunt in an apartment in Teşvikiye,' he said. 'She was away on holiday. He gave me a key. I ran there and changed my clothes.'

'He left a new set for you in the aunt's apartment?'

'Yes. He went to pick my old clothes up later. He told me he burnt them. Ali Reza plans well.' There was some admiration there, still.

'Murad, how did a boy like you with so much talent and such a bright future become involved with *jihadist* philosophy?' İkmen asked.

'When your parents are junkies,' he said, 'you need something to believe in. You need your religion to help you make it through.'

'Religion, yes, but . . .'

'When you see your mother letting men bugger her for money, you want to blow up the universe!' His face was purple with rage. 'You ask me how I came to be involved in *jihadi* things? I went out and I found them! I found the men who sell the DVDs, the pictures, who run the websites! I wanted to be like them! Not like the way I am, the . . .'

'What? The way you are what?' İkmen asked.

Murad turned his head to one side and said, 'Nothing.'

'Gay?' İkmen asked.

'No!'

'You love Ali Reza,' İkmen said. 'Even though he laughs at you, even though he betrays you. It's true, isn't it? Isn't it?'

Murad Emin turned back to look at him again, his anger obviously all burnt out, and said very simply, 'Yes. Yes, it is true.'

'You loved him before all the *jihadi* stuff, didn't you?' İkmen said.

Murad began to cry. 'I had to do something to make up for it!' he said. 'Such a terrible sin! Even thinking about it!'

'And so you lit a human blaze . . .'

'A noble blaze, yes,' the boy said. 'Yes, I did. I thought it would make up for it all.'

Only then did İkmen really feel any true sympathy for the boy.

'When you refer to something, meaning to be clever and cocky, it's just as well if no one else is listening,' Çetin İkmen said to Ali Reza Zafir.

'What do you mean?' Ali Reza said. He was so different from Murad Emin, so much more confrontational.

'We knew that you were hiding something,' İkmen continued, 'because you had to have hit your mother for a reason, which could only be connected to a desire to get away. You were dressed for the street, you had your passport and clothes in your bag.'

'I didn't mean to kill her,' Ali Reza said in a matter-of-fact way. He added impatiently, 'I hit her too hard. It was an accident.'

'Was it?' Süleyman, across the other side of the desk,

363

shook his head. 'Tell me, Ali Reza, when did you develop an ambition to be a hit man?'

The boy looked at him as if he was something disgusting and filthy. 'Don't be stupid!' he said. 'Some ridiculous peasant wanted a girl killed for no good reason; I did that using another stupid peasant and I got paid money for it. There was a market!'

'And what do you know about markets?' İkmen asked.

'A lot more than my father!' the boy snapped spitefully. 'Public service? Art?' He pulled a face. 'Yes, I like the piano. I'd like to be a concert pianist, but only because it pays well. Top musicians can live like footballers. But this was easier.'

'Which you found out when you killed Hamid İdiz?'

But still the boy wouldn't give that information up. He sat back in his chair again and smiled.

İkmen shrugged. 'We'll tie up the forensic evidence,' he said. 'You might as well tell me the truth now and save us all a lot of time later.'

Ali Reza didn't move.

'Oh well,' İkmen said. 'I'll just have to tell you how you've been stupid and then you can make up your own mind. Firstly you did protest rather too much about how your friend Murad might well be a dangerous fanatic when Inspector Süleyman and Sergeant Melik went to see you at your apartment just before you killed your mother.' İkmen waved an arm in the air casually. 'But that's a detail. Your main mistake was to mention two names that meant absolutely nothing to anyone when you were about to be transported over to Üsküdar.' He walked over to the boy and bent down to look into his face. 'Leopold and Loeb.

364

I knew of them, even if no one else did. A crime now widely accepted to have had homoerotic overtones.'

Ali Reza appeared mesmerised by İkmen's eyes. He looked up at him with a totally blank expression on his face.

'When I heard that you'd used those names, I knew,' İkmen said. 'We were not sure at the time what your connection was with Gözde Seyhan's murder, but I knew that you hadn't killed your mother for no reason. You needed to get away on your own account. We were pretty sure that Murad had actually killed Gözde, but what was your connection? More to the point, what was your actual crime? You shouldn't have tried to connect Murad Emin to Hamid İdiz's death, not after we'd taken his DNA. It wouldn't have shown up in the vicinity of Hamid's bed. But yours will. You shouldn't have tried to implicate Murad. That isn't the way to treat someone who is besotted with you. Not that I'm sure that bothers you in the slightest. And you shouldn't have brought out Leopold and Loeb. Why did you?'

Ali Reza Zafir glanced away for a few seconds and then looked back again at İkmen, smiling. He was a handsome, sensual boy, so different to the youngster Süleyman had first seen at his home with his parents. 'I read about them on the internet,' he said. 'So cool! When Murad bitched about how he'd got so upset about the girl's death, I had to see what would happen to me. It was just like Leopold and Loeb! Fantastic! I loved it!'

Furious, but fully in control, İkmen said, 'Oh, I'm so glad about that. But Leopold and Loeb failed because they just couldn't shut up about their murder. They talked and they bickered and they failed, just like you.'

365

'Well then,' the boy said cheerily, 'I'll know that for next time, won't I?'

'I don't think so,' İkmen said. 'Leopold and Loeb both got life imprisonment. They would have been executed if they hadn't been under-age. Loeb died in prison at the age of thirty because another inmate stabbed him. Rough places, jails. Guess what sentence I'm going to recommend to the prosecutor for you.'

Ali Reza leaned forward in his seat and, still smiling, said, 'Guess how much money my father is going to spend on my defence.'

Chapter 34

Even when summer burst out across the waters of the Bosphorus, the Golden Horn and the Sea of Marmara, the people of İstanbul were still under a metaphorical cloud. Between them the two young boys, Murad Emin and Ali Reza Zafir, had killed three people. They had also thrown a spotlight on the particularly ugly way in which some men resolved the problem of supposedly recalcitrant female relatives. Ali Reza had done it to get money, but he'd used his pious friend and would-be lover, a boy with a terrible home life and a wholly distorted vision of his religion, to actually perform the deed.

But where had the actual idea of honour killing for money originated? The notion of getting a young person to commit a murder and thereby, if caught, receive a lighter sentence was not new. People in the east had been doing it for years. But to actually pay someone, as in a business . . . Çetin İkmen still found himself wondering about the other families he had identified who had apparently fallen on hard times in the wake of a suspected honour killing. But there was no connection between any of them and Ali Reza Zafir or Murad Emin. Maybe lots of people were doing it? The thought made him shiver, and he consoled himself with the notion that at least

Ali Reza and Murad were on remand. Their trial was still months away, but the boys were off the street. That, especially in the case of Ali Reza, was a good thing. It was the boy's father he felt sorry for. He'd had what he thought had been the perfect family. But now his wife was dead and his son was awaiting trial charged with the deaths of his own mother and his piano teacher. Cold, sociopathic killings – that of Hamid İdiz at least – designed to be part of an experiment and a challenge to the authorities.

Murad Emin was another matter. Tortured by what he had done, he'd tried to kill himself twice since he'd been on remand and the prison authorities were considering a transfer to a psychiatric facility. In his desperate bid to make a life for himself away from his family's drug habits, he had fallen into error and become something truly monstrous: a person who could set fire to flesh. To İkmen such an act recalled the auto-da-fé, the burning of Jews and heretics that had swept Catholic Europe during the fifteenth century. Those hideous fires had driven hundreds of thousands of refugees into the Ottoman Empire, who had welcomed them. Now Turks were lighting fires of their own . . .

He hoped the young boys would go down for life, because a message needed to be sent, and if Ali Reza and Murad were to be martyrs to that cause, then so be it. Maybe in prison Murad Emin would get access to a piano and possibly play for the enjoyment of others again. He hoped so. Maybe that would take the boy's mind off where he was and the fact that for the last month his mother had been missing. The prison authorities had advised against telling him, but his father had done so anyway. She'd gone out one day to work and just

368

not come back. She'd probably been killed by some dissatisfied punter. That or she'd just finally died from illness and addiction. What a waste of life! Both hers and Murad's.

But there were some good things too. Saadet and Lokman Seyhan had left Fatih and gone to a small flat in Gaziosmanpaşa. Lokman had finally managed to get a new job and İkmen hoped that the two of them could maybe begin again. Young Sabiha, the intended victim of Cem Koç, was happy at the women's refuge where Ayşe Farsakoğlu had placed her and had decided to stay for the time being. But most importantly of all, Gonca the gypsy had survived. Against all odds she had come out of her coma and begun to heal.

Süleyman had seen her. She'd been leaning on the arm of one of her older daughters outside her house in Balat, taking some air. She had moved slowly and with difficulty and much of her hair seemed to have turned iron grey almost overnight. But she'd been alive, and although they hadn't spoken and might never speak again, she had smiled at Süleyman when she saw him. The gypsies for their part had left him alone. He had saved her life; what more could they do? İkmen wondered what Süleyman would do now that his affair with Gonca was definitely over, but he decided that was something that was unknowable and totally beyond him. He couldn't understand infidelity; he never had been able to. But he didn't judge it either. There was far too much real evil in the world to bother one's head with such apparent trifles. In a world where men burnt women to death and people were killed just for sport, adultery was very insignificant. Not that the men who did the burning would agree with him.

But now that his moustache had grown back again and his suit was crumpled, the world was not such a bad place. İkmen stood up from his office chair and put his jacket on.

'Ayşe,' he said as he put a cigarette into his mouth and lit up.

'Sir.' She stood as if to go too. İkmen offered her a cigarette, which she took with a smile.

'Tomorrow is the nineteenth of July,' he said.

Ayşe looked at the cigarette between her fingers and said, 'Smoking ban day.'

'Finally upon us,' İkmen said with a frown. Then he sighed. 'Enjoy it while you can, Ayşe.'

She watched him go, and then she smoked her cigarette right down to the butt. As she scrunched it out in İkmen's ashtray, she found that her eyes were caught by the tiny glowing embers at its heart. One by one, they all fizzled out.

Acknowledgement

I'd like to thank Fire Investigation Team Manager, Deon Webber from Greater Manchester Fire and Rescue Service for giving me so much information about the nature of fire and firefighting. If any of the details about fire in this book are inaccurate or wrong then that is entirely down to me and me alone.

Glossary

adhan – call to prayer. Performed five times a day by devout Muslims.

Bey – Ottoman title denoting respect, still in use today following a man's first name, as in Çetin Bey.

inşallah – Arabic, translates as 'As God wills'. Used by people all over the Muslim world to express the concept of divine direction. For instance, we will go to the cinema this afternoon, *inşallah*, if God wills. Christians often express the same concept by saying that they will do a certain thing only 'if I am spared'.

kapıcı – doorkeeper. Blocks of flats have *kapıcılar*, men who act as security, porters etc. for the apartment community. They are said to know all the tenants' secrets.

nargile – water pipe. Used for smoking plain and flavoured tobaccos.

yali – mansion, typically wooden, usually of nineteenth-century Ottoman vintage.

Zamzam water – from the Well of Zamzam in Mecca, Saudi Arabia. The water from the Zamzam well was supposed to have been produced by God for Ishmael, the thirsty infant son of the Prophet Abraham. The heavily salinated water is said to possess miraculous properties, and although it is not supposed to be sold outside the Saudi kingdom, small amounts of Zamzam water can be obtained in vials that can be hung around the neck. One of the things that pilgrims to Mecca always do is drink water from the Zamzam well.